JAMES HARPER

SACRIFICE

1

GEORGE WINTER FELT THE *DEAD OR ALIVE* DIP. A LARGE OR HEAVY man had stepped onto the stern deck. His pulse picked up, his mouth suddenly dry for no reason that he could explain. Except that there was something not quite right about the job, simple though it was.

He took a deep breath to calm his nerves, then slipped out from behind the galley table, went to welcome them aboard. He slid open the glass doors to the salon, stepped outside.

That's when he got his first surprise.

There were three of them. Bormann and Hitch he'd been expecting. The third man he hadn't, didn't think anybody ever would. Unless they were a mortician.

Bormann, a grim-looking man with a taste for mindlessness, that rare ability to do almost anything to anybody for no good reason at all, was in the fighting chair. Leaning back, feet pushed hard into the footrest, an imaginary rod in one hand, winding furiously with the other.

Dickhead.

'Whoa! Think I've caught myself a whale.'

Spoken around a mouth full of gum as always, the irritating

wet sucking sound as he chewed with his mouth open punctuating everything he said. Most of the time it made more sense than the words themselves.

Winter laughed dutifully.

Moron.

Bormann's partner Hitch was helping the third man into the boat. As you would a person who had to be over a hundred years old, more like a hundred and ten. He was so old, the warmth gone from his flesh so long ago, he wore a heavy overcoat despite the heat of the tropical Florida night. And a waistcoat under that, a strange-looking patchwork affair that Winter couldn't quite make out.

An aura of having cheated death for far too long clung to him. Maybe that was why Winter felt his stomach clench, knew he didn't want to look into the man's cadaverous eyes. Fragments of stories shared with good friends here on this very deck came back to him, made him shiver.

Strong hands streaked with dirt and grime hauled the three grunts into the back of the slick by their pack straps. Behind them the rotor wash bent the elephant grass flat, blew the marker smoke every which way.

The moron Bormann jumped out of the fighting chair and the old man took his place. Except he didn't grab an imaginary rod and reel. Just sat staring out over the dark ocean humming a song to himself.

Winter recognized the melody, couldn't put his finger on it. It took him back to when he was a young man, to a time when he'd have laughed in the faces of men such as these. It would come to him.

He ushered Bormann and Hitch into the salon. Bormann slid in behind the galley table, made himself at home.

'Nice boat. Got anything to drink?'

'Light beer,' Winter said.

Bormann gave him a look like he'd just offered to empty the chemical toilet into his mouth. He stuck his hand in his jacket pocket, came out with a pint of Johnny Walker.

'Lucky I brought this along, eh?'

Winter shook his head, went to fetch a glass.

'Not for me, thanks.'

Then he caught sight of Bormann's face, saw that he'd offended the man. He might be a moron, but he was a big moron and not somebody you wanted to upset.

'Maybe a small one. What about your friend outside?'

Jesus Christ! I'm not getting my ass shot to hell for that crazy son of a bitch.

Bormann shook his head, the light reflecting off the shiny bald dome. Winter had the sense to keep his thoughts and jokes to himself, knew that any crack about finding their master a pint of blood would not be well received.

He laid three glasses in a row on the table in front of Bormann, watched him carefully fill them. His more than the other two.

'To a job well done,' Bormann said and raised his glass, his eyebrow too.

'Absolutely,' Winter said, slopping some of his drink in his haste to pull the slip of paper from his pocket. He put it into Bormann's outstretched hand.

'Any problems?'

'Like a walk in the park.'

Bormann raised his glass again and Winter took a sip of the whisky, felt the burn all the way down his throat. It made him think of better times with better people, out on the deck under a perfect night sky. Like kids around a campfire, trying to scare each other with their ghost stories.

Drop it, you sick bastard.

After two more reluctant shots Winter at last began to relax, a gentle mellowness creeping through his body. Then the door to the salon slid open and that all changed. There wasn't a distillery in the world that could pump out sufficient booze to warm the chill that blew in with the old man.

He lashed out. A vicious open-handed slap across the mouth that grinned around its prize.

Winter dropped his eyes. Didn't want to look into the man's face. He knew he didn't want to hear him speak either, a sound that would be like shovels in the dirt.

But he was being melodramatic. Blame it on the whisky. The old man was more human than he looked, even made a joke. He shivered as he came in, hunched the collar of his overcoat up around his ears. Some impertinent bird had deposited a dollop of birdshit on the shoulder of his coat. From the size of the mess it must have been a big one, a seagull or a crow.

'Getting a bit chilly out there.'

Everybody laughed.

Winter, to let out the nervous tension building strength inside him.

Hitch, because he was a sycophant.

Bormann, because he laughed when everybody else did.

Everything would have been okay if it had stopped there. But it didn't. Because the old man laughed at his own joke.

And when Winter looked into the grinning mouth, he knew he'd gone to hell. Because where else would you meet a man with his teeth filed to points.

Like an animal that has returned to its natural habitat, the place where it can be what it truly is, do what it was brought into this world to do.

2

'I'm not going back in there,' Kate Guillory said. 'Not after what happened last time.'

Evan tried to look disappointed. The place was eye-wateringly expensive after all.

'If you're sure . . .'

'I'm surprised you want to.'

He shrugged, you've got a point, looked down at his newly-shined shoes. He was standing in the exact same spot where it had happened. A couple months back, he'd taken her to dinner at this very restaurant. They'd had a great evening—up until the point where he was tasered in the exact spot he was standing in now. And then abducted. It's not how anybody wants their evening to end. She'd been in the ladies' room at the time, hadn't spoken to him for days afterwards.

She put her hand on his arm, a smile on her lips.

'I know you've shined your shoes specially.'

He rubbed the toe of the left one against the back of his right calf. It had gotten scuffed already.

'It is your birthday, after all.'

She leaned away from him to get a better look at him, her eyes narrowing to see what else was different.

'Combed your hair too.' She flicked her head towards the restaurant door. 'Maybe we should—'

'No, you're right. Don't want to tempt fate.'

Neither of them could stop themselves from glancing around. Because both of them had their private suspicions that the events that followed that evening might not be as closed as they pretended to each other. They both felt a little stupid, nonetheless.

'So. Where shall we go instead?' Mr Disingenuous said.

'Idiot.'

She'd already looped her arm through his. He clamped it tightly to his side with his elbow, trapping it, avoiding the clip around the back of the head that generally accompanied the *idiot* accusation.

'Looks like it's the Jerusalem Tavern,' she said, trying and failing to put some resignation and disappointment into her voice.

'If you insist,' he said, trying and failing to keep the grin off his lips.

Despite his relief at the prospect of an evening in the Jerusalem instead of in an over-priced restaurant, he scanned the whole of the room quickly as they entered. Because in the course of the interrogation that followed his abduction, the man doing all the shouting and spitting in his face had made a very astute observation: *A couple of beers in the Jerusalem is more your style.* Just so that there was no misunderstanding about how deeply they'd dug into his life.

'There's nobody here,' Guillory said.

He hadn't realized she'd caught him looking. She peeled off to go to the ladies' room as he headed to the bar, got settled into his usual seat. Lucinda Williams' bittersweet *Lake Charles* playing on the jukebox set a nice, mellow tone, relaxing him. The manager, Kieran, wandered over, a frown on his face.

'I thought you were taking the lady to a fancy restaurant.'

'She didn't want to go.'

Kieran nodded knowingly.

'Is that so?'

'Uh-huh.'

Without saying anything more, Kieran went to pour their beers. A minute later he put a single glass in front of Evan, got some helpful advice back.

'It's a lot more efficient if you bring them both over together.'

'Yep,' Kieran said, turning to the cooler cabinet behind him, his voice muffled as he did so. 'If you're both having the same thing.'

Then he pulled a fresh bottle of champagne from the cabinet, placed a champagne flute on the bar in front of Guillory's empty chair. Evan watched as he popped the cork, then carefully filled the glass.

'You can thank me later,' Kieran said as he put the bottle back in the cabinet.

If you wink at me, I'll put my finger in your eye, Evan thought as he wandered away.

Guillory did a small double take when she got back from the ladies' room.

'What? Have they run out of beer?'

'I thought you'd like a glass of champagne instead. Seeing as it's your birthday.'

'Seeing as you're not having to shell out for dinner, you mean.'

She took a small sip, nodded approvingly.

'I could get to like this. Thank you, it was very thoughtful of you.'

He took an embarrassed mouthful of his beer. He felt

Kieran's grin as he watched them, all the way from the other end of the bar.

'I see you didn't put any lipstick on while you were in the ladies' room,' he said to get the attention away from himself.

'No dinner, no lipstick.' She held up the champagne. 'I didn't know about this at the time.'

He pulled something out of his pocket and put it on the bar. She stared at it as if it might explode in their faces. At that moment Kieran walked past them. He saw what was sitting on the bar. He paused, caught Evan's eye. Raised his own eyebrow.

'Looks like we'll be needing a lot more champagne.' Then to Guillory. 'Well, go on Kate. Open it.'

Guillory picked up the small black box with the name of an up-market jewelry store embossed in gold on the lid. It was as if everybody in the bar was holding their breath, the music on the jukebox paused mid-song. With her heart beating a crazy tattoo in her chest, she flipped the lid open. Stared at the contents sitting on a red velvet cushion.

Evan let the grin creep across his lips as her face relaxed, the frozen features softening.

'What did you think it was?'

'Damn,' Kieran said, moving away. 'I was sure it was an engagement ring.'

Guillory lifted out a pair of gold earrings.

'They're lovely, thank you.'

'So what did you think it was?' Evan said again.

'Just shut up. It might have helped if you'd said Happy Birthday instead of just putting the box on the bar with that stupid look on your face. Even if you can't help it.'

He called Kieran over, ordered two more beers while she held one of the earrings to her ear, tried to see in the mirror behind the bar. Kieran brought one beer back, topped off Guillory's champagne.

'That's two disappointments the lady's had in one night.'

'Hey!' Guillory laughed, 'less of that. That's what I call a close shave.'

But despite the banter and the joking, it was clear to Evan that her heart wasn't in it. It wasn't just tonight either. She'd been getting worse over the past weeks, becoming increasingly withdrawn and irritable. He knew what was causing it, too.

And he had plans to do something about it.

3

'YOU THINK SHE'S PLANNING ON DOING SOMETHING STUPID?'
Elwood Crow said.

Evan held up his hands, beats me.

'I'm not sure. But she's not herself.'

They were sitting in Crow's back room as usual. Crow was an ageing, semi-retired investigator who'd helped Evan out on a number of his cases. Particularly if they turned overly cerebral or required access to information that he wasn't strictly entitled to. Crow's pet bird, an American crow called *Plenty*, was sitting on Evan's shoulder, its new favorite position, watching Evan's ear as if something tasty to eat might poke its head out at any moment.

'You can hardly blame her after what happened,' Crow said.

Guillory had only recently returned to duty. She'd been suspended for attacking a suspect in custody, a convicted pedophile called Robert Garfield. During her suspension she was abducted by the pedophile gang. She was beaten and interrogated, then driven, hooded and bound, out to the woods to be executed. Through a combination of circumstance and a not-so-simple twist of fate, she'd escaped.

And while the visible cuts and bruises had healed, the psychological wounds had not. Nor would they for a long time. She had no idea who had abducted and beaten her. No idea who had given the order for her to be killed as if she were simply an inconvenient irritation to be dealt with. Or so she claimed.

Evan suddenly realized the possible double meaning in Crow's question.

'When you say do something stupid, you don't mean . . .'

Crow shook his head. But Evan saw that his words had put the thought into Crow's mind. And it hadn't been immediately dismissed.

'No. I didn't mean kill herself. I meant take things into her own hands. But now you mention it . . .'

The toxic thought hung in the air between them, palpable like a bitter taste in the mouth. It made Evan wish he never mentioned it. Then Crow put the spotlight on him to try to reverse the damage that the words had done to their mood. He put a lot of bright and breezy into his voice. For Crow, that is.

'That's why she needs you.'

'That's why I'm here.'

Crow's wrinkly brow squeezed in a few more creases, a new world record for one person's forehead. He made a show of looking around the room to see if Guillory was hiding in the corner or behind the drapes.

Evan got his wallet out, extracted a battered business card. He held it out towards Crow.

'Todd Strange,' Crow said, reading the name on the front. Underneath it was a cell phone number and a PO box address. He gave Evan a questioning look.

'He's the contract killer the pedophiles hired to kill Kate. Or, he was. He's dead now.'

'How did you get his card?'

'It doesn't matter.'

Crow looked as if he was going to object, thought better of it. Because Guillory wasn't the only one who'd changed. Evan had too. It was understandable. His search for his missing wife Sarah had recently come to an end. He'd found the answers to the questions that had plagued and tormented him since the day six years ago when she went to work and never came home. It hadn't been a happy ending, the answers not the hoped-for outcome that had kept him going during his long search. She had committed suicide while incarcerated in a state psychiatric facility and was buried in the hospital grounds. Kate Guillory had been there with him at the graveside when he'd learned the truth. It should have brought them together. For some reason it had so far failed to do so.

Crow had his suspicions about why. Nothing concrete, no evidence to base it on. Just a feeling in his wrinkly old bones based on a lifetime spent digging into other people's lives. He wasn't sure either of them believed what they'd been told.

So he didn't push Evan now, cut him some slack. As if it were the most natural thing in the world to have a dead hit man's business card in your wallet.

'You want me to find out where he lives? Lived.'

Evan shook his head.

'I know where he lives. I saw his driver's license when I found the card. I wrote the address on the back.'

Crow turned the card over, saw the hand-written address and a phone number. He leaned forward, elbows on his bony knees. He looked like an ageing vulture that had just seen the animal carcass in front of him try to get away. Things were getting interesting.

'Have you been around there?'

'Not yet.'

Crow didn't miss the *yet*. He'd have been disappointed if it had been omitted. He waved the business card in Evan's face.

'You don't think you should give this to the police?'

'There were more in his wallet along with his driver's license. They'll have found them. Who knows whether they'll have bothered to go around there. If you listen to Kate, it sounds as if nobody's very interested.'

'And that's where you come in.'

'Somebody's gotta do it.'

Crow slapped the card back and forth against the edge of his palm, making an irritating flapping sound. His pet bird launched itself from Evan's shoulder at the sound, left a reminder of its visit on his jacket.

'What about the phone number on the back?'

'And that's where you come in,' Evan said, mimicking Crow's remark of a moment ago.

Crow leaned back in his chair and studied the number. As if he could come up with the answer if he stared at it long and hard enough.

'Any idea who it belongs to?'

'Nope.'

'But you're hoping it's the people who hired him to kill Kate.'

'That, or I suppose it could just be his mom.'

Crow ignored the flippant remark, asked the obvious question.

'Have you tried calling it?' He held up a hand quickly before Evan had the chance to answer. 'No, let me re-phrase that. I hope you haven't tried calling it.'

Evan shook his head slowly.

'Once bitten, twice shy.'

It was the correct response.

'Good. We don't want to set off the same as happened last time.'

Last time was when Evan was tasered outside the restaurant and abducted. It had been a direct result of him doing an internet search for a name that had been on a watch list. Although much as Evan agreed that he had no desire to repeat the experience, neither of them could deny that it had set in motion a chain of events that resulted in him finally learning what had happened to Sarah.

If blindly calling the number on the card would have resulted in Guillory finding the same relief from her ordeal as he had, he'd have done it. And let them taser him until the cows came home.

All of this Crow knew and understood. Which was why he was keen to take on the task. Stop Evan from barging straight in, good old Buckley style. It was what he was good at, after all, now that he was too old for the rough and tumble of the job out on the streets. It was the prospect of that rough and tumble that gave him slight pause before he spoke again.

'There's something I want you to do for me in return.'

'I'M WORRIED ABOUT A FRIEND OF MINE,' CROW SAID, FEELING A small pang of guilt as he chose the word *worried* rather than admit to the fears that kept him awake at night. 'George Winter. I haven't been able to contact him for a couple of days.'

'Maybe he died in his sleep. If he's as old as you.'

Crow did Evan the favor of pretending he hadn't heard.

'He called me a week ago sounding more excited than I can remember him sounding for years. He was a private investigator too, until he retired.'

'Did you work together?'

It wasn't just an idle question, an invitation to an old man to share a few reminiscences from the glory days. From what little Crow had told him about his work, Evan knew that it had been very rough at times. Not the glory days so much as the gory days.

Anybody who'd worked with him would be cut from the same cloth.

'No.'

Evan waited for more but more didn't come.

'Okay, just a friend.'

Crow started to say something. Stopped. Then came out with it.

'He's someone I knew from the old days. But that doesn't matter.'

Evan knew that when Crow referred to the *old days*, he was being a lot more specific than it sounded. He was talking about his time in Vietnam. He was very aware of Crow's reluctance to talk about it. He'd tried on a number of occasions to pry stories out of the old dog. Crow always deflected the conversation. It made him wonder what he'd gotten into over there. Now it seemed his reluctance extended to talking about people he'd known there.

Much later, the reasons for that reluctance would become clear. The statement that it didn't matter wasn't so much disingenuous as an outright lie.

'After he retired, he sold up and bought a boat. Moved down to the Florida Keys. He makes a bit of money running fishing charters.'

The twist to Crow's lips and the wrinkling of his nose made it clear what he thought about such a lifestyle.

'He's filling in time waiting to die?' Evan suggested.

Crow nodded vigorously with all the conviction of a man who knows that the Devil can't catch you if you don't sit still.

'Exactly. There's only so many fish a man can eat.'

'I think you put them back these days.'

Crow looked at him as if he'd confirmed that the world had indeed gone mad. To spend time and money and effort to catch a fish and then throw it back again. Then to do it again tomorrow. And the day after. He was sure the fish got tired of it too.

'Whatever. Seems George finally realized it himself. He started doing a few bits and pieces of proper work again, anything that came his way.'

'That's what he was so excited about.'

'Yes. Just some chickenshit little job, he said. But it made a pleasant change from spending the day afloat with a bunch of drunken Midwesterners.'

'Did he say what it was?'

'He had to identify some people in a video.'

'Why not ask whoever took the video?'

Crow crossed one bony leg over the other, rested his hands on his knee. Stared at Evan, a long-suffering look on his face.

'I don't know, Evan. Maybe that's what he did. But that was the job. Identify the people in the video. Report back. As far as I know, he wasn't to approach them or make contact with them.'

'Who gave him the job?'

'I don't know.'

Therein lay the problem as far as Evan could see. Crow didn't know. And he didn't like it.

'Did you ask him?'

The long-suffering look grew longer and more suffering.

'Of course I asked him. He was very evasive. Just a friend of a friend.'

Evan smiled to himself, takes one to know one. If you put the word *evasive* into an internet search engine, you get a picture of Crow's face staring back at you at the top of the results.

'Does it matter?'

'Well it might if something's happened to him,' Crow snapped.

Since it was a day for letting things slide, Evan ignored the sharpness of his tone. Because he'd gained some information—Crow was more than just worried about his friend.

'The job shouldn't have taken him more than a day at most. Given how excited he was, I should've heard from him by now. He should be answering his phone if nothing else.'

Evan didn't bother saying that he was most likely enjoying his money, lying on a beach somewhere. A cold beer in his hand, his cell phone left far behind. Nonetheless, he felt bad about his crack that maybe he'd died in his sleep. Crow's demeanor suggested that he thought he may well have died. Just not peacefully in his sleep.

'I'd like you to check up on him. Make sure everything's okay. And'—he paused a moment, swallowed drily—'if it isn't, find out what exactly it was he was working on. And who gave him the job.'

'You sound as if you've already got your suspicions. You just want me to confirm it.'

Crow shook his head energetically which only proved it.

'Not at all. I'd go down there myself, but . . .'

He flicked his head towards the ceiling. His wife—also called Sarah—lay above them in her bed. She'd suffered from Alzheimer's Disease from before Evan first met Crow. Crow insisted on caring for her at home. Nor was he happy to entrust her wellbeing to professional carers. He looked a little uncomfortable putting Evan in a position where it was impossible for him to refuse, felt the need to explain.

As all people hiding something do.

'I thought about asking Caleb—'

'*Caleb?*'

'Evan. I've got *Plenty* here to repeat every word I say. I don't need you to do it as well. Caleb is my son.'

Evan hadn't been aware Crow had a son and told him so.

'No reason why you should.'

'Is he anything like you?'

Crow knew exactly what he meant. When they first met, Crow had indirectly admitted that in his younger days he had garrotted a degenerate and vicious man in the aftermath of one of his investigations, dispensing a rough natural justice like a self-styled avenging angel. And the world had not mourned his passing, had become a better place for it. That killing had never been officially solved.

'Oh yes.'

Good to know, Evan thought to himself. A man with skills like that would be useful when he went down the road that started with Todd Strange. He noticed that Crow was smiling now, a gleam in his eye, knew something was up.

'But then I thought, why not kill two birds with one stone? I know somebody who could use a short vacation in Florida. And I don't mean you. Take Kate with you. It'll do her good.'

He fished in his pocket and pulled out a bunch of keys, held them out towards Evan.

'George gave me a spare set of keys to the boat. He never married, didn't have anybody else.'

Evan took the keys and made a note of where the boat was moored. He was halfway to the door when Crow called him back.

'Don't worry, I didn't ask Kate on your behalf. But I will do if you're not quick about it.'

4

THE FILTHY HOOD OVER KATE GUILLORY'S HEAD SMELLED OF blood and sweat and vomit. Hers or somebody else's she couldn't remember, didn't want to know. In places it stuck to her skin as the blood soaking into it congealed.

In the darkness, her other senses heightened to compensate.

Thanks a lot, other senses.

She felt the grain of the hard wooden chair through the sweat-soaked seat of her pants, felt the coarse fibers of the rope biting into her wrists and ankles.

She heard them. Circling her like a pair of wild dogs, the gritty crunch of their leather-soled shoes loud on the rough concrete floor. Leather-soled, not because they were smart executive types, but because rubber-soled shoes aren't much good at hacking a person's shins.

She smelled them. Each as distinguishable as if she had a photograph in front of her swollen eyes.

Dog's breath and stale ashtray.

United in the common odor of unwashed body working too hard in a small airless room.

Already her subconscious brain had made the connections.

Told her what was coming next by their odor as one stepped forward, the other dropping back for a well-earned rest.

Dog's breath hit harder. Stale ashtray was more accurate.

They took it in turns.

What a team, get that on your résumé, boys.

Somewhere behind them, his presence as repugnant as abscessed gums, the man who screamed and shouted into her face. His voice an invasion of her body and mind, the hood for once a blessed protection from his flying spittle. Incoherent threats and unintelligible questions assaulting her senses. Over and over and over. Until all she wanted was for it to be over in any way at all.

But if they thought they'd get a cry or a scream or even a little squeal out of her, they were as stupid as they were abhorrent.

Then a heavy foot on her chest. Squashing her breast, heel bruising her ribs. Shoving her violently backwards. The chair toppling, the back of her head smacking hard into the concrete floor.

She jerked upright at the impact.

Looked around the too-bright bedroom in wide-eyed terror. Heart sprinting in her chest. Hair plastered to her scalp with sweat. She stared at the covers twisted around her legs as tightly as when she'd been tied to the chair, touched the back of her head gingerly where she'd banged into the wooden headboard.

Evan wouldn't want to take her home if he knew this happened nearly every night. One of these days he was going to give up trying.

She lowered herself back down. Turned her head to look at the alarm clock. 2:05 a.m. Later than most days. She stared past the clock to the Glock 22 sitting on the nightstand. Bigger and more powerful than the 19, it combines the power of a .45 caliber weapon with the size and flexibility of a 9mm gun.

One time, on a night like tonight, she'd picked it up, put the barrel in her mouth. Tasted the cold metal and gun oil, felt the front sight sharp against the roof of her mouth, hot salty tears running silently down her cheeks, soaking without trace into the sweat-soaked pillow.

She told herself it wasn't because she was weak—or was it strength that you needed to put a gun in your mouth and pull the trigger, she could never remember—but because she wanted to know what *he* was going to feel when she did the same to him.

Liverman.

The man whose voice, whose bloated presence, whose very existence on the same planet as her, had made her recoil in disgust even before the blows from his men came at her from out of the darkness.

That's another thing, Evan. You think you'll be able to sleep with the light on all night, every night? For the rest of your life?

There were times when she thought it might have been easier if they'd found his wife alive.

That thought opened up another can of worms. Standing with him at his wife's grave. Or the grave they'd been told contained his wife's remains. Evan's reaction, jabbing his finger angrily at the ground at his feet.

No! I don't believe that's my wife.

She couldn't blame him for the outburst. Because she had her own doubts. Memories of a face glimpsed at a high window. The man who took them to the grave had sensed their skepticism, had offered to let them see the autopsy report. To let *her* see it. So that she might convince Evan without him having to look at the photographs and read the clinical words to describe a body that once was a person carved up like a holiday turkey in the name of truth, then hastily stitched back together.

Yet for some reason she'd failed to take them up on the offer.

Maybe it was her own problems getting in the way. Or perhaps she was scared of what she might learn.

That wasn't all.

A slip of the tongue by the man they knew only as Smith at the graveside. Referring to her *condition*. Evan hadn't picked up on it. But to a woman, the word *condition* is very specific. She'd said nothing to Evan, of course.

Was it any surprise that things were difficult between them?

And now that his quest was supposedly at an end, she had one of her own. One every bit as blinding and all-consuming as his had been. One that she knew had no happy ending. And she'd be damned if she let it go on for six long years.

Liverman.

Liver. Man.

A horrible name. Slimy on the tongue like calf's liver. A name that defiled the mouth that uttered it. A name dropped in error. A careless mistake by Todd Strange, the man who came to bundle her into the back of his van and drive her out to the woods to put a bullet in the back of her brainpan. She'd have kissed him if she hadn't had the foul-smelling hood over her head.

Had Liverman noticed the slip?

Did he know she had his name?

She didn't know what would be better. To have him know and to spend his life looking over his shoulder. Or for him to be in a state of smug over-confidence, and then to see that look slide off his face like birdshit off a windshield when she caught up with him.

Because catch up with him she would.

Absently, she twisted one of the earrings that Evan had given her for her birthday. Smiled to herself as she remembered the initial shock at seeing the little black box. Thoughts like that would have to wait. As would Evan, for now.

Because the only man she had any interest in now was Liverman.

And the best way to find him was through Robert Garfield, the pedophile she'd assaulted in the interview room. Her knuckles throbbed with the memory of putting her fist down his throat, taking most of his front teeth with it. And her heart soared at the memory of it.

She knew she wasn't a bad person. But she couldn't have told you what it meant that she fell asleep again with those thoughts filling her mind.

THREE HOURS LATER CURTIS BANKS STARTLED AS GUILLORY climbed into the passenger seat of his car.

'Jesus, Guil, you gave me a fright.'

He was the only person who called her Guil or Gil and she hated it. But for tonight, she'd put up with it. What she couldn't put up with was the atmosphere inside the car. A mixture of stale body and food remnants with a hint of something acrid behind it. She buzzed the window down a couple of inches, let the cool early morning air in. He yawned, tried and failed to disguise it.

'I hope you weren't asleep.'

'No way.'

The look she gave him made him squirm in his seat, run his hand nervously through his hair.

'So?' she said.

'Nothing.'

Banks was one of her confidential informants, a petty thief and burglar. He was a hundred and forty pounds of attitude with a mouth at one end and an asshole at the other. Most of the time she couldn't tell which end was which. He'd been sitting in his car opposite the pedophile Robert Garfield's house for the past twenty-four hours. The passenger footwell was littered with the detritus of his vigil. Fast food containers and candy bar wrappers, crushed soda cans. And a larger plastic bottle half filled with amber-colored liquid that she pushed carefully out of the way with the side of her foot.

'Nobody has gone in or out of that house since I've been sitting here. No lights, no movement, nothing. Whoever it is'—he paused to give her the opportunity to enlighten him, carried on when she didn't—'is either dead or he's not in there.'

'Good.'

'Any chance I can go now, get some sleep?'

'In a minute. There's one more thing I need you to do for me first.'

He smiled, patted the lock picks in his pocket.

'I came prepared.'

She pulled a face. When don't you?

'I don't know why you need me,' he complained. 'I know you can do it.'

'Why keep a dog and bark yourself? Come on.'

They got out and crossed the street quickly, two figures dressed all in black.

'Nice house,' Banks said. 'What did you say he does?'

'I didn't. But he used to be a lawyer. You don't want to know what he does in his spare time.'

The tone of her voice told him everything he needed to know about asking more questions. They made their way down the side of the house and around to the back door, keeping to the shadows. He hesitated, his hand in his pocket.

'You sure about this?'

'Just get on with it. And keep your voice down.'

He pulled out a pair of latex gloves and his picks, pulled on the gloves and went to work on the lock. Guillory pulled on an identical pair as he worked. A minute later he gently turned the door handle, pushed the door softly open.

'You better hope there isn't an alarm.'

They stood in silence for a long moment, waiting for the fast beep of an alarm. She pushed past him when it didn't come, stepped into the darkened kitchen. Already she was thinking it was all going to be for nothing. How likely was it that Garfield would keep anything incriminating in such an unprotected house? Except she didn't want anything incriminating, just an address or a phone number, something to go with the name in her head.

Liverman.

Banks stepped quietly into the kitchen after her. She turned, hissed at him.

'Out! Now. I thought you wanted to get home to your bed.'

He shrugged as he peered around the kitchen, obviously expensive even in the gloom.

'Thought I might get a little something for my trouble. Seeing as I've just spent twenty-four hours freezing my balls off and not even any thanks from you. You're welcome, Detective, don't mention it.'

She gripped his upper arm, steered him back towards the door.

'I don't want you seeing anything you might regret.'

Banks wasn't sure what she meant by that. It would become clearer to him when he read the newspaper a couple of days later. For now, he allowed himself to be pushed out into the yard. She closed the door behind him, shooed him away through the glass. He got back to his car and drove away. But he didn't go far. Just far enough so that Guillory wouldn't see him waiting if she glanced out of the window. Then he adjusted the rearview mirror to give himself a view of the house he'd just let her into, settled back to wait and watch. Any hint of tiredness was gone now. Because something told him that this would be a house worth watching.

UPSTAIRS, ROBERT GARFIELD GROANED AS HIS STOMACH CRAMPED again and curled himself into a fetal position on the sweat-soaked sheets. For two days he'd been unable to drag himself out of bed other than to stagger to the bathroom as another bout of diarrhea turned him inside out. A foul-smelling bucket sat at the side of the bed for those occasions when the projectile vomiting caught him unawares, didn't give him time to make it to the toilet.

As if it wasn't bad enough that he lived every day of his life sick with fear and worry, never knowing whether that bitch Guillory or, even worse, the aberration of nature that was Liverman was coming up behind him.

Life was so unfair.

Now a sound from downstairs.

Was this when they came for him as he lay too weak to even sit up in his bed? Was this how it would all end, surrounded by his own filth, the smell of piss and vomit and human excrement clinging to him?

It couldn't be Liverman's men. They wouldn't creep around the house in the middle of the night. They'd kick the door down, drag him screaming from the bed. Never had he regretted anything as much as he regretted telling Liverman that Guillory had chased him in her car, that he'd barely managed to get away. And after their attempts to get rid of Guillory had been thwarted, had Liverman decided to go to the root cause of the problem instead? Him. Robert Garfield.

No more Garfield, no more problem.

He pictured Liverman's fat face as he flicked the back of his hand dismissively at his sidekicks—deal with it.

He froze, even his thoughts on hold, as the bottom stair creaked.

There was no mistaking it now. Somebody was in the house. Somebody creeping stealthily around. Not Liverman's men for sure.

Guillory.

Come to finish the job she started in the interview room. He swung his legs off the bed. Sat on the edge of it, a pathetic figure in sweat-stained T-shirt and dirty boxers, shivering as the sweat cooled on his skin. Then another violent cramp in his lower abdomen, a rapid building of pressure to vacate his bowels.

No. Not now.

He pushed himself to his feet, swaying gently. He needed a weapon. He didn't own a gun. His eyes flicked frantically around the bedroom. There was nothing. His foot bumped the bucket at the side of the bed, half full of his own vomit and bile. It wasn't a weapon, but thrown in a person's face it might give a few vital seconds. They might stumble as they crept up the stairs, fall and knock themselves unconscious.

He picked it up, the smell making him retch, increasing the pressure on his bowels. He took an unsteady step towards the door, then another, went to meet his maker in whatever form he'd chosen to come calling.

5

SITTING UP AT THE COUNTER IN THE DINER WHERE HE MET Guillory for breakfast every Thursday, Evan checked his watch. Again. She was late. He pushed his plate away, feeling comfortably replete after a breakfast of scrambled eggs and bacon and buttered toast with coffee and orange juice. If the counterman took his plate away before she arrived, he might pretend he'd waited for her, have it all over again. Maybe some link sausages this time.

Too late.

The plate was still sitting on the counter in front of him when she pushed in next to him, smelling of soap and shampoo. Her hair was still wet. There was a rosy flush to her cheeks as if she'd run all the way. Or taken a scrubbing brush to them.

'Oversleep?' he said.

She shook her head, don't ask.

'I went ahead and ordered.'

'So I see. I'm not hungry anyway. I'm just going to have coffee.'

Despite that she still wiped her finger in the bacon grease on his plate, licked it.

'If I had any bits stuck between my teeth you could have those.'

He'd have expected her to tell him not to be gross. It was as if she hadn't heard him. The counterman put a cup of coffee down in front of her, re-filled Evan's cup. He watched her as she took a sip, noticed that she wasn't wearing the earrings that he'd bought her. He didn't say anything. Maybe she was keeping them for best. Didn't want to risk losing them as she wrestled bad guys to the ground. Hopefully she hadn't lost one already.

'What are you staring at?' she said.

'Nothing.'

That wasn't true. He'd been staring at the cut on her cheek. He'd already written off asking if she was going to a pirates fancy dress party as a bad idea. Now he decided to say nothing at all about it.

'You're very quiet,' he said instead.

'Make the most of it.' She risked a small smile then, which was a start. 'We can't win.'

'Who can't?'

'Women. You complain we never stop talking and then when we do, you say *you're very quiet* and stare at us like you're thinking about calling the paramedics.'

He wasn't sure what to say to that beyond *okay*. She was in a strange mood.

'Crow gave me a job to do for him,' he said when the silence threatened to take over.

'He must be desperate.'

That was slightly better, more like her usual self.

'What's he want you to do?'

He didn't answer the question, said instead, 'He's got a son, you know. Caleb.'

That got a reaction at least. Her coffee cup stalled halfway to her lips. She put it back down.

'Really? Is he anything like the old man?'

'No idea. I haven't met him. Crow just mentioned him.'

Too late he realized that this line of conversation was leading him towards the outcome that Crow had suggested—taking her with him to the Florida Keys. From the way she'd been acting so far this morning, it couldn't have come at a worse time. She was staring at him, waiting for him to explain further.

'He's a private investigator too—'

'So why didn't Crow ask him to do whatever it is that he's asked you to do, that you still haven't told me.'

They were at the point of invitation already. So he told her what Crow wanted him to do to give himself a few more minutes.

'And he's asked you to do it instead of his son,' she said. 'It can't be because he thinks you're more capable.'

He let her have her little laugh at that. At least he'd manged to crack the stone face even if it was at his expense.

'Maybe it's because he doesn't think you'd want to go to the Florida Keys with his son.'

'I don't want to go to the Florida Keys with anyone.'

The words were out before she realized what she'd said. She bit her bottom lip, nodded to herself.

'He thought you might want to go with me,' Evan said. 'Thought you could do with a break.'

She was suddenly sitting very upright and very indignant. The flush on her cheeks had deepened. He held off telling her that it suited her, a bit of color on a face that for the past weeks had looked like it was carved out of alabaster. The raised hand helped keep his mouth shut too.

'Hang on. I hope the two of you don't sit around with that stupid bird of his talking about me—'

'No.'

'—and why is it his job to think about you asking me if I want to go to Florida with you?'

He sat still and bit his tongue, waited for her to run out of steam.

'It's not like that at all.'

'Sounds like it to me.'

He did some more sitting still and tongue biting. After a couple of moments silence he ventured back into the argument . . . sorry, conversation again.

'He just asked me to do this for him and said why don't I take you. That's it. It's not some conspiracy.'

He shook his head in exasperation, took a sip of cold coffee. He was tempted to pour it in her lap, give her something to be grumpy about.

'I'm too busy, anyway,' she said. 'And why is everybody suddenly so concerned about my welfare? Do I look like I need a vacation to you?' She thrust her face towards him.

'No, you're right. Those black bags under your eyes are just your age showing.'

If he'd been a tortoise or a turtle, he'd have pulled his head down into his shell at that point. But they were beyond the playful smacks around the back of his head that usually followed an impertinent remark.

Today things were serious.

He put his hand on her arm, felt as if he'd put his finger in the electrical socket. At least she didn't throw it off.

'So. Here's me, asking you something that just crossed my mind—do you fancy a couple of days in Florida with me?'

'I can't. I'm too busy at work.'

'Do you know if Martina is free?'

There was a stunned silence. Martina Perez was a patrol officer that they both knew. She also looked like she belonged on the catwalk and not in a police cruiser. Recently separated from her husband, she'd expressed a strong interest in Evan taking her out for a blast in his '69 Corvette Stingray. From blast around the block to two days away together wasn't so much of a leap.

Guillory's mouth didn't appear to open at all. Her lips remained a straight, un-lipsticked slash across her face when she spoke.

'That's not funny, Evan.'

For a second, he thought she was close to tears. She blinked rapidly a couple of times. Then the moment passed. He reckoned he'd have more chance seeing a tear leak out of a glass eye.

It was him who couldn't win. His attempt at lightening the mood had gone down like a dirty joke on the church steps. Nor would she accept any show of concern from him, from anybody, saw it as an indictment of weakness.

Selecting his left hand because it would be less of a problem if she stabbed it with a knife or fork, he risked putting his hand on her arm again, hoped it didn't fail the patronizing test.

'Do you really think we can't see the pressure you've been under the last few months. All this trouble with Garfield—'

That was it.

Everybody knows the F-word and the C-word but this was the G-word. She threw his hand off. Slipped off the stool, almost lost her footing.

'Jesus Christ! Can't you just shut up about Garfield?'

Her mouth opened and shut abruptly as her brain failed to supply the words necessary to do justice to the emotions running riot through her. Then she did them both a favor. She pivoted on the spot, marched across the room to the door, knocking a fat man out of the way as she went. Evan reckoned the guy was lucky he didn't have a Guillory-shaped hole in his body. He stared at her back as she blew through the door and then was gone.

'Is this seat free?' the fat guy said, standing next to him, indicating the seat recently vacated by Guillory.

'It is now.'

He didn't bother saying it probably would be from now onwards. Mind you don't set your pants alight sitting on it. He was too busy wondering how one mention of the name Garfield had provoked such an extreme reaction.

He wouldn't have to wait too long before he found out.

EVAN SPENT ANOTHER FORTY-FIVE MINUTES SITTING UP AT THE counter, drinking coffee and nursing his thoughts. He was no further forward when he left. The only thing he could say was that despite her indignant claims that there was nothing the matter with her, it was affecting her more than he'd realized. His thoughts on the matter were cut short the moment he stepped out onto the sidewalk. A large object was moving swiftly towards him like an out of control wrecking ball.

He squared up, prepared to meet the onslaught, verbal or physical.

'Hey, Donut. How's it hanging?'

Guillory's partner, Ryder, looked as if he couldn't decide what to do first—punch Evan or burst a blood vessel. He teetered to a halt inches away from Evan's face like a cartoon character arriving at the edge of a cliff. If Evan could have seen around his bulk, he reckoned he'd see a channel torn up in the sidewalk behind him. Not even nine a.m. and Ryder's tie was already undone, a sheen of sweat glistening on his face.

'No need to rush, you can have my seat up at the counter,' Mr Helpful said. 'It's still warm.'

Ryder rocked backwards and forwards on the balls of his feet, fists clenching and unclenching at his sides. It took him a moment to get his breath before he could speak coherently.

Even then the words were strained, the threat of impending violence the only clear thing.

'What have you been saying to her?'

Evan just stared at him for a long time. It was none of his business. He took a step sideways to get around him. Ryder did the same. The aggression in his voice had ratcheted up a notch when he spoke again.

'What—'

'It's none of your business.'

Ryder pushed his face further into Evan's until they were breath-mingling close.

'Really? Well I think it is. Especially when she tries to punch me afterwards.'

Evan grinned at him, a small ray of sunshine lighting up what had been a bad day so far.

'Oh, that. I gave her ten bucks to do it.'

Ryder put a meaty finger on Evan's shoulder. He pushed hard, his whole weight behind it. It was a lot of weight. Evan leaned into it.

'Take the finger away.'

'Or what?'

'I'll break it.'

The finger stayed. Evan clamped his fist around it, felt it hot and sweaty in his palm.

'Let go or I'll arrest you for assaulting a police officer.'

Evan didn't let go.

'Really? I don't think so.' He bent the finger downwards a fraction, saw the pain in Ryder's face as he refused to go with it. 'Seeing as this is personal. Even you wouldn't hide behind your badge over this.'

Ryder yanked his finger away with a loud crack of the knuckle, his mouth twisted.

'I told you before what I'd do if you hurt her—'

'Uh, oh. Movie dialogue alert!'

Ryder suddenly let out a startled *Ow!* His face jerked forwards, forehead banging Evan on the nose. A diminutive old woman dressed all in black was hidden behind him on the sidewalk. She was busy adjusting her grip on her walking stick, looking like she was planning on hitting him on the back of the head with it a second time.

'Out the way, Fatso. You're blocking the sidewalk. And stop acting like a pair of overgrown schoolkids.' She took a swipe at Evan with her stick. It caught him unawares, a solid blow landing on the side of his head. 'You too, sonny.'

As one they jumped two feet backwards out of her way, hands up in apology, a chorus of *Sorry Ma'am* on their startled lips. Unimpressed, she gave them the benefit of her wide and surprisingly profane vocabulary. Then she was gone, marching down the sidewalk, people parting before her like earth before the plow lest they get some of the same. They both stared after her feeling very childish. Evan broke the embarrassed silence first.

'You not going to arrest her for assaulting a police officer?'

'Don't be an ass your whole life, Buckley. But I still want to know what you did to Kate.'

Evan didn't say anything about how *said* had somehow morphed into *did*.

'Seriously?'

'Uh-huh.'

'I mentioned Garfield's name.' He held up his index finger. 'Once. And she walked out.'

'That's all?'

'That's all.'

Ryder shook his head, let out a long breath.

'She's been under a lot of stress recently.'

'She doesn't think you take her seriously about him.'

'Who?'

'Garfield. Who do you think?'

'Jesus. You know what happened. You were there. She imagined she saw a kid in the car with him. What are we supposed to do? She's obsessed with him.'

Evan held up his hands.

'I'm just telling you. Maybe it's not me that's the problem.'

For a moment Ryder looked as if he was going to take offence. He straightened up from the slouch he'd relaxed into.

'Can I ask you something?' Evan said before he got himself worked up again.

'Depends what it is.'

'How busy are you at the moment?'

Ryder snorted.

'I haven't got time to have coffee with you, if that's what you're asking.'

'No. Not right now. In general.'

Much as it pained him to make any kind of admission, Ryder wasn't stupid, knew there was no point in not answering truthfully. He rocked his hand from side to side.

'So-so. That's why she's got so much time to waste with you. Why?'

Evan shrugged, no reason.

'As you said, she's under a lot of stress. Maybe a short vacation—'

'With you? Don't make me laugh. I can't think of anything more stressful. She'd come back worse than she is now.'

With that he started to walk away, unaware of how helpful his comments had been. Even if Evan wasn't pleased to hear them. It wasn't that Guillory couldn't spare the time to go to Florida with him. She just didn't want to.

Then Ryder stopped, turned back towards Evan. Nobody could've blamed Evan if he'd thought that Ryder had one more snide comment to make. Except for some reason he knew it wasn't that at all. The way Ryder cleared his throat confirmed it.

'I just wanted to say I'm pleased you found out what happened to your wife. Even if it didn't turn out how you wanted.'

Although he'd seen it coming, Evan was still rendered speechless. One of the core elements of the animosity that had existed between them since the day they first met and which had festered ever since, was Evan's loudly-voiced opinion that the police hadn't done enough when Sarah first disappeared. After the childish spat of a minute ago, neither man could hold the other's eyes.

'At least you've got closure,' Ryder said to his shoes.

'Thank you,' Evan said to the crack in the sidewalk between his own feet.

Then Ryder spoiled it all.

'Even if it does leave you free to waste Kate's life.'

But there was something different now between them. There was none of the deep-seated animosity behind the words. Evan still doubted they'd ever end up going for a beer together. But the chances of a fist fight breaking out had diminished. Nonetheless, Ryder had another crack at it.

'It must be her self-destructive streak that attracts her to you. Like a moth to the flame. She gets it from her old man.'

There was something else behind the words this time. No animosity, no joking. Just the clear ring of the truth. The look on Ryder's face suggested he realized he'd gone too far. Evan was on it immediately.

'What are you talking about?'

'You don't know?'

Evan shook his head. Ryder looked very uncomfortable, took a strong interest in his shoes again.

'You'll have to ask her. It's not for me to say.'

Evan waited in case he changed his mind. It wasn't going to happen. There was one last thing he wanted to ask. He couldn't see any reason why Ryder would have a problem with it. He made sure he kept the smile off his lips all the same.

'What did you say to make her throw a punch at you?'

That got a satisfied grin from Ryder.

'It's like you upsetting her by bringing up Garfield's name. I mentioned another name she didn't want to hear.'

He was already nodding by the time Evan mouthed *me?* at him.

6

As soon as Evan inserted the tension wrench from his lock pick set into the lock on Todd Strange's front door and applied a gentle pressure, he knew something wasn't right. The door opened immediately. It hadn't been locked. He stepped quickly inside, closed the door behind him. Then stood with his back against it, head cocked, breathing on hold. Listening.

This was too easy.

And if something seems to be too good to be true, it usually is. But for now, there was nothing except the silence of an empty apartment. Maybe the police had been careless, left it unlocked. Because despite Guillory's belief that her colleagues weren't taking her or her abduction seriously enough, it was obvious to him that they were. Standing in the hallway of the small apartment, it was clear that the police had been here before him.

He guessed they'd had the same expectation of success as he was feeling now. None whatsoever. There would be no little black book of names and addresses with the names of the targets and amounts paid in the margins next to them. Besides, if the police had found anything, he'd have heard about it from Guillory.

Something immediately struck him as odd. From where he stood with his back against the front door, he had a line of vision into the living room. Sitting on a side table beside the sofa was a table lamp. It was on. The electricity hadn't been disconnected. Which meant that somebody was still paying the bills.

Taking a closer look, he saw that it was plugged into a timer in the wall socket, the sort of thing that turns the lamp on at a predetermined time to give the impression that somebody's at home. To deter burglars. Because that fools the burglars every time.

It might be that the payment was being taken automatically despite the account holder being dead. Or it could be that somebody else had a good reason to keep the power on. It sure as hell wasn't for security. There was an alarm control panel on the wall at the side of the door. The illuminated lights on the front indicated that it still had power. No doubt the police had disabled it, not bothered to re-set it when they left. Or lock the door.

All of which was an unexpected bonus. Nonetheless, a cold shiver rippled across the back of his neck. If an alarm, why not CCTV? Was somebody watching him at this very moment?

He glanced around the room, saw nothing obvious. But a camera can be hidden anywhere.

The spare bedroom had been turned into a home office. Looking around the room it was immediately obvious that Todd had been obsessive about everything in his life, a good trait in a man who kills people for a living. The desk was shiny clean and ready for business, everything on it arranged neatly around an empty space where a computer or laptop had sat, the power cord pulled out and left lying on the desk. On a shelf under the desk a wireless router was still connected to the phone socket. If he'd felt as if he was simply going through the motions earlier, that feeling now intensified.

Above the desk, the wall was crowded with framed photographs. There were lots of Todd, on his own or with other people. Two of those others were of interest, both of them women. The first one was significant because she was present in so many of the photographs. A woman in her late twenties who looked a lot like Todd himself. She was slim, almost emaciated, with a figure that lacked a woman's curves. Her dark red hair was cut close to her head and looked as if she'd taken the kitchen scissors to it herself after a night on the town. It was only the softer features and fuller lips that made you realize you were looking at a woman. It had to be his sister, if not his twin.

The other photograph that caught his attention was unframed, tacked to the wall with a thumb tack. That wasn't what made it interesting. What made his breath catch was that it was of Kate Guillory. Standing outside the Jerusalem Tavern. The neon sign over the door was clearly visible behind her. She had an expression on her face he recognized only too well. It brought a soft smile to his lips, a renewed determination despite the blatant futility of his current illegal search for information. Studying the photograph, he knew that if Todd had waited another minute before taking it, he'd have seen himself in it as well, having caught up with her after going to the men's room on the way out. Hence the long-suffering look, why do you always wait until it's time to go?

He was surprised the police had left it.

It seemed wrong in some way. Disrespectful. It said something about the man that Todd Strange had been, one of the runts of evolution who displayed an image of his next victim alongside all the photographs of family and friends. What it said was that for him, Kate Guillory had not been a person like all the others around her. She'd been an assignment, a job to be done. A way to make a bit of cash. Cash that could then be spent on the people he cared about, maybe take his sister on vacation for her birthday, or just because he was feeling generous, the going rate for a cop being so good.

Evan forced down the rising tide of anger that was surging up inside him, concentrated on the task in hand. Todd Strange was beyond his vengeance. The man who hired him was not.

He pulled the photograph off the wall. Held it by the edges in his latex-gloved fingers, turned it this way and that, angling it towards the light. It was spotlessly clean, not a fingerprint in sight. Whoever had supplied Todd with it had been careful. As you would if you were contracting to have a police officer killed. Even so, he'd have expected the police to take it for a more thorough investigation in the lab. It couldn't be that Guillory was right, that they didn't give a damn.

He tacked it to the wall again, then got out his phone and took a photo of one of the images of the sister. He enlarged it, studied her face, couldn't help but wonder again what kind of a person she was. Was she in the same line of business herself? A brother and sister team.

They were questions he would soon have answers to.

There was nothing else of any interest in the room. The lack of any paperwork told him that whatever information there might have been, it had been on the computer or laptop.

Another power cord was still attached to the electrical socket in the wall under the desk, the end that had been pulled from the piece of equipment lying on the floor. From the scattering of fine paper dust and small slivers around it, he guessed a small shredder had been plugged into it. Good luck to whoever had the job of piecing together the shredded paper only to end up with a bunch of last month's junk mail.

There was no point wasting any more time. Todd and whoever had employed him had been careful. The police already had what little information there might have been. He didn't know what he'd been expecting. Actually, he did. And he'd been proved right. It had been a complete waste of time.

But just because he thought that, it didn't mean everybody else did.

LYDIA STRANGE DIDN'T THINK IT WAS A WASTE OF TIME AT ALL.

With a cheese and ham sandwich clamped between her teeth, she fished her phone out of her pocket. At first, she hadn't realized what the sound was. It had never gone off before. It was the app that alerted her as soon as an intruder triggered the hidden CCTV camera in her brother Todd's home office.

She watched the guy as he poked around, wasting his time looking for things that weren't there. Then he saw what was there, the thing he was meant to see. The picture of the cop Guillory that she'd tacked to the wall after the police had finished with the apartment. She couldn't tell you what made her do it.

But now it had done its job.

The guy holding it, looking for prints that also weren't there, knew her. She saw it in his face. He wasn't happy at all, looked like he wanted to spit. He wasn't police. A friend, then. She opened the image gallery on her phone, found the copy she'd taken of Guillory's photograph.

The guy wasn't in it. But she had a funny feeling that the bar Guillory was standing outside was somewhere they frequented together. It was worth checking out. The name of it was highlighted in neon behind her head. Like an open invitation.

The Jerusalem Tavern.

7

Pushing open the door to the Jerusalem Tavern, Lydia knew she had to be careful. She'd seen the guy from Todd's apartment take a picture of her. So she'd put on a shoulder-length blond wig, stuck a baseball cap on top. Colored contact lenses stared out through several inches of plain glass in a heavy frame. Then she painted her lips bright red, made sure she went well over the limits of them. Got some on her teeth too. She looked like a freak but it would do.

As soon as she stepped inside, she got a good feeling about the place. Bob Dylan's original 1965 version of *Knockin' on Heaven's Door* was playing on the jukebox. It was an omen. Because somebody was going to be doing exactly that very soon if things panned out.

Nobody paid her any attention as she skipped across the room singing along softly to the words. She took one of the stools up at the bar. After she'd ordered a beer and the bartender had put it down in front of her, she got out an image she'd printed from the CCTV footage. One that didn't show Todd's apartment in the background. She pushed it across the bar towards him.

'I'm looking for this guy. I know he comes in here.'

The bartender gave her a look, one that said he hoped nobody looking like she did ever came asking after him. Then he picked up the photograph. He recognized the guy immediately, didn't try to disguise the fact. Instead he laughed.

'What's so funny?'

'Nothing. Apart from the fact that it's Evan and he spends most of his life doing what you're doing. Looking for people. He's a private investigator.'

Lydia laughed along with him, who'd have believed it. Then she took a calculated gamble.

'I'm guessing he comes in with Kate Guillory.'

He smiled as she said the name, nodded.

'Yep. In fact you're sitting in her seat. And that one's Evan's.'

Lydia jumped off the stool as if he'd just pointed her out coming back from the ladies' room, handbag swinging. He shook his head.

'I didn't mean now.'

Lydia worked an embarrassed smile onto her face, silly me. She rested one cheek of her skinny butt back on the stool.

'Oh. Right.'

He leaned forward, gave her a wink. It made her want to throw her drink in his face. What was it with men and winking? But she didn't. Because today, in here, she had to behave herself.

'Can't be too careful. They get upset if anybody sits in them.' Then he looked from side to side, like he was checking to make sure there was nobody close enough to overhear. 'Word of advice.'

'What's that?' Lydia said leaning in even closer, thankful that she didn't get another wink or, worse, a patronizing touch of the hand on her body.

'Don't let Kate catch you coming in looking for Evan. She's been acting a bit strange lately.'

'Really? Why's that?'

She was amazed at how keen he was to discuss the private lives of his regular customers with a perfect stranger. If she was a regular and she caught him doing it, she'd be waiting outside for him with a baseball bat. See how you get on pouring a beer with broken fingers.

She must have come across a little too eager. He suddenly got wary on her, maybe embarrassed at what he'd been about to divulge. He shrugged.

'No idea.'

Then he walked away to serve another customer. He hadn't even bothered to ask why she was looking for him. She had no doubt that the exchange would be reported back to Evan the Private Investigator, seeing as how he and Guillory seemed to be part of the furniture. She carried her beer over to the far side of the room, found a table the furthest away from the door and the restrooms.

The guy would be easy to find now. If he was John or Dave the Private Investigator it might take a little longer. With a name like Evan, a two-minute search on the internet would throw up his details. And seeing as it was such a nice place, even if it was full of old farts and dinosaurs and Bob Dylan freaks—they were playing *Blowin' in The Wind* now—she decided to wait a little longer, see if he turned up, then play it by ear.

Over the next hour the bar steadily filled up with an after-work crowd. She amused herself by smiling at the men when their girlfriends weren't looking, running the tip of her tongue along her lips in what she hoped was a provocative way but which just licked all the lipstick off. It made her glad she never wore it. It left a nasty sticky mess on the glass too.

At one point she had to move tables, take one nearer the door to make sure she didn't miss him if he came in. The last thing she wanted was for him to slip in unnoticed and then suddenly appear at her table, *I hear you were looking for me.*

Then, just after seven o'clock, Evan the Investigator walked in.

'On your own tonight?' Kieran said as Evan took his usual seat up at the bar.

'Looks like it.'

There must have been something in his voice that gave him away.

'Bad day?'

Evan shrugged, took a long mouthful of his beer, sucked at the foam on his top lip. Kieran grinned at him.

'What are you grinning at?'

Kieran shook his head, doesn't matter.

But Evan knew. Guillory always gave him a hard time for sucking the foam like that, said it made him look like a retard.

'I had an argument with Kate at breakfast, then nearly had a fight with her partner in the street.'

He didn't mention the fact that Guillory had said she was too busy to go to Florida and then Ryder had immediately contradicted her, told him they didn't have a lot going on. Nor did he say anything about his wasted trip to Todd Strange's apartment.

Kieran nodded like he knew how it was.

'So you won't be wanting the rest of that bottle of champagne I opened for her?'

'It'll be flat by now.'

Kieran placed his hands on the bar, fingers splayed. Like he was thinking of throwing Evan out for being so morose.

'You want to tell me what the argument was about? She didn't lose one of the earrings you bought her already, did she?'

Evan said he didn't know, made it sound as if he didn't care. Kieran gave up, started to move away. Then he came back, a smile on his face. As he had with Lydia, he leaned over the bar.

'I don't want to get you in any trouble with Kate—'

'More trouble,' Mr Morose corrected.

'—but there was a woman in here looking for you earlier.'

He took a small step backwards at the violence of Evan's reaction. It was as if he'd sat on a cattle prod. The long face of a moment ago was a distant memory. Suddenly he was all ears.

A small worm of excitement twisted in Evan's guts, set his heart racing. In all the years he'd been coming to the Jerusalem, he could count on the fingers of one hand the number of times somebody had come looking for him. He wasn't complaining. Because it had ended badly every time. He had a feeling that this time was going to be no different. Because it was too much of a coincidence coming less than twelve hours since his visit to Todd Strange's apartment.

'What did she want?'

The smile slipped from Kieran's face and with it some of Evan's animation.

'I forgot to ask. Sorry. But I haven't seen her leave.' He pointed over to the far side of the bar. 'She was sitting at a table over there.' He raised himself up onto his toes, moved his body from side to side. 'I can't see if she's still there for all the people in the way.'

Evan left his beer on the bar, walked over to where Kieran had been pointing. All of the tables in that part of the room were occupied by noisy groups of people. There were no single women. He made a slow lap of the bar on his way back to his seat, a mental image of Todd Strange's sister in his mind. There was nobody who looked remotely like her.

Kieran was still standing in the same spot when he got back to the bar, curiosity taking the place of the previous apologetic look on his face. Evan got out his phone, found the picture he'd taken of the sister. He showed it to Kieran.

'Is that her?'

Kieran shook his head, didn't even need to take the phone to get a better look.

'Nope. Nothing like her. This one was scary. And I mean scary. Long blond hair. Heavy glasses that looked like your granny should be wearing them. Lipstick smeared all over her face.' He shuddered, tapped the screen of Evan's phone with his finger. Then leaned away quickly in case Evan took a swipe at him. 'I'd go for this one every time. If things don't work out with Kate, I mean.'

Evan wasn't listening. He put his phone away. It didn't mean a thing that Kieran didn't recognize her. It sounded like a very bad disguise anyway. For once he was glad Guillory wasn't there to tell him to stop being so paranoid. His visit to Todd Strange's apartment hadn't been such a waste of time after all. He'd kicked something loose. Now that he thought about it, he realized that the police wouldn't have left Guillory's picture still tacked to the wall. It had been put there afterwards.

As bait.

And he'd swallowed it whole.

8

THE NEXT MORNING EVAN FLEW INTO THE SUN AND WARMTH OF Miami International, leaving behind for a couple of days the unanswered questions surrounding Todd Strange and his sister. He rented a Ford Mustang Cabrio to make the most of the weather, put the roof down, then headed south. He took the Ronald Reagan turnpike, then picked up US-1 just before it turned into the Overseas Highway at Key Largo.

He was on his own of course. He hadn't spoken to Guillory since she walked out of the diner the day before. At least it gave him time to think and reflect, with the sun warm on his face, the wind in his hair. That didn't mean he wouldn't have preferred to feel the weight of her head on his shoulder, her hair flicking in his face, tickling his nose.

But time alone with your own mind isn't always a good thing. Because the drive without her brought to mind another car journey, one made with her. One without sun and the sea and a sporty convertible car to enjoy it in. The two of them in the back of a government-issue sedan. Driven in silence by stony-faced men in cheap gray suits to a state psychiatric hospital. Then walking with her to his wife's grave. A solemn procession on legs made from rubber hose, the wind in their faces, cold this time, whipping her hair into his eyes as she pressed closely into his body, the strength of her arms the only thing keeping him upright.

And his reaction, standing at the desolate graveside. Jabbing his finger at the unkept ground at his feet like he was trying to poke it through to the body buried below.

No! I don't believe that's my wife.

Then later in the Jerusalem with Guillory. Seeing the same doubts in the denim blue of her eyes, clouding them. Pressing her until she gave in.

It's nothing. I got a feeling someone was watching us from one of those little windows, that's all.

So what? he'd asked her.

Exactly, she'd replied. Nothing. Like I said.

That should have been that. Except you don't get to decide what your mind serves you up when you close your eyes at night. Small doubts and minor misgivings, the sort of vague anxiety that comes calling at four in the morning before the gray dawn light seeps through the gap in the curtains, bathing the room in a creeping pale radiance, leaving you unable to say what was real and what was a dream. A slight inconsistency here, an incompatible detail there.

In the cold clear light of day they were nothing at all, didn't give him a moment's pause.

Until time weighed heavily on his hands.

The sudden blare of a horn as he drifted into the path of a passing car snapped him out of it, jerked him back to the sun and warmth of the present, sent the demons scuttling back into their hidey holes to bide their time. Not that they minded, they knew they'd be seeing him again soon enough.

He turned on the radio, didn't care what station. Cranked up the volume and sang along to keep them at bay. He took it easy, a steady sixty as the big trucks blew past him. And not just because the new Mustang didn't drive like the Boss 302 he'd owned some years ago, a long pause when he put his foot to the floor while the engine woke up, stretched, and scratched itself before eventually getting around to accelerating. So he went with the flow, passing through Key Largo and Tavernier and Plantation Key. After a couple of hours he started looking for a place to eat, pulled off the road into a roadside bar and grill sandwiched between the highway and the ocean just before Islamorada.

He sat at a table on the upper deck, the black thoughts of earlier left far behind. Leaning back in his chair, hands clasped behind his head, he looked out over a small marina and then the endless flat turquoise water beyond. All the way to The Bahamas and Cuba somewhere over the horizon. He ordered a club sandwich with grilled Wahoo and crispy bacon served on Texas toast with a slice of Key Lime Pie to follow, washed it all down with a couple of ice-cold beers.

It beat working any day.

Then he got back on the highway for another thirty easy miles to Marathon. At the end of town, right before the start of Seven Mile Bridge, he turned left onto 11th Street Ocean. He passed a trailer park, continued on down towards the Marathon Marina and Boatyard. He parked in a lot on the left which for some reason had a boat with a blue and white hull sitting on boat stands on the far side. Then he continued on foot to look for Crow's friend Winter's boat, the *Dead or Alive*.

He couldn't remember when he'd had such a relaxing easy day. It was good that he'd made the most of it. Because it wasn't going to last for much longer.

Strolling past a small, unmanned wooden security office, he felt as if he belonged. He hoped he looked like it too, ostentatiously swinging Winter's spare set of keys on his finger.

He found the *Dead or Alive* almost at the end, a seventy-eight-foot sport fishing motor yacht complete with fighting chair on the stern deck and tuna tower up top. It was a beautiful boat. He could think of worse ways to while away the twilight years of your life, despite what Crow thought.

He stood on the edge of the dock a moment looking for any signs of life on board. There weren't any. Just standing there he could tell it was unoccupied. The same couldn't be said of the boat on the other side of the shared jetty. The sliding glass doors to the cabin—what purists call the salon—were open, music playing softly inside.

Then a middle-aged man in shorts, T-shirt and boat shoes came through the door, noticed Evan standing there. In one hand he held a glass filled to the brim with white wine, a pair of sunglasses in the other. Some of the wine slopped onto his hand in his surprise at seeing Evan standing there. They stared at each other for a couple of beats, the contented smile on the guy's sun and wind beaten face hardening to a look of wary suspicion.

'Can I help you?'

Evan did the translation from alcohol-slurred nautical to English.

What are you doing there?

Evan racked his brains, tried to remember Winter's first name. It was right there on the periphery of his memory, wouldn't come. The guy transferred his sunglasses to the top of his head, the now empty hand settling on his hip in a mildly aggressive stance. He looked like the sort of guy whose hands spent a lot of time there. Again, the gesture was easy to interpret.

You're one lame excuse away from me calling security.

'George!' Evan said, the name exploding from his mouth.

'What?'

'I said George asked me to check his boat. Make sure everything's okay.'

The guy's face suggested he might have had a drink or two but did Evan think he was born yesterday?

Evan showed him the keys, stepped onto the jetty. It seemed he didn't show them clearly enough. All the guy saw was a raised hand and a man he already thought was up to no good taking a step towards him. He took a step backwards with a quick glance into the salon.

Evan held the ring of keys up by his finger and thumb, jangled them, almost dropped them in the water.

'I'm not breaking in. George gave me a set of keys.'

The guy nodded, unconvinced. Half a million dollars' worth of sport fishing boat was as good a reason as any for mugging an old man in an alley, stealing his keys. Evan walked further down the jetty.

'Call George if you don't believe me. I assume you've got his number, seeing as you live next door to him. Or next boat or mast or whatever you nautical types say.'

He pulled out his phone, found the number Crow had given him. He'd already tried it after he'd finished his lunch. It had gone straight to voicemail. He held the phone towards the guy.

'You want it or not?'

The guy shook his head, worked a nervous smile onto his face.

'No, that's okay. You go ahead, do what you have to do.'

Then he ducked quickly back into the salon behind him, slid the glass doors closed. With the light reflecting off the smoked glass, Evan couldn't see what he was doing in there.

Not that he needed to. He was thankful that they were all the way down the end of the dock. Even so, it wouldn't take long for security to get there. He stepped onto the stern deck, unlocked the door to the salon, slid it all the way open.

Standing looking in, two things immediately hit him. First, George wasn't at home. Or, at boat. Or whatever. From the lack of any odor apart from a faint mustiness from the lack of fresh air, he knew he wasn't going to find poor old George lying on the bed in the stateroom with his head caved in. Or even having passed away peacefully in his sleep. At least he'd be able to put Crow's mind at rest on that front.

The second thing made his heart sink. More so because he could almost hear the urgent, whispered phone call the suspicious neighbor was making to security, hear the fast, excited footsteps as they rushed to investigate something more interesting than a drunken sailor driving into somebody else's boat. Looking around the salon, he reckoned there must have been a million places to hide something. Boat interior design is necessarily a lesson in efficient use of limited space, carefully designed and concealed storage everywhere. The number of hiding places that resulted from the design was bad enough, let alone all the secret places a paranoid owner could devise.

Unless George had left his laptop or his phone lying around in plain sight—which was unlikely—there was no way he was going to find anything before security got there. He hadn't got further than down the stairs and into the master stateroom when the boat dipped slightly.

Security had arrived.

Then a shout from outside.

'Come out with your hands where I can see them.'

Evan retraced his footsteps, stepped out onto the stern deck with his hands at shoulder height, palms forward, the glare of the sun blinding him momentarily. The security guard stared at him from behind mirrored sunglasses, his hand resting loosely on the holstered gun on his hip. The name badge sewn onto his shirt said Rodriguez. Behind him, the neighbor watched smugly from the safety of his own boat, his glass now almost empty. Evan dropped his hands, gave a flick of his head towards him.

'I already told him George asked me to check on his boat. I've got a set of keys.'

Rodriguez looked as unconvinced as the other guy who had now moved out of the safety of the salon to get a better look.

'Really? What's to say you didn't mug him, steal his keys? And his wallet which gave you his name?'

'What? Then made a really good guess about which one of the thousand boats was his?'

'You could've been watching him. There's not a thousand anyway.'

'Uh-huh. And he could've given me the keys and asked me to check his boat.'

Rodriguez nodded, it's possible. Evan felt like flicking his sunglasses off so he could see his eyes.

'Except he didn't say anything to me about going away. He always lets me know if he's going to be away for any length of time.' He jabbed his breastbone with his thumb. 'So I can keep an eye on his boat. Because that's my job.'

They weren't getting anywhere. Going around in circles. Evan got the impression Rodriguez was happy to do exactly that, was just filling in time.

'Yeah? Well I've got a job to do as well.'

He turned his back on him, headed towards the salon. Then the reason for Rodriguez's dawdling became clear.

A police cruiser screeched to a halt on the dock above them. It skidded on the loose gravel, made Evan think that the white concrete bollards evenly spaced along the edge of the dock weren't just for show. The doors swung open. Two police officers climbed lazily out in marked contrast to their excited arrival. They hitched up their belts in unison as if it was a routine they practiced regularly when things were slow.

'How's it going, Luis?' the driver called down from the edge of the dock. 'Looks like you've caught yourself a boat thief, eh?'

His partner parked his butt on one of the concrete bollards, arms crossed to show off his well-muscled arms. Everybody was wearing mirrored sunglasses except Evan and the owner of the neighboring boat whose designer shades were still perched, jerk-style, on the top of his head. He was now sitting comfortably on a padded couch watching the proceedings. Evan promised himself if he got the chance, he'd throw him into the water.

'Hey, Ricky. Mr Segal here caught this guy snooping around. He says the owner asked him to check on the boat.'

Ricky was a caricature of a small-town cop. A cocky extrovert who wore his holstered thirty-eight special like a loincloth and divided his time almost equally between polishing the squad car and drinking free beer in the various waterfront bars. He looked over at Segal who raised his glass in greeting and nodded, that's right officer, happy to do my duty.

Ricky waved an acknowledgement, turned his attention to Evan. Gave him a long sunglassed stare.

'You've got keys?'

Evan held them up.

'I thought maybe he'd stolen them,' Rodriguez called up to Ricky, his self-esteem slipping away like fish guts hosed off the wooden deck.

'Nothing's been called in.'

'Wouldn't be if the owner's lying unconscious or worse in some alley.'

Ricky jumped down onto the jetty between the two boats. He pulled off his shades to get a better look at Evan. From the look of boredom on his face and the way both the cops seemed to be just going through the motions, Evan reckoned he viewed all rent-a-cops like Rodriguez as a waste of space. Wannabees who liked to spice up their boring jobs by wasting the real cops' time, making a mountain out of a molehill over every little thing. Even

Segal was yawning, looking bored seeing as nobody had wrestled Evan to the ground yet, didn't even look as if they were about to.

'Haven't heard anything about that either. Unless you think they dumped him in the sea.'

Rodriguez's jaw tightened, not happy that they weren't taking him seriously.

'You check his ID?' Ricky said.

He climbed into the boat, made a give-it-here gesture with his hand towards Evan without waiting for Rodriguez's mumbled *no*. Evan pulled out his wallet, held out his ID. Ricky took his time carefully folding his sunglasses and slipping them into his top pocket before he took it. Then he nodded to himself as he read it, like his day had just taken a turn for the worse.

'Private investigator, huh?'

Evan didn't bother to confirm it. Ricky's tone of voice implied that he was having trouble getting the correct ranking in his mind about the jobs of rent-a-cop and private investigator. That it didn't much matter anyway. One was right at the bottom of the pile, the other one immediately above it. And if he had his way the pair of them would be looking for a new job.

'That's what Winter used to do before he moved here,' Rodriguez chipped in.

Ricky carried on nodding with as much interest as if Rodriguez had told him that, once again, the sky was blue and the sun was shining down here in sunny Florida.

'That how come you know him?' Ricky said to Evan.

'Through a mutual colleague, yeah,' Evan said, the words feeling ridiculous in his mouth.

Seemed Ricky thought so too.

'A *mutual colleague*.' He looked up at his partner still sitting on the concrete bollard, got a sorry headshake back. 'What? He used to call you up when he needed somebody to go undercover in the public toilets?'

They all snickered. Including Rodriguez, who was pleased to have the ridicule aimed at Evan instead of himself for a change. Evan pulled out one of Guillory's business cards, held it towards Ricky.

'Call her. She'll vouch for me.'

Ricky took the card, climbed back up onto the dock. He shooed a gull off the next bollard along from his partner and perched on it himself. Then pulled out his phone and made the call. At one point, he looked directly at Evan, eyes narrowed. Presumably as Guillory described him. Then, just before they ended the call, his face split into a wide grin. His day had suddenly improved unexpectedly. Evan let out a weary breath, didn't need to ask what that was about. Ricky was busting a gut to let him know anyway. He jumped back down onto the jetty.

'Up on the gunwale.'

He patted the upper edge of the side of the boat in case Evan didn't know what the gunwale was.

'You don't have to do everything she says.'

Ricky grinned wider.

'She's a police detective. That makes her my superior. She tells me to push you in the water, I gotta push you in the water.'

He shrugged like it was a rotten job but somebody's gotta do it. His partner had stopped picking at his nails, looked a lot more interested now. So did Rodriguez and the interfering neighbor for that matter. Evan didn't move, crossed his arms, feet planted. They all stayed like that for what felt like a very long time. Then Ricky got bored, the grin fading.

'Only kidding.'

He held Guillory's card out towards Evan. He had his shades back on now. Evan couldn't see his eyes. He took the card, not expecting him to grab his arm but ready for it if he did.

'She says to tell you that you should've brought her down here with you. It would've avoided all this trouble. And she said she could do with a break.'

Evan worked a big smile onto his face, wondered what the hell Guillory was playing at. Even though he didn't think Ricky would be calling her back, he had a little fun of his own just in case.

'Yeah, well, she needs to get in line like everybody else.'

Ricky raised an eyebrow, then climbed out of the boat when it became obvious Evan wasn't going to say anything more. He gave Rodriguez a consolatory slap on the shoulder, maybe next time, and called his thanks to Segal sitting disappointed in his own boat. Then they were gone in another screech of gravel and dust, back to their free beers and real police work.

9

'NO NEED TO APOLOGIZE,' EVAN SAID TO RODRIGUEZ'S BACK AS HE climbed sullenly out of the boat.

'I wasn't about to,' drifted over his shoulder.

'You got a minute anyway?'

Rodriguez turned around slowly. His expression suggested he didn't know if Evan was having fun at his expense, implying that he had nothing better to do than cause trouble.

'I want to ask you about George.'

Rodriguez relented, the scowl on his face softening. Even so, he didn't get back on board, stood on the jetty with his arms crossed, hands tucked into his armpits.

'You said George always tells you if he's going to be away.'

'Yeah. But it's nothing official, not like I said. If business is quiet, he takes me out for free sometimes. So I look out for him. I've got a bunch of his cards. If somebody comes around looking to go fishing, I give them one of George's cards, point them in this direction. There's a lot of competition. He tells me if he's not going to be here so I don't send them down here for nothing, send them to someone else.'

He shrugged, that's the way it works.

'And he didn't tell you he was going away.'

'Nope.'

Rodriguez rolled his neck, stretched the muscles in his shoulders. Maybe he got stiff sitting in his little hut all day long. Evan didn't think so, reckoned he was doing it while he made up his mind whether to say more.

'Are you really a friend of his?'

'A friend of a friend. But he couldn't make it. Why?'

Rodriguez looked up at the dock behind him, his mouth turning down again. Evan felt like saying to him, don't worry, you'll know about it if they come back. We'll have another dust shower landing on our heads. He sat down in the fighting chair, put his feet up on the footrest, swiveled from side to side. Then Rodriguez climbed back into the boat, rested his butt against the padded cushions that ran all the way around the stern of the boat.

'It's not like that *pendejo* Ricky thinks. That I make a fuss over nothing, call them every time the slightest little thing happens. But the guy who works the night shift said he heard something going on down here a couple of nights ago. When he got here, there was nobody around. George's boat looked like it was shut up tight. Except the lights were on. And it was rocking like people were moving around inside. But you can't go knocking on the door every time you see a boat rocking in the middle of the night. That's what half the owners buy them for.'

He pushed himself off the side of the boat, made an obscene thrusting gesture with his hips, a smile creasing his face for the first time. Evan smiled with him.

'But not George?'

Rodriguez shook his head.

'No. He told me he's too old for all that. He'd rather be on the water fishing. Fish don't answer back.'

Evan glanced at Rodriguez's hand where it was tucked under

his armpit, couldn't see if he was wearing a wedding ring or not. The heartfelt emotion behind his words made him wonder if it was George who preferred being out on the water where the fish didn't answer back or Rodriguez.

'I haven't seen George since then. So when Mr Segal called me about you snoop . . . sorry, looking around, I called the cops.'

Evan nodded like it was understandable, he'd do the same.

'Is Segal here all the time?'

'No.'

'Was he here the other night?'

'You'd have to ask the night guy. But I don't think so.' He glanced over his shoulder at the boat behind, dropped his voice even though Segal was nowhere in sight. 'The amount he drinks, the gas tank could've blown and he'd have slept through it.'

Evan sat up suddenly in the fighting chair as if a big fish had just taken the bait. The mention of drinking had kicked loose something in his mind. Something that had registered as he walked through the salon earlier.

'Don't take this the wrong way, but did George drink a lot?'

'He liked a cold beer when he was out on the water as much as the next guy.'

'But not hard liquor?'

Rodriguez shook his head.

'I never saw him drink anything stronger than a light beer. Why?'

Evan nodded backwards towards the open doors to the salon.

'There's an empty whisky bottle sitting on the counter in the kitchen—'

Rodriguez stifled a laugh.

'Galley.'

'Right. Galley. Maybe he kept it for the guys who chartered the boat.'

Rodriguez wasn't buying it.

'No. Nobody wants a bunch of drunks on board. A couple of cold beers, sure. But not hitting the hard stuff with the sun beating down on your head.'

Neither of them said anything for a while, the potential implications of the unexplained empty bottle on their minds.

'I gotta get back,' Rodriguez said. 'Who knows, maybe somebody's cat has fallen in the water. That's what that *pendejo* Ricky thinks I do all day.'

He handed Evan a business card with the contact details for a number of the marina's administrative officers, including a couple of cell phone numbers for security. He'd circled the top one in red.

'Give me a call if you find anything.'

There was one more thing Evan wanted to do before he knuckled down to the massive task ahead of him. He climbed up to the flybridge for the best view, pulled out his phone. Then he framed a shot of the view across all the other boats gleaming in the sun, their masts swaying against the pure blue of the sky, the perfect turquoise of the water stretching to the horizon beyond. He considered taking a video to catch the sound of the rigging clanking in the breeze and the noisy squabbling of the gulls wheeling overhead, decided a photo would do. He sent it to Guillory with a brief message signed by Mr Dry-As-A- Bone.

Thanks for getting me off the hook. BTW, I thought you were too busy to come.

10

BEFORE GETTING DOWN TO THE SERIOUS SEARCH FOR ANYTHING that might give a clue as to what George Winter had been up to, Evan poked through the galley cabinets and the refrigerator. As Rodriguez had said, he found nothing stronger than light beer. There were a couple of cans of it in the fridge and that was all. No doubt Winter stocked up when he had a charter booked, preferring the company at one of the many bars in town to drinking alone on his boat when he was moored up. There was no hard liquor on board at all. Just the empty whisky bottle.

Faced with the daunting task ahead of him, he appropriated one of the cold beers from the fridge. Even though he knew it was stupid, he didn't want to take it outside and sit in the fighting chair drinking it in the sun in case Segal came out again and saw him. Why he should care what a drunk like Segal thought, he didn't know. But he did. So he slid into the bench seat behind the polished teak table in the galley instead.

From there he had a good view of the whole of the salon. It depressed the hell out of him, the number of potential hiding places. Then there were the staterooms downstairs. And then outside. And what about the engine compartment, why not there while you're at it?

Finally, he couldn't put it off any longer. He crumpled the empty can in his fist, slid out from behind the table. It was a low table, bolted to the floor. And he had long legs. So his thighs brushed the underside of the table as he half stood and slid out.

That was when his day took another turn for the worse.

A piece of chewing gum was smeared across his thigh. Some slob had stuck it to the underside of the table. The beer can in his hand crumpled noisily as he stared angrily at the gum, thinking how he'd like to grind it into the dirty, lazy bastard's hair if he got hold of him. Maybe use his face to clean the residue off the underside of the table.

It couldn't have been Winter who'd stuck it there. Nobody does that to their own property. The rest of the boat was spotless. Someone he'd taken out on a charter, then. Thinking they'd paid for the use of the boat, they'd do what they damn well liked.

He picked it off carefully, rolled it into a disgusting little ball in his fingers. Tried not to think about it having been in some slob's mouth. Probably while he swilled his beer and smoked at the same time. Then, almost as an over-compensation for what the slob had done, he found a knife in one of the galley drawers and scraped the last of the gum from the underside of the table.

However, there is a limit to what a man will do with a piece of another man's gum. He wasn't about to climb back up to the dock and go searching for a trash can. So he went outside, balanced the sticky little ball on his fingernail, tensed the finger against his thumb ready to flick it far out into the sea. Then stopped. Not because of a last-minute pang of conscience. He smiled to himself, looked to his right. At Segal's boat. The open door to Segal's salon would be an easy shot.

He didn't do it, of course.

That would have made him as bad as the slob who stuck it to the table in the first place. He flicked it far out into the water of the marina without another thought, happy in the knowledge that a hungry fish or a crab would eat it.

It would've saved him a lot of trouble down the road if he'd indulged his childish thoughts and flicked it onto Segal's boat instead.

He started with the exterior of the boat because he reckoned it had fewer hiding places and the added advantage of working in the sun. He soon found out that he'd been wrong about the number of hiding places. There were locked storage compartments everywhere for rods and tackle, the keys to them on the ring Crow had given him. There were a number of livewells too—tanks used to keep bait fish healthy and frisky by pumping water through them. They had clear acrylic tops and side windows to monitor the bait, make sure it was healthy. That made life a bit easier. Evan could see with a quick glance that most of them were empty and dry. Although one was full of water. He couldn't stop himself from laughing when he saw the solitary fish inside floating dead on the surface, its white belly distended. So much for a livewell. More like a deadwell.

Apart from the fleeting amusement caused by that discovery, there was nothing of interest. After a couple of hours' fruitless searching he fetched the last remaining beer from the fridge and sat in the Pompanette fighting chair to take a break, enjoy the warmth of the afternoon sun rather than just work in it. After the last two hours he didn't give a damn whether Segal saw him or not.

And just occasionally, not giving a damn is exactly what's called for.

Swiveling around to face the glass doors leading into the salon, he saw another door to the side of them, underneath the steps leading up to the flybridge. He guessed it was the day head

—the bathroom used by everyone on board, not located in one of the staterooms. Leaving his beer in a drinks holder clipped to the back of the chair—the most sensible accessory he'd seen on the boat so far—he went to take a closer look.

The lock had been forced. He pulled the door open gingerly expecting to be assaulted by the stench, to find nothing but a chemical toilet full of shit and piss courtesy of whoever had been taken short and broken in. Instead, he was surprised when a load of diving equipment came tumbling out, landed at his feet. He was looking at two or three thousand dollars' worth of gear at least.

His heart, instead of sinking at the discovery of an overflowing toilet, picked up. Because in all the neatness and order of the rest of the boat, something wasn't right. Nobody stores that much expensive equipment in a toilet with a broken door.

He stepped backwards, spread it out on the deck. There was a BCD, the lifejacket lookalike that allows you to control your buoyancy underwater. And a regulator, the piece you put in your mouth with its attached hoses and dials, plus assorted small equipment—mask, snorkel, fins, knife. Everything but the oxygen tanks themselves. The BCD was the most likely candidate to conceal something in, with a number of zippered compartments. He sat on the deck with his back against the glass salon doors and started to go through them. It didn't take long to determine that they were all empty.

Then he worked his way methodically across the surface of the BCD with his fingers. Squeezing and feeling for bumps that would indicate something inserted into the fabric of the jacket. As he did so, a vague thought scratched at the back of his mind, a feeling that he was missing something obvious.

He looked up suddenly from concentrating on the BCD, saw Segal watching him from the cockpit of his boat, the wine glass in his hand full once more. Evan raised his arm, waved at him good-naturedly. After discovering the busted door, it seemed the guy wasn't so paranoid after all. But Segal didn't acknowledge him, didn't ask what he was doing. A minute later, he drifted back inside the salon.

Then it came to him, sitting on the deck with the BCD in his hands. Like a small boy playing with his new toy and finding a part was missing. Because the oxygen tanks weren't the only piece of equipment missing.

People are buoyant. So are aluminum tanks full of air. Strapping on a BCD only increases the tendency to float on the surface. Scuba diving wouldn't be nearly as much fun if all you did was float around on the surface. You need something to weigh you down, to counteract all that buoyancy.

The weight belt was missing.

When he'd picked up the BCD, he hadn't noticed the weight of it—or the lack of weight. It was only after going over it inch by inch with his fingers that it struck him that there were no integrated weights. Anybody wearing this particular BCD would need a separate, old-fashioned weight belt—a canvas belt with heavy lead weights threaded onto it.

What better to tie a sealed waterproof container to, submerge it in the water under the boat? Attached to a length of heavy-duty fishing line, the other end tied off on one of the many cleats around the boat, it would be almost invisible. The weight would be sufficient to hold something as large as a laptop —certainly something as small as a phone or a USB thumb drive—hard on the bottom.

Knowing he was right and pleased that Segal had gone back inside the salon and wasn't watching his every move, he made his way slowly around the perimeter of the boat, checking every cleat and handrail support for unexplained fishing line disappearing into the depths like a forgotten crab line.

And found nothing.

Feeling deflated, he dropped into the fighting chair again. The beer he'd left in the drinks holder and forgotten about was now too warm to drink. He let his head loll backwards and closed his eyes, felt the sun warm on his face. He'd been so sure he was right, was doubly glad Segal wasn't watching him chase his tail. He'd be calling the men in the white jackets, not security, if he was.

There was nothing for it now but to make a start on the inside. He'd be spending the night on the boat at this rate. Instead of driving down to Key West, only an hour away, which is what he had planned. A photo sent to Guillory from the bar of Jimmy Buffett's Margaritaville would teach her to think twice before she pretended to be too busy next time.

Feeling as if he'd just finished fighting a world-record-beating Marlin, he pushed himself out of the chair, headed towards the salon. The diving equipment littered the deck at the entrance to it. He shoved it aside with his foot. Then stopped. Looked at the mask, an idea popping into his mind.

He'd stick his head in the water, take a quick look under the boat. Maybe the fishing line had snapped as the boat moved with the swell, anchored too securely to the bottom by the heavy weight belt.

A buzz of nervous excitement started up in his gut. This time he was right.

He kicked off his shoes, stripped down to his boxers in case he accidentally toppled in, hoping nobody was watching him from the dock. Standing stripped-off on the deck a shiver rippled over his skin despite the warmth of the sun.

Something was waiting for him under the boat.

He pulled on the mask, adjusted the strap. Didn't bother with the snorkel. He wasn't going to be looking for that long.

He had no idea how right he was about that.

Then he maneuvered himself carefully into position, balanced his body over the gunwale. Gripping the underside tightly with his fingers, he lowered his face slowly towards the water. A couple of inches above the surface he took a big juddering gulp of air right down into his lungs, his chest expanding, then submerged his face, the cool water fresh and clean on his skin.

He'd been right. The weight belt was down there.

But it didn't bring a smile of satisfaction to his tightly-clamped lips.

Because it wasn't weighing down a waterproof container.

George Winter was wearing it.

11

EVAN'S HEAD EXPLODED OUT OF THE WATER AS IF A DEPTH CHARGE had gone off under the boat, a stream of water droplets flicking in a graceful arc high into the air, glittering in the sunlight. He ripped off the mask. Heaved air into his lungs like he'd been underwater a couple of minutes or maybe hours, not a few measly seconds. The sun was in his eyes, the salty water running into them, blinding him. It didn't stop him from seeing the image of George Winter's face staring back at him, what little there was of his thin wispy silver hair moving gently in the currents like delicate seaweed stretching towards the light above.

He allowed himself a minute to get over the initial shock, his breath ragged and rasping like he'd swum a circuit of the marina with a weight belt around his own waist. Then he pulled the mask back on, got himself back into position on the gunwale. He heaved air deep into his lungs, expanding them, forced it out again. Over and over until he felt he could hold his breath for a week. Then filled them to bursting, lowered his face back into the water, water that was no longer cool and fresh and inviting, but cold and soul-numbing, nothing more than one big watery open grave.

Winter was directly under the boat. Unlike his neighbor Segal and most of the other men and women Evan had seen on the other boats or walking around the marina who favored shorts and T-shirts, Winter was dressed all in black. Long black pants and long-sleeved black shirt. The weight belt was clipped around his waist, the dull gray lead weights resting on his hips. His body was upright although he appeared to be thrusting his pelvis forwards as the intestinal putrefactive gases concentrated in his belly tried to lift him towards the surface. Under the bulging stomach the legs were bent at the knees from the weight of the belt, the inflexibility of his leg muscles preventing them from collapsing entirely.

Above the black clothes, his face was startlingly white. There was no trace of lividity. Because blood after death adheres to the laws of gravity and, his body being upright, it had drained from his face and neck. His mouth was wide open. As were his sightless eyes. Small, inquisitive fish made tentative forays into his hair, nipped at his skin and hunted even smaller creatures that had already colonized the new arrival in their domain.

But the thing that struck Evan more than anything else was his hands and arms. They floated freely at his sides. Made him look as if he'd been crucified, not drowned. Cadaveric spasm had turned the fingers into claws, and maceration, the skin change which characterizes immersion, had begun. The skin on the tips of his fingers and his palms was whitened and sodden, thickened and wrinkled like an old washerwoman's, not yet to the point where the epidermis becomes loose and peels, the nails and hair detaching.

It wasn't the physiological effects of Winter's time in the water on his hands and arms, fascinating as they might be, that demanded Evan's attention. It was the fact that they weren't tied behind his back or constrained in any way. He could have unclipped the belt at any time. He'd either gone in of his own free will or he'd been unconscious. There were no obvious cuts or wounds on the front or the top of his head, visible through his thin hair. Time would tell whether he'd been hit from behind.

Or maybe the unexplained empty whisky bottle was now unexplained no longer. A pint of whisky either drunk voluntarily or administered forcefully would render most people unconscious. Certainly a man not accustomed to hard liquor.

He'd seen enough. More than enough.

He pulled his face out of the water, less violently than last time, maneuvered himself back into the boat. Looking down into the gap between the boat and the jetty, Winter's body was invisible, even to someone looking for it. Totally inappropriate for the climate, the black long-sleeved top and long pants did a great job of making him almost invisible in the shadows under the boat.

He, or somebody else, hadn't wanted his body found too quickly.

The half-empty can of warm beer was still in the drinks holder behind the fighting chair. He downed it in one, belched loudly, wished he hadn't bothered. Then he dressed again quickly which did nothing to lessen the shivers that had taken hold of his body despite only his head having gotten wet. Sinking into the fighting chair, he angled his face towards the sun and closed his eyes.

Then opened them again. Fast. Just not fast enough to stop him from seeing Winter's face staring at him from the back of his eyelids. There would be no peace or rest for him, not for a while yet. So he pulled out his phone and made a call. Crow answered immediately as if he'd been expecting it. His opening words confirmed it, not even a *hello*.

'Bad news?'

'I'm sorry.'

He told him what he'd found, kept it brief. Then he backed up, ran through the events leading up to the discovery. Crow was silent for a long while. Evan gave him time, leaned back in the chair. Almost forgot himself and closed his eyes again. Around him the everyday sounds of the marina as people went about their business and their pleasures seemed too loud, too intrusive, a stark, rude contrast to his brief visit to Winter's silent underwater world.

When Crow eventually spoke, Evan would not have been surprised if he'd heard the voice that came down the line coming from Winter's own mouth.

'It's not suicide.'

'I knew you'd say that.'

'That's because it's obvious. And because you think so too.'

'You want to tell me why you're so sure?'

In the background he heard the clink of ice in a glass. Then the sound of a generous measure of liquid poured over it. Unlike his friend George, Crow was not averse to a drop of the hard stuff. It made Evan wish there were some cold beers left. He had a feeling a long night lay ahead.

'Because he wasn't the type,' Crow said.

Evan didn't say anything. He knew what would happen if he tried to get away with something as wishy-washy as that. Crow knew it too.

'If you knew what we went through together, you'd know it too.'

Wishy-washy times two, Evan thought to himself. He felt as if his head was underwater again and it was Winter talking to him. He could see the mouth moving, hear strange indistinct sounds resonating in the water all around him. And he was supposed to make sense of them.

'Seeing as I don't know what you went through together but I *do* know that you're not going to tell me, how about giving me some concrete reasons? Because the police are going to be asking me the same things very soon—'

'Did you call them yet?'

'No. I called you first.'

'Good boy. There's hope for you yet.'

'So. Some reasons?'

'I told you how excited he was about getting this job. Some real work for a change, he said. Why would he suddenly kill himself when his life's just taken a turn for the better.'

Evan shook his head even though Crow couldn't see him.

'That's just more of the same. He wasn't the type. He was so *excited*. They're going to want more than that.'

Crow thought for a while, the sound of him slurping his drink loud in Evan's ear. If it went on too long, Evan would be hopping onto Segal's boat, asking him if he had any beers in the fridge as well as all the wine.

'That wasn't his diving equipment, for one,' Crow said.

'How do you know?'

'Because he couldn't swim.'

'What? A man who spends his life on the water can't swim?'

Crow said there was nothing strange about that. Floating around on top of the water was better than getting in it, certainly preferable to going under it. Assuming you've forsaken the even more sensible option of not going anywhere near it in the first place.

'I take it you can't swim either.'

Crow ignored the question which was confirmation enough.

'And he didn't drink hard liquor. So that wasn't his whisky.'

They both knew that the autopsy was likely to show that

George was full of it nonetheless. The point they were arguing was how it had gotten into him. They also knew there was no point in them trying to convince each other. Because, despite playing devil's advocate, Evan was of the same opinion as Crow. Unfortunately, it wasn't Crow who was going to have to convince the police.

'I know you have to call the police now,' Crow said, 'but see if you can have a quick look around before they get there.'

Evan bit his tongue. Didn't ask what the hell Crow thought he'd been doing all afternoon. If Crow had been there with him, he'd have been taking his first involuntary swimming lesson right about now. In his clothes, like his old friend George.

'I'll do that. Just one other thing. Why did he call the boat the *Dead or Alive?*'

He couldn't say what made him ask the question. Maybe it was the way that it mirrored the task Crow had asked him to perform. Find George . . .

Whatever it was, it would turn out to be the most pertinent thing he'd asked Crow the whole conversation.

'I never asked him,' Crow said. 'But he did a lot of work as a bounty hunter at one point. I suppose he thought it seemed appropriate.' He chuckled, a sound that had more than a hint of fond reminiscence about it. 'Not that you're allowed to bring them in dead these days, of course.'

'Not like when you first started out, eh?'

Not surprisingly, the line went dead at that point.

12

DESPITE TELLING CROW THAT HE'D DO IT, EVAN DIDN'T START over searching the boat. It would be a waste of time. Even if the million-to-one chance came off, he'd have to hand over whatever he found as evidence. Instead, he called the security guard, Rodriguez, seeing as he didn't have the number for the local police department. Besides, Rodriguez needed a break, a chance to look like he wasn't the idiot the real cops thought he was. Evan knew the feeling well.

From the noisy background sounds when Rodriguez answered the call, either his patrols included the neighboring bars and restaurants or he'd gone off shift. Evan had to shout louder than he'd have liked in the circumstances to make himself heard.

'I found George Winter. Can you go somewhere quieter?'

The background noise cut off abruptly as Rodriguez stepped outside. Evan lowered his voice to a more normal level, told him what he'd found. A stunned silence came down the line. Then Rodriguez said he'd be there in ten minutes, don't ring the other number for security on the card.

Ten minutes. Longer than Evan had anticipated, the security

office being no more than a thirty-second walk away. Winter had been down with the fishes a couple of days at least. Another ten minutes wouldn't hurt if it helped put a spring back into Rodriguez's step.

Ten minutes was something else as well as longer than thirty seconds. It was useable time. Because the decision of a moment ago to not waste more time looking was based on thirty seconds. Now a picture of Crow's disapproving face popped unbidden into his mind, the disappointed tone of his voice as clear as the screech of the gulls overhead.

You didn't bother looking?

It wasn't just that.

Typical is what it was. Before finding Winter, when he had all the time in the world to look, his mind was a blank. An idea-free zone like no other. Now, with Rodriguez already on his way and the clock ticking, something at the back of his mind was working its way forward.

It was to do with the boat's name. The *Dead or Alive*.

He jumped up from the fighting chair, the weariness and apathy of a minute ago gone. Across the jetty, on his own boat, Segal was staring at him. The self-filling wine glass was still in his hand. His face had the dreamy look of a man who's spent all afternoon, maybe longer, drinking. But however much or little was going on behind them, his eyes were boring into Evan.

Forget his eyes, how well had his ears been working? Had he overheard the conversation with Rodriguez? From the way he was sitting with his legs splayed, sprawled on the couch rather than standing on the jetty staring horrified down into the water under the *Dead or Alive*, Evan guessed not. He'd find out soon enough anyway.

Segal was the last thing he needed. With the idea now fully formed in his mind, he didn't want him watching his every move. He thought about starting an argument, tearing him off a strip for calling security in the hope that he'd retreat again into the safety of the salon. But it would waste too much time, might not even work. So let him watch. Maybe he'd fall asleep in the sun.

Earlier, when he'd been searching the exterior of the boat and before he'd found the scuba equipment, he'd come across a number of livewells, all but one of them empty. Ignoring the curious looks from Segal he now made his way towards the one that wasn't.

Dead or Alive.

The livewells were supposed to keep the bait alive. The fish floating on the surface of the water in the tank that he'd seen earlier most definitely wasn't. Not unless live fish enjoy lying upside down sunning their distended bellies.

He raised the lid. A faint odor of dead fish rose up to greet him as the lid's seal let out the air inside. He scooped the dead fish out—

'What are you doing?'

Segal. Standing now, bobbing up and down. Evan ignored him, his body blocking Segal's view. He concentrated on the small fish in his hand.

Why keep one tank full of water with a dead fish in it when the rest of the boat was so shipshape?

'Hey! I'm talking to you.'

Segal again, the booze lending him Dutch courage, putting the aggression into his voice. He was leaning on the gunwale now, trying to see around Evan's body.

Evan hunkered down, held the little fish close in to his body. Tuned out Segal's increasingly irritated voice. He put a finger on the top of the fish's head, another under its lower jaw. Squeezed. The fish's mouth popped open. A rush of fetid air escaped with a quiet hiss, more than he'd have believed possible for such a small fish. He peered into its mouth. Squeezed harder, opening up the gullet.

There it was.

A small Ziplock plastic bag stuck in the fish's gullet. As if it had choked to death trying to swallow its prize. He stood and fumbled his keys out of his pocket, worked the plastic bag out of the fish's mouth with one of them. Inside it was a USB thumb drive. And some water. The little fish didn't look as if it had any teeth. Something had ripped a hole in the plastic bag nonetheless.

'Hey, there!'

Not Segal this time. The shout rang out from the edge of the dock. Evan recognized Rodriguez's voice. He pushed the plastic bag back into the fish's throat, dropped the fish into his pocket. Then he turned, waved at Rodriguez who was already on the jetty, peering under the boat. Evan joined him. As did Segal, stumbling as he climbed out of his boat. Rodriguez steadied him with a hand on his elbow, told him to get back on his own boat. Which he didn't do, the alcohol bringing out the stubbornness in him as well as the aggression.

A short, undignified scuffle followed that ended with Rodriguez manhandling him back on board, trying to tell him it was a crime scene now. Segal wasn't listening, too busy yelling at him. Telling him how he'd have his job just as soon as he could find his damn phone and call the manager of the marina who was a personal friend of his and take your hands off me—

There was a satisfying clunk as Rodriguez slid the door to Segal's salon shut, cutting off the flow mid-abuse. He turned to Evan, smoothing his shirt, tucking it back into his pants where it had pulled out. His face was flushed with excitement, his voice breathless from the tussle with Segal.

'Sorry about that. And thanks for calling me first.'

Evan gave a no-problem flick of the hand.

'Deputy Dawg on his way?'

'Afraid so,' Rodriguez said, the words riding out on the back of a snicker. 'Don't worry, they're sending some grown-ups too. Detective Cortez is on the way. Everybody likes Cortez. You two will get along like a house on fire.'

He didn't mean anything by it, but it would turn out to be a very unfortunate choice of words.

13

'I CAN SEE WHAT SHE MEANS,' DETECTIVE CORTEZ SAID, JUMPING lightly down onto the jetty and studying Evan as if he were a new species of brightly-colored tropical bug. Evan half expected to feel the grip of fingers on his chin, his head turned from side to side, like he had a price tag hanging off his ear.

Cortez believed in the benefits of good preparation. Find out what you're dealing with, act accordingly. Evan's slightly sunburned forehead had creased into a frown. Cortez explained.

'Ricky might be a borderline retard, but he's still got redial on his phone. I spoke to Detective Guillory. You want to hear what she said about you?'

'No thanks.'

Cortez smiled, revealing perfect teeth. They set off the perfect tan nicely.

'Didn't think so. Lucky for you she can vouch for your whereabouts for the whole of the relevant time period. You spend a lot of time hanging out with police officers? Or just Guillory?'

It was a strange question. And not one that Cortez was interested enough in waiting for the answer to.

'You want to tell me what happened.'

Evan ran through the whole story, starting with the connection to Crow and his concern for Winter's welfare. He omitted to mention why at this stage. Nor did he mention what he'd found in the livewell. Or what was stuffed down the fish's gullet. In a perfect world—one in which he'd be able to keep everyone, including Crow, happy—he would've liked to take a copy of the contents of the thumb drive before surrendering it to Cortez. However, he was acutely aware of the damp patch on the front of his pants, soaking through from the dead fish in his pocket. How long that went unnoticed was anybody's guess. He ended the account with his and Crow's opinion on the matter.

'We don't think it's suicide.'

Cortez nodded, thanks for the information, I'll file it appropriately.

'Why not?'

Already Evan felt himself fighting a losing battle. He gave Crow's nebulous reasoning first—he wasn't the type, he was excited about what he had going on. Then he gave the only slightly less vague facts that he couldn't swim and didn't drink hard liquor. He felt as if he was working towards the punchline of a joke that the audience had already seen coming and weren't going to laugh at anyway.

Cortez listened politely without interruption. At times nodding along, sounds reasonable, before summing up, the points counted off on long, slim fingers.

'So. For your theory to work, Mr Winter would have needed to keep Mr Crow up to date on everything going on in his life. Not just the work he was so excited about. But also his ability to swim, his interest in diving, the clothes he liked to wear. And . . .' Cortez paused to let him know that the best was coming next. 'Most importantly, how much, and what, he drank. In my experience that's something a lot of people keep a secret. Even from their spouse, let alone an old friend from the glory days. Hey! Remember what we used to get up to back in the day? Now I just sit and drown my sorrows on my boat.'

Evan found himself nodding, couldn't help himself. It sounded pretty far-fetched.

'What about leaving two or three thousand dollars' worth of scuba gear lying around in a toilet with a busted lock?'

'And that suggests to you that the perp brought all the gear with him to make it look as if it was Winter's, and then busted open the day head because he didn't have the key?'

That was exactly what he thought. He wasn't about to admit it to Cortez.

'Did you find a note?' Cortez said.

'Nowhere obvious, no. It's not tied around his neck.'

Cortez nodded at the unsurprising answer, put a consolatory hand on his arm as if the discussion-cum-argument was already at an end.

'Don't worry, we'll be looking into Mr Winter's personal and financial affairs. See if he was in financial difficulties, that sort of thing. A boat like this is a money pit. A lot of people don't realize it until it's too late. But at the moment, it looks like a pretty clear-cut case of suicide.'

Up until that point Evan could see what Rodriguez meant about everybody liking Cortez, a picture of calm reasonableness. Then it was as if the wind had suddenly changed direction, blowing in from a colder place to leave them standing at the point where the paths of truth and untruth diverged.

'Unless you know anything we don't, of course.'

There was a harder edge to the voice now. The eyes too had changed. The almost friendly sparkle in them was gone, replaced by a sharper glint. The sort of eyes that didn't miss a thing. He knew they were about to drop at any second to the wet patch spreading out from his pocket, the guilty clue growing steadily bigger. He'd have expected to see noses wrinkled by now, was sure everybody must be able to smell the odor of rotting fish.

A noise told him he didn't have to worry about any of those things. The sound of the door to Segal's salon sliding open. And here Segal was now, come to drop him in it. Fed up with being banished to his own boat, unable to hear anything that was said through the glass doors, he made his bid for the spotlight.

'I saw him find something. He put it in his pocket.'

Cortez stiffened, didn't turn to face him. There was no need. Evan's face gave him away. *Bad face.* He stuck his hand in his pocket, pulled out the stiff slimy fish. Held it out towards Cortez by the tail, biting his tongue to keep the smile off his lips. Because it was no laughing matter.

Cortez stared at the fish, didn't make a move to take it. A raised eyebrow asked Evan if he'd like to explain himself.

'There's a plastic bag with a USB thumb drive inside stuck in its throat. But the water got in.'

Cortez nodded like that explained everything, why didn't you say so earlier?

'That's why you didn't mention it. You didn't want to waste our time seeing as it's useless anyway. You're worried about the best use of your tax dollars. You want to tell your story again? With all the facts this time? We could do that down at the station if you like.'

Evan felt ridiculous holding out the fish that Cortez still hadn't taken. He dropped his arm, felt just as stupid. A man holding a dead fish at his side instead of out in front of him. He was tempted to throw it back in the sea.

'The only thing I didn't say is that Crow thought Winter might be in danger because of what he was working on. That might be what's on this.' He held up the fish again, waggled it in Cortez's face.

Finally Cortez got sick of the sight of the fish. And Evan by the look of it.

'Ricky! Bag this up.'

Deputy Dawg aka Ricky swaggered down the jetty, a fine example of modern-day policing with his mirrored shades and an unlit cigarette stuck to his bottom lip. Evan wouldn't have been surprised to be told to get off his horse and drink his milk. Ricky held an evidence bag open towards Evan. Evan dropped the fish in, looked around for somewhere to wipe his fingers. Not comfortable asking either Ricky or Cortez for a kleenex, he gave up and wiped them on his pants. They were going to stink anyway.

He caught sight of Cortez's face watching Ricky as he sauntered back towards the cruiser, the God-help-us despair. Good to know, he thought. A cop after Guillory's own heart. A potential ally should things develop the way they looked like they were going to. Then Cortez turned the glare back on him.

'Now you know everything we do,' Evan said.

Cortez gave him a hard stare, a chance to add more. Everybody was holding their breath, waiting to see if Evan was going to be arrested. For having a pocket full of fish slime in a public place if nothing else. Then Cortez's shoulders relaxed. The moment passed.

'I hope for your sake that's true. Because we can always take you down the station for a strip search, see what else you've got secreted about your person.'

Evan didn't like the sound of *your person*. On the neighboring boat Segal liked the sound of it a lot. He looked as if he wanted to add something to his earlier statement. But Cortez was only joking, carried on before Segal could open his mouth.

'I have to tell you, I know how in your world it's all secret agents and cloak and dagger stuff, but to me it still looks like a sad old man with a ton of debt and a drink problem who decided to call it a day. So we'll take a look at what's on that thumb drive, but I'm not going to hold my breath. I suggest you don't either.'

He reckoned he'd just been told they weren't going to throw the book at him, decided now wasn't a good time to ask what happened if it turned out the information on the thumb drive linked directly to Winter's death.

'We'll need you to come in tomorrow morning and give a formal statement,' Cortez said. 'You can go now. We can take it from here.'

There was one thing Evan was dying to ask before he went. The hardness in Cortez's eyes had softened sufficiently for him to risk it.

'What did you mean when you first arrived, when you said I can see what she means? You were talking about what Guillory said about me.'

Cortez gave him another flash of the perfect teeth against the full lips.

'That's just between us girls.'

Evan reckoned it must be hard-wired into him, his attraction to female police officers. Because if it hadn't been for Guillory, he'd have asked Ana Maria Cortez if she wanted to drive down to Key West with him once she'd finished putting poor old George Winter to bed. The strip search didn't sound so bad either.

14

LEAVING MARATHON AND THE MIDDLE KEYS BEHIND, EVAN started the drive over Seven Mile Bridge, the start of the Lower Keys, the last remaining slice of Old Florida. With their unspoiled charms and the many ramshackle restaurants and residences, the whole place had the feel of a Jimmy Buffett song come to life. He turned the radio on but it wasn't Jimmy singing, of course. That sort of thing only happens in movies. Instead it was The Band Perry's version of *Gentle On My Mind*. He switched it off immediately even though it was one of his favorite tracks. It reminded him of Guillory. And the fact that the last thing he was at the moment was gentle on her mind.

Looking to his right, that's to say north, he saw the remains of the old Seven Mile Bridge, closed to traffic in 1982 when the new bridge was opened. Originally built as a railroad bridge, part of Henry Flagler's first land route ever from Miami to Key West, it was sold to the state of Florida and converted to an automotive bridge. Closed to traffic a couple of years before he was born, Evan reckoned it must have been more like driving on an old wooden pier than a highway, a white-knuckle ride on the way to Key West, the end of the line in more than just geographical terms, a very different place to the cruise ship destination it had become in recent years.

Passing through Big Pine and Summerland and Cudjoe Keys and all the others, he was in Key West in an hour. He took Flagler Avenue downtown, checked into a bed and breakfast towards the southern end of Duval Street, then took a cab into the heart of downtown. Passing Jimmy Buffett's Margaritaville and Sloppy Joe's, the driver dropped him outside the Hog's Breath Saloon without being asked.

'You look like a man who needs a beer,' he said by way of explanation.

Evan took a seat at the raw bar. Not just because he liked the food. He'd be able to pass the blame if somebody sitting near him started asking what that fishy smell was. He hadn't missed the way the cab driver's nose had wrinkled when he got into the cab. He ordered a dozen oysters and a half pound of Stone Crab claws, washed it down with a draft beer. The first one barely touched the sides so he ordered another. Then he called Guillory.

He hadn't spoken to her since she walked out of the diner after he mentioned the pedophile Robert Garfield. So he was determined that he'd avoid anything to do with that, leave it well alone until he got back.

As it turned out, he needn't have worried. The conversation was going to take care of itself.

'Thanks for getting me off the hook with Cortez,' he said.

It seemed it wasn't the best way to start.

'Is she as good-looking as she sounds?'

He didn't bother asking how a person can sound good-looking. Because that would have been missing the point. He'd actually just been invited to explain—in some detail—what an absolute horror Cortez was, what with the extra eye in the middle of her forehead and the boil on her chin just above her beard. And so on.

But it had been a long day. He was tired. He'd found a dead body and been caught concealing evidence. Which he could still smell despite his best efforts to mask it. The two beers inside him weren't helping any as far as saying the right thing goes. Being Evan Buckley didn't help either but there wasn't much he could do about that.

'You want me to take a photo when she gets back from the ladies' room, send it to you?'

The heavy silence that came down the line told him that maybe he'd overshot the mark a little. She soon recovered.

'You win. So where are you? That sounds like live music in the background.'

He told her where he was, what he'd had to eat. It made him hungry again just talking about it. He could hear her salivating on the other end of the line.

'I did ask you if you wanted to come.'

There was a slight pause when he thought she was about to say that she wished now that she had. But the only one doing any wishing was him.

'I told you, I'm too busy.'

He took a long swallow of his beer, thought carefully before he replied. It wasn't something he was known for. It didn't come out any different.

'That's not what Donut said.'

'What do you mean—'

'We almost had a fight in the street.'

Then he told her what had happened, how the old woman had broken it up, hitting them both with her walking stick. Guillory was laughing by the time he'd finished. Which was just before he got to the awkward bit.

'I wondered why he kept complaining and touching the back of his head,' she said, sounding more like her old self.

So he spoiled it all.

'I asked him about the caseload.'

The gentle laughter that had continued in the background stopped as if the connection had been cut. He dug the hole a little deeper.

'He said things were as quiet as they get.'

Not as quiet as her, he thought, as the silence bounced back at him. This time it was even longer than the last one. It wasn't a comfortable silence either, the reminiscing sort that comes with a soft smile and follows one of you saying, *hey, remember that time we ...*

She went to say something but he talked over her. He also forgot all about not mentioning the G-word.

'You don't have to make excuses. At the risk of you hanging up at the slightest mention of Garfield, I understand if you want to just curl up and do nothing and hope it all goes away. Cold beer and oysters and crab claws and more beer and live music and the sea and the amazing sunsets down here probably wouldn't do you any good anyway. Hold the line a sec, I've got to order another beer.'

He heard the familiar accusation of *idiot* in the background as he did just that. Then he ordered another dozen oysters to go with it.

'I've just ordered some more oysters. They're really good.'

'You'll make yourself sick.'

'And mommy's not here to look after me.'

'*Aw*. I'm glad now I pretended to be too busy. Maybe Cortez can rub it better.'

They were back on track. For now.

'So tell me about your day,' he said. 'After you tried to punch Donut.'

A nervous stuttering laugh came down the line.

'He told you about that, huh?'

'Remind me to pay you the ten bucks I told him I offered you to do it when I get back.'

Then he listened as she talked, tipping the oysters into his mouth and washing them down his throat with cold beer, content just to hear the sound of her voice and the music playing behind him, the happy chatter of people all around. Sounds idyllic. It would've been if he'd asked the guy shucking the oysters if he could borrow his knife for a minute, then used it to dig his brains out of his ear.

Because despite their conversation taking a long-overdue turn for the better, he couldn't shift what had been going through his mind since he'd said he understood if she just wanted to have it all go away. Bringing Ryder into the conversation hadn't helped either. Because his words kept repeating over and over in Evan's mind.

It must be her self-destructive streak that attracts her to you. Like a moth to the flame. She gets it from her old man.

Then his refusal to explain. Not that it was difficult to work out. Luckily he'd only had three beers and not the three dozen it would take for him to ask her what was on his mind.

Did your father kill himself?

And the logical follow-on given the way she'd been lately.

Do you feel that way too?

Would it ever be possible for him to ask her that? How do you even go about it? Trouble was, there are some people who want to keep all that stuff bottled up inside. Until it's too late.

One of them was chattering away happily on the other end of the line.

She'd have just pointed the finger straight back at him, talk about the kettle calling the pot black.

He slid the last of the oysters into his mouth and was

chewing it, enjoying the fresh saltiness, when he realized she'd stopped talking and was waiting for him to say something. So, feeling his nose growing as he said the words, he told her, 'I'd rather take Donut for a night out than Cortez.'

He could say the right things if he put his mind to it.

15

LIAR, LIAR, PANTS ON FIRE. THE STUPID PHRASE KEPT GOING through his mind as he sat opposite the very attractive Detective Ana Maria Cortez the next morning to give his formal statement. A small smile curled her lips when she saw his face. She raised her hand, counting off on her long slim fingers the way she had the previous day when destroying his argument that Winter's death wasn't suicide.

'So. Margaritaville, Sloppy Joe's, Hog's Breath'—he thought the last one might actually be a personal comment as she said it, tried to keep his breathing shallow—'anywhere else? They bury people looking better than you do.'

He admitted that the Schooner Wharf Bar seemed to ring a bell. And somewhere else he couldn't remember the name of.

'Sounds like a fun night,' she said. 'Shame I was working or I'd have tagged along.'

He tried a noncommittal *that would've been nice*, hoped his tongue wasn't lolling too obviously. He wasn't sure he pulled it off. One thing he did know—that particular remark would *not* be relayed to Guillory, no sir. It would be their secret. Then it was down to business.

'Hopefully you haven't erased too many brain cells and your memory's still working okay.'

He tried a small laugh.

'Some people say that boat sailed a long time ago.'

She smiled back, the white of her teeth against her lips too bright for this early in the morning.

'Yeah. Detective Guillory said something along those lines.'

It was enough to make a man paranoid. Then he ran through the events of the previous day for her again.

'You still suspect foul play?' she said when he'd finished.

He hadn't given it a moment's thought since he last saw her. What with enjoying the drive down through the Lower Keys and then immediately hitting the town in Key West. She didn't give him a chance to think about it now either. She picked up her notebook, a pointless thing to do seeing as she didn't consult it.

'Because what I've learned since we last met makes me more convinced that Mr Winter took his own life.'

He expected to see the fingers at work again, bet she'd need both hands from the satisfied look on her face. But he was wrong. The fingers stayed holding the notebook.

'In addition to the empty whisky bottle and the lack of any restraints, the ME's initial inspection revealed no head wounds, no indication of him being knocked unconscious. I'm convinced the autopsy will show that he was the one who drank the whisky. I think he numbed the pain with it, strapped on the weight belt and jumped in. If the shock of the water gave him any second thoughts and he tried to unbuckle the belt, his manual dexterity was shot to hell by the whisky.'

She put the notebook back on the desk. That's when the fingers came into play again. He smiled. Maybe not the best thing to do.

'Something funny?'

He shook his head. Sorry.

'No, please. Share it with me.'

'You like to count things off on your fingers, that's all.'

She gave him a look like she was wishing she'd asked Guillory a few more in-depth questions before she started the interview. He was thinking about Guillory too, her remark of the previous evening—maybe Cortez can rub it better.

'Right,' she said, letting go of the little finger that she'd been holding. He noticed that there was no wedding ring on the finger next to it. 'Getting back to what I was saying. The weight belt had twisted around so that the buckle was in the small of his back, making it more difficult to undo. And if he couldn't swim, he'd be more likely to panic. That would only make things worse. And he wouldn't be accustomed to holding his breath for any length of time.'

Evan listened in silence, not bothering to interrupt or say that he didn't deny any of it—although he doubted a heavy weight belt would move itself all the way behind him. It was more a question of how the whisky had gotten into him in the first place.

'Okay, let's assume I accept that's how it happened. What about why?'

She smiled at him again. It was still a nice smile, she could use it on him any time she liked. But it was different. This one said, I'm glad you asked that. She leaned back in her chair, hands clasped behind her head. Only for a second though. She realized about the same time as he did what a provocative pose it was, stretching the crisp white fabric of her blouse tight over her body. She leaned forwards again, elbows on the desk.

'We talked to Mr Segal.'

A smile crept across Evan's lips.

'Last night?'

'Uh-huh.'

She knew exactly what he meant, refused to acknowledge it.

'Did you happen to check the trash? Seeing as empty booze bottles seem to be playing a large part in this. I think you'll find a couple of wine bottles at least in there. He'd been drinking all day. I could smell it on his breath when he shouted—'

'When he dropped you in it, you mean? About the fish in your pocket.'

That shut him up.

'We'll be getting onto that soon.'

Despite the vague fuzziness clinging to his mind after his night out, he didn't think there was any suggestion of a threat, or of dire consequences to come for him, in her voice. That could all change in the blink of an eye of course.

'But, no, I didn't miss the fact that he'd been drinking. Talking to the security guard Rodriguez, it seems he's like that most of the time. What?'

She'd seen something in his expression that she didn't like.

'Nothing.'

Again, she wasn't having it.

'Tell me.'

'You want it all your own way, that's all.'

She crossed her arms over her chest, the full lips not so full now. Pursed was a better word.

'Go on.'

'Winter was unaccustomed to hard liquor so it incapacitated him to the point where he couldn't even unbuckle a belt. But Segal's drunk most of the time, it's his normal functioning state, so you can believe everything he says. That's some logic.'

The look on her face suggested that sometimes fate knows best, that the drinks in Key West together if she hadn't been working might not have been such a good idea after all. It certainly wouldn't be happening now. She carried on without acknowledging his point.

'Segal told us that he'd seen the scuba gear before.'

'Really? Ignoring the fact that most of the time he probably can't see the boat next to his, let alone what's on it, Segal is the sort of sycophantic creep—'

'You really don't like him for dropping you in it, do you?'

'—who'd say whatever he thought you wanted to hear.'

He almost said, *especially given what you look like*, caught himself in time.

'Moving on,' she said, 'we talked to—'

'Rodriguez told me Winter didn't dive. He'd been out fishing with him on the boat a number of times. He knew what he did and didn't have on board.'

It was as if he hadn't spoken for all the attention she paid.

'We talked to Rodriguez. He told us that business has been bad for some time. And getting worse. There's a lot of competition. As I told you yesterday, a boat like that is a money pit.'

Again, his face had given him away. She looked at him, eyes narrowing.

'What now?'

He shrugged, what's the point?

'Say what's on your mind. Guillory says you're never normally reticent about saying whatever comes into your head.'

He made a mental note to have a word about telling tales out of school.

'I want it all my own way again, is that it?'

'Actually, yes. Seeing as you ask. How is it that everything Rodriguez says is gospel when it relates to Winter's business going down the drain, but you don't believe him when he says Winter didn't dive? You'd rather believe that drunk, Segal.'

Her weary smile wavered then resumed its post, except this time it said I know things you don't, buddy.

'Well, seeing as *you* ask, maybe it's because what he says about the business side of things ties in with other information that's come to light.' She paused for a moment, that shut you up. 'You want to hear it?'

He wasn't sure how things had turned around. Suddenly he was the one with a closed mind, not her. It was a trick Guillory had pulled on him a number of times. He wondered if it was a female detective thing or just a woman thing.

'Sure.'

'You may already know this'—the tone of voice suggested *I know you don't*—'but Winter wasn't the sole owner of the boat. In fact, his partner owned a bigger share.'

'Who's the partner?'

'I'm not—'

'At liberty to disclose that?'

'So why'd you ask? Anyway, we've spoken to his partner. As a result of the way business has been going, he told Winter that he was thinking of selling the boat.' She leaned back, a satisfied gleam in her eye. This time she couldn't stop herself from lifting her hand to count off the points on her perfectly-manicured fingers. 'Let's see what we've got—'

'Okay, okay.'

But she was determined to rub it in. Again he wondered if it was a female detective thing or just a woman thing. She ran through all of the arguments they'd already covered first in case he hadn't been paying attention.

'On top of all that, the guy's about to lose the roof over his head as well. I think I'd kill myself.'

No, not you. Not someone so similar to Guillory.

The thought came out of nowhere, hijacked him. It took him right back to his conversation with her the previous evening and the thoughts that had gone through his mind. Six months ago, he'd have said never in a million years. Now? He wasn't so sure.

Cortez took his sudden quietness, the way his face fell, as evidence of the way she'd demolished his arguments, overcome his objections. The realization, false though it was, made her soften and thaw towards him. It was as if somebody had switched off the air conditioning. Her voice lost all of the aggressive edge to it.

'Winter's partner even gave me the name of the yacht broker he's put the boat with. They're in the historic seaport in Key West, just along from the Schooner Wharf Bar. You probably walked or staggered past them last night.'

He nodded mechanically, doesn't prove a thing.

Loathe as he was to be the one to bring it up, given his behavior the previous day, he had to ask her about the dead fish and the USB stick. The smile on her lips—a better one this time —told him she was thinking along the same lines.

'There's nothing on that USB stick either. I'm afraid that's your conspiracy theory gone up in smoke. There never was anything on it either. I don't know whether you know, but water doesn't damage a USB drive, not unless it's powered up.'

'So why'd he hide it?'

She stuck out her bottom lip, shook her head.

'Beats me. Maybe he had two thumb drives, hid the wrong one. Maybe after he'd drunk some of that whisky he never touched.' She held up her hand before he could say anything. 'That doesn't mean there's a *right* one which is still hidden somewhere with all your cloak and dagger stuff on it.'

He wanted to pull out his phone, call Crow, put her on the line to him.

Convince him.

Because that was the job he had ahead of him. He knew exactly the reaction he'd be getting too. It made him wonder if it was even worth going home before being sent back down.

The last piece of information was the final nail in the coffin as far as she was concerned. She had a *we're all finished here* look on her face. Then suddenly a light edged into her eyes, a look of almost salacious mischievousness. He sniffed surreptitiously, knew what was coming.

'Do you mind if I ask you something?' she said.

Might as well meet it head on.

'Yeah, I had to wear these pants with the fishy stain on them when I went out in Key West last night.'

Her eyes crinkled as she nodded, good to know.

He knew he'd be getting a hard time about it from Guillory in the near future.

16

EVAN WAS ACUTELY AWARE OF THE FISHY STAIN ON THE FRONT OF
his pants when he walked into the offices of Conch Yacht Sales
in Key West just over two hours later. He'd been skulking
around outside for the past hour until he'd seen a man wearing
a yellow polo shirt over tan linen trousers with a gold Rolex
wristwatch worth more than his car on his well-tanned wrist—
Mr Conch presumably—escort another, similarly-attired man to
his Mercedes and hold open the passenger door for him. A real
customer.

Not that the stain bothered Evan unduly. It was more the
knowledge that he'd have gotten a similar reception even
without it. He half expected to be told that people who cleaned
the boats should use the back entrance. If he was ever offered a
ride in the Mercedes, it'd be in the trunk.

'Can I help you?' the young woman on the front desk said in
the tone that a certain type of receptionist reserves for those
whom she has no intention of helping at all. A little name sign
on her desk said *Amanda* in a curly girly script.

'Are you the broker selling the *Dead or Alive* that's moored in the Marathon marina?' He'd almost said *parked* which would've given him away.

She said they were. Her expression said she wished they weren't at this particular moment.

'I was talking to one of the owners, George Winter, about it. He's a friend of my father. But now that . . .' He made a meaningless gesture with his hand, meant to imply a whole host of emotions—embarrassment, frustration, irritation.

'Now that what?'

'You didn't know?'

'Know what?'

'He's dead. I found him dead on the boat yesterday.'

Amanda's mouth opened into a perfect circle. He felt like saying, don't let your boss catch you with your mouth hanging open like that in front of the paying customers.

'What happened?'

'He drowned. They think it might be murder.'

The relief on the girl's face was plain to see. *Thank God. Drowned.* No damage to the boat, no blood to clean up. Not like somebody blowing his brains out in the master stateroom.

'I'm surprised you didn't know. Everybody in the marina is talking about it.'

The subtext—*it's going to be a bitch to sell now.*

He saw a second emotion cross Amanda's face as the implication of his words sank in. Righteous indignation. Old George Winter got what he damn well deserved. The cheek of it, trying to make a private sale under their noses.

'I'd already made George an offer. He said he wanted to think about it.'

Amanda smiled thinly, the smile of a person who likes to deliver bad news.

'It wasn't Mr Winter's decision to make. He only owned a part share.'

Evan twisted an annoyed frown onto his face, this is all getting too complicated. All I want to do is buy the damn boat.

'So who the hell do I talk to now?'

'You need to make an appointment with my boss. You've just missed him.'

'Who? Mr Conch?'

She gave him a tired, withering look, we've got a right one here.

'No. Mr *Romano*.'

'Right. He's the fat guy with the Rolex who just left?'

He leaned towards her as he said it to stop himself from being blown back outside by the weary exhalation.

'*No*. That was another client.'

'Can't I talk directly to George's partner if Mr Conch is busy?'

Amanda looked at him as if he'd just put his hand up her skirt. A hand with a Timex on the wrist it was attached to.

'Good heavens, no.' Then her eyes narrowed as she realized what he'd been trying to do. 'And if you think that you're going to trick me into revealing the other owner's name, you're going to have to try a lot harder than that. All'—she tapped the desk top with a bright red fingernail to reinforce her point —'negotiations are handled by Mr Romano. Mr Winter should have known that too.'

He had to admire her for the amount of disapproval she got into those few words, hoped Guillory never ran across her and picked up some tips. Just for the fun of it, he glanced around the reception area, asked if he should wait. She looked horrified. Her eyes dropped to the suspicious stain on his pants—what if another client were to come in?

'He's only just left. He won't be back for a couple of hours at least. Probably longer.'

'Taking one of the boats out for a test drive, eh? Good idea.

Try before you buy. Book me in for one this afternoon, will you. Maybe you'd like to take me out instead of Mr Conch.'

He tried a lascivious wink, one that would have Guillory poking him in the eye with a cocktail stick. Amanda was looking exactly like he'd felt when he first woke up that morning after all the beer and oysters.

'I'm off to the Half Shell Raw Bar now. Get a few drinks inside me, loosen up the old muscles.' He grabbed an imaginary ship's wheel with his hands in front of him, wrestled with it from side to side. 'In case it's rough out there. See you later.'

The sound of the door bolt sliding firmly home behind him was the last he ever heard from Amanda. Or anybody else at Conch Yacht Sales. Not that it really mattered. Crow would be able to dig up Winter's partner's name without much difficulty.

That's when the trouble would really start.

17

Despite Elwood Crow's proficiency with all things computer and internet related—particularly those things he didn't strictly have permission to stick his prominent nose into—his expertise did not extend to the telephone. And certainly not texting. Paranoia was his watchword if not his middle name. As a result, Evan was unable to send him a text telling him the bad news about the blank thumb drive. He was going to have to do it in person.

Crow welcomed him in with a big smile, one Evan was going to wipe off his wrinkly old face very soon. He followed him down the hallway to the back room where Crow sank into his favorite chair.

'What have you got for me?'

'The police are more convinced than ever that it's suicide,' Evan said, then told him the new information about George Winter only owning a minority share in the boat and his imminent eviction.

Crow's dark eyes lit up as he listened. He put Evan in mind of an ageing vulture, one who's just been told by another ageing vulture about a new, quicker way to get at all the juicy morsels inside the carcass in front of them.

'Interesting. I didn't know that. It explains how George managed to buy such an expensive toy. It won't take long to find out who it is. Not that it makes any difference. It still wasn't suicide.'

Evan was tempted to get out his phone, book his flight back down to Florida already.

'Cortez—'

'Cortez?'

'She's the detective in charge down there.'

Crow nodded to himself as if that explained a lot.

'Is she pretty?'

Evan made a show of looking under his chair, then behind it.

'What are you doing?' Crow said.

'Looking for Kate. She said exactly the same thing.'

Crow said *ah* in a way that implied everything was now crystal clear. It was also a way that would have had Evan punching a younger man.

'I was about to say Cortez wasn't impressed with your counter-argument that he wasn't the type to kill himself. A little lacking in hard evidence.'

'He wasn't. That's all there is to it.'

Evan stared at the brick wall sitting in the chair opposite him. Took a deep breath before he banged his head against it.

'You said on the phone that if I knew what you went through together, I'd know it too. What was that all about?'

'Did I? Are you sure?'

The only thing Evan was sure about was that he wasn't going to get an answer.

'There's something you're not telling me.'

'Uh-huh,' Crow said, as if it were the most natural thing in the world to not tell people the most pertinent information until it was squeezed out of them like blood from a stone.

He pushed himself out of his chair, crossed the room to where his laptop sat on the table. Then he brought something back, held it towards Evan.

'This came in the mail today.'

Evan took it—an identical USB thumb drive to the one he'd found in the fish's gullet. A frown creased his forehead as he looked to Crow for an explanation.

'George left it and some other papers with a friend. Told him to mail it to me if he didn't check in with him every day. The friend got the address wrong so it took an extra couple of days to get here. I think even your Detective Cortez would agree that George was worried something might happen to him.'

'You couldn't have told me that earlier.'

Crow shrugged, it passes the time.

'What's on it?' Evan said.

'It's the job he was given. A video of a couple of people. And their names. He obviously succeeded in identifying them.'

He paused, waited for Evan to make the connection.

'You think that's why he was killed? Why would you pay somebody to identify a couple of people and then kill him? And make it look like suicide too.'

Crow didn't answer the question. Evan knew him well enough to know that there was more that he was holding back, that it wasn't worth trying to get it out of him until he was good and ready.

'You want to watch it?' Crow said instead.

Evan said why not. They both went over to Crow's laptop where he'd already made a copy. Paranoid *and* careful. Crow hit *play*.

'What do you make of that?' Crow said when it was over.

'Not much. It's a couple of people taking a selfie video on

vacation. Looks like Key West to me. It makes sense, explains why George was given the job. I can't see anything in it that would make you want to kill the person who identified them. Besides, why would you even need to hire somebody to find out who the people are if you've got the phone in the first place?'

The look Crow gave him suggested that while it was sweet that Evan still maintained some of his boyish innocence, it was worrying that he should be so naive given the sleazy divorce work that he had spent so long doing.

'It's a burner phone. Look at them.' He pointed at the screen with a long bony finger where the couple were frozen in time and motion waiting for someone to hit *play* again. 'Down in Florida for a weekend of sun and sex. I'd put money on them being married. And not to each other. I bet his wife thinks he's on an aluminum siding conference.'

Evan looked at the way they were holding onto each other, the rapt smiles on their faces. He couldn't disagree.

'Yeah. Even if that's not the case, lots of people who use dating apps use a burner. So they don't have to give out their primary number to someone they might not end up with. Everybody's seen the movie *Fatal Attraction*.'

Nobody could deny the truth in that. Never had anything as inconsequential as a movie contributed so much to the sanctity of the marriage vows, to the marital fidelity of the American male.

'None of which explains why the person who identified them would be killed for his trouble,' Evan said.

Again, Crow didn't explain. He opened up a text file on the laptop, invited Evan to take a look.

'Elliott Turner and Grace Davis,' Evan read out. 'I assume those are their names.'

'Were.'

Evan had been about to say the names meant nothing to him when his mind rewound.

'Were? As in, they're dead too?'

Crow nodded, in his eyes a mixture of satisfaction that he was being proved right and sadness that it should be so, that this is what it took.

'Died in a house fire a couple of nights ago. In Key West as you correctly identified.'

'How do you know?'

Crow shook his head, the youth of today, God help us.

'I don't know about you, but if I get a video through the mail from a friend who's already dead with a couple of names as well, I stick them straight in a search engine, see what pops up. He clicked on the internet browser window, held his hand open towards the news article on the screen. Voilà.

Two dead in house fire.

Evan skimmed the article, found it short on facts beyond the conclusion drawn by both the police and fire departments that the cause of the fire was a cigarette left smouldering in an ashtray while the couple lay passed out on the bed from an excess of alcohol and drugs. There was nothing to indicate that it was anything other than an unfortunate accident, although it appeared that the smoke alarms had been disabled. The owner of the property hadn't been available for blame. Sorry, comment.

A nervous laugh slipped out of Evan's mouth.

'That's a strange reaction,' Crow said. 'Remember not to do it if you meet the next of kin.'

'Sorry. I got a mental image of Detective Cortez's face when she hears about it. I'd like to be the one who tells her.'

That got a knowing smile from Crow.

'For purely professional reasons, of course.'

'Of course. Even she can't deny that Winter being found dead as well as the people he was paid to identify is too much of a coincidence. Except she'll probably say Winter was hired to kill them, not just identify them. Then he killed himself out of remorse. Nice and tidy, case closed. *Next!'*

He suddenly realized they were getting ahead of themselves.

'If the fire wasn't an accident, why were they killed?'

'Jealous spouse?'

Evan knew he was only joking. There was no way Crow could know why. He was wrong.

'Watch the video again.'

Evan watched it again. He saw it this time. As the couple panned around with their faces in the foreground, the scene behind them moved slowly across the screen. It started with the gravestones and vaults of the Key West Cemetery stretching away into the distance. Then it swung around so that the street and the parked cars were behind their heads, then the sidewalk, then, finally, the houses facing the cemetery. Suddenly a door in one of the houses burst open as if a bomb had gone off inside. A man fell out, stumbled. Another man who'd been waiting with his back against the wall to the side of the door, came instantly to life, his reactions those of a well-trained professional. He caught the man's arm, helped steady him. Steered him towards a car idling at the curb. The first man's face had been completely obscured behind the faces of the couple taking the selfie. As the bodyguard—because that's what he was— straightened up after helping his charge into the back seat, he looked directly at the couple taking the selfie. Anger clouded his face. They were too busy smiling at themselves to pay any attention. He started towards them, immediately breaking into a run. Before he'd taken more than a couple of paces, the video ended abruptly. Elliott, the young guy in the video, shouted at somebody to *piss off*. There was a quick, blurred view of the sidewalk and two pairs of sneaker-clad feet. Then nothing.

'It must be because of whoever came out of that house,' Evan said. 'And what happened inside it.'

He got a slow, deliberate nod back from Crow.

'You know who it is?'

Crow's expression said he could no more see through other people's bodies than Evan could.

'No. But whoever it is, is very keen to make sure nobody saw him coming out of that house.'

'And he's the one who hired George to find out who the witnesses were . . .'

He left the rest of the sentence unspoken—who then got rid of them. And after that got rid of the only person who could tie him in to them.

'What about the guy shouting *piss off* at somebody?' Evan said.

Crow shook his head, said he had no idea. His tone implied that the practice of photographing and videoing oneself at every opportunity and in front of the most mundane backgrounds was so alien to him that for all he knew it was customary to end such videos with a loud shout of *piss off*, a modern-day equivalent of *Bravo!* Then he pulled the thumb drive from his laptop, handed it to Evan.

'You better give that to your new friend, Detective Cortez. And I still want to know who owned the other half of George's boat.'

On the subject of Crow delving into the nether regions of the ether where much and varied information was to be found by those who knew how to look, Evan asked him if he'd found a name and, better still, an address to go with the phone number that he'd found on the back of the contract killer Todd Strange's business card.

'Not yet, no. But I did find the other information you wanted.'

He dug in the pocket of the tatty cardigan sweater that he always wore, produced a folded slip of paper. He handed it to Evan, everything that needed to be said passing unspoken between them.

The unspoken *Good Luck* or *Be Careful* could never do justice to what Crow had just set in motion. Or the repercussions it would have for all of them.

Then Crow saw him to the door.

'Watch your back. Whoever killed George and the two witnesses might already know that you've been poking around, that you don't buy the suicide angle.'

Evan couldn't help but notice the lack of the word *we*, the emphasis on *you*, as the door closed in his face. He supposed that was how Crow had managed to live so long.

18

CROW WAS RIGHT. EVAN SHOULD HAVE WATCHED HIS BACK. EXCEPT Crow had been talking about down in Florida, not at home. His mind was too full of the task ahead of him, the address on the slip of paper Crow had given him. And the way that prospect made his heart sprint in the tight, breathless cavity that was his chest, left his mouth dry. His plan was to grab a few hours' sleep before heading out again in the small hours of the morning.

So much for plans.

He knew something was up the minute he stepped into his apartment, closed the door behind him. A woman with a gun in her hand and a twisted scowl on her face was sitting in his favorite easy chair like she owned it.

'You're the sister,' he said after he recovered from the initial shock.

'*The* sister?'

She had a point. It was rude. And it's never a good idea to be rude to the person holding the gun. But he was dog tired, didn't have the energy to give a damn.

'I'm Todd's sister, yes. Lydia.'

'Hello Lydia.'

She looked exactly like the photo of her he had on his phone, nothing like the description he'd been given of the woman looking for him. Her hair was the sort of dark red color that only comes in a bottle, short like a boy's and hacked into a shape that made him think she'd fallen asleep in a field on the day the combine harvester was working. But she had nice eyes. On the surface at least. You knew on a primeval, subconscious level that you didn't want to look too deeply into them. She was slim too, again like a boy, with shapeless, unflattering clothes hanging off her.

Some vague intuition told him that the whole effect was deliberate, to eradicate all vestiges of her femininity. There would be some root cause behind this desire to make herself unattractive. It wouldn't be anything good. Nor would it be safely squared away in her past. It would be something to be very wary of in the future.

'You were looking for me in the Jerusalem Tavern.'

She nodded, motioned with the gun for him to sit down. He considered the distance between them. Decided it was a bad idea. The relaxed way she held the gun told him she was comfortable around guns. Comfortable with putting a bullet in his gut if that's what it took. He sat, closed his eyes for a moment.

'Why were you in Todd's apartment?'

He couldn't see any benefit in not telling the truth. Some people would say he should try it more often.

'Looking for information.'

'About what?'

'The person who hired him.'

She let out a short stutter of a laugh, shook her head.

'Like he'd just leave that lying around. And after the police had been all over the place.'

'Gotta start somewhere.'

His phone chose that moment to ring. It startled them both. They stared at each other a long moment.

'Aren't you going to answer that?'

'No.'

She waved the gun at him, irritation on her face as if the sound was grating on her nerves.

'Answer it.'

'No.'

The phone stopped ringing before things could escalate. A few seconds later a double beep announced the arrival of a text message. It was from Guillory. He recognized the ring tone he'd assigned to her. He smiled at the thought of what she'd say if she ever found out what it was.

Bad move.

'You think this is funny?'

She raised the gun. He took a better look at it, his mouth suddenly dry. Her brother had been a paid assassin. He'd have had a lot of guns, a lot of equipment to go with them. He wouldn't have been so stupid as to leave it in his apartment. Presumably his sister had access to it now. Hence the suppressor on the gun, an accessory that was illegal in some states, a pain in the butt to acquire in the others.

He shook his head, showed her his palms in apology.

'Let me see the phone.'

He pulled it out carefully, threw it gently to her. She let it land in her lap, didn't try to catch it. Then she checked the display.

'Kate Guillory. That's the cop—'

'Your brother was paid to kill. And whose picture you tacked to the wall in his apartment.'

It was her turn to smile then.

'And look what it got me. I was watching you on CCTV when

you pulled it off the wall, saw what a soft spot you've got for her. It almost brought a tear to my eye. Why's she calling you?'

'No idea. See what the text says.'

She brought up the message and read it, her eyes flicking up and down between it and his face, never leaving him for more than a split second.

'*Call me.* Is she always so blunt?'

'Tell me about it.'

'Better call her, then. Before you get in trouble.'

She threw the phone back to him. He caught it, didn't make a move to do anything with it.

'What do you want me to say?'

'Invite her over.'

That surprised him. He couldn't stop it showing on his face.

'What for?'

'Because I want to know how she got from a situation where it was meant to be her dead and my brother alive to the opposite way around.'

'She didn't kill him.'

'No?'

'No.'

'Then who did?'

He knew who. Francisco Garcia, a gangster known to everybody as Chico, in the aftermath of an ambush gone wrong. But he wasn't going to tell her that. Not now, anyway. And not because of any loyalty to Chico, a ruthless thug who deserved anything that Evan or fate itself might send his way. But because an idea was forming in the back of his mind, one that would allow him to forget about what Crow had just given him. He was thinking more along the lines of trade, rather than tell. It all depended on how close she'd been to her murderous swine of a brother, how much information he'd shared with her.

She took his hesitation as an admission that he didn't know.

'Call her.'

He called her, held the phone out between them so they could both hear it ringing.

'I hope you've changed your pants,' Guillory's tinny voice said from the small speaker, proof of the fact that Cortez had called her again to share the fish story with her. She sounded as if all the problems of their past conversations were just that—a thing of the past. Nothing like a fishy story to put everyone in a good mood.

Time to change all of that.

He raised an eyebrow to Lydia Strange. Got a nod back. He put the phone to his ear.

'Piss off, Kate.'

He killed the call, knew she'd kill him next time she saw him. He gave Lydia a guilty smile.

'Oops. Don't suppose she'll be coming over now.'

Lydia was on her feet before the words were out of his mouth, face twisted, fury and frustration colliding in her features. The whole of her slim body shook like a young tree in a gale, her anger lighting up the room like a flare. The gun quivered in her double-handed grip, way too big and unpredictable in the small hands, silenced barrel aimed directly at the middle of his face, wavering, pointing first at the bridge of his nose, now at his front teeth.

'You think you're clever, you fuck? You—'

She never got to finish.

He hooked his leg around in a wide fast arc. Caught her hard and low on the back of the leg. A startled yelp erupted from her mouth as she toppled backwards, fell into the easy chair behind her, gun arm waving crazily in the air as she tried to keep her balance.

By the time her butt hit the seat, he was out of his, moving fast. Adrenalin sledding through his veins. Heart racing, pulse loud in his ears. Leg muscles contracting, ready to leap at her, smother her with his superior weight and strength.

Then a noise like a distant thunderclap, still loud as if the suppressor were nothing more than an empty tin can.

Behind the shot, the sound of her voice screaming at him, knuckles growing ever whiter on the gun grip as dust and plaster drifted down from the ceiling.

'Stop!'

The force of it slammed into him like a second shot hitting him in the chest, left him teetering on the verge of falling onto her below him in the easy chair. Now the gun arm was worryingly steady, the barrel that had been pointing at his face dropping to the bigger, unmissable target of his mid-section. He froze, a hard-wired natural instinct, a subconscious survival mechanism kicking in, telling him that she would not hesitate to fire again if he moved another thousandth of an inch.

Her voice was raw, hysterical with rage and frustration as she screamed into his face, so loudly he heard the rasping suck of air down her throat between every word spat at him.

'Get. On. The. Floor.'

He backed off, palms towards her. Lowered himself carefully down, his movements smooth and unhurried for fear that any sudden movement might be misinterpreted. He lay on his front. Turned his face to the side, cheek on the floor. Looked up at her as she sat in the chair, tight lips flecked with spittle, eyes that he had thought pretty now pits of molten hatred.

He watched the small chest under the shapeless top rise and fall steadily, her lips parted now as she fought to control her breathing. It worried him that maybe she should be popping some medication right about now and who knows what would happen if she'd left it at home.

After the noise of the gunshot and the raw emotion of the screaming it was strangely peaceful in the room, his own heartbeat slow and steady. It wouldn't take a lot for his eyes to close, a natural reaction to rest and recuperate after the danger has passed, the adrenalin leached away.

Except the danger hadn't gone far if it had gone anywhere at all. She was staring intensely at him. He didn't want to know what was on her mind. So he pre-empted her.

'I can tell you who killed your brother. But I want information from you first.'

There's nothing like negotiating from a position of power, he thought and bit down on a nervous smile.

He'd misjudged her.

Despite the outward show of calm that she'd achieved, she was still beyond words, beyond thinking. She got out of the chair, edged cautiously around him, the gun aimed at his head the whole time.

A sudden weight landed on his back and legs as she upended the easy chair he'd been sitting in on top of him as she passed. He threw it off, heard the front door slam, then the sound of her footsteps disappearing rapidly down the hallway.

There was no point going after her.

He had no doubt they'd be meeting again soon enough. And he had things to do that wouldn't wait. The only difference being, his mental preparation was now shot to hell.

Thanks a lot, Lydia.

It wouldn't have mattered if there hadn't been so much riding on what he had to do tonight.

19

UNLIKE GUILLORY, EVAN DIDN'T HAVE A CURTIS BANKS, THE confidential informant, petty thief and burglar she'd used to watch Robert Garfield's house for her. He had to do it all for himself. Nor did he have the luxury of spending twenty-four hours to make sure the house was empty. Rather than sit in the relative comfort of his car watching the house and risk the unwanted attention of a nosy neighbor, he'd crept into the overgrown back yard, hid in the dense bushes at the bottom.

For two hours he watched and waited in the cold and dark. A chill worked its way into his bones to match the cold dread that gripped his stomach and squeezed his heart. For two hours he stared at the house that was as lifeless as a mausoleum and tried to still his mind.

Because in the neglected, overgrown jungle of Robert Garfield's yard he couldn't shift from his mind the memories of the last time he'd waited in preparation for breaking into a deserted house—and he didn't mean Todd Strange's apartment. It was ironic that Kate Guillory had been at his side on that occasion to lend emotional and physical support.

Because the house they'd broken into had been one where

his dead wife Sarah had spent time growing up. One in which she'd suffered the most traumatic experience of her young life. A trauma that had contributed to her taking her own life in a state psychiatric institution more than twenty years later.

Or so they'd told him.

Because at times like this his mind would give him no peace. Now here he was, alone, on a mission to try to find for her some of the peace she'd helped try to find for him.

It was time.

If he didn't make a move now, his doubts would weaken his resolve to the point where he'd give up altogether. He encountered the first surprise at the back door. It was unlocked. And while it was an unlooked-for bonus, it also made his stomach turn over.

Had somebody been here before him?

Because it couldn't be that Garfield left his house unlocked. It sent a wave of revulsion crashing through him to think of the sort of things that a man like Garfield might keep in his house. The sort of things he was going to have to dig through himself in his search for information. That sweaty, gorge-rising wave of nausea told him that Garfield would never leave his house unlocked. Not unless he was stupid. They knew for a fact that he was far from that. It was the smug confidence in his own cleverness that had gotten under Guillory's skin to the point where she'd attacked him in the first place.

Somebody else had left the door unlocked.

And that person or persons might still be inside.

He eased the door open. Stepped lightly into the kitchen, breathing on hold. Silence. Complete stillness. Not even a startled cockroach scuttling for the safety of a dark corner. He couldn't explain the aura of hollow emptiness that immediately enveloped him. Not just in the kitchen. In the whole house. As if he could see through the walls and the ceiling. His shoulders relaxed, his breathing easier. He'd put money on the fact that he was the only living thing in the house.

There was something else as well as the sense of abandonment. Not strong or overpowering, but it was there. A sharpness in the air. Like the smell of spilled milk gone sour. Except it wasn't that. He recognized the smell. It awakened memories that he couldn't put his finger on, of sweaty nights spent tossing sleeplessly in tangled sheets.

It was coming from the hallway. Leaving the kitchen, he crept silently into the increasingly pungent atmosphere. He closed the kitchen door behind him to block out the kitchen window, flicked on his flashlight.

An up-ended bucket sat at the bottom of the stairs. Around it, a congealing pool of vomit, the source of the acrid smell. More of it streaked the wall leading up the stairs to the landing. As if the bucket had been thrown down the stairs, its foul-smelling contents spattering everything.

Or everyone.

Amongst the bile and partly-digested food particles that lay at the bottom of the stairs, he saw something that was out of place. Something bright. He ignored it. Concentrated instead on the task ahead—getting across to the other side of the sea of vomit in front of him.

Because whatever might have happened here, it had happened upstairs. He wouldn't be able to search for information until he knew what it was. He already had a bad feeling about it.

That was when he caught the smell of soap. Just a hint, then it was gone. So fast that it might have been nothing more than a remembered smell, his nose working with his subconscious mind to put thoughts into his head he refused to acknowledge.

He gripped the banister tightly with his left hand. Bent his knees, tensed, then leapt across the pool of vomit, thigh muscles exploding into adrenalin-fueled action. He landed on the second step with a heavy thump, wobbling precariously. Shot out his right hand to steady himself against the wall. Then froze, head cocked, alert for any reaction to the unavoidable noise he'd made.

No sound came from above, just a deeper silence.

He got up on his toes to avoid the spills on the stair treads, pressed his fingers against the wall for balance. Ever mindful to avoid the streaks slashed across the wall, he made his way upstairs. As he climbed, the acrid smell receded, only to be replaced by one far worse, one that told him what he was about to find. As if, in the darkest places of his mind and heart, he hadn't already known.

The smell of death.

Of rotting flesh and putrefaction over a backdrop of rotten eggs and feces. He pulled out a handkerchief, clamped it tightly over his mouth and nose.

He paused at the top of the stairs, tried to slow his heart and his breathing. On the other side of the landing the door to the master bedroom was closed. He ignored it. Put off approaching it, even thinking about it, concentrated on looking for Garfield in the places he knew he wasn't.

He wasn't on the landing. So much for the theory that he'd dropped the bucket as he collapsed at the top of the stairs. He wasn't in the bathroom. Not slumped clutching the toilet pan like a prized possession to be carried with him to the next world. Or even stabbed to death in the shower stall in a frenzy of murderous rage. He wasn't in the second or third bedrooms either, both of them empty and unused, their doors wide open.

He was all out of places Garfield wasn't.

He stood for a long time in front of the closed door to the master bedroom. His nose told him that his irrational hopes that he wasn't only seconds away from finding Garfield dead behind this door were in vain. Not because he gave a damn whether Garfield lived or died. But because his mind would give him no rest from the thoughts that tormented him, from what he so desperately wanted not to be so.

The smell of soap. And something shiny where nothing shiny belonged.

Gently, he pushed the door open with his finger.

Then rocked violently back on his heels. An odor straight from the pits of hell rushed out to embrace him like a long-lost friend, to smother him with its foul embrace, the chemical compounds and particles released by Garfield's decomposing body eagerly searching out a new home in his hair, his eyes, his pores. Who'd have thought that an inch of wooden door could keep such a monstrous thing at bay.

Robert Garfield's unseeing eyes stared back at him as he lay in his bed, propped up on pillows as if waiting for a friend or a kindly neighbor to bring him a hot drink and his medication. Except he'd had a very different sort of visitor. Even from the doorway, the dark stain on the pillow around his head was clear to see. Still Evan's mind clung to its desperate hopes of natural causes. It was vomit. He'd choked on it. In his sleep or as he lay too weak to move.

Those hopes died a peaceful, easy death as he crossed the room, saw that it wasn't so, that the dark stain was blood and not bile.

Garfield's death had been neither peaceful, nor easy. His throat had been slit, an open wound from ear to ear like a second obscenely grinning mouth. His eyes were like those of a dead bird, reflecting the world but with no life within, just the remembered horror of his passing. A crudely-written placard sat on his chest.

So many perverts, so little time.

He stared at the words, a thousand thoughts fighting in his

brain. Was it the work of some vigilante group or individual? Or was it somebody who wanted it to look that way? His own people perhaps, worried he'd become too great a risk.

Or somebody else altogether, somebody with an axe to grind.

All thoughts of searching the house for the names of the men higher up the food chain, the men who might well have sanctioned what lay before him, went out the window. The house was a crime scene now. He'd contaminated it unwittingly, didn't want to compound his guilt.

He backtracked carefully out of the bedroom and across the landing, made his way down the stairs. It was obvious now what had happened. The bucket of sick had been Garfield's last-ditch attempt to fight off an intruder intent on killing him, buy himself a few moments' time.

As he descended, carefully avoiding the splashes and stains, his mind went into overdrive. All his senses conspired against him, each contributing its own small piece of a picture that made him wish that he'd never set foot in this house, never heard of Robert Garfield.

The sight and smell of Kate Guillory in the breakfast diner. Her skin, usually pale, looking like it had been scrubbed raw with a stiff brush. Hair smelling of soap, still wet.

The unexplained cut on her cheek.

Snapping at him. Irritable. Stressed. So out of character.

Her lack of appetite, an inability to face a plate of greasy food. He'd just seen and smelled something that had stolen his own appetite. And he was a mere spectator.

On the bottom stair he tensed momentarily, then leapt to the far side of the mess at the bottom, stumbled and fell headlong into the wall as he landed.

Don't look.

He picked himself up, shook his head clear.

Don't turn around.

He had to call it in immediately.

Keep walking.

On leaden legs he took a step towards the kitchen, then another.

You don't want to know.

That was the trouble. He *did* want to know, couldn't help himself. Who the hell did he think he was fooling? He turned around. Stared without seeing at the pool on the floor. He'd rather drop to his knees and lap up the filthy mess like a half-starved dog than do what he had to do.

Something shiny and bright.

Around him the room blurred and faded to black as he squatted down. The blood roared in his ears as he reached out his hand for the thing that would bring his world crashing down.

Something that doesn't belong in a puddle of sick.

Carefully so as not to get his fingers wet, he took hold of what he'd noticed earlier and forced himself to ignore. A small, glittering object so very out of place in the bile surrounding it.

He pulled it free, didn't need to look closely at it.

Why would he?

He'd bought the damn thing. He closed his eyes, choked back a strangled sub-human cry.

Kate Guillory had lost one of the gold earrings that he'd bought her for her birthday.

Careless bitch.

Lucky for her he'd found it.

20

EVAN STARED AT THE EARRING IN HIS HAND, HIS MIND A MERCIFUL blank, a temporary lull before all hell broke loose.

What should he do?

Choose the option of a person without a vested interest, without an emotional connection—put it back.

Or the alternative—put it in his wallet for safekeeping.

Then deal with the fallout. Because one thing he knew for sure. He'd never survive the first meeting with Guillory without it coming out.

To his guilty mind the spot from which he'd plucked the earring was like a gaping hole, as obvious to even a casual observer as a sign hammered into the wooden floor: *This is where the removed evidence was.*

What did he know? The earring placed Guillory in the house.

What did it prove? Nothing beyond that.

It was at the bottom of the stairs. Not in the bedroom or on the bed, on the dead man's pillow. She might have come to the house, meaning to search it as did he. If Garfield had thrown a bucket of sick over her, maybe that was shock enough for her to come to her senses, get the hell out of there.

The earring went in his wallet, another notch on his conscience. But that was beyond repair, had been for years.

He pulled out his phone. Called Ryder. Got an earful of abuse for his trouble.

'Do you have any idea what time it is?'

'Do *not* hang up.' He yelled it into the phone, a stunned silence bouncing back. 'Get over here now.' He told him where *here* was, then told him not to call Guillory under any circumstances.

He couldn't stay in the house a minute longer. He needed fresh air, to breathe it deeply into his contaminated lungs. But even though he might scour his insides clean with the fresh night air, drawing it down into the deepest depths of his body, he knew he could stand in the face of a raging hurricane and it would never blow the poisonous thoughts from his mind.

He sat on the front step waiting for Ryder to arrive, head in his hands. He felt as dead inside as the corpse upstairs on the bed. He almost envied it. At least it was at peace now. Things weren't only just beginning for it.

The sound of a vehicle approaching made him look up. A police cruiser drove slowly down the street without lights or siren. It jerked to a sudden halt at the curb in front of the house as if it had been about to drive past, then saw him at the last moment. Two officers got out, hands resting loosely on gun butt or nightstick.

He stood up, showed them his hands. From the look of wary suspicion on their faces, he guessed Ryder had omitted to tell them that he'd be at the scene.

'I'm the one who called it in,' he said.

'What?'

'I called Ryder.'

They shared a look—careful, he's on something.

'Turn around please sir,' one of them said. 'Hands against the wall.'

He was too tired and stressed for this shit. Had Ryder told them to give him a hard time just for the fun of it?

'Didn't you hear what I just said? I called—'

It wasn't the response they were looking for. Strong hands spun him around, cut off his protests, nose squashed into the front door as they kicked his legs apart. Despite the tiredness and irritation and the numbness inside he knew better than to resist. He relaxed into the position, let them get on with it.

'Something must have happened to your voice in the last ten minutes. Seeing as it was a woman who called us.' The cop patted him down as he spoke. 'Saw somebody creeping around. What looked like a flashlight flicking on and off in the house—'

Evan didn't need to look at him to see the sudden triumphant look on his face.

'Well, what have we got here?'

'Looks like a flashlight,' his partner said.

Evan didn't bother to say anything, waited for them to find the latex gloves. It didn't take long.

'Gloves too,' the first cop said.

It wasn't a good time to say forget about gloves and a flashlight, there's a dead body in the bedroom. These guys liked to jump to conclusions. He almost laughed, caught himself just in time, as a thought crossed his mind—never had he been so keen to see Ryder in all his life.

Where was the lazy bastard anyway? Probably grabbing a quick breakfast before heading out. Hopefully not calling Guillory despite being told not to.

The thought of Guillory coincided with the cop finishing patting down his upper body. With that his stomach turned over, his breath catching in his throat, as those two independent factors collided in one inescapable conclusion. Any second now the cop would start to pat down his lower body. He'd find his wallet in his pants' pocket. He'd pull it out, check his ID. And he'd find the earring in it, small though it was. When he did, he wouldn't miss the sticky residue of vomit clinging to it, might even think it was blood.

All his worries about being caught in the middle of the night with flashlight and gloves breaking into a man's house were as nothing compared to the consequences for Guillory of such a discovery. He stood, barely breathing, every muscle rigid as the cop's hands moved down his body, stopped as he felt the bulge of the wallet. The cop pulled it out. Handed it to his partner.

The partner rifled through it, pulled out Evan's ID. Evan waited for the predictable response. The guy didn't disappoint.

'Ha! A private investigator.'

He made it sound like the man who swabs out the toilet stalls in a strip club. But amongst the scorn and derision Evan saw a way out.

'Yeah, well, somebody's got to do the job while you lot are just sitting around with your thumbs up your asses.'

The cop's mouth hung open a couple of beats, at a loss for a suitable reply. Then it snapped shut into a tight line. The one patting him down had also paused.

Had they heard that correctly?

It wasn't what they were expecting from a guy they were about to haul down to the station. Not what anybody would call passing the attitude test. He sure as hell wouldn't be getting the best cell in the block. Or a kiss goodnight from the Captain. Even so, he decided to make sure.

'And I know exactly how much cash is in that wallet. So don't think about an unofficial on-the-spot fine because your wife needs a new dress after she put on an extra thirty pounds.'

The cop looked as if he was going for his nightstick until he heard his partner stifle a snicker. In the end, he stuffed Evan's ID back into the wallet, all thoughts of looking through it more thoroughly forgotten. Then jammed it back into his pocket hard enough to rip it with a look on his face that said he could afford to wait until they got back to the station. The one patting him down finished, straightened up. He put his mouth close to Evan's ear.

'You want to explain what you're doing? What you're *investigating*.'

Even if he could have found his voice through the relief that washed through his veins, left him feeling a little shaky, what would he have said?

I wanted to search the house. But I found a dead body instead.

'Cat got your tongue?' the partner said, a mocking satisfaction in his voice.

They took his silence as an admission of guilt.

Then things got a whole lot worse.

As the first cop pulled his arms down and around behind his back ready to cuff him, the partner stiffened. Then pulled his own flashlight from his belt. Played the beam over the door frame.

They all saw it at the same time. It looked like a bloody smear. Even with the knowledge of what waited upstairs, Evan knew it couldn't be. They'd used the back door, same as he had. But the two cops were looking for something like it. Now their suspicions had been confirmed.

'What's that?'

It was a stupid thing to say. But Evan couldn't say anything, not without the whole story coming out. It didn't make any difference either way.

Next thing he knew, he was on his face on the ground. A knee dropped heavily onto his back in the middle of his shoulders, cuffs clicked tightly around his wrists. Then they hauled him up, dragged him to the cruiser.

'You're making a mistake,' Evan said as they dipped his head and bundled him into the back seat.

They looked at each other. *We're* making a mistake? Then a couple of *I don't think so* head shakes as they got in the front. The partner was just about to get on the radio and call it in when another cruiser pulled up alongside facing the opposite way. The two drivers started talking through their open windows like a couple of old fishermen stopping to discuss how good a day they'd had.

The cop in the driver's seat in front of him was just telling the other guy what they'd caught with a jab of his thumb in Evan's direction, when Evan saw the lights of an unmarked car approaching. It pulled to the curb immediately in front of the cruiser he was in. The second car's flashing lights reflecting off the windshield made it impossible to see how many people were inside.

He held his breath as the driver's door swung open and Ryder hauled his bulk out. His eyes went to the passenger door, praying that it didn't swing open and Guillory climb out. But Ryder wasn't stupid, much as it pained him to admit it. The significance of the address wasn't lost on him. The passenger door stayed shut.

He stood with his fists on his hips, looking at Evan in the back seat of the cruiser, enjoying the moment. Evan didn't look at him, didn't want to see the grin he knew would be plastered all over his face. It wouldn't have surprised him if he'd pulled out his phone, taken a photograph.

'What a beautiful sight,' Ryder said, pulling the back door open. 'I can't tell you how much it upsets me to spoil it.'

'Good to see you too, Detective.'

Ryder laughed, resisted the temptation to point out how

polite Evan had suddenly become, the *Donut* moniker notable by its absence.

'I think you actually mean it for once.' He turned to the cops in the front. 'I can vouch for him.'

If his hands hadn't been cuffed, Evan would've given him a round of applause for getting those words out. Even so, he looked like he wanted to spit. He pulled Evan out of the car, uncuffed him.

Evan told him what he'd discovered.

Apart from the earring, of course.

All traces of the grin were gone from Ryder's face by the time Evan had finished.

'It's good you told me not to call Kate. I didn't think you had that much sense in you.'

Evan shrugged, if only you knew. He'd just done the most stupid thing in his life. Guillory would've said the competition for that particular accolade was stiff. Now it seemed that the way his last conversation with Ryder had ended without its usual acrimony, plus his good sense in calling him out alone, had stood him in good stead. Ryder put a hand on his elbow. Steered him out of earshot of the patrol officers.

'You want to tell me unofficially what the hell you were doing here in the first place?'

He didn't. But he didn't have a choice. So he told him he'd been hoping to find information on the men further up the food chain to Garfield—or down, considering the sort of people they were.

Ryder listened in silence. Astonishment, amusement and pity all collided in his doughy features. Evan expected to feel a condescending hand on his shoulder at any second. Then Ryder surprised him.

'I guess your heart's in the right place. Even if you act like a fucking idiot. Does Kate know what you're up to?'

Evan shook his head, are you kidding me?

It struck him then how screwed up everything was. That both he and Guillory had come up with the same idea—not killing Garfield, of course—and hadn't said a word to the other. The thought squeezed a laugh out of his mouth, a short sharp bark of a sound.

'What?'

He could hardly tell Ryder. The police might discover that Guillory had been there. She might even admit it. But he wasn't going to say.

'It's nothing.'

Ryder looked at him a long while. As if he was re-evaluating his opinion on a species of bug that hitherto he'd squashed without a second thought, but was now seeing things more from the bug's point of view.

'You're a strange guy, you know that?'

'I prefer complex.'

'I'm sure you do. It doesn't make you any less strange.'

Then Ryder suddenly laughed to himself, gave a sorry sad shake of the head at the ways of the world. Without knowing how, Evan knew that what he said next would not be funny at all. He didn't ask him to explain. Ryder wanted to share it anyway. Because he was in a state of beautiful ignorance. Evan would have given anything to swap places with him, even to be him if that's what it took. He flicked his head up at the bedroom window. Leaned in closer to make sure the patrol officers couldn't overhear.

'I'd only say it to you seeing as the two of you are so close'— he swallowed, the word *close* giving him some difficulty to get out—'but I hope Kate's not too pissed when she discovers somebody's beaten her to it.'

21

EVAN COULDN'T GET RYDER'S WORDS OUT OF HIS HEAD. HE walked the length of the block back to his car with his head held low, his heart lower. He was tired. He'd had a long day. An eventful day. That was his excuse for not being more vigilant. In case the long, eventful day wasn't quite over yet.

He dropped wearily into the seat of the courtesy car he was driving while his '69 Corvette Stingray was in the shop. Thank God he didn't have to wrestle with an ageing muscle car to get home.

A '69 Corvette Stingray doesn't have any back seats. Sometimes that's a pain in the butt, sometimes it's a good thing. It would've been a good thing tonight. Because that way Lydia Strange couldn't have been hiding in the back waiting for him. Lydia didn't wear perfume. Or smoke. There was nothing to give her away.

He rested his hands on top of the wheel, threw his head backwards against the headrest. Closed his eyes and took a deep breath, wondering what the hell he'd gotten himself into.

He barely flinched when Lydia rose up silently behind him and touched the cold steel of the suppressor on the back of his neck. Like why wouldn't this be happening? How else could his day have ended? She must have waited outside after leaving him earlier, followed him here.

'Hello Lydia. Missing me already?'

She twisted the suppressor harder into his neck.

'You hit the horn or do anything else stupid I'll put a bullet in the back of your head and take the consequences. What's going on down there?'

'A man's been murdered in that house.'

'Did you kill him?'

It was a stupid question. But even stupid questions deserve an answer when the person doing the asking has a gun to your head. And is a little unbalanced.

'No. I'd have liked to. He's a pedophile. But somebody beat me to it.'

The words sent a shiver through him that made the gun on his neck seem like a minor irritation, no more troublesome than a mosquito bite. Too late he realized he'd said too much. He was tired, after all.

She came alert at the mention of pedophiles. In the mirror her eyes clicked into sharper focus. She didn't say anything. He knew she recognized the importance of the information to her own single-minded purpose.

'You found him.'

'Yep.' He gave a small laugh that didn't start to do justice to the situation. 'I seem to be good at finding dead bodies at the moment.'

'Why'd they let you go?'

'Because the fat detective knows me. He likes me.'

He should have known *detective* was another trigger word, had her sitting forward in the seat, an excited edge to her voice.

'Is Guillory there?'

'Why don't you go take a look for yourself?'

She drew back her arm sharply, slashed him across the cheek and ear with the gun. The additional length and weight of the silencer gave the blow added momentum. It hit hard, made his head ring. Then she said something that did a damn sight more than make his head ring, made him feel as if he'd been punched by an angry bear.

'Give me your wallet.'

'What?'

He tried to fill his voice with confusion, hoped it didn't sound to her like dread, as it did in his own ears.

'Throw it on the back seat.'

She couldn't know what was in it. Already he was learning not to underestimate her. She'd piece it all together as soon as she saw the earring. He tried stalling nonetheless.

'Why do you want it?'

'Because I caught you creeping around Todd's apartment looking for information on the pedophiles who hired him. Now here you are breaking into a pedophile's house in the middle of the night. I want to know what you found.'

'I told you. A dead body. That's kind of difficult to ignore when you're trying to search a house.'

'Give it here anyway.'

He met her eyes in the mirror, wasn't sure what he saw staring back at him. An undeniable determination to kill him if necessary, if that's what it took. There was something else behind it, a hint of desperation that she'd gotten herself into something that had spiraled out of control and she didn't know how to make it stop. That maybe she'd happily pull the trigger and blow his brains all over the windshield because that would put an end to it if nothing else.

Or maybe she just had crazy eyes.

He pulled out his wallet, threw it over his shoulder.

She picked it up off the back seat, went through it with a lot more thoroughness than the cop had. He guessed she was looking for a slip of paper, some information scribbled down.

She certainly wasn't looking for an earring. But when she found it, she knew she'd hit pay dirt. It was the only thing you wouldn't expect to find in a man's wallet.

In the mirror he watched her lift it out, saw the *aha* moment register in her face. Then a slight frown on her forehead as she felt the stickiness of it. Although this time he guessed she was wrong in the conclusion she jumped to. He'd bet she thought it was blood, not bile.

So what? One bodily fluid is much the same as another. Both are sufficient to place a person where they shouldn't be.

'What's this?'

'What's it look like?'

She hit him again with the gun even if her heart wasn't in it. Because she wasn't a stupid woman, far from it. Her mind was too busy pulling together the information she already had. Suddenly she let out a whoop of almost girlish joy.

'Ha! It's Guillory's earring. She killed him. You're trying to protect her.'

He kept his eyes on the dash, wouldn't meet hers in the mirror.

'Look at me and tell me I'm wrong.'

He knew there was a spiteful gleam in her eye to match the breathless excitement in her voice. Then it was as if a switch had been flicked, all the girlish charm gone.

'Did she kill him?'

'You tell me.'

There was no need to flinch this time, no need to worry about her striking him. Because she had ears that worked every bit as well as her mind. She knew the ring of truth—and the myriad emotions behind it—when she heard it. She held the earring between her finger and thumb, dangled it where he could see it in the mirror.

'Maybe I should take a walk down the street, give this to the fat detective. Tell him where I got it. And where *you* got it.'

He ignored her. She was only taunting him. She was less likely to hand it over than he was. For him it was something he wished he'd never found. Something that would only bring him pain, strike a wedge between himself and Guillory. For her it was an unlooked-for piece of luck. It was a weapon.

'Just get out the car,' he said, wanting her gone now.

'In a minute. Give me your phone.'

He knew why she wanted it. She wanted Guillory's number. So that she could put her new-found weapon to work. The thought of what it would do to Guillory's fragile state of mind when she received a text from Lydia out of the blue—*guess what I've got*—made him feel sick.

He was taking too long thinking about it, heard the sound of the back door opening. He knew what was coming.

'Detective Fatso is going to think it's his birthday.'

She won't give it up.

'So give it to him.'

That wiped the smugness off her face. But only for a second. The back door opened a little wider.

'If that's the way you want to play it.'

She won't give it up.

'Go if you're going to.'

Said with more conviction than he felt. Holding her eyes in the mirror. Neither of them blinking. Then a change in hers.

'Prison's a bad place for a cop.'

And now he wasn't so sure. Maybe she'd give Ryder the earring after all. Sit back and watch the fireworks. Knowing all the while that if that didn't put Guillory behind bars, condemn her to a living hell, she could revert to plan A and do whatever she had in mind before the unexpected earring bonus. Win-win all round for the psychopath.

'I'm glad you're not my friend. Last chance.'

The maddening confidence in her voice, the knowledge that out of all of them she had the least to lose, made him squeeze the wheel until it flexed to stop himself from spinning around, flailing wildly at her head. Because she'd be expecting it. She'd duck under the blind swing, put a bullet in his spine through the seat. What good would that do any of them?

The door was all the way open now. He stared through the windshield at the group of cops down the street. Any second, one of them would look their way, see the open door. He'd stride down the street to investigate. Face twisted in disgust, thinking it was some rubbernecker or ambulance chaser to be sent on their way with a righteous foot up their ass.

Speak of the devil and he shall appear.

Or if not appear, then at least look up. Which is what one of them did now.

At the same moment, in the absolute quiet, he heard the gritty crunch of Lydia's shoe on the sidewalk.

The cop leaned towards his colleague. Pointed at the car. Lydia now standing half in, half out of the car saw it too.

'I'm going to wave to him in five seconds.'

Without warning she banged hard on the roof with the side of her fist.

'Five!'

In the quiet of the street it was like a scream.

'*Okay.*' His voice an insistent hiss.

She brought her fist down again, harder still, rocked the car on its suspension.

'Four!'

'I said okay. Get in the damn car. Close the door.'

He pulled out his phone, threw it on the back seat.

It didn't take her long to find Guillory's number. For a brief moment he prayed that she'd be stupid or careless, would forward the number to her own phone, leave a trail. But she wasn't either of those things. She took a quick photo of Guillory's details, her eyes lighting up at the second unlooked-for bonus of the night—an address to go with the phone number she was after. Then she was gone.

He pulled away, drove slowly past Garfield's house. Ryder was on the sidewalk, raised a hand as he drove by. It was the friendliest gesture he'd ever made towards Evan.

If only you knew what I've done.

22

'Piss off Kate?' Guillory said. 'You sure know how to make a girl feel good about herself.'

He wished he hadn't answered the damn phone, had kept his head buried under the pillow until it stopped ringing. The only reason he didn't was because it wouldn't have done any good, would only have put off the inevitable. But now was not a good time. He'd only had a couple of hours' sleep, hadn't had a chance to get things straight in his mind. He doubted he'd ever have that much time unless he lived to be as old as Crow, something that felt very unlikely at the present time. But they needed to be a lot straighter than they were now for him to have any chance of negotiating the minefield of their conversation.

'Sorry. I needed to get you off the phone in a way that wouldn't have you calling back.'

A sharp bark of laughter crackled unpleasantly in his ear.

'Mission accomplished.'

He didn't mention that she was calling him now, less than twelve hours later, didn't think that would be helpful.

'You want to explain why?'

He vaguely remembered back in the good old days when he

might have made a joke about it—one in very poor taste, of course—along the lines of him being busy with Detective Cortez. Just not today. Or any time soon now he thought about it.

But he had a problem. How to tell her any of it without it all coming out, unfiltered by time and reasoning? So he resorted to the tried and trusted mix of vagueness with some outright lies and omissions of fact thrown in.

'You remember Todd Strange...'

It was a stupid way to start. Like saying, you remember the guy who was going to put a bullet in the back of your head, bury you in a shallow grave?

She told him that, yes, she remembered. Thank you for the reminder.

'He's got a sister. Had. Because he's dead. But she's alive.'

She filtered the gibberish, told him she didn't know that. If you can hear patience wearing thin, he heard it now coming down his telephone line at 6:30 in the morning. It's actually quite a loud sound. A bit like an angry bull snorting down the line at you. He swallowed drily—the effect of sleeping with his mouth open, nothing more—and dug the hole a little deeper.

'She was waiting for me when I got back to my apartment yesterday.'

He held his breath, was tempted to bite the pillow to stop himself from saying too much.

Never forget, vagueness is your friend.

'What did she want?'

He let out a relieved sigh. Spat out the pillow—he'd bitten it after all without realizing it—thankful that she hadn't come out with any awkward questions. Like why has she come looking now? Why you?

It was only a temporary reprieve, he knew that. He could sense those difficult questions huddled together in the background, plotting his downfall, waiting for the perfect opportunity to blindside him.

Despite the reprieve, he didn't give her the short answer to what Lydia wanted.

You.

But he couldn't give her the long answer—she wanted to know what he'd been doing in Todd Strange's apartment. Not without it all coming out.

Again vagueness came to the rescue.

'She's trying to find out what happened to her brother.'

'He's dead. She knows that.'

You can't beat a discussion with an angry pedant first thing in the morning, he thought to himself.

'I meant who killed him.'

'Did you tell her?'

He couldn't see where this was going. It seemed she couldn't either. She changed tack abruptly.

'Forget it. I don't see why that made you tell me to piss off and hang up on me.'

Saying the words crystalized it in her mind. There was a long, uncomfortable silence. Then she backed up to her previous line of questioning but with a different line of attack. And a harder edge to her voice.

'You didn't tell her that I killed him, did you?'

'Of course not. Why would I do that?'

'Because sometimes you're an idiot.'

He felt like asking her if that was just a plain, garden variety idiot or a *fucking* idiot like Ryder had called him. At least Ryder had said his heart was in the right place. Guillory sounded as if the only interest she had in his heart was in seeing it ripped out by wild dogs. If he'd had some lipstick, he'd have drawn a face on the pillow, tried having a conversation with that instead. He took a deep breath.

'Be careful, that's all. She's got a habit of sneaking up on you.'

'On *you*, you mean.'

'Yes, on me. Anyway, why were you calling when I told you to piss off?'

He knew what it was without asking, was only asking to change the subject. She'd been calling to give him a hard time after Cortez called her and told her about him trying to hide the rotting fish in his pants pocket. If he was hoping it might lighten the mood now, he was going to be disappointed.

'It doesn't matter now.'

There was an awkward silence.

'Really,' she said. 'It's not important. So what are you up to?'

He groaned inwardly, wanted to know what he'd done to deserve this. With his heart in his mouth he told her that he was heading back down to Florida.

If an alien had hacked into the line at some point in the last few minutes, it would naturally assume that long excruciating pauses were a normal part of everyday human communication. That perhaps information was passing back and forth on a non-audible level, maybe even blamed it on an inability for its alien ears to pick up all levels of human speech.

It wouldn't have been wrong. There were plenty of unspoken emotions in the early morning air.

'Really? Why's that?'

Translation: *You're going back to see Detective Cortez.*

He told her about the thumb drive Crow had received in the mail, how they believed it was relevant to Winter's death.

'Postal workers on strike so you can't send it on?'

He didn't say anything.

'Email not working?'

'I was going to ask if you're free.'

'Liar. Anyway, three's a crowd.'

He'd known when he told her to piss off that there'd be

trouble down the road, even though he'd done it for all the best reasons. But he'd never have thought it would be like this.

'Crow wants me to ask around some more down there, okay? I'm doing it as a favor to him. He's lost an old friend and I want to help put his mind at ease.'

He wanted to tell her he was trying to do the same for her. To find out who had put her through the ordeal that had turned her into the person he was having this verbal confrontation with now. To hopefully get the old Kate Guillory back. It seemed she was intent on making the job more difficult every step of the way.

He didn't say any of that, of course.

'Okay. Have a nice time with Ana Maria.'

It was only after she'd ended the call that it struck him. He'd never mentioned Cortez's first name to her. She'd looked her up.

23

THE FIRST THING CORTEZ DID WAS DROP HER EYES TO HIS CROTCH. He did a little wiggle to show off his fishy-stain-free pants, got an appreciative nod back.

'You think I've only got one pair?'

She shrugged.

'Some of the men I know do.'

'That's the laid-back Keys for you. And thanks for calling Guillory, keeping her abreast of the important developments in the case.'

She smiled, you're welcome. She had very nice teeth.

'Us girls have to stick together. Hope she didn't give you too hard a time.'

'Nothing I'm not used to.'

He didn't tell her she didn't get a chance, that was when he told her to piss off. He certainly didn't tell her that the only thing she was giving him a hard time over was her, Detective Ana Maria Cortez. Nor did he spoil the illusion, didn't say try calling her now, see how much *us girls* camaraderie there is coming from Guillory's end of the line.

The thought depressed him, reminded him of his last conversation with Guillory. It had knocked most of the stuffing out of him, all of the *joie de vivre*. As a result, a long drive down from Miami on his own hadn't held many attractions. Instead he'd flown into the Florida Keys International Airport at Marathon, picked up a car there. Not a convertible either.

'Anyway, you look a bit better than last time I saw you,' she said.

'That's because I don't have a hangover today.'

Then her face turned serious.

'I hope you're not here to tell me you need to change that hangover-induced statement.'

He shook his head, dug the thumb drive out of his pocket.

'No. I'm here to give you this.'

She took it with less enthusiasm than he'd have liked. Didn't exactly push him out of the way as she dived for her computer to plug it in.

'At least this one's not covered in fish slime. Anything on it?'

'Why not take a look.'

She told him to pull over a chair. They both sat in front of her computer as she inserted the thumb drive. Squashed into the small cubicle, sitting up close next to her, he caught the scent of her perfume, was very aware of the heat of her body. It made him feel as if they were about to curl up on the sofa together for a night in watching a movie. He almost asked her when was the pizza going to be delivered.

It would've been a very lackluster start to the evening if that had been the case. They watched the short movie clip in silence.

'Two people on vacation in Key West,' she said when it was over. 'Wow! You've cracked this one wide open.'

She was tapping a pencil impatiently against the desktop, a gesture he correctly identified as *say something relevant or leave*.

At that moment a young woman stuck her head around the side of the partition. Leaning in close to Cortez, she said the captain wanted a word with her. Cortez told her that she'd be there in a couple of minutes, the implication being, as soon as she'd gotten rid of the time waster. The young woman didn't leave. Smiling in embarrassment, she silently mouthed the word *now*.

Cortez told Evan to wait there and not touch anything. Then she followed the young woman across the bullpen area and into another office with large windows facing the bullpen. Inside the office an older, heavier man in shirtsleeves spoke briefly with her, while Cortez kept nodding. Finally Cortez left and retraced her steps back to where Evan was waiting.

She dropped into her chair, anger and embarrassment colliding in her face.

'I've just been informed that the Winter case is closed.'

The pencil was busily tapping on her desk again. In frustration this time. Evan decided to make matters worse.

'I'd have thought you'd be pleased. Seeing as you don't think there's a case in the first place.'

He didn't know why he said it. It was obvious what the problem was, one that he had no difficulty in understanding. She didn't like to be told what to do. Especially not in front of a member of the public. She didn't answer him, the pencil still going *tap, tap, tap*.

'Who closed it?' he said, feeling like he was going to snap the damn pencil in half any second.

She shook her head, enough of the stupid questions.

'Who do you think? He also said to show you the door.'

The *tap, tap, tap* got faster. He grabbed the end of the pencil, held it still. He could feel her body vibrating through it.

'How does he even know who I am?'

'How the hell am I supposed to know?'

His long association with Guillory had prepared him well for times like this. The words *don't take it out on me* never got further than the confines of his mind. Despite her snapping at him and the inadvisability of pushing her, he'd have liked an answer to his question. How *did* the captain know who he was? Was his presence there in any way connected to the abrupt closure of the case? Cortez didn't give him time to think about the implications of either question.

'Come on.'

The tone of voice didn't leave any room for discussion. Definitely not refusal. They both stood.

'It's okay, I can find my own way out.'

She put a hand on his elbow, steered him towards the door.

'I said *come on*.' Then she dropped her voice. 'I assume you've got a copy of that video on your phone.'

He came on, amazed at the power of pride, especially when pricked. Whoever promoted it to one of the seven deadly sins didn't miss a trick. They went to a diner a couple of blocks away, took a seat in the window. Once they were settled in, he tried a different version of his earlier question.

'Do you know who's behind the captain closing the case?'

'No. He didn't see fit to share that information with me.' The thin line where her lips used to be and the flaring of her nostrils indicated that she didn't want to be asked a third time. 'Let me see the video again.'

He studied her face as she watched it again, thinking that the residual flush on her cheeks from the anger and embarrassment suited her. She must have read his mind.

'Stop staring at me.'

He stopped staring, concentrated on getting the menus lined up neatly. Out of the corner of his eye he could still see her touch the tip of her tongue to her upper lip. She paused the video in the same place he had, trying to see the face of the man obscured by the couple taking the selfie. She gave up, pushed the phone across the table.

'I still can't see the connection. How are these people linked to Winter and to the guy in the video coming through the door?'

He turned the phone towards her, pointed at the young couple who were only ever going to move again when somebody pressed *play*, their actual lives on hold forever.

'Those two are now dead as well.'

A light edged into her eyes, a bit more interest now.

'How?'

'They died in a house fire in Key West.'

Something else took the place of the interest in her eyes. The gleam was still there but it was more mocking amusement than professional interest.

'Let me get this straight. Winter's job was to identify the couple in the video. They were then killed because of whatever they caught on the selfie that was going on behind them. And then Winter was killed to tidy up any loose ends.'

'You forgot the aliens.'

Her face compacted into a frown. Suddenly she looked a lot older.

'What?'

'Your tone of voice is the same as if we were talking about aliens doing it.'

She pushed her coffee cup away. Leaned back in her seat. Let out a weary sigh, one that said she'd already had enough of being caught between the hardass captain on one side and the lunatic sitting opposite her on the other.

Then she leaned forwards again, put her elbows on the table. He leaned in to make a cozy little huddle like they were making plans to run away together. She dropped her voice to a whisper as if the words she was about to utter could get her fired.

'Any proof?'

She didn't give him a chance to say *no*.

'Hey! I've got one. How about Winter was paid to kill the couple in the video and then topped himself out of remorse?'

'Possible. But I prefer mine.'

'Want to flip a coin?'

'Good to know I won't be getting you in any trouble with the captain. I wouldn't have wanted that on my conscience.'

They stared at each other for a long moment. Then she put her hand on his arm, made him wonder if a male detective would've done the same or just told him to drop it and not tried to let him down gently.

'Look, I'd like to help. If I had the captain's blessing or you'd come up with some hard evidence, or even a bigger coincidence like they'd all been drowned, to make me go against him . . .' She held her hands open wide, now's the time to give it to me. 'But seeing as I've got neither, there isn't anything I can do. I'm sorry.'

They paid and left. Standing on the sidewalk outside, she asked him what he planned to do next.

'Head down to Key West.'

''Cause more trouble, you mean.'

For a moment he felt as if Guillory had had a last-minute change of heart, had come along for the ride after all. He frowned, not aware of having done anything. Yet.

'We got a complaint from Conch Yacht Sales.'

'*Ah*. From Mr Conch?'

She smiled, her accusation confirmed.

'From Mr *Romano*, yes. Apparently, we sent some lunatic down there trying to wheedle confidential information out of the girl who works there—'

'Amanda.'

'Amanda, yes. Seems this particular lunatic propositioned her as well, wanted her to take him out on a boat. He pretended he wanted to buy one but she said she wouldn't have trusted this guy to clean one.'

He shook his head sadly at the wicked ways of men.

'Key West attracts all sorts, I suppose.'

Then he headed off to find out just how true that was.

24

EVAN HAD THREE THINGS TO DO IN KEY WEST. HE DECIDED ON A decreasing temperature scale to prioritize them. He'd start warm with the house fire location, drop down to frosty at the Key West PD and finish up cold as the grave at the Key West cemetery.

The news article that Crow had found reported that the fire had occurred at a small guest house at the top—or Atlantic Ocean—end of Duval Street, not far from where he'd stayed on his previous visit. The exact address wasn't given. But the blackened property wasn't hard to find amongst all the white clapboard bungalows surrounding it.

He parked across the street, stayed sitting in his car. It was immediately apparent that the property was a privately-owned house available as a vacation rental. The owners lived elsewhere, taking advantage of the lucrative rental market. As a result, there was no reception, no staff on site. In the relaxed Key West environment, check-in often consisted of a key left in an envelope for guests to pick up on arrival, particularly if arriving late. There would be nobody on site during the night apart from the guests themselves. Nobody to lend assistance if those guests had already passed out through smoke inhalation.

A perfect setup for somebody up to no good.

He waited for a lull in the traffic and pedestrians on the street, then scooted down the side of the house where he vaulted over a low white picket fence into a secluded yard. Dense planting surrounded the small pool and the pool house at the bottom end providing sufficient cover for half a dozen men to hide.

He dropped into a patio chair pushed hard up against the side of the pool house. Even in broad daylight, in its shadow and with the greenery affording almost impenetrable screening, he was all but invisible from the street and neighboring houses. In the dark that invisibility would have been guaranteed. The relentless chirping of the cicadas in the tropical night would have provided an audible cloak to match it.

The blinds on the windows at the back of the house were closed. It wasn't a problem. What could he have learned from sticking his nose up against the glass? Or breaking in for that matter. Charred furniture and ash in a gutted house wouldn't tell him anything.

He sat thinking in the chair for a while longer. Arms hanging down at his sides, he tapped a meaningless beat on the underside of the chair with his fingers. The sort of thing that would make anybody sitting in the chair next to him want to throw him in the small pool. But it helped him think, to picture what might have happened. Think *perp* he told himself. Think like a person who's prepared to burn a young couple to death.

Like somebody who might have been sitting in this very chair. Somebody getting bored waiting. He stopped tapping the beat on the underside abruptly. Leapt out of the chair like somebody lit a fire under it. Flipped it over.

Gum.

Stuck to the underside of the chair.

It couldn't be coincidence that he'd discovered the same

disgusting thing on Winter's boat. Anybody could have stuck the gum to this chair. A succession of people passed regularly through the house. It wasn't their chair, what did they care? Let the greedy owner clean it off, do something for the three thousand bucks a week he charged.

That's all there would've been to it—if he hadn't found a similar piece of gum on the underside of a table on Winter's boat. Winter sure as hell wouldn't have done it to his own table, not given how shipshape the rest of the boat was.

And Evan didn't believe in coincidence. Coincidence is just life's way of telling you that you haven't been paying enough attention.

The same person had sat in this chair and at the table on Winter's boat. A person who owned neither the house nor the boat. But who had killed all of the people. The elation he felt at the realization was short-lived, replaced almost immediately by the prospect of what lay ahead, the ridicule that would be raining down on his head very soon.

It was the gum, officer.

Gum, you say? That clinches it.

Coming hard on the heels of Cortez's rejection of his theory, he doubted he'd fare any better with his tale of the mysterious chewing gum. In its favor, gum is a good source of DNA. Against that was the fact that he'd thrown the gum from Winter's boat into the sea.

Not wanting to repeat his error, he left it where it was. The visit had been more productive than he'd expected. He toyed with the idea of calling Cortez to see if it would make a difference to her attitude. Then he got a mental image of the captain in his office, the animation in his face and hands as he told Cortez that the case was closed. He decided against it, drove instead to the Key West PD which sits behind a small pond on the corner of North Roosevelt Boulevard and Jose Marti Drive to bang his head against a different brick wall.

'GUM?' THE BRICK WALL, AKA DETECTIVE DEUTSCH, SAID, HIS JAW working tirelessly on a piece of it in his own mouth. A piece that Evan could clearly see by virtue of the fact that he failed to close his mouth when he chewed.

Evan nodded unhappily.

'I've seen a lot more disgusting things than gum stuck to the underside of a chair, working in this town.'

Evan said that he could believe it, listened patiently while Deutsch ran through a few of the more lurid examples. Evan agreed it was shocking, the sort of things people did in the name of a night on the town.

Then Deutsch opened his mouth fully, pulled out the gum. Held it for Evan to see.

'Like this you mean?'

Evan got the impression he wasn't being taken seriously. So he felt comfortable doing what he did next. He squeezed the piece of gum between his finger and thumb before Deutsch realized what he was doing.

'Yeah, like that. A bit harder. Not so warm.'

Deutsch scowled at him, dropped the gum in the trash.

'Lucky I didn't stick it to the underside of the chair, eh?' He held out his arms, wrists together to accept imaginary handcuffs as he said it, eyes full of amusement. 'Then you'd be thinking it was me.'

Evan had already taken him through the details of Winter's death. Deutsch, who knew Cortez by sight only and had attempted a man-to-man leer when Evan first mentioned her name, then went to some pains to have Evan admit that no,

Cortez didn't buy his cock-and-bull story either. And yes, it was true that the case was now officially closed.

'Do you know how many people die in house fires every year?' Deutsch asked him instead of answering whether he thought there was anything suspicious about the one in his jurisdiction.

Evan admitted that particular statistic had slipped his mind.

'Two and a half thousand. That works out at seven people every day.'

Evan nodded, that's a lot of burned people.

'And do you know how long it takes before you pass out and die of smoke inhalation?'

Evan couldn't help himself, had suggested two to five days? Deutsch had then accused him of not taking things seriously.

'Two to ten *minutes*, smartass. It's not just the fire eating up all the oxygen in the room. There's hydrogen cyanide and a bunch of other toxic gasses that you're sucking into your body. So if you happen to be not just asleep but passed out from too much booze and drugs like these jokers were ...'

He ran a finger across his throat rather than finish the sentence. Then he leaned back, spread his fingers on his pot belly, a smug look on his face.

Stick that in your pipe and smoke it.

'So there was nothing suspicious about it? Like they'd been knocked unconscious instead of passing out. Maybe the tooth fairy put a spell on them. Or they'd been drugged.'

Deutsch shook his head continuously as Evan ran through the possibilities. He didn't bat an eyelid at the mention of the tooth fairy, proving to Evan that not only was he dismissing them before Evan uttered them, he wasn't even listening.

'No, nothing like that. There were no bruises or contusions, no ligature marks. Nothing to suggest anything other than they'd overdone it on the booze and weed while they were out and carried on when they got back. At some point they passed out with a joint still smoldering in an ashtray. It got kicked over and *whumpf*, the whole place went up.'

'What about the smoke alarms?'

'They took the batteries out.'

'They did? Or—'

'Your mystery assailant?' He shrugged noncommittally. 'There's no smoking allowed in the house. They liked a toke in bed.'

His tone of voice suggested that the case was as closed as his mind. It was at that point that Evan got his phone out, showed him the video.

'That's the Key West cemetery,' Deutsch said.

Evan could see they'd made the right decision promoting him to detective.

'The point is, the person who was paid to identify the people in the video who are now dead, is also dead. Drowned on his boat in Marathon as I told you.'

Deutsch sat upright as if Evan had finally said something of interest, a light in his eyes. But it wasn't that at all, which became clear when he stretched and yawned.

'Cortez's closed case, you mean?'

He then started to inspect his fingernails, never a good sign. Evan should have cut his losses. Instead, he mentioned the gum. He didn't say anything about throwing the other piece in the sea, of course. He'd already given Deutsch enough to laugh about for one day.

From the Key West PD, Evan drove the few blocks to the cemetery, then drove slowly all the way around it. Covering nineteen acres and with an estimated one hundred thousand people buried there, it houses more than three times the thirty thousand living residents of the island. Established in 1847, it was built on the highest point in Key West after a hurricane wiped out the old graveyard and scattered the bodies the previous year. The final resting place of slaves and Civil War soldiers alike, many of the graves are ornate and above ground as in New Orleans. Amongst the many winged angels is a figure that's less demure than the rest. On the grave of Archibald John Sheldon Yates sits a statue known as *The Bound Woman*. Rumored to be his wife Magdalena, she sits nude above his head. Her hands are tied behind her back, her face in distress as she struggles against the constraints of her bonds.

Had Evan seen her it might have put him in the right frame of mind for what he would later discover.

On Passover Lane he saw a house that he was certain was the one in the background of the video. He carried on without stopping, parked further down the street. Then he entered the cemetery on foot. Walking back the way he'd just driven, he stopped opposite the house, pretended to study the grave markers and above-ground burial vaults. He got out his phone and angled it towards one of the tombs as if he was taking a photograph. In fact, he was watching the video, pausing it when the house came into view.

It was the same one.

There was nothing unusual or remarkable about it. Nothing to indicate what might have gone on inside it. Something that was so sensitive that everybody who'd come into contact with it, no matter how obliquely, was now dead. There was no way of telling just by looking at it. After what he'd found at the last house he broke into—Robert Garfield's decomposing body—he wasn't tempted to repeat the experience.

His mind ran riot with possible scenarios as he stood amongst the graves staring at the house, each more sinister than the last. Now that he was here, he couldn't decide what to do.

Wait a while longer to see if anybody went in or came out? Come back once darkness had fallen? What he really needed was to see the curtains twitch. Or a face at the window. Somebody watching him as he watched them.

There was nobody inside watching him.

But there was a man coming up fast behind him.

25

EVAN DIDN'T HEAR A THING. LOST IN HIS THOUGHTS AS HE STARED at the house, the background noises of the street and people in the cemetery merged into one, masking individual sounds. Then a sudden squawking beep of a horn. A man on a ride-on mower swerved violently around him, close enough that the grass cuttings peppered the back of his legs. He jumped, heart in his throat, let out a surprised yelp. The echoes of the man's irritated words carried clear over the noise of the mower's engine.

Head up your ass.

Evan watched him spin the mower around in a tight arc, two wheels lifting off the ground, the way any municipal worker livens up a tedious job. He stepped out in front of the mower as it bore down on him. If ride-on mowers have gears, the driver changed down, accelerated at him. Evan held his ground, saw the grin on the driver's face turn to panic. He stomped on the brakes, the mower skidding to a long, fishtailing halt as he turned the wheel at the last minute. He leapt from the seat before it stopped moving, mouth open as he stared in horror at the twin skid marks snaking across the freshly-mowed grass.

'What the fu—'

He caught himself, remembered that the City doesn't like its employees cussing at grief-stricken members of the public paying their respects at the grave of a loved one.

'What the hell do you think you're doing?'

He didn't wait for an answer, frantically tried to smooth the furrows flat with his foot. He ran his hand through his hair, shook his head in disgust as he only made it worse.

'Sorry,' Evan said. 'I was miles away.'

He saw Mower Man's earlier way of describing that state of mind go through his thoughts once more, put a half-smile on his face, both apologetic and conspiratorial.

'Head up my ass, I mean.'

Mower Man didn't know whether to laugh or not, unsure whether Evan would report him to his supervisor.

'Don't worry about it.'

Evan dialed the conspiratorial grin up a notch.

'Makes the job more exciting, huh? See how many old folks you can run down. Maybe give somebody a heart attack.'

The guy was eyeing him now as if maybe Evan had climbed out of one of the graves while he wasn't looking. The one where they threw all the retards in together in the old days. He sure as hell didn't know how to respond.

'I'd get bored too,' Evan said. 'Driving up and down all day, nothing ever happening.'

He was getting bored now in fact, trying to prompt the guy into saying, no, you'll never guess what happened the other day. Then the guy obliged. He pulled a crumpled pack of Marlboros out of his pocket, offered one to Evan.

Evan shook his head, no thanks.

'Funny you should say that.' He took his time lighting the cigarette. Then he sucked half of it down in one hit, let it out slowly. Coughed for a minute or two, made Evan think about asking if he knew why they were called coffin nails. 'This place is normally quiet as the grave.'

Evan laughed dutifully. He tried smoothing the furrows in the grass—did a better job than Mower Man had—to give himself something to do while he waited for the guy to get to the damn point.

'Hell of a coincidence, standing right here, too.'

Evan forced himself not to turn his head. Not to look directly at the house. A hot worm of excitement twisted in his gut.

'Really? Why's that?'

'There was this homeless Cajun guy called Armand used to hang around by the gates.' He waved off towards the gates behind Evan, might as well have been throwing Evan's hopes into the trash can over there while he was at it. 'He used to sleep in the vaults some of the time. Smelled like it too. In the daytime he'd sit by the front gate. I reckon he thought people coming to visit a grave would feel sorry for him. Maybe give him more money so he didn't end up in here permanently.'

Evan agreed that was most likely the case.

'I asked him one time how much he made, what his best day was.'

'Bet he didn't tell you.'

'Nope. Reckon it was more than I make.'

He took another long hit on his cigarette. Evan breathed the smell of freshly-cut grass deep into his lungs. He was tempted to suggest the guy could save money and his lungs if he did the same instead of smoking. He felt the conversation sliding towards one long gripe about the wages the City paid, and from there onto a thousand other grievances.

'You said it was a hell of a coincidence.'

Mower Man looked at him for a moment as if he didn't know

what he was talking about, his weathered face creased into a frown.

'Standing here.'

'Right. About Armand. I was on my break, sitting over there.' He pointed towards one of the larger vaults. 'I was sitting on the ground, leaning against it. Having a quick smoke.'

He held up his almost-finished cigarette to help Evan get into the story. Evan was having trouble not laughing out loud at the words *quick smoke*. Looking at the vault the man had pointed to, he knew he'd chosen it because of its size. It was big enough for a seated man to sit behind and have a very long smoke safe from prying eyes.

If the conversation ever headed the way he was hoping it would, that vault had saved Mower Man's life.

He wandered over to it. A large Iguana sunning itself on the rough stone watched him approach, then darted away when he got too close. He sat down with his back to the stone wall of the vault. Mower Man was looking at him now as if it was time he got back into whichever grave he'd climbed out of. From where he was sitting Evan had a direct line of sight to the house on the other side of the street. He'd have had a perfect view of the couple taking the video as well.

But nestled down amongst the graves, nobody would have noticed him, given his express purpose of remaining hidden.

'Good spot,' Evan said, re-joining him.

'Anyway, I was finishing my break when I saw this young couple taking a video of themselves.'

A buzz kicked in with a vengeance in Evan's gut. He kept his face deadpan.

'That's young people for you. They'll video anything.'

'You're not kidding. Anyway, I stayed where I was. Didn't want to get in their video, spoil it for them.'

Evan did the easy translation from Municipal Employee to

English: *Didn't want to get caught on film taking an unauthorised break.*

'Then Armand walks up to them. I think maybe he said he'd take it for them for a couple of bucks. The guy told him to piss off. So loud I heard it from where I was sitting. That wasn't necessary even if Armand does smell pretty bad. I reckon Armand thought the same thing or maybe he was having a slow day, I don't know, but the next thing, he snatched the phone out of his hand and runs off with it.'

Evan felt as if he'd run into a mental brick wall. *What?* Mower Man was really getting into his stride now, re-living the most exciting day since he'd been hired.

'At the same time, something's going on in that house.' He nodded sideways towards it, rather than point, made Evan wonder if he knew what went on in there, didn't want to be caught pointing at it. 'The door burst open and this guy almost falls over himself coming out. He must have been somebody important because he's got a bodyguard waiting for him outside the door.'

He glanced surreptitiously at the house now, just a quick flick of the eyes. As if he was scared he might still be there now. He took a step closer to Evan so that his back was to the house now, dropped his voice. Evan huddled in. To a casual observer they looked like two men deciding how best to explain the twin skid marks in the grass to their supervisor.

'The thing is, the bodyguard caught his boss to stop him from falling flat on his face, helps him to the car, then leaves him there. He sets off running after Armand. He pushes the young couple who are standing in a daze out of the way and goes tearing down the street after him. He'd seen him steal their phone.'

'So what happened then?'

'No idea. The young couple started to have an argument

about whether they should go after him or not. Then the woman walks off in the other direction. The guy's standing there with his head going side to side like he's watching a tennis match. Then he goes after the woman. Maybe it was a cheap phone and he didn't care.'

'What about the bodyguard? Or Armand?'

Mower Man put a mildly indignant frown on his face.

'I couldn't just sit around waiting all day. I had work to do. Anyway, I thought I'd ask Armand the next time I saw him. Except then I thought, he might be homeless but he ain't stupid. He's not gonna come back here right after he stole a phone. And I was right, I haven't seen him since.'

Evan could have told him he probably wasn't going to either. He also could have told him his laziness and the animal cunning that had helped him find the perfect spot for shirking had saved his life. He didn't think scaring the guy was going to help, asked him something else instead.

Because something had just struck him. In the video the body of the man taking the selfie had obscured the face of the man who fell out of the door. What were the chances that he had also been in a direct line between Mower Man leaning on the vault and the man leaving the house? Because unless he had been in that direct line, Mower Man would have had a view of the man as he emerged.

'Did you recognize the guy who came out of the house?'

It appeared he did. Because of the way he said *no*. Very quickly. Evan felt as if he was back with Detective Deutsch, being given negative answers to his questions even before he asked them. It was that same animal instinct for self-preservation.

'Never seen him before in my life. Now I've got work to do, if you'll excuse me.'

Then he leaned in closer. Evan's stomach did a flip. Was he

just being cautious? A loudly-voiced denial followed by a whispered secret—*here, write this down.*

It wasn't to be.

'Pay more attention in the future or somebody's gonna run you over.'

26

'WHAT IS IT NOW?' DETECTIVE DEUTSCH SAID WHEN EVAN CALLED him. 'You discovered what brand of gum it was?'

'No. I wanted to ask you something. Has a homeless guy been found dead in or anywhere near the cemetery?'

He knew it was a mistake as the words came out of his mouth. He pictured Deutsch's face on the other end of the line. Deutsch didn't disappoint.

'A dead body in the cemetery? Now you're talking. Last count, there were approximately a hundred thousand of them.'

It struck Evan that Deutsch must spend all of his spare time trawling the internet for useless statistics. He was full of them. Seemed he thought Evan was full of something else. But for some reason his curiosity was aroused.

'Why do you want to know? Lost a friend of yours?'

'It doesn't matter if there wasn't. Sorry to waste your time.'

Maybe it was a slow day. Or maybe he just didn't like somebody else telling him what did and what didn't matter.

'Hang on. I've been off for a couple of days.'

The sounds on the other end of the line muted as Deutsch placed his hand over the mouthpiece. Despite that, Evan still heard the amusement in his voice as he asked around. When he came back on the line, most of it had slipped away.

'There was a guy found dead a few days back. In the cemetery itself. Looked as if a couple of winos had gotten into a fight over a bottle of Thunderbird. One of them cracked his skull open on one of the big stone vaults. The other one must have dragged him out of sight because he wasn't found for a couple of days. Must have been a big guy too. And strong. The deceased had only been hit once, a punch to the middle of his face. Sent him flying backwards into the stone vault. That was all it took.'

It was time to play Deutsch at his own game, have a little fun.

'Okay. Thank you for that, detective. You've been very helpful.'

'Hey! Not so fast. How come you're asking?'

'I thought you weren't interested in talking about closed cases. Or gum.'

The mention of gum made him realize that Deutsch was chewing it now, an irritating regular lip-smacking noise in the background. He couldn't stop his mind from taking the various facts that he knew and trying to mash them together. Was it possible that the man on the other end of the line was the gum-chewing assassin? Was that possibility more likely in the light of Cortez's investigation into Winter's death being so abruptly shut down? But Deutsch would have said millions of people chew gum, probably given him the exact number.

'Spit it out,' Deutsch said.

Evan resisted saying *only if you do.*

'I don't know if it's the same guy, but a homeless man called Armand snatched the phone of the two people who made that video, then ran off with it.'

Deutsch thought about it for a moment. Evan felt a tide of skepticism washing down the line towards him.

'And you think they chased after him and caught up with him in the cemetery. Killed him, either accidentally or otherwise.'

Something made Evan bite his tongue momentarily, not immediately put him straight. Deutsch hadn't finished talking anyway.

'And then what? The bum's friends decided to kill the people who killed him by setting fire to their room? I don't think so.'

Put like that, Evan had to agree. It sounded like an unlikely chain of events, too complicated to be plausible.

It was a whole lot simpler if you accepted that one person was behind all of the deaths.

There was no point suggesting Deutsch interview Mower Man. He must have known Armand's body had been found dead in the cemetery he maintained, might even have found it himself. Yet he claimed that he'd not seen him again after he stole the phone. He was distancing himself from the whole situation, a wise move under the circumstances. Evan considered asking Deutsch who had discovered Armand's body. What was the point? Even if it turned out to be Mower Man, all he'd have done is prove that the guy was determined to keep out of it.

Which may well have been the same as keeping alive.

'If it's not fish slime, it's gum,' Cortez said. 'What is it with you and sticky things?'

He'd felt obliged to call her, let her know what he'd found out. Even if nobody was taking any notice. He smiled to himself at her words, thinking it could've been Guillory on the other end.

'You don't have to answer that,' she added quickly with a shudder he felt all the way down the line. 'You're suggesting I go down to Winter's boat to find a piece of chewing gum stuck to the underside of a table?'

The time for complete honesty had arrived. He wasn't very happy about it. So he eased into it gently.

'You know how cleanliness is next to godliness?'

'Uh-huh.'

Just from that one guttural utterance, the wariness of it, he could tell that she was already putting it together, didn't like the feel of where it was going.

'My mom drummed it into me,' he said, feeling like someone was hammering nails into his coffin. Him, in fact.

'Uh-huh.'

Again the wariness.

'And the rest of the boat was so clean and sparkling . . .'

'You pulled it off?'

It was his turn to say *uh-huh*, not so much wary as wishing he'd never made the call.

'Threw it in the trash?'

'Sorry.'

'You threw it overboard?'

'Why wouldn't I?'

'Please. Feel free to pollute the ocean. And lose evidence in the process, why don't you?'

He didn't say anything. Certainly not what was going through his mind. Ask the divers who recovered Winter's body if they saw any crabs with their claws stuck together. Or maybe a fish with a constipated look on its face. Some things you just know won't help the situation.

'You said two things,' she said, a hopeful note in her voice.

He told her about the homeless guy, Armand. She perked up at that. Then he told her that in his opinion Mower Man would probably deny ever having had the conversation with him. Not only because he wanted to distance himself from whatever went on in the house, but also because any official investigation that started with the question, *what were you doing when you witnessed the incident?* was unlikely to enhance his career prospects with the City.

'Right,' she said. 'So all we've actually got is a dead wino. Who obviously didn't have the phone on him when he was found, that being the reason he was killed in the first place. So no connection to anything.'

Well summed up didn't feel like it was going to help any either.

'Anything else to brighten up my day?'

'No, that's it from me.'

She surprised him then.

'You can do something for me.'

'What?' said Mr Amenable.

'You can buy me a drink before you fly home. Meet me at The Marathon Grill and Ale House in an hour. It's on your way to the airport.'

SOMETHING WAS WRONG. THE GUILTY HALF-SMILE ON CORTEZ'S face when he saw her sitting at the end of the bar told him something bad had happened since their phone conversation. He sat on the seat next to her, took his time ordering himself a beer from the selection of thirty craft beers on tap. A growing sense of trepidation stopped him from picking at the nuts on the bar.

'Tell me.'

She took a small sip of her own drink, placed it carefully back down on the scarred bar top.

'I think you might be in trouble when you get home.'

Trouble.

There was only one thing she could be talking about.

Guillory. An unpleasant burning sensation started up in his chest. It almost put him off his beer as well as the nuts.

'Okay.'

Meaning, *tell me what you've done.*

'I called Detective Guillory on the way over.'

'One of *us girls*?'

She laughed nervously, you got me.

'Maybe not any longer. I felt as if I'd gotten locked in an industrial freezer. There's still ice on my phone.'

She lifted her hand, was about to rest it on his arm. Then she caught herself, dropped it into her lap.

'Why'd you call her?'

He couldn't believe it. She looked even more embarrassed as he asked the question. What next? Had she called Guillory to ask if she'd mind if she invited him to spend the night with her?

It wasn't that of course.

'I told her I was meeting you. I wanted to ask her how much I could trust you.'

That sure as hell wasn't what he'd been expecting. It stole the words out of his mouth for a moment. He filled the lull with a swallow of beer. Then he asked the question he didn't want the answer to, instead of just asking her why.

'What did she say?'

Cortez smiled at the memory. Not the guilty half-smile of a minute ago, more the sort of smile that had Guillory worrying in the first place.

'She asked me how much trouble I wanted.'

'And did you quantify that?'

She shook her head, ran a fingernail along one of the scars on the bar top.

'Let's say the coolness of her tone of voice discouraged further conversation.'

He knew that the next time he saw her that coolness would

be matched in equal measure by the roasting heat in his ear. Staring at his reflection in the mirror behind the bar, he reflected on how it was often thus. Cortez hadn't even gotten the answer to her enquiry, but had managed to drop him in it just by asking. Sometimes it amazed him that the human race had continued for so long given the obstacles men and women put between themselves at every opportunity.

It was at that point that his phone rang. They both heard it, shared a look.

'Don't worry, I'll speak to her later.'

She nodded, good call. They sat there waiting for it to go to voicemail as if continuing to talk while it was ringing would be rude or might make things worse.

'Now you've got a problem too,' he said.

'I'm not—'

She realized too late he didn't mean the same sort of problem as she'd given him.

'You've got to decide how much to trust me without the benefit of inside information.'

She swiveled on her seat, rested her elbow on the bar. He did the same so that they were facing each other. Brass tacks time.

'I figured anybody who could provoke such strong reactions in a person had to be worth a gamble.'

He wasn't sure how to take that, whether it was a backhanded compliment or not.

'Deutsch is a dick,' she said.

It took him a moment to connect the dots, realize she was talking about the detective he'd met with in Key West. One of the many people who didn't take him or the situation seriously. He was regretting now squeezing the man's gum between his fingers. He wiped them on his pants leg without thinking.

'I'm guessing you don't just mean in his attitude towards female police officers.'

The lecherous camaraderie Deutsch had tried to establish with him at the mention of Cortez's name made his skin crawl thinking about it. From her downturned mouth, he guessed Cortez felt the same.

'No. I mean professionally. He's lazy. And stupid. Everybody knows it. I don't know how he ever made detective. Well, I do. But I don't want to go into that. Anyway, I didn't want you flying home thinking we're all the same down here, that everybody's treating you like an idiot.'

He tried his best to keep the smile off his lips, took a swallow of beer to hide it. She didn't need to know that he didn't have to come down to Florida for that to happen.

'Don't look so smug. I know I didn't believe you at first either. But now?' She gave a gentle shrug, we'll see. 'I'm not going to be looking for that gum you threw overboard—'

'Some hungry fish has probably gobbled it by now.'

'Exactly. It's amazing what fish will eat. Chewing gum, thumb drives . . .'

He let her have that one.

'Anyway, no point crying over spilled milk. But I'll see what I can do. Maybe get the case re-opened.'

It seemed like a better time to ask the question that had caused her to snap at him the last time he asked.

'You really don't know why it was closed so suddenly?'

She shook her head slowly, holding his eyes. He got the impression he was being told not to push it, she'd already said she'd see what she could do.

'Sorry about getting you into trouble,' she said as they got up to leave. This time she did put her hand on his arm.

'Don't worry about it. I just wish I could go back, tell her you're the dick and it's Deutsch who's smart and keen to help.'

He kept the *and good-looking* to himself.

27

EVAN WAS IN MORE TROUBLE THAN HE KNEW. GUILLORY PICKED UP her phone when she heard the double beep announcing the arrival of a text message. Having tried to call Evan the previous day and having it go to voicemail, she expected that the text was from him.

The thoughts running through her mind were far from complimentary as far as Mr Buckley was concerned. She didn't think she was a jealous person, didn't *own* Evan after all. She could even be accused of pushing him away at the moment.

But to have her call go to voicemail shortly after receiving a call from Ana Maria—what a *lovely* name—Cortez with her oh-so-sexy voice coming down the line making her think she'd accidentally called a premium rate phone sex number, telling her she was meeting Evan—in some idyllic bar on the waterfront watching the sun sink slowly below the horizon of the perfect azure sea, no doubt—and wanting to know if she could trust him—words failed her!

She reckoned she deserved a promotion. Or at least commendation for not yelling down the line at her: *you can trust him to cause trouble*. Which is what she'd said, just not shouting.

She'd tried to keep her voice friendly, wasn't sure she managed to pull it off.

The phone flexed in her hand as she glared at the display, imagining that it was his neck in her strong fingers. It wasn't him, wasn't any number in her contacts. It wasn't anybody she was going to want to add to her contacts either. She stared at the words, her mind temporarily blank, all thoughts of what she wanted to do to Buckley suddenly gone.

I've got something that belongs to you.

She didn't know exactly what it meant. She didn't need to. It was enough to know that it was nothing good. Her stomach tightened, her legs suddenly weak, crazy thoughts she'd never have believed possible just a minute ago now filling her head. She would rather it had been from Evan. Telling her that he'd spent the night in Marathon or Key West or whatever romantic location in bed with his new-found friend Ana Maria.

Because, if she was honest, ever since the events of a few nights ago, she'd been expecting something like this. She'd expected Curtis Banks, the petty thief and burglar who'd let her into Robert Garfield's house, to try to put the squeeze on her. Except this wasn't him.

This was a whole lot worse.

It was more than that. Because the feeling had been building inside her since she couldn't remember when, since some former life that was unrecognizable to her now. From *before*.

This was what she deserved.

Because she didn't believe in salvation, or if she did, she lived her life knowing that its light would not shine upon her.

And while it was her emotions, her subconscious that gave her no peace, that made her feel that way, it was her mind, her intellect and years of experience that told her something else as well.

It was only the beginning.

In her experience, things generally start easy and then get worse. The only positive thing that could be said about the whole situation was that at that point, she wasn't aware that the item of hers that the unknown person who sent the text had in their possession had been supplied by Evan, however unwillingly.

Trouble likes to save the best—or worst—until last. Just like anybody else.

GUILLORY WASN'T THE ONLY ONE TO GET A TEXT FROM LYDIA THAT morning. When Evan heard it arrive, he jumped to a similar conclusion to the one Guillory had made. That it was her. The only difference was, when he saw from the display that it wasn't, he knew exactly who it was.

The text was similar too. Except that it was the other way around.

You've got something that belongs to me. I want it back.

He knew exactly what she was talking about too.

In the course of the investigation that had involved Guillory being abducted by the pedophile gang, he had ended up driving the killer Todd Strange's van—with Todd dead in the back. He'd been shot by the gangster Chico—the very detail that his sister Lydia wanted to know. While waiting for the final showdown with Chico, he'd searched the van. He'd made a very interesting discovery. A Nemesis Arms Vanquish, a lightweight, take-down sniper's rifle. He'd hidden it in the undergrowth, then come back for it later. Because you never know when a sniper's rifle is going to come in handy.

It never had of course. Broken down into its component parts, it fitted neatly into a carrying case that looked for all the world like an executive briefcase. It had been sitting on the top shelf of his closet ever since. He'd almost forgotten about it, certainly never bothered to get it down and assemble it. Or feel the perfect balance of it in his hands, maybe even imagine blowing Ryder's fat head apart with it on those occasions when their relationship was at a particularly low ebb.

Now it seemed Todd's sister Lydia was well aware of all of her brother's lethal toys, knew which one was missing. It wasn't a huge leap for her to figure out that he had it.

And now she wanted it back.

No way. He wasn't about to hand it over to anybody harboring suspicions—justified or otherwise—about Guillory's involvement in her brother's killing. She already had the earring. He wasn't going to give her a ready-made backup plan as well. So he ignored the text, knowing that he'd be hearing from her again very soon.

Sooner than he thought. Another text came in almost immediately with details of a time and location. He didn't even read it all the way through, deleted both messages.

Then he got the rifle in its case down from the closet. He couldn't keep it in the apartment any longer. Lydia had broken in once already. And he couldn't carry it around with him. He'd take it to Crow who never left the house.

As he headed out, he looked as if he were about to make his first sales call of the day on a hapless homeowner, his briefcase full of kitchen worktop or aluminum siding samples, his mind full of dirty tricks.

Except it was Lydia's mind that was full of dirty tricks as she watched him leave the apartment.

28

'No thank you,' Elwood Crow said and started to close the door in Evan's face.

Evan waited patiently on the step for Crow to have his fun. The door opened again, Crow's grinning face behind it.

'Sorry. Thought you were selling something.'

Evan laughed dutifully, glanced quickly up and down the street before stepping inside and closing the door behind him.

'Got a new job?' Crow said. 'You look very professional.'

Wait to see what kind of professional, Evan thought to himself as he handed the case over.

'For me? You're too kind.'

'I'd like you to keep that somewhere safe for me.'

'What is it?'

Evan invited him to see for himself with a sweep of his hand. Crow popped the latches, lifted the lid.

'A Nemesis Vanquish. Very nice. Should I ask where you got it? Or why?'

Evan told him the story, most of which Crow already knew. Crow gave an admiring dip of the head as he finished, you're a quiet one.

'You never said a word about this little beauty before.' He closed the case, put it on the floor at the bottom of the stairs. 'So now his sister wants it back. Don't worry, I'll find somewhere safe for it later. Come on.'

Neither of them knew it, but later would be too late.

They went into the back room as usual. Crow closed the door as he always did, concerned about drafts and the spiraling cost of heating the big old Victorian property. He kicked an old-fashioned draft stopper into place that looked as if his grandmother had knitted it to celebrate the end of the Civil War.

Had Evan ever looked to buy one of them, he'd have seen that they were advertised not only as draft stoppers, but as sound stoppers too.

'So. How are things between you and Kate?' Crow said, once they'd gotten settled. 'Managing to act like a couple of grown-ups yet?'

Evan stared at him a long time before speaking. Not that Crow even noticed, concentrating instead on his pet crow *Plenty* which had landed on his knee and was pulling at a loose thread in his cardigan sweater. Crow pulled back the other way in a mini tug of war.

'I thought you said last time that you were going to keep your nose out of it.'

Crow conceded the match to the pet bird, sucked air in through his teeth as if he'd touched a hot stove. He held up his hands.

'Sorry. Didn't realize it was such a sensitive matter.'

He changed the subject in an attempt to appease Evan. From Evan's point of view it was more of the same.

'Did you make use of the information I gave you?'

Because it was Crow who had given Evan Robert Garfield's address and unwittingly set in motion the events that left Evan in the position he was now in.

'Yes.'

Crow studied him. Evan got that laboratory rat feeling again. He shifted uncomfortably in his chair. The bird *Plenty* hopped victoriously onto his knee as if it wanted to be close to the action, to get the tastiest morsels, when Crow opened Evan up for inspection, started poking around in his innards.

'Hmm.'

'What do you mean, *hmm*?'

'What happened?'

'Nothing *happened*. Can we talk about something else?'

'There's not much left, is there? Can't talk about Kate. Can't ask what happened when you broke into Garfield's house. It's not like you to be so close mouthed. Generally you just open it and let the wind blow your tongue around. Besides, I'm interested to know what you did in that house. I don't want anything coming back to bite me on the ass.'

Evan didn't say that anyone or thing that tried biting Crow's skinny ass would only get a mouthful of old bones, would break their teeth, figuratively. Because nothing Crow did ever linked back to him. Instead he was getting the first vague suspicion that Crow was talking for the sake of it, was doing his best to put off what they should be talking about—the results or otherwise of his latest trip to Florida.

So he didn't volunteer the information for the moment, knowing that there was something at work in the background. He tried a different tack instead.

'Did you find out who owns the other half of George Winter's boat?'

Now it was Crow's turn to be close mouthed. He looked uncomfortable too as far as Crow ever looked uncomfortable. He pulled the thread on his sweater that the bird had unraveled.

'I did.'

Evan cleared his throat noisily as if preparing himself for an important announcement.

'Hmm.'

Crow nodded his acknowledgement of the point, gave him a wrinkly grin.

'No flies on you, eh?'

'So who is it? The President? The Pope? Someone important anyway.'

'Vaughan Lockhart.'

Evan's face compacted in confusion.

'Should that mean something to me?'

'No reason why it should.'

'Then why the face as if your dog just died? Why—' He stopped abruptly, nodded to himself. 'It means something to you.'

'Oh, yes.'

It struck Evan then what a difference one little word can make. If Crow had simply said *yes*, he'd have paid it no particular heed, waited for him to elucidate. But the addition of the exclamatory *Oh* made him think that everything he'd discovered in Florida paled into insignificance compared to Crow's one small discovery, a name on a boat's ownership documents.

Something else he knew—he wasn't going to find out the significance of the name until Crow was ready to divulge it. Crow confirmed it for him.

'Tell me what happened in Florida. Did you find out anything interesting?'

'Not as interesting as whatever it is that you're not telling me about Vaughan Lockhart.'

Crow shrugged amiably, that's the way it goes.

There was no point arguing. Evan told him about his discussion with Mower Man, how the homeless man was found dead after snatching the phone and being chased by the bodyguard of the unknown man caught on video.

'That's four people dead now,' Crow said. 'We've got a fight between two bums, an accidental house fire and a suicide.'

He got an *I don't think so* shake of the head back from Evan.

'Anything else?'

Evan didn't answer quickly enough to stop Crow from leaning back in his chair, spreading his fingers across his stomach, a knowing gleam in his eye.

'What else? And why don't you want to tell me?'

'Gum,' Evan said.

'Gun?' Crow's eyebrows gave a startled leap. Suddenly he wasn't leaning back anymore. 'You found a gun?'

Evan thought about playing along for a while, decided against it. It would be bad enough when he admitted to what he'd done. No need to make things worse by getting Crow overexcited. He leaned forward himself, put his mouth to Crow's ear.

'Gum. G. U. M for mother.'

He wished the word had the letter *D* in it so he could've said *D for deaf old fart*.

Crow jerked his head away.

'No need to shout. You should speak up a bit. I assume you meaning chewing gum.'

The emphasis he put on the words, the way his bottom lip turned almost inside out, suggested he'd rather chew on a mouthful of the detritus at the bottom of his pet bird's cage.

Then Evan told him about the gum he'd found on the boat and at the rental house in Key West where the fire had occurred. Crow's face, still bearing the signs of his disapproval of gum in general, turned sourer still as he listened to Evan describe how he'd found the gum stuck to the underside of the table and chair. If it hadn't been for the admission that he was going to have to make any minute, Evan would have laughed. Crow looked like a vulture who'd pecked too hard and too deeply, had split open an organ normally left for the flies, letting loose the dead animal's waste all over its beak. He only had one thing to say after Evan had finished.

'Disgusting.'

'Yes.'

'But useful. It could place the same person at two of the scenes. Surely the police can't ignore that.'

Evan let his silence answer for him. Crow got hold of the wrong end of the stick to begin with. His eyebrows went up into his wrinkly forehead.

'You haven't told them? Why not?'

'I told them. But I—'

Crow extended his arm, elbow locked, his palm towards Evan. As if he were trying to stop a brick wall from falling on him.

'I don't want to know.'

'I threw the gum from Winter's boat overboard.'

Crow dropped his arm, the danger gone, let out a relieved sigh.

'Thank God for that. I thought you were going to say you ate it.'

Evan wasn't sure if he was being serious or just being deliberately provocative, suggesting that nothing would surprise him from the kind of person who chews gum in the first place. Crow didn't give him time to think about it.

'It was very stupid, nonetheless.'

Evan suddenly cocked his head.

'What was that?'

A self-satisfied smile appeared on Crow's face. As if to say, at least I'm old and have an excuse for being hard of hearing.

'I said—'

'No.' He strained his ear towards the door. 'I thought I heard something.'

Crow shook his head, don't worry about it.

'It's an old house. It creaks and groans all the time. As I said—'

'I heard you the first time. I hadn't found the gum at the house by then.'

Crow shook his head again, no excuses please.

'And you told the police all this. What was their reaction?'

'The guy in Key West, Deutsch, virtually laughed in my face. At least Cortez—'

'Ah! The problem is revealed.'

Evan was tempted to ask him was he interested in who killed his old friend George Winter, or did he just want to give him a hard time over Guillory? But Crow wasn't finished.

'Don't let Kate see your face go all gooey like that when you mention Cortez's name. Try to keep it more professional.'

Evan counted slowly to ten in his head until all thoughts about giving him a professional poke in the eye had subsided. Trouble was, Crow's irritating refusal to stop linking everything he did or said to his relationship with Guillory made all thoughts about the noise he thought he'd heard go out the window. At least later, when they discovered what had happened, he could justifiably say it was Crow's fault.

'Thanks for the advice, I'll try to remember that. Cortez'—he twisted his mouth as if he'd just drunk sour milk—'has more of an open mind, but the case is closed.'

'What? Already?'

'Her boss called her in while I was with her.'

'That's better.'

'What?'

'Your face. You almost scowled then. Keep it like that when you're telling Kate.'

Not for the first time Evan wondered if Crow was playing with him. If he'd had a wager with himself over how much he could say before Evan leapt out of his chair and throttled him.

'The reason I was scowling was because it seemed that the Captain who closed the case from under Cortez's feet also knew who I was, told her to throw me out.'

'Hmm.'

'Yes, *hmm*.'

'Four people dead and strings being pulled. Interesting.'

Evan asked him if he was spelling that w-o-r-r-y-i-n-g. Crow's expression told him not to be such a big baby.

'Nothing to worry about.'

'Unless you're the one getting sent back to Florida.'

'*Sent*? And I never said anything about going back.'

'No. That comes after you tell me about Vaughan Lockhart. You think I don't know how your mind works?'

Crow smiled at him like his slow-witted but favorite grandson had just produced a correct answer.

'It'll give you another crack at getting Kate to go with you. Put this silliness with Cortez behind you.'

Evan was on his feet by the time Crow's words were out, looking around for something suitable to stuff down his throat. The pet bird looked the best bet if it would just sit still for two seconds. Crow held his hands in front of his face as if the Grim Reaper had just come knocking.

'You want me to tell you about Lockhart or not?'

29

THEY WERE BOTH QUIET FOR A LONG WHILE AFTER CROW STOPPED talking, the only sound Crow's pet bird chattering to itself as it hopped sideways along its perch. Crow raised his hand and the bird lifted off, flew silently to land on it, wings beating a low cadence against the air, flapping in Crow's face as it steadied itself. Crow stroked the back of its head with his finger.

Evan sank back into his chair like a deflating blimp as the tension that had built inside him as Crow told his tale leeched slowly away. He felt as if he should be snuggling down into his sleeping bag under a star-filled night sky as the campfire spat and crackled.

His Zippo lighter was in his hand, a relic from the Vietnam war that had belonged to his wife. He'd carried it around with him for years and it had ultimately led him to her. Or at least to her final resting place. It had been a comfort to him during his long search. It was a comfort to him now as he listened to Crow's story, running his thumb over the faded inscription that he knew better than his own name.

But more than that it was a comfort to him as he looked at what he held in his other hand. A faded photograph. Crow had fetched it part way through his story so that Evan might have a face to go with the words and the emotions those words brought out. It had been taken almost fifty years previously in the jungles of South East Asia. In the foreground two men stood side by side. An M60 machine gun was balanced on one man's shoulder, his right hand gripping the integrated bipod, the 7.62mm cartridge belt wrapped twice around his body. This was Vaughan Lockhart. The second man's M16 rifle was held loosely in his right hand. In his left hand he held something that either time or the photographer had rendered difficult to identify. Behind them wooden huts burned fiercely, the intense orange red of the flames easy to imagine despite the black and white of the photograph.

Crow had said he didn't remember the second man's name. That he was nobody important.

Evan hadn't been sure he believed him.

Crow had seen it in his eyes and had sought to reassure him. The man was not important. The only thing Crow remembered about him was that he'd been one of the many who had not made it back home.

Evan looked again at the photograph. Even though Lockhart should have been the focus of his attention, his eyes went once more to the unidentified man's unsmiling face. He got the impression that the reason he wasn't smiling like Lockhart next to him was smiling around the cigarette in his mouth had nothing to do with him being angry or harboring dark thoughts. The opposite in fact. Because Evan knew without knowing how that the man was afraid. Afraid that if he allowed himself to smile, his true self would shine through for everybody to see. And that was something he would not endure. So he glared at the camera with flat, dead eyes and a mouth like a knife slash while Evan tried again to see what he held in his left hand.

He was suddenly aware that Crow was waiting for him to say

something in response to his story. To give some indication that he had understood the lesson that had been delivered for his benefit, a lesson in personal sacrifice and hardship for the greater good of his fellow men.

'That'd create a bond between you.'

Crow nodded gravely, be careful what you say. Choose your words carefully as it would be unwise to mock.

'It did.'

Those two words carried a lot of unspoken meaning. They implied the world would be a better place if all young men were required to don a uniform in defense of their country or their country's beliefs and get something in return for themselves— some backbone and moral fiber, two commodities sadly lacking in the modern world.

'Which is why you said Winter would never have killed himself.'

'Exactly. If you endured what we did, you don't kill yourself because money's tight. The worst thing you do is swallow your pride and ask an old friend for help until you get back on your feet.'

Without realizing it the pressure of the finger stroking the bird's glossy head had increased. The bird squawked loudly in protest, tried to flap away. But Crow had his thumb over the top of its feet, pinning them to his hand. It flapped its wings more frantically like a hooded falcon attempting to escape its tether. Then Crow lifted his thumb, released it, watched it fly lazily around the room.

Evan thought he'd most likely agree to go back to Florida for a third time when that old friend asked him to.

'It's why the story about Lockhart selling the boat and putting Winter on the street is rubbish. If that boat's up for sale, it's because they both decided to sell it. Somebody put that story out there as a smoke screen.'

'Lockhart?'

Crow shook his head as if his favorite grandson had returned to his usual dull-witted form.

'If only life were so simple. No, there's somebody else involved here.'

'Who?'

It was as if he hadn't spoken. He had more chance of getting an answer out of the other crow, *Plenty*, that was now sulking on its perch, watching its master with hatred in its beady black eyes.

'You're right about one thing,' Crow went on, 'Lockhart is your best bet going forward.'

Evan didn't miss the *your*, the lack of *our* in Crow's words. It seemed Crow had him trained better than the bird. He didn't even question being sent on an errand with the most important fact withheld from him. It was no different to any other chain of command. The rookie cop and army grunt don't expect the Commissioner or General to keep them in the loop, so why should he? Crow had one final piece of advice for him.

'And take Kate with you this time, for Christ's sake.'

If they hadn't been standing at the door at that moment, if Evan hadn't just kicked the draft stopper out of the way and opened the door, he might have punched Crow on the nose.

But he had just done all those things. Now he was staring open-mouthed at the empty space at the bottom of the stairs where the Nemesis Vanquish had been until somebody—Lydia obviously—had picked the ancient lock on the old front door and stolen it. Or taken it back. Didn't matter. She had it.

It didn't take a rocket scientist to work out what she planned to do with it. He got out his phone and dialed Guillory's number.

GUILLORY TOUCHED HER EAR AUTOMATICALLY. LIKE YOU WOULD when somebody taps you on the shoulder, *excuse me, is this your earring*? You can see it in their hand, maybe you've just watched them bend and pick it up off the floor. You know it's yours. And yet you still touch the place where it ought to be.

Stupid. But that's human nature.

She did it now, staring at the new text that had just arrived.

Recognize it?

Of course she recognized it.

It was one of the earrings Evan had given her for her birthday. She hadn't even noticed that she'd lost one of them. Then one of those totally inconsequential thoughts that pop into your mind at the most inappropriate times blindsided her. He was going to be so upset when she told him. She saw his face sag already, heard him ask *where did you last have them*? Until this morning she couldn't have told you where.

She could now.

Now she knew exactly where and when she last wore them. The disastrous night she broke into Robert Garfield's house. She'd been in such a state when she got back home, she didn't even notice she'd only ripped one of them off before she dived headlong into the scalding water of the shower in a vain attempt to wash and scrub away the horror of that night.

Now somebody had found it.

Somebody who planned to use the knowledge of where they'd found it against her. To blackmail her. Or worse. She had a good idea of who that might be. Liverman. Who else? The pervert at the top of the pedophile gang. The man who gave the order for her to be taken out and disposed of like so much trash. Trying a different tack after that didn't pan out the way they planned.

The text contained detailed instructions as well as the image and the mocking *recognize it*? Details of where and when she was to meet with them. Some of it was good. Or not as bad as it might have been. She groaned when she saw the location. They'd specified a diner which was better than some dark alley. Trouble was, it was one she used regularly with her partner Ryder. At least it meant the first stage was to talk. Which was a relief. Unless all that was said was *follow us*. Then a hood over her head in the back of a car or van.

The other instructions were to be expected. Unarmed. Obviously. Come alone. She couldn't contain the strangled shriek that burst from her throat as she read the words.

Come alone!

Who was she going to bring for Christ's sake? Bring to a meeting where her crimes would be laid before them in all their shameful glory?

Her eyes were suddenly moist, her throat thick. She drew back her arm to hurl the spiteful little phone against the wall, threw it on the bed instead. With the knuckle of her thumb she wiped away the tears. Because she knew who she could ask to come with her. To hell and back if necessary. The person who would do it without question or concern for his own safety despite the hard time she gave him over Ana Maria Damn Your Eyes Cortez.

She couldn't ask him. Couldn't drag him into the mess she'd created for herself, the mess that had turned her into the nervous wreck she was now. The mess that was destroying their relationship as inexorably as day follows night.

Then something happened that made her want to drop to her knees and howl at the ceiling, tear her hair out by the roots and stuff it down her own throat until she choked and died.

Her phone rang.

She knew who it was before she looked at the display.

Because she'd been around the block a few times, knew how fate likes to pick its moments. She looked anyway, saw it confirmed. Evan. She let it go to voicemail. She knew that if she heard his voice, heard him come out with some ridiculous excuse about how he couldn't avoid going for a drink with Cortez, how he'd hated every minute of it and the beer had tasted like piss, she'd end up laughing until she cried. Then, when the laughter subsided, the truth would come pouring out until there was nothing left of her but a hollow empty shell. Because he'd sense it, would tease it out of her like his friend Crow's stupid bird pulling a fat worm from its hole.

She couldn't do that to him. Not coming so soon after his long search for his wife had come to its sad ending. For a brief moment she was back there with him. Standing beside a lonely grave in the grounds of a state mental asylum, the wind in her face, her hair in her eyes. Finding his hand and holding it in hers like a small dead animal as a stony-faced man with a voice full of false sympathy talked of suicide and being at peace at last. She still had the man's card. And if she ever got past the current mess, she'd be having a talk with him. Because something didn't ring true.

But she wasn't past the mess yet. So she replied to the

mystery text, a terse *okay*. She wasn't surprised when Evan's text came in as she was typing. She didn't read it. Nor did she look in the mirror in the hallway as she headed out to her clandestine assignation. How could she look herself in the eye knowing full well that on the other end of the unanswered line Evan was climbing the walls?

THANK GOD IT WASN'T THE DINER WHERE SHE MET EVAN FOR their weekly catch-up. But the smells were the same. Of bacon frying and coffee, and the sounds too, the everyday bustle of people getting on with their lives. Eating and drinking and talking, some laughter and the wail of a spoiled child making disapproving heads turn. If they'd wanted to make a point, show her the stark contrast between her life now and how it would be going forward, they couldn't have picked a better location.

She took a seat in the window as the text had specified. A shiver rippled across the back of her neck. Were they watching her from somewhere across the street? Framing her head in the crosshairs of a rifle's sights? An easy shot in the big window. She glanced across the street at the buildings opposite, scanned the windows. Some of them were lit, some of them dark. One caught her eye. *That's the one I'd choose.* The window was half open, the darkness of the room beyond it impenetrable.

She'd have sworn she saw the sunlight catch on metal as she stared at it. Just a quick flash, then it was gone. As if a man with a gun had adjusted his position, gotten himself more comfortable for a better shot. She looked away, wished she hadn't looked at all. It didn't stop her from pulling a small mirror from her bag, propping it on the table, adjusting it until she could see the window reflected in it with just a quick glance down.

She sipped her coffee, her appetite having deserted her.

Tried to tell herself she was being paranoid. Glanced quickly at the mirror. Looked away again. From the exposed seat in the window she concentrated instead on studying the people on the sidewalk. The knot in her stomach grew tighter by the minute, her mind a place you didn't want to go.

Because even though she'd never seen the faces of the men who had beaten her, had only the smell of them burned into her subconscious, she knew she would recognize them the minute they came into sight, wouldn't need to wait for them to slip into the booth with her. She saw it in her mind as if it had already happened. One of them sitting next to her, boxing her in. Pushing up too close, the heat of his body against hers sickening her. His partner taking the seat opposite. Both of them with a filthy smile on their lips. Maybe a subconscious massaging of their knuckles, a sardonic greeting spat at her—*you're looking a lot better than the last time we saw you.* Then the laughter. Making her wish she'd ignored the instruction to come unarmed and damn the consequences, pushing the barrel of her gun down their throats, make that two guns, pulling the triggers—

A sharp bang on the window made her jump. She gave a startled yelp, coffee slopping on the table as her whole body jerked. Her head snapped sideways, fully expecting to see the faces of the two men staring back at her. Then a finger beckoning—*come with us.* Instead it was a solitary man trying to get the attention of somebody behind her. She forced her shoulders to relax, her heart still racing. Then looked casually around the room to see if anybody had noticed her over-reaction. She met the eyes of a young woman sitting at a table on the far side, a smile on her lips. She'd been staring at her ever since she came in.

She felt like jumping up, striding across the room. Getting into her personal space, shouting into her face, *what is your problem?* But that wouldn't have helped anything. Instead she slid out of the booth, slid back in on the other side. The woman could look at the back of her head for a change. If she'd had her number, she'd have sent her a text, *stare at that all you want, you stupid cow.*

As it happened, she did have the woman's number in her phone. She just didn't know it yet.

Feeling a childish pleasure at stopping the woman's intrusive and rude staring, she returned to her thoughts. They hadn't improved any during the short interlude. Nobody on the street matched her expectations of the men she expected to see. She checked her watch. They were late. Was it a deliberate ploy to prolong and intensify her unease, increase the chances of her compliant cooperation? Or were they waiting for the perfect moment to take the shot from across the street? She glanced down at the mirror. It was angled the wrong way now that she'd moved seats. An irrational spike of fear went through her as if the mirror had somehow been protecting her. They wouldn't shoot while she could see them. Now she was exposed. She grabbed it, twisted it. But she couldn't get the angle right. Couldn't find the dark, half-open window. The one that she knew a rifle barrel was now poking out of while she played with a stupid mirror. She slammed it into the table top, mirror side down.

She was panting now, her breathing fast and shallow. She was suddenly aware of a presence at her shoulder. She spun around, her heart lurching. It wasn't a pair of large men looming over her, telling her to shift along.

It was the young woman from the other side of the room. She slid into the seat opposite, a cup of coffee in one hand, her bag in the other. As if she'd just spotted an old friend at a table on her own.

Guillory's mind and mouth froze momentarily. That same phrase, *what is your problem?* did battle with the more direct, *piss off!* In the end she controlled her anger, forced out a strained polite response.

'That seat is taken.'

The young woman took no notice, her hands clasping her bag beneath the table as she studied Guillory. Only then did the penny drop for Guillory.

'You sent the text.'

The woman nodded slowly, enjoying the effect her entrance had produced. Guillory's shoulders relaxed, her pulse subsiding. It had to be a good thing. They'd sent a woman and not a pair of thugs. It gave her a small feeling of confidence, enough for her to take the initiative.

'I don't know what you want. But before I talk to you, I want to know where you got that earring from.'

The woman considered the question for a short while, then confirmed Guillory's suspicions.

'Somebody gave it to me.'

A small smile crept onto her lips as she said the words. Guillory let her smile, let her think she was being so clever.

'Really? Who?'

'That doesn't matter. What matters is that I've got it.'

'Only if you know where they got it.'

Again the slow nod.

'I do. The pedophile's house. The one who was killed. The one whose house you were in when you lost your earring. An earring that's got dried stains on it. Bloodstains.'

It didn't matter that the girl had jumped to the wrong conclusion. She was close enough. Close enough to take Guillory right back to Garfield's house, to bring a cold sweat out on her neck. Suddenly she needed fresh air, water on her face, breathing space. She slid across the seat.

'I have to go to the —'

'Stay where you are.'

There was an edge to the girl's voice that made her stop sliding across the seat. The girl's hands were still hidden under the table. Their eyes locked. For the first time it struck her that the girl looked familiar, a vague feeling that she was missing something here. The girl dropped her voice to a low hiss.

'Why do you think I told you to sit in the window?'

Without thinking Guillory started to twist to look out of the window. Then caught herself. It was enough. She didn't need to look up at the buildings opposite for the girl to know that she understood. Now the girl brought her hands out from under the table, laid them flat on it. They were empty, obviously, in such a public place. She nodded to confirm the understanding in Guillory's eyes. Then she tapped the face-down mirror with a short, chewed fingernail.

'I was watching you. Which window do you think it is?'

Guillory ignored her, the pointless stupidity of trying to see which particular window a bullet might come from making her feel stupid, made worse knowing the girl opposite her had been watching her. Laughing at her.

'Want me to tell you?'

'No.'

'You know what a Nemesis Vanquish is?'

'No. But I can guess.'

The girl suddenly stifled a laugh. Not the sort of behavior you'd expect from somebody who's just made you aware that you're a sitting duck for a man with a sniper's rifle. More the action of a person who's left their meds at home.

'Sorry. I know it's cheesy, but if I scratch my nose, then you won't have one any longer. Or a face for it to sit on.' She wrinkled her nose a couple of times, stretched it as you would if you were trying to hold off a sneeze. 'Better hope I don't get an itchy nose, eh?'

'You've made your point,' Guillory said, glancing up into the corner of the room. 'You know there's CCTV? I don't know what they're paying you but it's not worth spending the rest of your life in prison for.'

It was what the girl said next that stopped Guillory dead, not a bullet in the head. And the way she said it, a bare fact plainly stated.

'I don't know what you're talking about. Nobody's paying me. This is about my brother.'

Realization hit Guillory like a freight train blowing through a disused station, sent her spinning like a rusty old sign. The vague memory crystallized with the mention of a brother. She was the sister of Todd Strange. The man paid to kill her. The one Evan had warned her about and she'd ignored. She slumped back into her seat, let out a rush of air that could have blown the slim girl away.

'You're not working for pedophiles?'

From the look on the girl's face it was as if she'd asked her how long she'd been one.

'I feel like my nose is getting itchy just with you saying that.'

Guillory had the sense to swallow the words, *your brother did*. She held her hands up in apology. Asked something that had just crossed her mind now the relief was flooding through her in the knowledge that her life did not belong to the pedophile gang and Liverman who ran it after all.

Because something didn't make sense now.

'Were you in the pedophile's house?'

'No.'

'So how did you get the earring?'

'I *told* you. Somebody gave it to me.'

'Not the pedophiles?'

'No.'

'Then who?'

'It doesn't matter. And I'm sick of your questions. I want to know what happened to my brother. How come he ends up dead and you're still alive.'

That's when it struck Guillory that unless she had a good answer for the crazy young woman opposite her, that wasn't going to be the case for much longer.

'Now give me your phone.'

31

'I'm not her,' Lydia said, cutting off the flood of Evan's desperate warnings as he answered his phone, didn't even say *hello*. A stunned silence filled the void between them for a couple of beats. 'It's Lydia.'

'I'd worked that out,' he snapped.

Then he asked the question he didn't want the answer to, his mind full of thoughts he didn't want to think. Of Kate Guillory lying crumpled on the ground, what was left of her head lying in a pool of blood. Lydia rifling through her bag and pockets, finding her phone. Calling him to gloat.

'How did you get Kate's phone?'

She ignored the question as if he hadn't spoken.

'You shouldn't have made it so easy for me to get the Vanquish back.'

And he ignored her taunts, the mention of the sniper's rifle. He couldn't shake the image of Guillory lying dead on the ground, the denim-blue eyes flecked with blood, staring sightlessly at the sky. All her worries and fears proved right and taken mercifully away with the same sharp crack of a high-powered rifle. All of it his fault. Because she still hadn't said whether Guillory was alive or dead. His voice when he found it was a dry rattle.

'Where's Kate?'

It seemed to him that the silence that followed lasted a lifetime or more. He felt himself growing old and weak as he waited, the phone growing heavy in his hand, while she kept him twisting in the wind. In truth it was no more than a split second, the time it takes an unbalanced mind to decide that the time for games is over, the time to get down to business has arrived.

Her voice had lost all of its mocking quality when she spoke.

'We're in the Bluebird Diner.'

With that one small word, the *we* and not *I*, his legs became rubber hose, unable to sustain his weight. His whole body sagged. As if it had been his own head that had taken a direct hit from the Vanquish leaving him suspended for a brief moment before he collapsed to the ground.

He knew it was only a temporary reprieve, too early to allow the relief to dull his senses. He shook the lethargy from his limbs, pushed all thoughts of what might have been from his mind.

'It doesn't sound like it.'

'I stepped outside to make the call.'

In the background he heard a sound like somebody rapping their knuckles on a window, pictured her grinning smugly at Guillory inside, the sour grimace she'd get back.

'What do you want?'

'You. Here. Right now.'

'What else?'

A confused silence came down the line.

'Why did you go outside to make the call? There must be something you don't want her to hear.'

She laughed, a recognition of his perception mixed with pleasure at the devious workings of her own mind.

'I'm not going to tell her how I got hold of the Vanquish, that's all. It's up to you whether you want to. Seeing as it's aimed at her head right now.' Then she snickered again. 'I don't suppose we're going to be able to keep her from finding out how I got the earring though.'

GUILLORY WASN'T SURPRISED WHEN EVAN SLID ALONG THE SEAT opposite her. She'd guessed that was why Lydia wanted her phone. They exchanged a small, almost shy, smile as Lydia followed in after him, didn't say anything. For once, their minds were aligned along the same track. They both knew the shit was about to hit the fan. Even if neither of them knew of the other's complicity.

'What's he here for?' Guillory said to Lydia instead.

Lydia smiled the smile of the person with all the answers at her.

'In case you decide you're in it too deep, might as well go down in a blaze of glory and try to jump me. We'll shoot him instead.'

As one, they looked out of the window at the buildings opposite, two of them wondering if there really was a man with a gun trained on them, the other one knowing. Evan avoided Guillory's eyes, the guilty knowledge eating away at him that if there was, it was his fault. If he'd left the Vanquish in Todd Strange's van where he found it, it would be locked away in a police evidence room somewhere. Not aimed at their heads.

'Now tell me,' Lydia said. 'How come you're alive and Todd isn't? And it better be good.'

She spread her hands wide towards Guillory, over to you. Then folded her arms across her small chest, leaned back in her seat. Sitting next to her, Evan felt like he was on an interview panel and his colleague had just delivered the killer question to the hopeful applicant. Except in this case a lot more than a new job rested on the right answer. A vein in his neck was throbbing, muscles rigid from the strain of not looking sideways out of the window.

Still his guilt stopped him from looking at Guillory for fear that she might see it flicker in the depths of his eyes, like a small stray fish sensing the approach of a predator. So he looked out of the window anyway, kept his eyes down. Watched the passers-by on the sidewalk, didn't look up at the windows opposite. Then wished he'd just sat with his eyes closed, hadn't looked anywhere at all. A sharp intake of breath like his coffee was too hot burst from his mouth.

Lydia mistook his reaction. Thought it was a play of some kind.

So did Guillory. Anger and astonishment at Evan's stupidity collided in her features.

'*No* '

An urgent hiss at both Evan and Lydia. To stop him from doing anything stupid. Stop her from giving the signal to blow her or Evan away, splatter them across the walls of the diner and the other customers happily eating and drinking, unaware of the unordered side dish that might at any moment land on their plates.

Everybody froze.

Evan and Guillory expecting the window to explode inwards, not knowing whose head would follow, maybe both.

It didn't happen. Nobody relaxed. Hearts sprinting, mouths dry. Sitting staring at each other in silence. As if it might still happen if somebody broke it.

Then Evan looked out of the window again. Hoping he was mistaken. He wasn't.

'What?' Lydia said sounding as shaken up as the rest of them.

'Ryder.'

This to Guillory more than Lydia.

'Shit.'

'He's headed this way.'

Lydia looked, not knowing who Ryder was. Then a smile curled the corners of her mouth. Evan felt the shitstorm gathering strength over his head. She'd recognized Ryder from when she ambushed him in his car.

'The fat detective.'

Confusion clouded Guillory's features momentarily. But there was no time to ask anybody to explain how come Lydia knew who Ryder was. She leaned over the table towards Lydia, her voice low and urgent.

'Let me go to the ladies' room unless you want this to turn into the biggest clusterfuck ever.'

Lydia's gaze flicked from the brisk rolling gait of Ryder's approach to the nervous tension in Guillory's face and back again, indecision in her eyes. Evan upped the pressure.

'He's definitely coming in.'

Guillory stuck her hand out, palm-up on the table towards Lydia.

'Give me my phone. So you can let me know when he's gone.'

On the other side of the room the door opened, the sounds of the street adding to the noise inside.

Guillory hissed at Lydia, thrust her hand more insistently at her.

'Quickly!'

Lydia snapped out of her indecision. Shook her head.

'Go! But no phone. I'll get you.'

Guillory slid out of the booth as Ryder turned the other way towards the counter. Head down and hunched over, she scooted across the room to the ladies' room. Concentrating hard on the door ahead, she didn't give her immediate surroundings her full attention. Her thigh crashed into the corner of a table as she weaved her way across the room. Bolted to the floor, it didn't budge. But the empty plate pushed to the side after the guy sitting there had finished eating went flying. The crash that followed sounded to Evan like Lydia's partner in the building opposite had gotten bored and shot out one of the windows just for the hell of it. He almost ducked, expected to feel a shower of glass rain down on his head. The guy at the table had his nose in the newspaper. He jumped at the sudden noise.

'Hey! Careful.'

To Evan it sounded as if he'd just leapt onto the table and yelled across the room.

Hey Ryder, look what your partner just did.

But Ryder was too busy digging his wallet out to pay any attention. Guillory stepped over the pieces of broken plate and left-over food and dashed for the safety of the ladies' room.

With Guillory gone, it left Evan sitting next to Lydia on one side of the table with nobody on the other side. Nobody to shield them from Ryder's view should he turn to look around the room while he waited for his order to be filled. Which he did. Just as Evan was about to tell Lydia to move seats to block him from view. Or so that he could go to the men's room. Or whatever. It didn't matter because Ryder had already seen him, was already making his way towards them, negotiating his bulk between the tables a lot more adroitly than Guillory had.

That was when Evan noticed Guillory's coffee cup on the other side of the table. A momentary spike of panic went through him. But why shouldn't there be a third person at the table? There was nothing to say it was Guillory. It was only his guilty conscience. It didn't make the smile he managed to put on his face feel any less strained.

'Good to see you, Detective.'

Ryder did a small double take, then recovered.

'Don't be an ass all your life, Buckley. I just wanted to say, don't forget to come in and make a formal statement.'

Evan wasn't sure if Lydia had slipped something into her coffee while he wasn't looking or whether she just liked to have fun at his expense, but she joined the conversation, a look of surprise-cum-excitement on her face as she turned to Evan.

'What have you been up to?'

Ryder seemed to notice her for the first time, gave her a patient smile. She looked up at him overshadowing the table, stuck out her hand.

'Hello, I'm Lydia. He's not in any trouble, is he?'

She could never have guessed the thoughts going through each man's head. Ryder thinking, no, but I'm working on it. Evan thinking now would be a good time for the window to explode as Lydia's partner took a shot at a target a six-year-old child couldn't miss.

Ryder shook her hand, a spasm of irritation rippling across his face when she wouldn't let go.

'No, it's just a routine matter.'

Lydia's face fell as she continued with her charade. She still hadn't let go of Ryder's hand.

'Oh. So it's not something exciting. Like a murder.'

Ryder wrenched his hand out of hers, gave her a strange look. He shook his head without bothering to answer. Then he noticed the third coffee cup on the table. Lydia saw him looking.

'Our friend is in the ladies' room. She'll be so sorry to miss you. She's got a thing about police officers. Why don't you have a seat?'

By now Evan's fingers which had been resting on his thighs

had gone through his jeans and his skin and the first layer of muscle and would soon touch bone. But he didn't know what to do to shut her up. He considered throttling her, taking his chances with a bullet through the window. In the end he decided if you can't beat 'em, join 'em.

'Kate not with you?'

That shut Lydia up, a look of genuine surprise taking the place of all the faces she'd been pulling for Ryder's benefit.

'No. She called in sick.'

His expression suggested she'd been acting so strangely recently he wouldn't have been surprised to find her here with Evan and his unusual friend.

'Who's Kate?' the unusual friend said.

'His partner.'

'My partner.'

The slight pause that followed them both answering at the same time was broken by the sound of the ladies' room door opening. Evan's head had snapped around before he could do anything to stop it. The suddenness of the movement registered in Ryder's face. He turned to look, see what had caused such a violent reaction.

Lydia was watching the door now as well. Like Evan, she was pale with worry. Worry that all her careful plans were about to go up in smoke as Guillory came out of the ladies' room and told her partner everything.

The door stopped moving when it was halfway open. The person behind it wasn't visible. Everybody's heart was in their mouths, all for different reasons. Then the door slammed decisively shut again. Evan slumped into his seat as if somebody just pulled the stopper out of an inflatable mattress. He'd have expected Lydia to do the same, but she was back to her game.

'Looks like she didn't want to meet you after all,' she said to Ryder.

But Ryder wasn't paying any of them any attention. From the other side of the room somebody was yelling that his order was ready. He glanced briefly at the third coffee cup on the table, then left with a final reminder for Evan to come in to give a formal statement. Evan and Lydia sat side by side without saying anything until he'd collected his order and left. The moment the door banged shut he turned to face her.

'What the hell was that all about?'

Lydia gave him a look like he was simple.

'Just a little demonstration of how easy it would be for me to bring your friend Kate's career to an end.' She put a lot of mocking emphasis on the word *friend*, like it was something to be ashamed of. 'That's if she doesn't end up in prison for the murder of the pedophile. I'm sure you know police officers don't have such a great time in prison. Just think how old and wrinkly she'll be by the time she comes out. I was her, I might even choose a bullet in the head, get it over with. I'll go get her now. Then we can have a proper talk.'

She slid out of the booth, stared out of the window for a long moment. A satisfied half smile appeared on her lips. His back was still towards the window. He didn't bother to turn around to see what had put the smile on her face. He didn't need to. Maybe her partner had just waved to her, given her the thumbs up. What did he care?

He was wrong.

He should have cared.

Because if he had turned around, he'd also have seen Ryder pull to the curb on the opposite side of the street.

32

EVAN WATCHED GUILLORY FOLLOW LYDIA BACK FROM THE LADIES' room, trying to see her face. At first, she kept her head bowed. As someone might if they've decided to do the right thing about something, then backed down. And because he was watching her, he wasn't looking out of the window, still didn't see Ryder parked opposite them. With her head down, neither did Guillory.

But if either of them had looked out and seen Ryder pull away a moment later, they'd have known that he'd seen them, their guilty secret, secret no longer.

Then she looked up, met his eyes. He knew then that she'd made up her mind. She would tell Ryder what she'd done. But at a time and place of her own choosing.

And he would tell her what he'd done, here and now if necessary.

She was still only halfway to the table when a red Ford Transit van, the model with the extended high roof, climbed the curb and parked immediately in front of the window shielding them from view from the buildings across the street.

He slid out from the booth.

'Come on, let's go.'

Lydia jumped in front of them as Guillory joined him, her phone in her hand. She held it towards Guillory, the image of Guillory's earring on the screen.

'You really want me to show this to your fat partner?'

A frown creased Guillory's forehead as she remembered Lydia's previous reference to him—*the fat detective.* Somehow the girl knew they were partners. How and when she'd found that out was irrelevant now. Now that she'd made her decision.

'She's going to tell him herself,' Evan said for her.

Guillory nodded.

'Better coming from me.'

They both thought it would knock some of the confidence out of Lydia as her last card proved redundant.

But it was Lydia's reply that hit harder, delivered with a shrug.

'He's probably expecting it. He just drove off after watching you come back.'

Guillory kept her face deadpan. Didn't let the girl see the damage she'd done, the realization of the effect her deception would have on her relationship with her long-term partner.

'Let's go,' Evan said again.

He knew that Lydia hadn't played her last card. And there was nothing redundant about the one she had left. If she chose to play it, so be it.

Which she did now.

'Don't you want to know how I got hold of this?'

Momentarily, anxiety and anger tightened up Guillory's face as she stared at the girl's smug half-smile and the mocking eyes. The hollow void in her gut told her she was missing something here.

'You didn't get it from the pedophile gang?'

Lydia didn't answer. Evan did, talking over her, silencing her with a voice that proclaimed that the time for lies and deception was over.

'She got it from me.'

Her mind froze, refused to process the information, as she watched Evan's mouth moving. Looking as if he had to wrestle every word out into the widening void that lay between them.

'Tell her where you found it,' Lydia chirped with all the malevolent enthusiasm of a mischievous imp busy doing the Devil's work.

'In Garfield's house?' Guillory said for him.

He worked a sad smile onto his face, nodded.

'In a puddle of sick.'

She almost laughed then, knew he would too if she started it. Instead they just stared at each other as the understanding of what the other one had done sank in, the laws they had broken for all the best reasons but which had conspired to bring about a lose-lose situation all round.

'What were you doing there?' she said.

'Same as you.' He hesitated as the image of Robert Garfield with his throat slit wide open suddenly filled his mind. It was only a split second. Still, it was enough. She'd noticed. It seemed to him that something died in her eyes. So he quickly finished the sentence with words that were too little, too late. 'Looking for information.'

'You found the body?'

'And called Donut.'

Any other time she'd have told him not to call Ryder that. Just not today.

'Does he—'

'Of course he doesn't know.' He didn't care that he snapped, let out an aggravated sigh at the stupidity of the question, the stupidity of the whole crazy situation. 'Why would we have gone through all that nonsense with you hiding in the ladies' room if he did?'

'Who else knows?'

'Just the three of us,' Lydia sang out. 'And I'm bored with this tearful confession shit. Now you tell me what happened to my brother.'

Guillory gave her a look. A god-give-me-strength, withering look and Evan prayed that she never used one like it on him.

'Or what? I told you, I'm going to tell them myself.'

'Come on,' Evan said. 'We're done here.'

Lydia had done her worst, had nothing more to use against them. What she'd already done and said would do for now, would give him and Guillory plenty to be going on with.

They were both wrong.

Lydia sat down and slid along the seat as if she knew they'd be following in after her.

'I can tell you who hired my brother to kill you.'

If she expected to see Guillory's knees buckle, feel the table rock as she clutched at it for support, she was mistaken. So was Evan. He expected to see her go flying across the table, arms outstretched and mouth open in a demonic howl, fingers tightening around Lydia's neck until the name popped out.

Instead she gave a small shrug, that's yesterday's news.

'Liverman.'

Evan's head jerked around at the name. Not that he recognized it. Just that she knew it at all. Guillory met his eyes. There was no apology there for not telling him despite the many occasions he'd asked her about it. Instead, an understanding passed between them on a level that didn't need words.

We all have our secrets.

So he just nodded mechanically, wondered why the hell he'd broken into a house in the middle of the night where he'd found the corpse of a murdered pedophile and evidence of Guillory's possible complicity in that deed, all in the hope of finding a name she already knew. He didn't know about God, but fate certainly moved in mysterious ways. He realized that he'd missed what Lydia had just said in response to the name Liverman. But he saw Guillory's open-mouthed reaction to it.

'What was that you said?'

'I said that's what she knows him as. But it's not his real name.' She turned her attention to Guillory who stood frozen as if she was waiting for the music to start again. 'Had much luck tracing the name Joseph Liverman?'

Guillory's silence answered for her. Lydia gave her a tight smile, tapped the table with her chewed fingernail.

'So why don't you two sit down and stay sitting down until I tell you that you can get up. You tell me what I want to know and maybe I'll give you his real name. And how to find him.'

Evan had never wanted to be the man at the top of a pedophile gang. Not even once. The look in Guillory's eyes made him especially glad today that he wasn't the man known to her as Liverman. He'd have sworn he heard the wooden table splinter as she gripped it to lower herself slowly down.

Despite the anger and loathing and hatred burning in her eyes that might cause a person who didn't know her to think that she'd built an impenetrable shell around herself to protect her from the memories, he knew that the last thing she needed was to run through the events that followed her abduction for the benefit of the crazy young woman sharing their table. He lifted his hand before she had a chance to begin.

'Let me tell it.'

She nodded gratefully, sank back into the seat. She didn't close her eyes. He guessed that was when the horrors crawled out of her subconscious to torment her, make it real again.

'I found him,' he said to Lydia by way of explanation as to

why he was qualified to tell the story. 'And there isn't much to tell. He got a flat.'

Lydia's features collapsed into confusion, then rebuilt themselves into an expression of suspicion.

'What?'

'He dumped Kate at a cabin in the woods'—Lydia nodded at the mention of the cabin, a detail she clearly recognized—'then headed off for something, don't ask me what. That's when he got a flat. It must have been from the rough track leading up to the cabin. Unfortunately for him, the first person to happen along was a low-life gangster called Chico who'd just been ambushed. His own car was shot to hell. So he shot your brother and took his van.'

'How do you know all this?'

'Because I was the one who found your brother's body and a flat tire in the back of the van.'

'And—'

He shot her a warning glare, knew that she'd been about to say *and the Vanquish*. She caught the flash of his eyes, clamped her mouth shut. Next to him Guillory now had her eyes shut and damn the demons.

'We found Chico's car shot to pieces hidden nearby as well as the aftermath of the ambush. So we put it all together. That's all there was to it. Wrong place, wrong time.'

He made it sound as if her brother had been an innocent casualty, not some murdering bastard himself who deserved everything he got. He let his story sink in. Held his breath, hoping she wouldn't ask how come he was the one who found her brother. That was a story he didn't want to get into.

Beside him Guillory suddenly came awake. Her eyes showed the remnants of what had been going through her mind as she listened to Evan talk about the day she nearly died as if he was telling Lydia about a great movie he'd watched the previous week.

He couldn't begin to imagine what must be going through her mind. The situation was surreal. To be sitting in a diner with the sister of the man who'd been paid to kill her, trying to convince the girl that she wasn't the guilty one. In those few seconds as they all sat in silence, he understood the depths of her hatred for the man she knew as Liverman, that she would suffer the outrageous situation. He felt it like a fourth person at the table with them, the malevolent presence that now lived inside her.

'What happened to this guy Chico?' Lydia said finally.

'He's gone to ground,' Guillory said. 'Either that or somebody's done to him what he did to your brother.' She put a lot of spiteful emphasis on the words, something Evan reckoned she wouldn't have risked earlier. 'It's dog eat dog. They screwed up the ambush, maybe they got him another time. Either way you're not going to find him. And anyway, what would you do if you did?'

Evan had a pretty good idea. But he kept it to himself. He doubted there would ever be a good time to mention the Vanquish. Now definitely wasn't it. Seemed Lydia agreed with him. She gave a small shrug, that's the way it goes.

He knew that she hadn't dropped it just like that. But for the moment they all played along. Then she stood up, clutched her bag tightly to her.

'What about Liverman's real name?' Guillory said, her voice proclaiming zero expectation of a positive response. 'Or was that just another lie?'

Lydia shook her head solemnly.

'No lie. But I need to think things through.'

Evan and Guillory both did the translation from crazy to English: *I need to think of a way to make this work for me.*

Guillory lifted her hand, let it drop again, words on her lips that she swallowed back again. There was no point in wasting any more breath. Lydia would give them what they wanted or she wouldn't. There was nothing they could do to influence the decision either way.

They sat in silence until Lydia had gone, thankfully turning left out of the door so that they didn't have to watch her walk past the window, maybe give them one last unbalanced smile. Guillory broke the silence with the only words that needed to be said.

'Ask me, Evan.'

So he asked her.

'Did you kill Robert Garfield?'

33

ELWOOD CROW SAT WITH HIS NEW BURNER PHONE IN ONE HAND and the number that Evan had given him from the back of Todd Strange's business card in the other. His bony fingers hovered over the phone's keypad as they had at least a half dozen times previously.

He didn't want to make the call.

But he had no option. For the past two days he'd tried unsuccessfully to trace the number Evan had given him. From the total lack of information, he could only assume that it was another burner phone, exactly like the one in his hand. He may as well have let Evan call the number in the first place and see what shook loose, not wasted two days for nothing.

There was another option. Do nothing at all. At least that way there was no chance of causing more trouble. But that was like admitting defeat, something he'd never done and didn't want to start doing now. He could call Evan, ask him which way he wanted to play it. But after the hard time he'd given him over his recent inadvisable internet searches he didn't want to give the impertinent boy any ammunition to come back at him with.

Later, he would regret not making the call.

His pet bird cawed loudly as if telling him in its own way to get his finger out, make the damn call. So he got up and left the room, closing the door firmly behind him so as not to be disturbed by the bird making a noise at an inopportune moment.

Just closing the door made him feel guilty, a constant reminder of the Vanquish sniper's rifle Evan had brought to him for safekeeping being stolen from under their noses within five minutes. It was naive to think that there would not be consequences for somebody as a result of that carelessness.

So he tapped out the number carefully, held the phone to his ear, his breath even shorter than after a trip upstairs.

It was answered immediately.

He waited for the *hello* or perhaps a gruff *yeah?*

Silence.

And it wasn't that his hearing was failing him. The knot in his stomach tightened as the seconds stretched out.

Still nothing.

He knew then that the person on the other end of the line was waiting for him to say something. Trouble was, he'd been around the block enough times to know that it had to be the right something.

So it didn't matter what he did. Say nothing or say the wrong thing, the end result would be the same. A dead connection. And the people on the other end more suspicious than they had been before the call. Because anyone innocently dialing the wrong number would tire of the silence, would come out with an irritated *hello? hello?* and not just return the silence.

Then the person on the other end of the line made the decision for him, cut the call.

Crow almost threw the phone at the wall, a whispered *damn*

on his lips. He returned to the back room where it seemed to him that the pet bird was shaking its head at him.

He just hoped he hadn't done too much damage.

ROACH, THE MAN ON THE OTHER END OF THE LINE WHO'D CUT THE call dropped the phone back in his pocket, a frown clouding his large features. He wasn't the sharpest tool in the box but he knew a genuine wrong number when he heard one. And that hadn't been it. Nobody sits in silence for twenty seconds, the time he'd been told to wait before hanging up.

Roach liked rules and procedures, orders too. They made his life easy, meant he didn't have to think. Hit this person, get rid of that body. He was happy to let somebody else make the decisions, the difficult part. So he didn't have to think about what to do next.

If you receive a suspicious call, tell Mr Liverman.

Mr Liverman was sitting behind his large desk when Roach entered the room. Sometimes Roach thought it was because he was so fat that he'd gotten permanently stuck under the heavy oak desk. He hoped he never dropped dead sitting there. It'd be a hell of a job getting him out from under it. They'd need a chainsaw—and not to cut up the nice old desk. Trouble was the teeth would probably clog on all of Liverman's blubber. For those reasons alone he wished Mr Liverman a long and healthy life.

Liverman had his phone clamped to his ear, his little finger with the big ruby ring sticking straight out like he was sipping tea with the Queen of England. At least Roach thought it was his phone. It could have been a growth he was scratching. It was hard to tell amongst the overlapping rolls of flab that hung over his collar like wax running down a candle. Liverman raised a finger for Roach to wait then continued with his conversation.

Roach tried not to listen, tried not to think about what was being said. He didn't like working for Liverman. Didn't like him period. Didn't even like the feel of the name Liverman on his lips, even if he knew it wasn't his real name. What sort of a person chooses a name like that? A pervert and a degenerate who ought to be in prison where he wouldn't last five minutes, that's what sort. So Roach passed the time thinking it'd be fun to dig Liverman out from under the desk with that chainsaw after all. But while he was still alive.

'What is it?' Liverman said, finishing his call and snapping Roach out of his reverie.

Roach told him about the call. Liverman nodded to himself as he did so, the rippling effect of the flesh overhanging his collar making Roach feel ill.

'They didn't say anything?'

'Nothing. For twenty seconds like you told—'

'Yes, yes, I know all that.'

Roach waited while Liverman thought about it, the pinkie with the ruby ring now digging at something in his ear. Roach stifled a laugh, turned it into a cough. Maybe Liverman had lost his phone somewhere in there. He didn't offer to see if he could find it for him.

'So,' Liverman said, leaning back and spreading his fingers over the suit vest that he always wore, 'what have we got?'

'Well—'

'No, no, no. I'm not asking you, you idiot. I'm thinking out loud.'

Roach's mouth clamped shut, his teeth almost cracking as his jaw clenched. He controlled his anger, thought of new places he'd stick the chainsaw when the day came.

'We've got all that trouble with the cop Guillory and that idiot Garfield. Then we've got another idiot Todd Strange making a complete mess of dealing with Guillory . . .'

It seemed to Roach that as far as Liverman was concerned everybody was an idiot except him. He waited patiently while Mr Big Brain thought it through.

'Does Guillory seem the sort to give up easily?' Liverman said.

Roach kept his mouth shut. Once bitten, twice shy.

'Well, does she?'

Roach jumped as Liverman barked at him. How the hell was he supposed to know which question to answer and which one to ignore?

'No, Mr Liverman.'

'Exactly. And now we get a strange call. I don't believe in coincidences like that.'

Roach said he didn't either, a fact that appeared to be of no consequence whatsoever to Liverman.

'Give me the phone.'

Roach dropped it into Liverman's sweaty palm. He felt a small pang of sorrow at the thought of what those hands liked to touch. They'd be the first things he'd take off with the chainsaw when the time came. Liverman found the number and made a note of it.

'I'll see if we can trace that. If they've got any sense it'll be a burner but it's worth a try.'

He stared at the phone for a long while. Call the number or not?

'Should I call them back, Roach?'

Roach shifted uncomfortably from one foot to the other. *Shit.* A decision. Liverman watched him squirm for a while longer, a mocking sneer on his face.

'No, I don't think so either,' he said as if Roach had responded. 'There's nothing to gain from it. Going forward, we need to be even more cautious than usual. Everything should be viewed as suspicious until proven otherwise.'

Roach nodded enthusiastically, happy to get a straightforward instruction for once instead of all the other airy-fairy bullshit Liverman normally came out with.

'Especially any attempts to set up a meeting by anybody we haven't dealt with before.'

34

'NOT HERE,' GUILLORY SAID. 'I CAN'T TALK ABOUT IT IN THE middle of all this . . .' She waved her arm in a broad sweep, took in the diner full of everyday people going about their everyday lives. It was no place to talk about the deviants and the degenerates of the world and the death of one of them, however little the planet might mourn his passing. Or however eagerly the diners might raise a glass of juice or cup of coffee in celebration if they knew.

'Not the Jerusalem, either,' she added before he could suggest it.

It made him wonder, worse, it made him dread how bad it could be. Because they'd had many a serious discussion propping up the bar in the Jerusalem with liquid backbone on hand. Instinctively, he knew where she wanted to go. To a place perfectly suited to thoughts and talk of death and depravity.

To her brother's grave.

Known to everybody as Teardrop, he'd been a police officer himself, working undercover until his recklessness betrayed him and the gang he'd worked to infiltrate had butchered him, his death a lesson in cruelty. Guillory had called Evan Teardrop for a while in recognition of his own reckless and pig-headed nature. And as a reminder of what happened to those who rushed in blindly, who ignored all sensible advice.

'Teardrop,' he said.

She nodded. That small dip of the head and the soft smile that accompanied it made him think that things could still be good if they could only get over their current problems. He didn't dwell on the question of whether that would still be the case if she admitted to him in the next five minutes that she had indeed killed Robert Garfield in cold blood, slitting open his throat as he lay in his bed.

He couldn't get out of his mind the way she was on the morning after the night he now knew she'd been in Garfield's house. The freshness of her hair and body as if she'd scrubbed herself clean for hours. The quickness of her temper, understandable in a person with a weight on their mind and another scar on their conscience. Or soul, if you prefer.

Not surprisingly, they walked to the cemetery in silence. Side by side, separated by an inch or two that might as well have been a wide ocean, one filled with doubts and recriminations and what should have been.

Neither of them was surprised when a car pulled to the curb beside them before they'd gone a quarter mile. The passenger door flew open, blocking the sidewalk.

'Get in Kate,' Ryder said, leaning over from the driver's side.

'Not now.'

She stepped around the door, carried on walking as if nothing had happened. Ryder stared after her for a couple of beats, then turned on Evan.

'That was her with you in the diner.'

There was no point in denying it. Lydia had told them Ryder had been watching from across the street.

'Yep.'

'What's this about?'

Evan shook his head.

'I wish I knew.'

He didn't bother to add what he felt. That he didn't want to find out either. Ryder wasn't prepared to be brushed off so easily. His gaze flicked back to Guillory disappearing down the street. Then he seemed to become aware of where they were, the direction she was headed. His face fell.

'She's on her way to her brother's grave.'

'Uh-huh.'

'Jesus. It's something to do with that pervert Garfield and all the other deviant bastards, isn't it?'

Evan said nothing.

'I just knew it.'

You have no idea, Evan thought to himself as Ryder gave him a hard stare.

'There's something you're not telling me.'

Again, Evan said nothing. Ryder didn't bother to repeat that he just knew it. They both knew he knew it anyway.

'Get in,' Ryder said.

'Why?'

Ryder looked like he wanted to bite something. The steering wheel. Evan's head. Anything. He held his breath which only made his face redder.

'Because I'll arrest you if you don't,' he yelled.

'For what?'

'For being a fucking idiot in a public place.'

Evan couldn't deny that one. He slipped into the passenger seat.

'And leave the damn siren alone.'

Then, in the twenty seconds it took for Ryder to make up the distance between them and Guillory striding out up ahead he told Evan exactly what he'd do to him if whatever half-assed scheme they were up to backfired and ended up making her worse than she already was.

But Evan wasn't letting him have it all his own way, told him he'd like to see him try and there wouldn't be a problem in the first place if Ryder and the rest of her fair-weather colleagues got a bit more behind her and didn't treat her like a pariah.

So the windows were misted by the time they caught up with her, both men having done nothing more productive than let off steam in frustration at their own inability to help. Neither of them felt any better for it.

Guillory stopped as they pulled up alongside her so Evan didn't have to pull the same stunt with the car door. That was a lucky break for the car door. He climbed out and Ryder leaned across.

'We've got to talk, Kate. There are some things I need to bring you up to date on.'

Then he was gone in a squeal of rubber and black smoke. It would have been a lot better all-around if he'd insisted that she get in the car and told her then and there. But things don't work like that.

'Nice chat with Donut?' she said.

'That's the first time you've ever called him that.'

She gave an uninterested shrug, started walking again. He fell into step beside her. The unexpected interlude had failed to break the tension between them. It was back to silence for the rest of the way.

'I had the name Liverman,' she said once they'd wound their way between the graves to stand in front of her brother's small plot.

'How did you get it?'

She laughed, a strangled sound that didn't do justice to the screwed-up way things had turned out.

'I heard our friend Lydia's brother Todd say it when he came to pick me up. To take me for a one-way ride out to the woods. It was careless. But they didn't think it was going to matter.' Her voice sounded as full of satisfaction that she'd proved them wrong as it was for staying alive. Then it dropped a notch. 'That's one mistake they're going to regret.'

Evan reckoned that if he'd been one of the residents of the graves that surrounded them, he'd have been looking forward to welcoming a new neighbor or two in the near future. Ones who'd met a very violent end.

'Like Lydia said, I wasn't getting anywhere with it. There aren't many people called Liverman and none of them fit the profile. I was starting to think it was a fake name myself.'

'You didn't say anything to anybody else?'

She shook her head, stared through the grave marker in front of them, her thoughts somewhere he could only guess at.

'I *told* you. They treat me like I'm making it all up. I wasn't about to say I thought I heard a name while I had the hood over my head and they were beating the shit out of me. It would've been straight back to that patronizing bitch of a psychiatrist to see if we could work through my feelings of anger and confusion.'

For a moment he thought she was going to spit her mouth was so twisted. Whether in disgust with herself or the psychiatrist bitch he couldn't say.

'What would you have done if you'd found him on the system?'

She pulled her eyes away from her brother's grave, turned them on him. He felt as if he'd taken a wrong turn somewhere, strayed into a different part of the cemetery and was looking down into an open grave. One that seemed to have no bottom. Only darkness, thick and welcoming.

'Lucky I didn't have to find out.'

He didn't say what a non-answer that was. Or that it was a

stupid thing to say. Because if Lydia gave her Liverman's real name as she'd promised, she'd be faced with that exact same decision once again.

'That's why you decided to break into Garfield's house,' he said instead.

'Seemed like a good idea at the time.' Then she laughed again. A proper laugh this time, one that made him feel good inside. 'Maybe Donut's right. I spend too much time with you. The half-assed must be rubbing off on me.'

Good as her laughter had made him feel, it was time for him to spoil everything, drag them both back to the question that stood between them like something that had crawled out of one of the graves.

'You want to tell me what happened in Garfield's house?'

'Jesus, Evan, I thought you'd never ask.'

35

SHE COULDN'T BREATHE. THROAT DRY, CHEST TIGHT. HEART thumping so hard it made her head throb, fighting desperately to control the panic that threatened to overwhelm her. She felt as if she was in a cheap pine box at the bottom of an open grave. Lid nailed down tight, no light penetrating, the only sound the regular thump of dirt landing on the wood an inch above her nose.

She was back in the dark of Robert Garfield's kitchen. Waiting for her vision to acclimatize while somewhere in the distance a door banged in the wind. She'd just sent Curtis Banks, the petty thief and burglar who'd let her into the house, on his way. He was up to something. She should never have sent him away with the words *I don't want you seeing anything you might regret*. She might as well have said *stick around to watch the fireworks*. It couldn't be helped. But if he thought he was going to use any of what he'd seen happen tonight, he was in for a very unpleasant surprise.

Never in her wildest dreams could she have imagined exactly what he was up to.

Banishing all thoughts of him from her mind, she stood

stock still, concentrated on the house around her. Banks better have watched it for the last twenty-four hours as she'd told him to do, not snuck off to the nearest bar instead. Again, he'd regret it if he had.

None of which would help her now if Garfield was in the house.

She padded silently across the kitchen. If she stayed standing still too long she'd come to her senses, turn around and get the hell out of there before it was too late. Before she did something she might regret herself, forget about Banks.

She searched the ground floor rooms quickly and efficiently. As quickly and efficiently as anyone can when they don't know what they're looking for. When they're only doing it to be doing *something, anything,* to stop their mind from driving them crazy. Whatever it was that she had no idea what she was looking for, she didn't find it.

One corner of the living room had been made into a small home office. There was a cheap desk and office chair but no computer. She was sitting in the chair now, having just finished searching the desk. Swiveling gently back and forth, the movement comforting, calming her.

Bringing her to her senses.

Was there any point in searching upstairs? Would he be so stupid as to leave something incriminating lying around? Or not even incriminating, just something to go with the name Liverman. The name that ran through her mind constantly like the words to a song that you hate but can't stop singing in your head.

It wasn't the words to a song in her head that told her that she had no choice other than to search upstairs as well. It was the nagging head voices that would never give her a moment's peace if she gave up now.

Why didn't you search upstairs?

The answers were in the bedroom nightstand.
Why did you give up?
Why did you let them win?
Just do it!

She jerked herself violently out of the chair. The cheap piece of junk flew across the floor behind her, banged into the table at the side of the sofa. Cheap and lightweight it might have been, flexing as you sat in it, but it still had enough weight to topple the lamp that stood on the table. She watched it fall. Slowly. Gracefully. Like the leaning tower of Pisa had finally given up its long fight with gravity. In the quiet of the room, it sounded to her as if that ancient tower had just fallen on the roof.

She froze.

But if the house was empty, what did it matter?

Then a noise from upstairs.

It sounded like a low groan. Like a person in pain. Or was it just the creak of timbers in an old house? She strained her ears, breathing suspended in a chest that was as tight as if the falling tower had landed on her. If anybody was up there, they'd have to shout to make themselves heard over the pounding of her blood in her ears.

Silence.

Deep and comforting, slowing the racing of her heart. She waited a couple of minutes longer, heard nothing more. Do it. Now. She crept silently across the room, out into the hallway, made her way to the bottom of the stairs.

She felt his presence before she saw him.

Felt his fear flowing down the stairs to embrace her. She looked up. Saw Robert Garfield staring back at her, his face frozen in horror. Dressed in a sweat-stained T-shirt and boxer shorts that looked as if he'd soiled himself in them, he was a pathetic sight with his little pot belly and his hairless spindly legs that were so pale they almost glowed in the dark.

His mouth opened but nothing came out, his eyes wide with terror. In his shaking hand he held a bucket. An old-fashioned metal one with a wooden grip on the handle. The sort of thing that arty people use to plant flowers in, to brighten up a drab corner.

Except this one wasn't full of flowers. Nor were its contents about to brighten anything up.

As Guillory found out.

He didn't wait for her to make a move towards him, to start climbing the stairs. He heaved the bucket and its foul contents at her.

Standing at the bottom of the stairs she watched it fly through the air almost as if it were in slow motion. Even as the bucket turned in the air, all the clues came together in her mind before it unleashed its filthy load.

Nobody entering or leaving in the past twenty-four hours. The unclean smell pervading the whole house. Garfield's sweat-stained T-shirt and dirty boxers. His pallor even allowing for his terror. And the bucket. Letting loose its load now. A shower of vomit and bile raining down on her head before she had a chance to move. Splashing her face. Soaking into her hair. Running down her cheeks and her nose and behind her ears and in her eyes. Seeking out every open pore to fill to overflowing with the still-warm, foul-smelling mess.

She bit back a surprised yelp, kept her mouth tightly shut. Thank God for small mercies. Then the bucket hit her full in the face. Sent her staggering backwards into the wall behind her, the rough edge of the lip opening up a shallow cut on her cheek. Without thinking she clawed at her face, tried to clear the sour filth from her eyes and ears, stop it from running down her neck.

She hooked one of the earrings Evan had given her with her fingernail, ripped it out, never even noticed in her desperate panic to clean herself. Swiping and slapping at her skin as if a swarm of angry bees were attacking her, wishing it was nothing more than bees or hornets or any of the other creatures God himself regrets creating and not the excreta of this deviant man's body.

Above her at the top of the stairs that deviant man exploded into movement, turned tail and dived back into his bedroom. The door slammed with a crash that shook her whole body. As if even the house itself were mocking her futile attempts to creep around.

As the sound of the door banging faded away something happened to Kate Guillory.

It was as if the rancid contents of the bucket had achieved their aim, had permeated her skin and flesh, leached into her blood, poisoning it, filling her with a madness that was beyond controlling by rational thought. She kicked the bucket angrily away, did nothing more than hurt her toe, then started up the stairs. The whole house seemed to shake as she stomped up them, ignoring the spatters of sick that lined the wall.

She felt a mean satisfaction deep in the pit of her belly as she pictured Garfield cowering behind the door. As if that would protect him, don't make me laugh. So she stomped harder and more deliberately with every step, tried not to think about the sight or smell of his boxer shorts when she kicked the door in.

She stood in front of the closed door. Breathed deeply. Not to calm herself. Why would she want to be calm? No, to infuse her body, her muscles, with extra oxygen, feel them swell and respond as she prepared herself physically and mentally for what was to come next.

A pitiful wailing sound came from behind the door. She'd never heard a sound so sweet. You can shove your dawn chorus or the crash of the waves on a shingle beach where the sun don't shine. And it sure as hell wasn't shining in Kate Guillory's heart.

'Open the door, Garfield.'

'Leave me alone.'

It was a pathetic sound. All it did was fuel the anger and loathing still building strength inside her.

'That's what the children you abuse say, I'll bet.'

She kicked the door hard, rattled it in its frame. The wall too.

'And what do you do when they say it? Do you leave them alone? Or do you put your filthy fucking hands all over them?'

'I'll give you whatever you want.'

She almost laughed. He didn't know what he was offering. Because all she wanted in this world was the feel of his scrawny neck in her fingers as she squeezed the worthless life out of him until his eyes popped and his body spat out the last of the filth inside him.

So consumed was she by the red mist that had descended on her, she was blind to what was staring her in the face. Because she was never going to find a piece of paper or a computer file labeled *Mr Liverman's contact details*. The only place information like that existed was in the mind of the pervert behind the door.

But she couldn't see it. So she shoulder charged the door. Burst it wide open, banging hard against the wall behind it.

It made a hell of a noise. What did she care? She should have cared. Cared a lot. Because behind the splintering of wood and the crash as the door hit the wall, another door opened quietly downstairs. The back door. And neither of them heard it.

Sometimes you can't help but admire fate's timing.

She stood in the doorway like a Viking queen surveying the last survivor of her merciless raid, the smell that greeted her like a charnel house. And it wasn't the vanquished king who cowered before her, but the lowliest knave. Garfield huddled in the far corner of the room, squatting, back against the wall, arms around his head. An incessant jumble of words and meaningless sounds spewed out of his mouth, a mixture of crying and pleading and begging and offers of anything she might desire.

It sickened her.

She felt again the hood over her head because it was that time of night after all. Only this time she was wide awake. Or was she? Tears of anger pricked at the back of her eyes as she remembered how she'd bitten her tongue in two, tasted now the blood in her mouth, rather than give in to her own body's desire to beg and plead. She'd taken the worst they could give without a sound to compete with their noisy grunts and the heavy slap of fists against flesh. Not once had she cried out or whimpered through swollen lips and loosened teeth.

And Garfield expected her mercy?

You make me sick.

Have the balls to take it like a man. Not that you'd recognize a man if he punched you in the face.

She took a step into the room and it seemed a smaller space, her righteous anger filling every inch of it. With his head buried between his knees Garfield felt her presence looming over him. Like the Angel of Death come to claim him, for what purpose God or the Devil only knew.

With his butt almost on the floor and his knees up in front of him, she could see his boxer shorts stretched tight over his body. As she looked a dark stain appeared and spread out from between his legs, growing rapidly. Then urine dripped through the sodden fabric, soaked into the carpet.

In that moment she felt sick to her core. Not with Garfield. With herself. A self-loathing so all-encompassing she felt words form on her lips, a plea for him to forgive her. But the words didn't come because she was beyond words, beyond anything other than the shame of what he had brought out in her.

She left the room.

Tried to ignore his pitiful crying as it followed her down the stairs. She stepped carefully over the pool of vomit that lay at the bottom, surprised there was so much of it. She'd have sworn every last drop had landed on her head. She looked away, didn't see the glint of a gold earring half submerged amongst the semi-digested food.

As she made her way towards the kitchen and the back door and the fresh air beyond, a different smell seemed to assault her senses. A remembered smell. One she didn't want to remember. Like unwashed teeth and stale ashtray. She paused. Sniffed. No, it was nothing. Just the remnants of what Garfield had thrown over her still clinging to her skin. It would still be clinging to her every night when she closed her eyes and prayed for sleep.

Now she had an appointment with scalding water, a scrubbing brush and bleach.

36

Evan relaxed, the tension in his rigid muscles releasing as Guillory's fingers loosened their grip in his hair, her nails withdrawing from the refuge they'd sought in his flesh. At some point during the telling of her story, he'd pulled her into his body, held her tight.

He'd felt his ribs move in the strength of her desperate embrace, felt the horror and loathing flow from her body into his as if he'd been there with her. It had saddened him, brought a lump to his throat, that it might flood into his veins and fill every cavity of his body until he was huge and bloated and finally exploded but it could never lessen what was still left inside her.

So he'd held her tightly to him, looking out over her head at the rows of graves stretching away into the distance, knowing that the relief was only temporary and it was going to take a lot more than a sympathetic ear and a comforting hug to mend her.

He'd have felt a lot better about it all if he'd only known that very soon he would be given the opportunity to do just that.

For the moment, they disentangled themselves from each other and stood with their own thoughts in the quiet of the cemetery beside her brother's grave. He was the first to break the silence.

'That explains your bad mood when we met for breakfast.'

Guillory allowed herself a small smile.

'Bad mood? Yeah, you could call it that.'

He took hold of her chin, turned her face to get a better look at the scratch on her face.

'It makes you look pretty tough. I wouldn't mess with you.'

Two things he wasn't saying. One, he wouldn't have messed with her before the scratch. And two, he couldn't stop himself from wondering if any of her blood was on the bucket. Ryder's parting words to her were stuck in his mind.

There are some things I need to bring you up to date on.

Had they found her DNA on the bucket? If so, all of the ridiculous charade with Lydia had been for nothing. Not to mention him having tampered with a crime scene by removing her earring.

'You think the people who killed him were in the house while you were there?' he said.

She gave a gentle shrug, one that said less about not knowing the answer and more about wishing she'd been more focussed, less wrapped up in herself.

'I don't know. I thought I recognized the smell of the guys who beat me. But I was so desperate to get out and clean up. And with all the other stuff still on me ...'

He did something then that he wouldn't have risked in the recent past. He put his arm around her shoulder, gave her a squeeze. And got it thrown off again for his trouble.

'I don't need sympathy. Or pity.'

He held up his hands, heaven forbid. The woman who'd poured her heart out to him with her head on his shoulder a minute ago had clearly left the cemetery while he wasn't looking, her place taken by a prickly creature that would bite if you weren't careful.

They started walking, her with one last look over her shoulder at her brother's grave. They weaved in and out of the graves, pausing at some of them, then moving on. Like two people trying to find the oldest one or the most poignant epitaph. Not much was said. Then they were at the entrance to the cemetery.

'The Jerusalem's only a couple of blocks away,' he said.

She gave him a look that said she might have just re-lived one of the worst days of her life, but she wasn't directionally challenged to go with it.

'No, maybe not,' he said.

He put a sad, downcast expression on his face. It didn't do him any good.

'Sorry,' she said.

'You know I've got to go back to Florida—'

'To see your girlfriend, Ana Maria.'

It struck him that the last time he spoke to her before everything kicked off with Lydia, she'd said something similar: *Have a nice time with Ana Maria.* The sentiment behind the two remarks couldn't have been further apart. They'd definitely moved on. Or was it so far away that she no longer cared?

'You looked her up.'

Guillory spotted a speck of mud on her shoe that had gotten stuck there as they wandered on the grass between the graves. She made a point of rubbing it clean on the back of her leg.

'Might have done,' she said to the newly-shined shoe.

'You missed a bit.'

Then he wiped some from the edge of his own shoe onto hers.

'Idiot.'

She didn't bother to clean it off.

'You want to come with me?'

She shook her head.

'I can't. I've got to tell them what happened before they find out anyway.' She pointed to the scratch on her cheek, let him know that she was well aware of all the implications. 'My DNA is probably on that bucket. I'm sure that's what Donut wants to talk to me about. What's she like?'

The abrupt change of direction threw him for a moment until he realized what she'd really said.

I don't want to talk about it anymore.

'She's nice.'

'Pretty?'

'I thought you looked her up.'

'It's an old photo.'

'She's not wearing well.'

'Idiot. You can tell me the truth.'

'It's nice and warm down in Florida.'

'I'm not going to get any sense out of you, am I?'

'Did you ever?'

'You've got a point. Is she pretty?'

'Very.'

It went on like that until they said goodbye, went their separate ways. Him down to sunny Florida and her to bring about what could be the end of her career. If he'd thought it would do any good, he'd have stayed around to lend moral support.

Or what she'd call sympathy and pity.

37

'DID I GET YOU INTO TROUBLE?' CORTEZ SAID.

Evan had just joined her at the bar in the Marathon Grill and Ale House where they'd had their last meeting. So much had happened since that meeting, he didn't immediately know what she was talking about.

'With Guillory,' she prompted.

'Oh, that.'

He took a leisurely sip of his beer, almost laughed to think how ridiculous the situation was—that Guillory's biggest worry might be caused by petty jealousy. He realized now that it was the events that occurred in Garfield's house and the stress she'd been under ever since that had fueled the hard time she'd given him over Cortez.

'No more than usual.'

'That bad, huh?' She waited, but from the way he took another swallow of beer it was obvious that she wasn't going to get any more details. 'I'm afraid it's bad news from me too.'

'They won't re-open the case?'

'No. And I'm not surprised.'

Nor was he, his guilt at throwing the gum he'd found stuck

to the underside of Winter's table into the sea kicking in. He could tell from the tone of her voice, the lack of room for any discussion on the matter, that it wasn't just what he'd done. Something else had happened.

'The captain made it very clear that he didn't want me to waste any more time on it. He made some very uncomplimentary remarks about the source of my information.' She took a small sip of her drink in an attempt to hide the smile on her lips.

'Me?'

'Uh-huh. Want to hear what he said?'

'No thanks.'

'Nothing you haven't heard before, I'll bet. Anyway—'

'You don't like to be told what to do.'

Her drink stalled halfway to her lips which he'd already noticed had a nice red lipstick on. Then she put it down on the bar again.

'I don't know what you're talking about.'

His eyebrows went up an inch, is that so?

'Of course you don't. I bet you had a day off the following day. Decided you hadn't been down to Key West for a while. Maybe check out the guest house where the fire took place, see if there's any gum on the underside of a chair.'

She gave him a guilty smile, you got me. But he hadn't finished.

'And it'd be an added bonus to stick it to that dick Deutsch. That's what you called him wasn't it?'

She nodded enthusiastically, then asked him if he was so clever, what happened next? He shook his head.

'No idea. It obviously didn't pan out.'

'Nope. The owner was there when I got to the burned-out house, making arrangements for the repairs, that sort of thing.'

He knew what was coming now, the reason for the finality in her voice.

'Let me guess. Throwing out all the old pool furniture while he was at it. Claiming it on the insurance too.'

'You know, you might make a good detective one day. The yard was empty, everything cleared out. Even the pool was drained. So all I've got is maybe some residue of the gum you threw in the sea still stuck to the underside of the table on Winter's boat and nothing to match it to.'

Evan washed the disappointment down with another mouthful of beer.

'I don't suppose I'd re-open the case, either. That still doesn't change the fact that it was closed for no good reason before any of this happened.'

Cortez nodded, can't disagree with you.

'Maybe you'd like to take that up with the captain?'

'That'd be the captain who made the uncomplimentary remarks about me?'

'That's the one. My boss.'

The last two words had a definite washing-of-hands feel to them. He couldn't blame her. At least it meant he wouldn't be compromising an official police investigation. That fact wasn't lost on her either. The mischievous gleam in her eyes told him that.

'It's back to what Guillory said. How much trouble do I want?'

If that wasn't an official endorsement to create as much trouble as he liked, he didn't know what was. He finished the last of his beer in one swallow, believing that their meeting was at an end. When she didn't follow suit and finish her drink too, he thought for a moment that she was going to suggest another one, maybe a bite to eat. Except it was something very different, something that was very out of character for her. Something that made him think she knew more than she was saying.

'Watch your back.'

38

———

FROM THE BAR HE WALKED THE FEW BLOCKS TO THE MARATHON Marina, Cortez's warning still echoing in his mind. Crow's vagueness about what he wanted him to do wasn't helping—give things a poke, see what comes back at you. The only thing he'd said was that he believed Vaughan Lockhart, the man who owned half of the boat with Winter, knew what was going on. And if he wasn't there, have a proper look around this time, don't waste any more time doing something as inconvenient as finding an old friend dead underneath the boat.

The security guard, Rodriguez, wasn't in his office when Evan walked past. He continued down to where the boat was moored. Or used to be. The slip was empty. On the adjacent boat, Winter's old neighbor Segal watched as Evan stared at the empty space.

'He's gone,' Segal said, his voice already showing signs of the alcohol that was his staple diet.

For a moment Evan wondered if he was talking about Winter, the *gone* referring to his death. But even Segal couldn't think that Winter had taken his boat with him to the big ocean in the sky. He must be talking about Lockhart.

'Where to?'

'No idea.'

The satisfaction on his face suggested that he wouldn't tell him even if he knew.

'Any idea when he'll be back?'

Segal just shrugged, do I look like my brother's keeper?

'And who is *he*?' Evan said, the irritation in his voice showing.

Again the shrug.

Evan gave up, headed back towards the security office. Rodriguez had returned from his rounds when he got there. He greeted Evan warmly. Evan couldn't help but wonder how much the story of Winter's discovery and in particular Rodriguez's part in that discovery got exaggerated as Rodriguez went from boat to boat.

'I see the boat's gone.'

'Yeah. It went out early yesterday. Before I started my shift. Hasn't been back since.'

'You know who took it out?'

'The other guy who owned it with George, I reckon. Saw him on the boat the day before he left, stocking up with provisions.'

Evan fished the photograph Crow had given him out of his wallet. He was glad it was Rodriguez he was showing it to and not Deutsch in Key West. Or even Cortez who would have given him a hard time over it. Even so, Rodriguez laughed when he handed it over.

'What is this? It looks like it belongs in a museum.'

Even though he'd studied the photograph a number of times Evan couldn't stop his gaze from settling on the grim-faced man next to Vaughan Lockhart, the one Crow had written off as *nobody important*. And what was in his left hand. Again he got the impression of barely-contained glee behind the unsmiling features. He felt a sudden urge, inexplicable words on his lips that he bit back to stop himself from blurting out *he doesn't belong in a museum, he belongs in a cage.* He forced himself to point to Lockhart.

'Is there any chance that's a younger version of the guy you saw? I know it's old so don't worry if you can't identify him.'

Rodriguez took a closer look anyway, then shook his head.

'Like you say, it's an old photo. Could be anyone.' He looked again. 'Where was this taken?'

'Vietnam.'

Rodriguez nodded like he'd heard of it, recognized it because of the new restaurant that had opened up, did great spring rolls with peanut sauce. He went to hand the photo back, then decided against it, looked for a third time.

'What?' Evan said.

Suddenly Rodriguez looked as if he'd eaten too many of the spring rolls too quickly without chewing properly.

'Can't be,' he said more to himself than Evan. 'It's too old to tell.'

Now it was Evan's stomach that made its presence felt, a gnawing hunger, an emptiness.

'Can't be what?'

Rodriguez glanced around quickly as he thrust the photo back at Evan. Anybody watching might have thought something illegal had just changed hands. Rodriguez looked like he wanted to disappear back into his office, shut the door until Evan had gone.

'There were a couple of guys.'

No story that ends well ever starts that way. Nobody ever said, there were these two guys who walked up to me and handed me a hundred bucks, told me to enjoy myself. So the gnawing feeling in Evan's gut intensified.

'They were asking the same questions as you. Except I didn't tell them jack shit. They had a photo too, but it was a lot more recent than that.' He pointed at the photograph now safely in Evan's hand.

'Was it the guy who took the boat out?'

Rodriguez scrunched his face up, rocked his head from side to side.

'Could've been.'

'You tell them that?'

Rodriguez pulled a face, are you serious?

'I wouldn't piss on them if they were on fire.'

'You didn't like them?'

It looked to Evan as if Rodriguez was about to launch into a long diatribe on exactly what he didn't like about them. It would have been better if he had, would've saved some time, but for the moment he asked him something to head him off.

'You reckon they could've been the men you said the night guard thought he heard on Winter's boat?'

The unspoken implication was clear.

The ones who filled him up with whisky and most likely drowned him.

'Could've been,' Rodriguez said again. Now it seemed he wasn't going to be put off by Evan from running through exactly what he didn't like about the two men asking questions. Evan listened patiently as he complained about their bad attitude in general and towards Latinos in particular and how it wouldn't have hurt if one of them had paid a little more attention to personal hygiene and as for the other one chewing gum the whole time with his mouth open making this irritating smacking sound as he talked to you so you could see everything inside his fat mouth and still get a kick in the face from his breath despite the gum.

Evan felt like he'd had a kick in the head from a horse. It couldn't be coincidence. It had to be the same man who'd been on Winter's boat before, who had most likely drowned him. Now he was looking for Lockhart.

'You okay?' Rodriguez said, thinking maybe he shouldn't have gone on so long, bored the guy so much. He looked like he was punch-drunk.

'Yeah, I'm good. You didn't tell them anything?'

Rodriguez shook his head proudly.

'Not a damn thing. Pretended to look at their photo. Told them I'd never seen him in my life.'

Evan couldn't help but glance around, a shiver rippling the back of his neck despite the warmth of the sun. Because if they hadn't gotten the answers they were after from Rodriguez, there was every chance they were hanging around somewhere, waiting to see if anybody else came looking for Lockhart. The thought clearly hadn't crossed Rodriguez's mind. Otherwise he wouldn't be laughing the way he was now. Evan realized he'd missed what Rodriguez had said, what he thought was so funny.

'What was that?'

'I said I sure as hell didn't tell them where he's gone.'

Evan resisted the temptation to grab his throat and shake him.

'You know where he is?'

'Yep. Guy I know runs fishing charters. He said he saw the boat anchored at Bird Key Harbor. That's out by the Dry Tortugas, about seventy miles away. It's as good a place as any if you're looking to keep your head down. That's why the guy I know recognized the boat, because of all the fuss. It's not every day I find a guy drowned under his boat. You can't blame his partner for wanting to get away from all the rubberneckers.'

Evan smiled to himself at how Rodriguez had assumed full credit for discovering Winter's body, forgetting that it was Evan who had alerted him to it. What wasn't so amusing was the fact that Rodriguez had it completely wrong. Lockhart hadn't taken the boat out to avoid unwanted attention from people who had nothing better to do than stand and point at the spot where a man had drowned. He'd done it because he was worried it was his turn next.

He was about to leave Rodriguez to it, maybe to make another round of the marina in case there was anybody he'd missed, anybody who hadn't heard his story, when something struck him. Something that had been pushed aside at the mention of a man chewing gum.

Rodriguez's smiling and slightly flushed face was very different to five minutes ago. Then, he'd looked like he was the one who'd swallowed a couple of gallons of salty seawater, not Winter. It was when he'd taken a third and final look at the photo. Evan held it up again. All the pleasure slipped off Rodriguez's face, the sickly pallor creeping back.

'What did you mean when you said it's too old to tell? Right before you told me about the two guys asking around.'

Rodriguez swallowed, his Adam's apple bobbing above his now-too-tight collar and tie. He worked his finger down under the collar, stretched it, the relief showing in his face.

'I told you. I couldn't be sure if that's the guy I saw on Winter's boat.'

Evan shook his head, you're not getting off that lightly. He pointed at the younger version of Lockhart in the photo.

'That was him. You said it after you looked again. You did a double take, then said it's too old to tell. Come on, Luis. It was me who called you when I found Winter under the boat, turned you into a local celebrity.'

Rodriguez gave up trying to get his fingers under his collar, undid his top button instead. He glanced over to the visitors' parking lot, then back to Evan. The corners of his mouth turned down.

'It wouldn't have happened if they hadn't been so cocky, if

they'd parked like normal people in one of the spaces. Not these guys. They drive up and stop right there.' He pointed to a place a couple of yards away, his finger quivering with indignation or fear, Evan couldn't tell which. 'Like they own the place. Lucky nobody else wanted to come in. I reckon they'd have thrown anybody who honked at them to get out of the way into the water. So then they get out and start asking questions, showing me their photo. And there's this old guy sitting in the back seat, staring straight ahead. Now I know how old people feel the cold but he's wearing this big black coat and under it he's got on a leather waistcoat that looks like it's made from lots of little animal skins all sewed together. Rats if you ask me. Then he turns to look at me. It's like they've been out robbing graves and they've got one of the stiffs they just dug up in the back seat because they couldn't fit them all in the trunk and they didn't want to have to go back twice. I swear to God if I woke up in the middle of the night and saw this guy standing at the bottom of the bed I'd think the Grim Reaper had sent his granddaddy to get me. Then he smiled at me. Like I'll be coming for you. *Real* soon. Like I say, he was old and he didn't have many teeth left. But the ones he did were filed to points.'

Evan let him ramble on, not wanting to break the flow of words pouring nervously out of his mouth, knowing what was coming, needing to hear the words spoken. Wishing he knew what the hell it meant when he did. Rodriguez took hold of the photograph. Pointed to the man standing beside Lockhart. The one Crow had explained away with a flick of the hand and a dismissive *nobody important*. The one who never came home.

Then a sudden gust of wind whipped up and the sun disappeared behind a cloud while they stood there, two men holding a faded photograph between them as it fluttered in the wind. It seemed to Evan that a chill descended on them that was deeper than could be explained by the temporary obscuring of the sun and a sea breeze, one that he felt in his bones. He understood then why Crow might have lied to him. Rodriguez cleared his throat, swallowed hard. He lifted his hand as if to cross himself or touch the gold crucifix around his neck, for fear that he was tempting fate, speak of the Devil and he shall appear.

'I couldn't tell you if that one'—he tapped his finger on Lockhart's face—'was the one I saw on the boat. But I'd swear on my mother's life the other one is the old guy in the car.'

The sudden raucous shriek of a gull overhead made both men duck instinctively, snapping them out of the chill private world that had enveloped them as Rodriguez told his story. They grinned sheepishly at each other. Maybe even thought about punching each other playfully on the shoulder to cover their embarrassment. Then the cloud overhead moved away and they felt the sun's warmth on their skin again.

The Devil hadn't put in an appearance, nor the Grim Reaper. But the man with the pointy teeth who'd caused those childish fears to take hold of Evan and Rodriguez for that brief moment, who'd made Rodriguez seek the comfort of his religion and Evan to wonder what the hell Crow had gotten him into, wasn't far away. He was watching them now from the back of his car, his men silent in the front seats. Bormann, the one who liked to chew gum with his mouth open had it respectfully closed now, his teeth moving slowly and carefully so as not to make a sound. His partner, Hitch, the one that Rodriguez thought should pay more attention to his personal hygiene, was busy with his camera.

The man in the back had no idea where Vaughan Lockhart had disappeared to. But he had a good idea who was going to lead them to him. And what would happen when he did.

39

EVAN MADE THE NOW-FAMILIAR DRIVE FROM MARATHON DOWN through the lower keys to Key West in just over an hour. He kept a careful eye on his rearview mirror the whole way. The men who questioned Rodriguez might well be following, looking for alternative ways to locate Lockhart after he refused to tell them anything.

What he couldn't have known was that as soon as those men had seen him show Rodriguez the photograph, one of them had slipped out of their car and attached a GPS tracker to the underside of his rental. So they were able to stay a long way back as they followed him to Key West and let the electronics do the hard work.

According to Rodriguez the easiest way to get to the Dry Tortugas was to take the *Yankee Freedom III*, a luxury catamaran that departed for Fort Jefferson at 8:00 a.m. each day. But after Rodriguez told him about the men, he knew he didn't have the luxury of waiting another day.

As it turned out, he had no choice. He toured Garrison Bight and the Historic Seaport, going from boat to boat in an attempt to rent a suitable craft. Most weren't capable of making the one-hundred-and-fifty-mile round trip. Of those that were, none were prepared to let him take the boat out alone. And he had a feeling that he wouldn't want a charter boat skipper looking over his shoulder when he got there.

Parking in the lot of the Key West Ferry Terminal on Grinnell Street, he thought nothing about the Mercedes sedan that pulled into an empty space a couple of cars down.

If he'd been there, Rodriguez would have thought something about it. He'd have approved of the way it parked properly in one of the designated parking spaces this time. Not just driven up and stopped, blocking the whole damn road, like it had when the men inside had questioned him. He'd also have approved of the way that the large man who quickly jumped out and followed Evan into the terminal building kept his mouth shut while he chewed his gum. In fact, standing a little way behind Evan watching him to see whether he would buy a ticket to Fort Myers or to Fort Jefferson on Garden Key in the Dry Tortugas, he pushed it up into his gums with his tongue, stopped chewing altogether.

So when Evan suddenly turned to look at him—for no reason that he could explain other than a vague impression of being observed—he didn't see a man chewing gum which would have instantly alerted him. He saw instead a large man with a confused look on his face. As if he was thinking that he'd wandered into the wrong building. So he thought nothing of it and joined the line to buy a ticket on the *Yankee Freedom III* for the next day. When he looked again the man was nowhere in sight.

Because the man had indeed been in the wrong building. Having established Evan's destination, he had no interest in buying a ticket for himself and his partner on the ferry to wait until the next day and then to make the trip with a bunch of excited kids and their stressed parents. Instead, he returned to the Mercedes sedan to collect his partner. Then, together, they went in search of an appropriate boat to rent. One with a two-hundred-gallon gas tank sufficient to take them the seventy nautical miles to the Dry Tortugas and back again once their business was concluded.

They were more successful than Evan had been. Mainly because threats of physical violence by men who are clearly prepared to use it to get what they want are more persuasive than polite enquiries. Nobody wants to be towed to the Dry Tortugas by their neck.

The Topaz 28 Sportfish that they eventually rented was slower than the high-speed catamaran with a comfortable cruising speed of twenty knots. It would take them four hours to get to their destination. Setting off immediately, they had plenty of time to get there, do what they had to do, and then get a few hours' shut-eye before the man they'd followed from the Marathon marina turned up.

That man, Evan, now left the terminal building and stood looking out over the water, deciding how to fill his evening. That wasn't strictly true. He knew how, it was just a question of where. Looking to his left he saw the Half Shell Raw Bar, no more than eighty yards away. It was one of the few bars he hadn't made it to the last time he was down. That made it a no-brainer. He got a table overlooking the water and ordered a beer and a bucket of middle neck clams steamed in garlic. Then he called the same bed and breakfast he'd stayed at last time to book himself a room.

If he hadn't been busy with his phone and had looked directly ahead of him, out over the water towards the entrance to the Historic Seaport, he'd have seen the Topaz 28 Sportfish leaving the marina to begin its four-hour trip. On board Bormann chewed happily and noisily on a fresh piece of gum, the previous piece now stuck to the underside of the captain's chair.

Not that Evan would have been able to see him chewing from that distance even if he'd been looking. As it was, his mind was too preoccupied with a nagging unease that every minute was a minute wasted. That somehow the men who had been behind were now ahead. If that wasn't bad enough, as the first swallow of the ice-cold beer slipped down his neck, his thoughts turned to Guillory. They were not good thoughts. The location didn't help. He looked around him. Took in the people laughing and talking in noisy groups, the tables in front of them groaning under the weight of plates piled high with shrimp and crab, oysters and clams, all washed down with beer or crisp white wine, while above them the gulls screeched and swooped, fighting over the scraps, and all of it played out before the perfect backdrop of the spotless white boats in the marina and the endless blue of the sea beyond.

Then he thought of Kate Guillory.

He didn't suppose there was much laughing and shouting going on where she was. Waiting to meet with her partner Ryder for a confrontation that could only end badly. Or sitting in the aftermath of it. Not much of a choice. Not much in the way of plates of seafood either. Or cold beers and wine. No sea or gulls at all.

The stark contrast depressed him, his own beer turned to ashes in his mouth. Except it was worse than that. Because the thought of Ryder brought back a memory that had slipped unnoticed into the back of his mind with all the events of the past few days. Now it was back with a vengeance. The memory of Ryder's words as they stood in the middle of the sidewalk and almost came to blows.

It must be her self-destructive streak that attracts her to you. Like a moth to the flame. She gets it from her old man.

Meant as an insult to himself, it had pierced him deeper than any insult ever could. It wasn't only the petty feelings of jealousy or hurt pride that Ryder should have knowledge of her past that she hadn't shared with him. Those he could deal with. It wasn't anything from her past that he feared. It was what that spoke of the future that made him push aside the bucket of clams, his appetite deserting him.

So he called her.

Before she said a word he knew she wouldn't be starting the conversation with another crack about his *girlfriend*, Ana Maria Cortez.

'How's it going down in sunny Florida?' she said instead.

He told her about the setback with the chewing gum evidence and the resultant washing of hands.

'No more Ana Maria for you,' she said, unable to stop herself.

'Not in an official capacity, no.'

The comment passed her by. Or she chose to ignore it. He told her the positive news about Lockhart's whereabouts and his plans to find him in the morning.

Which would of course be too late.

If you can hear somebody listening politely and making all the right noises in the right places, that's what she was doing now, her mind elsewhere. So he went to that place himself.

'Did you talk to Ryder yet?'

He might as well have asked did the axe fall yet?

'Not yet. He's picking me up later.'

That was when he realized that she wasn't sitting at home alone with only her thoughts for company. He heard background noises, voices he recognized, a song on the jukebox —Nathaniel Rateliff's *Howling At Nothing*—that made him wish he was sitting up at the bar next to her.

'You're in the Jerusalem?'

'Uh-huh.'

'Not with Donut?'

Maybe it was the horror in his voice, but she laughed out loud.

'No.'

'You had me worried there.'

'Don't be. He hates it here. Says it reminds him of you, puts him off his beer. Anyway, he's picking me up later.'

The constant talk of Ryder only brought his words back to Evan.

It must be her self-destructive streak that attracts her to you. Like a moth to the flame. She gets it from her old man.

But the words he wanted to ask wouldn't come. Neither of them said anything for a couple of beats. She broke the silence first and it was as if she knew what was on his mind.

'Why were you calling?'

'Just to see how you are.'

The brief silence that followed made him think of lips without lipstick pressed tightly together and the memory of his arm thrown angrily from her shoulder.

'You don't have to worry. I'm not sitting on the bed looking at my gun and picking it up and putting it in my mouth and then putting it down again.'

He wanted to shout down the line at her, *Jesus Christ Kate, let somebody show a little concern.* But his guilt that it was exactly what he'd been thinking before he made the call stopped him. That, and wondering if she'd unknowingly answered his unasked question about her father. A question that would most definitely remain unasked for the time being. So he made light of the situation.

'Good. They don't allow guns in the Jerusalem.'

'Lucky for you, eh?'

He pretended he didn't know what she meant, didn't know

that what she was saying was she'd have shot him a long time ago if they did. Then, seeing as he didn't feel comfortable asking her about her father, he asked the other question that was never far from his mind

'Did you hear from Lydia about Liverman yet?'

There was a pause. Which he didn't like. Then something that he liked even less. Her response.

'Gotta go. Ryder's just stuck his head around the door.'

'They must have enlarged the doorway then,' he said, so as not to blurt out an accusatory *prove it!* If he remembered, he'd ask the manager Kieran if he could take a look at the CCTV footage.

Because he'd put good money on the fact that he'd just heard an excuse to get off the phone rather than answer the question.

40

RYDER WAS BACK IN THE CAR BY THE TIME GUILLORY CAME OUT OF the Jerusalem Tavern. She climbed into the passenger seat, filling the car with the smells of the bar.

'You okay?' he said.

'I'm fine.'

He didn't believe a word of it. At least she didn't say what she was really thinking.

Cut the pleasantries and the concern, get to the damn point.

Because once he did, it wouldn't make much difference how she'd been before. She was being unfair, knew he was genuinely concerned about her. So she played the game, the one where you dance back and forth, slowly moving in for the kill.

'Why wouldn't I be?'

She almost laughed out loud as she said it. His face looked like he'd never laugh again.

'Because the last time I saw you, you were charging down the street towards your brother's grave. Like you were going to walk straight through anyone or anything that got in your way.'

'It helps me think. Get some perspective on my life.'

He didn't push it. With what she had on her plate at the

moment, she'd have to visit the Arlington National Cemetery to give her all the perspective she needed. So he avoided coming right out with the real reason for wanting to talk to her, asked her something he thought was a little more straightforward. Shows how much he knew.

'What was all that with Buckley and the weird girl in the diner, hiding from me in the ladies' room?'

She shook her head, eyes down. Ashamed at the things she'd kept from him, the things she was still keeping from him.

'Believe me when I say that it doesn't matter.'

'Whatever.'

He drummed his fingers on the steering wheel, stared out through the windshield. She wanted to shout at him, *just spit it out, tell me about the DNA.* Except that would have been too quick. Too good for her.

'There's been a development in the Garfield killing. Something you can help with.'

Something she can help with!

She didn't know if she wanted to laugh or cry or scream. Help how? By admitting it first? Might as well get it over with.

'There's something—'

'It's to do with Curtis Banks. He's one of your informants, isn't he?'

The name stopped her dead. How much worse could things get? Not only was her DNA on the bucket, Banks had come forward, told them he'd let her into the house. She squeezed out a confirmation, her voice a strangled croak, her mouth dry.

'He read about the killing in the paper. Then, being the fine upstanding citizen that he is, he sat around for a couple of days, no doubt trying to figure out how to turn the situation to his advantage. Maybe go to the papers first.'

He buzzed the window down to let in some fresh air, let out his disgust. It was going to take a lot more than an open window in a stationary vehicle to cope with the heat that was coming off her body. He took a deep breath, carried on.

'You always said he was a douchebag.'

She was going to punch him in the side of the head in a minute. She had an almost irresistible urge to bang his face into the windshield.

'But for once he decided to do the right thing.'

He turned to face her directly then, shifting his whole body in the seat. To get a better view of the reaction when he delivered the killing thrust.

'He's got some photographs.'

He was smiling openly now, no shame. They'd been partners for more years than she could remember. Didn't that count for anything?

'They're grainy. He's got a shitty old phone and he didn't want to use the flash. Obviously. But they're good enough.'

She couldn't believe Evan had been so right about him for all these years. How could he take so much pleasure in doing this to her?

'I don't know what he was doing there, but he's got photographs of a couple of guys going into Garfield's house on the night he was murdered.'

Everything stopped.

Her mind. Her breathing. All motor functions. She sat frozen for a period of time that seemed to go on forever. Then it was as if the man who had pumped her full of fear and worry until she was huge and bloated and fit to burst had pricked her with the pin he'd held against her skin for the past days, sent her flying around the interior of the car until eventually she dropped flaccid and empty onto the passenger seat.

'You okay?' he said to the boneless mass of flesh collapsed in the seat beside him.

'Yeah. It's just a bit warm in here.'

She buzzed down her own window. Stuck her head out like an excited dog, convinced the thump of her heart against the door must be rocking the whole car.

'We've matched one of them to a guy on file, haven't managed to locate him yet. We're still working on the other one. We've got a partial print in the bedroom that matches the first guy...'

She tuned his voice out as he continued to run through the evidence that had been amassed against the two men, nodding as appropriate on autopilot, feeling guilty about her earlier thoughts, that he would take pleasure from bringing her down. It only reinforced what an impact the whole situation had had on her, the way it twisted her view of the world and everything and everyone in it. She was suddenly aware of a change in his tone, more than a change in the words. It was less positive enthusiasm as he ran through the evidence and more cautious doubt as he made a suggestion.

'I'm sorry,' she said, 'I missed that.'

That seemed to make it worse, to have to repeat something he was unsure about the first time around.

'I said I've got copies on my phone. You can take a look if you like.'

What he didn't say: *it might be the guys who abducted and beat you.*

She stuck out her hand, let me see. He found the photographs, handed the phone over. She'd never seen the men who beat her. But she knew she'd recognize them when she did, couldn't have told you how.

She looked at the image on the screen, saw a garden variety thug.

'That's the first guy, the one we've identified. His name's Roach. As in cockroach.'

She knew instinctively, from the coldness that started in her gut and sent its chilly fingers out into every part of her body that it was the one she'd named Dog's Breath. She knew for sure that he'd been in the house when she was there. Hiding until she'd gone, then heading upstairs to put the pathetic wretch that was Robert Garfield out of his misery.

She swiped across to the next image, saw the man who'd smelled like a stale ashtray. They both looked very ordinary as she sat next to the reassuring bulk of Ryder, looked like the sort of creeps who'd beat a woman tied to a chair with a hood over her head. He was right, they were grainy. They were still good enough to put faces to the faceless demons that visited her every night. She handed the phone back. She wouldn't need it again, wouldn't easily forget.

'I never saw their faces,' she said in reply to the unasked question.

But I know it's them.

He took back the phone. Studied the face of the man on the small screen in his large hand. She watched the change in his face out of the corner of her eye. The tightening of his jaw even under the heavy jowls, the flaring of the nostrils. It made her feel bad all over again. She hadn't deserved what she'd gotten. But she sure as hell didn't appreciate what she had.

She swallowed hard, looked away out the window at the ungrateful bitch staring back at her.

'You said there's something I can help with.'

'Yeah. Curtis Banks. He gave us the photographs, told us where he took them. But he won't tell us anything else, what he was doing there. He says he'll only talk to you.'

She kept her face deadpan, her eyes flat, shifted seamlessly into deception mode. Seamlessly on the face of it. Underneath not feeling so proud of herself.

'I'll talk to him.'

He nodded, satisfied.

Or so it seemed for just a moment. Then he must have decided it was time to make her feel *really* bad about herself, worse than she did already. That was going to be some party trick. He eased her into what was coming by swallowing nervously himself, giving a little cough. By this time most of the color had gone from his normally florid face and his hands wouldn't do what he wanted them to. Unless he wanted them flapping like a fish in the bottom of a boat.

Then he cleared his throat again and she wanted to scream.

'I just wanted to say I don't need to know what's going on with you and Buckley and whatever you're up to. I don't want to either. Because you've still got a way to go before you're thinking straight.'

He paused, allowed her time to give a small nod of acknowledgement or gratitude. Then he held up his phone.

'We're concentrating on the men in Banks's photographs at the moment. I don't even want to start to think about what misguided, half-assed notions made Buckley break into that house in the middle of the night. But I'm happy that's all it was. Buckley thinking he's the Lone Ranger, no real harm done.'

She made a vague, noncommittal grunt, thinking just give him time.

He pretended he'd finished, slipped his phone back into his pocket. She waited, played the game. His face suddenly lit up as if an amusing anecdote had just crossed his mind.

'You'll never believe the stuff those crime scene geeks get into. Seems they measured the line of dried sick on the inside of the bucket to work out how much was in it. Then they compared it to what was on the floor and down the walls. It came up short.'

He shook his head and she agreed with him, that's crime scene geeks for you.

'They reckon half of it went over some poor schmuck's head. So when we catch up with this guy we'll be sniffing his hair, combing it for bits of carrot.' He ran his fingers through his own hair as he said it, sniffed them, his nose turned up in disgust. 'Can you imagine it? A head full of that deviant Garfield's puke. Probably went in their eyes and ears, maybe even got some in their damn mouth. That's punishment enough for anybody. I don't reckon you'd ever be able to get the stench off you. Christ, I think I can smell it now, just talking about it.'

'Me too,' she said with heartfelt conviction, wondering if that absolution covered sins yet to be committed as well as those past, 'me too.'

41

After leaving the Half Shell Raw Bar Evan collected his car from the ferry terminal parking lot, then drove the length of Duval Street to check into his bed and breakfast. That was all he did. Check in, throw his bag on the bed, then head back out again on foot. Not because he planned on carrying on drinking. But because it was a beautiful evening. One that made you want to stretch your legs, fill your lungs with fresh sea air. And because he might end up someplace where he didn't want the inconvenience of a car license plate advertising his identity.

It wasn't that he didn't believe Detective Cortez when she'd told him that she'd visited the burned-out guest house. He had to walk past it anyway to get to his second destination. As on his previous visit, he scooted down the side of the house, then vaulted over the low white picket fence into the secluded yard. It was exactly as Cortez had described. Pressing his nose up against the window, he saw that the room had been gutted. All the burned and sodden furniture had been removed and carted away, the blackened wallpaper stripped from the walls. In the yard the small swimming pool had been drained. The pool furniture was also gone—along with the chewing gum. He checked the small pool house in case it had been stored in there, out of the way to protect it while the soot-stained contents of the house were brought out. It too was empty.

Climbing back over the fence he felt a little stupid. But he'd been passing, so what the hell. It made him feel better about Cortez, knowing that she wasn't part of the cabal that had gotten the case closed so abruptly. With that thought came a reminder of her parting words to him.

Watch your back.

Seventy nautical miles away on board the *Dead or Alive* anchored in Bird Key Harbor, Vaughan Lockhart would have done well to heed that advice.

For the moment, in Key West, Evan continued on his way towards the cemetery. Instead of heading directly to the house on Passover Lane, he cut across town through the back streets, ended up on Olivia Street just past where a number of houses were built on the cemetery side of the street, surrounded on three sides by the graves and burial vaults. He moved further down the street away from them, then made use of a convenient road sign to vault over the iron railings. From there he wound his way through the graves, heading on a diagonal course across the cemetery towards Passover Lane. He found the location where he'd almost been run over by the guy mowing the grass, then got settled into the hidey-hole where he took his unauthorized breaks. Like the last time, he had a perfect view of the house that had set in motion a killing spree that had claimed four lives. And counting.

Two hours later, he was sick of the sight of the perfect view of the house. He'd have happily swapped it for a crap view of something going on. As it was, his butt was damp from the grass, his back cold and stiff from the stone vault he was leaning against. All around him pairs of disembodied red eyes watched him, gradually drawing closer as the rats' courage and inquisitiveness increased.

There was no point waiting any longer.

He stood and stretched. At his feet the grass came alive as the rats scattered in every direction, their hopes of a warm meal dashed. He picked his way carefully between the graves for fifty yards, then clambered over the railings into the street. Keeping to the deeper shade of the mature trees and palms in the front yards, he headed back to the house he'd been watching. He swung his legs quickly up and over the low picket fence, darted down the side of the house.

'The hell you think you're doing?'

The voice came out of nowhere, somewhere in the darkness of the yard next door. Evan jumped as if the lid of the vault he'd been leaning against a minute ago had opened and a dry, bony hand had reached out and tousled his hair. A man stepped forward out of the bushes, a shotgun held loosely in his hands. For the moment it was pointed at the ground.

'I've been watching you for the past hour, sitting in the graveyard. What are you? Some kind of ghoul? You're not a burglar.'

It was a strange thing to say to a man caught on somebody else's property in the middle of the night. Evan didn't think it was his open, honest face that made the guy say it. He struggled for a moment as his pulse subsided, then found his voice.

'Why's that?'

The guy's teeth suddenly appeared in the dark as he smiled. It made Evan think of the rats in the cemetery.

'Because no burglar is gonna be stupid enough to break into that house.' He swung the barrel of the shotgun up towards it as he spoke, sent Evan's pulse racing again. 'Not anybody who knows who owns it, that's for sure. Besides, there's nothing in it. Apart from a bed and some booze, of course.' The last words came out on the back of a laugh, the sort that follows a dirty joke. Except there was nothing funny about what the guy was implying.

'So who does own it?'

The neighbor dropped his voice.

'Phil Kovitz.'

The name meant nothing to Evan. The lack of recognition on his face surprised the guy with the shotgun, his voice going back up a notch.

'You don't know who that is?' He sounded as if they were talking about the President. 'Florida Phil?'

Evan shook his head slowly. He'd still never heard of him. Not that he needed to. It was enough to know that you don't mess with a guy who's got a state as part of their name. Or break into his house. The neighbor's smile got wider.

'Then maybe you're stupid enough after all. You're not a reporter, are you?'

Evan shrugged, kept his mouth shut. The guy was unlikely to shoot him or even call the police if he thought he was something as legitimate as a reporter. So let him think it. Not only that, he didn't reckon he'd have to wait too much longer before the guy asked and answered all of his own questions. It seemed the guy assumed he'd hit the nail on the head.

'Thought so. Well you're not going to find out much. Not with who Phil's got on the payroll.'

Evan was tempted to take a gamble, say *who, Deutsch?* It would explain his dismissive and obstructive attitude. But he didn't. Because the neighbor was shaking his head now, looked as if he was about to spit.

'Bastard shouldn't be allowed to get away with it.'

'One rule for them, a different rule for us,' Evan suggested.

'You got that right.' Now the guy did spit, as if he was getting rid of all the world's unfairness and corruption. 'Who'd you say you worked for?'

'I didn't.'

Again the guy jumped to conclusions.

'Freelance, huh? Well, you won't—'

'I know. Not with who Phil's got on the payroll.'

The guy squinted at him. Like he wasn't sure whether Evan had just made a joke at his expense.

'You're from out of town.'

'That's right.'

'So how'd you hear about it?'

Evan was hoping they'd move on soon from the current situation of two guys discussing something they both assumed the other man knew all about and as a result didn't actually say anything. So he kept it going, kept it vague. And took another gamble.

'You know, rumors. We're always on the lookout for stories about the guys with all the money getting away with murder.'

It wasn't just an everyday phrase, the use of the word *murder* a deliberate encouragement for the guy to open up. Then he worked a worried look onto his face. As if he'd just realized that what he said could be misconstrued.

'Not literally, of course.'

The neighbor gave him a look. Like he wasn't just from out of town, more like from a different planet. One where the inhabitants manage to live long and full lives without the benefit of a brain.

'Are you serious?'

Evan put a bit more stupid in his expression. Guillory would've said she couldn't tell the difference.

'What?'

The guy was shaking his head now, good one, you nearly had me there.

'You're saying that's what happened?' Evan said, squeezing some incredulous in with the stupid.

From the way the guy was gripping the shotgun more tightly, Evan guessed he was getting bored or annoyed with the conversation, maybe both. He held up his hands.

'Seriously. I didn't know. I just heard there might be a story.'

The guy's grip relaxed on the shotgun. Even if the suspicion that Evan was jerking him around was still on his face.

'Yeah, well, you're not gonna hear it from me. You'll have to make up some lies for yourself. Like you normally do.'

He spat again, this time ridding the world of sensationalism and the gutter press, having already put unfairness and corruption to bed.

Suddenly a woman's voice cut through the night air. It was the sort of voice that makes a man wish he'd stayed single, makes him feel a shriveling sensation in his underwear.

'Walter! You out there?'

Walter's voice dropped as low as his face.

'Yeah, I'm here.'

Evan felt like saying he could see why he spent his evenings in the yard in the dark.

'What you doing?'

Walter didn't answer quickly enough. But it wasn't an irritated repetition of the question that came back. It was laughter. Laughter that made you think of a head shaking at the ways of men and how the world hadn't changed one bit despite what the politicians and the feminists and all the rest of them wanted to tell you.

'You ain't gonna see no titties through that window. Not now she's dead. Or were you hoping he's moved another one in already?'

Then the banging of the screen door, the laughter still audible behind it. The two men stared at each other for a long moment. Evan didn't think it was worth asking who the woman who was now dead was and how she got to be that way. Walter confirmed it for him with a wave of the shotgun in his direction.

'Just piss off and don't come back. Unless you want to hang around while I give Phil a call.'

If it hadn't been for the shotgun, Evan would have told him not to take it out on him just because his wife knew what he did hiding in the bushes in the dark. But the gun was for real and Walter looked as if the idea of calling Florida Phil was getting more attractive by the minute, maybe earn himself a spell inside the house when they got around to moving a new woman in. So he backed away slowly, taking his new-found information with him.

The house was owned by a man called Phil Kovitz. As you'd expect from a man who'd appropriated the state as part of his name, he enjoyed the respect and fear of criminals and honest citizens alike. His house contained nothing more than a bed and some booze. It wasn't too difficult to work out what went on in there that kept Walter's nose pressed tight up against the glass. And a woman had died.

That'd make you come crashing through the front door in your panic to get away.

But who was it?

Somebody who knew people who could make it all go away. Somebody who operated in a world where people dying was the standard means of making a problem disappear. He didn't want to be cynical but that narrowed it down to two possibilities—organized crime or politics. Or, hush your mouth, maybe the two of them in bed together.

At least Walter could rest easy that Evan hadn't heard it from him.

42

EVAN HEADED BACK TOWARDS HIS BED AND BREAKFAST, WALKED straight down Olivia Street and hit Duval directly opposite the Old Town Tavern & Beer Garden. It was an omen. He deserved a beer after two hours sitting in a graveyard, needed the noise and celebration of life. His mental state was in better condition than earlier too. The morbid thoughts of suicide by a gun in the mouth had been replaced by a more wholesome apprehension about what waited for him at the Dry Tortugas.

That apprehension wasn't helped by two men standing at the bar. One of them had a logo for a fishing charter boat on his shirt and a fresh black eye on his face. He was complaining loudly to the second man who had enough facial hair to stuff a small sofa about the two thugs who had forced him to rent his boat to them.

'I wouldn't have let them have it,' the bearded man said, full of beer-fueled bravado.

'You'd have let these bastards have it,' Black Eye assured him. 'One of them stuck his chewing gum up my nose.'

Evan could have told him he'd made a very good call, be thankful it was only chewing gum. He ordered a beer and took it outside onto the deck to get away from them and the thoughts that their conversation put into his head. He found a table next to a tree that grew through the overhead awning. Then he called Guillory. She answered immediately, background sounds as noisy as those that surrounded him.

'Where are you?'

'Where's it sound like?'

'The Jerusalem.'

'Yep. Kieran's just put another beer in front of me. I like Kieran.'

She sounded too bright and breezy to have spent the past hours drinking herself into a pit of depression. There was a noisy slurp in his ear, then a satisfied *aah*. Much as he hated to risk destroying her good spirits, he had to ask the question on his mind.

'What did Donut have to say?'

'He knows I was in Garfield's house.'

For a long moment he didn't know what to say. The words didn't fit with her tone of voice. She sounded as if Ryder had told her they'd all just gotten a raise.

'You mean you told him.'

'No.'

'Then how?'

'He just put it all together.'

It was time to say something stupid.

'Did you admit it?'

The long silence that followed spoke of compressed lips and long-suffering looks, of glancing around the Jerusalem for a suitable alternative to his head to smack.

'Good,' he said quickly. 'That would've been a bad idea.'

The noisy swallowing sounds that came down the line were her way of washing any remarks she might have back down her throat, drowning them before any permanent damage could be done.

And he was learning. He didn't compound matters by asking if Ryder thought she'd slit Garfield's throat. He kept it vague. Because there are times when vagueness is your friend.

'What about Garfield?'

She told him about her informant coming forward with the photos he'd taken of the men entering the house.

'He's happy that's the only line of inquiry that needs to be pursued.'

'And—'

'What about you?' There was a pause which he didn't like. Especially since he knew it was deliberate. 'Ah.'

It was a very different *ah* to the earlier *aah* that had followed her drinking her beer. The loss of an *a* makes all the difference, turns an expression of satisfaction into *oh dear.*

They sat without talking for a while. He let her play her little game. Then yawned noisily into his hand.

'Time for bed?' she said.

'Early start in the morning.'

The light-hearted tone of the ridiculous conversation didn't stop his stomach from tightening as he said the words.

'Okay, night, night,' he said.

Finally she gave in, let him off the hook.

'He said he didn't know what misguided half-assed notions made that ass Buckley break into the house in the middle of the night, but he was satisfied it was just you being an ass like usual.' He suspected that there were at least two additional *asses* in her version, didn't mention it. 'At least you called it in. But I think he knows the reason you called him was because you knew I'd been in there.'

What she didn't say was that everybody was being given a hell of a lot of slack over their misguided and illegal actions, all in the interests of preserving her sanity. Because if she'd spoken the words, she didn't think she'd have been able to stop the tears.

He cleared his throat, knowing what she was thinking without her having to say it. So he didn't ask her again if she'd heard from Lydia Strange. Because they both knew that if and when she did, more and worse things would happen. Things that would stretch the limits of professional blind eyes. Maybe to a point where they would snap.

What they both also knew was that if Lydia didn't make contact with information about Liverman, nobody was going to see the real Kate Guillory ever again.

He couldn't leave it like it was, the up-beat mood of a few minutes ago having somehow slipped away unnoticed.

'So you went back to the Jerusalem.'

'Yeah. But it's not the same without you.'

That wasn't what she said at all. That was just in his head. What she said was very different.

'Yeah. Seemed like a good idea after my reprieve. So we came back for a quick celebratory beer.'

It took a second to sink in. But only a second.

'We?'

'Uh-huh.'

'I thought you said he hates it in there. Because it reminds him of me.'

'He does. He made an exception. It's been an exceptional day.'

A sharp snort of laughter hit him in the ear before she smothered it. He had a bad feeling about what had caused it.

'I hope he didn't—'

'He did.'

'No.'

'Yep. He sat on your stool.'

He groaned so loudly the people on the next table turned to stare at him.

'It's never going to be the same.'

'It is a bit wobbly now,' she admitted.

'While he was sitting on it, he didn't—'

'Enough now,' she said and ended the call.

He felt a lot better having salvaged the conversation. Good enough to get out the photograph Crow had given him that he'd shown to Rodriguez. He stared at the two men in it, one of whom he'd be meeting in less than twelve hours' time. But again it was the other man who demanded his attention. Maybe it was two hours sitting in a graveyard with only the red eyes of the rats for company as they watched and waited, but he couldn't get Rodriguez's words out of his mind.

He held the photograph closer to the string lights suspended from the tree to get a better look. He stared hard at the man's left hand. Still he couldn't see what he held in it. As the light played over the photograph, flickering erratically as a sudden gust of wind caught and tossed the bulbs, he imagined the man's predatory face with its dark and knowing eyes smiling at last to reveal a mouthful of teeth all filed to points.

He knew by the chill in his stomach that had nothing to do with the cold beer that he'd drunk that Rodriguez had been right. He was looking at a younger version of an old man who chose to wear a patchwork leather waistcoat in the Florida heat.

He didn't want to think about the implications that had for tomorrow.

It wasn't the best thought to take to bed with you.

But it was a damn sight better than what was happening seventy nautical miles away.

VAUGHAN LOCKHART LAY ON THE BED IN THE MASTER STATEROOM of the *Dead or Alive*, staring up at the ceiling. With his hands behind his head and his ankles crossed, he had the look of a man without a care in this world or the next, bobbing gently on the calm waters of Bird Key Harbor with nothing but the sound of the sea lapping at the side of the boat to disturb the tranquillity.

His mind was as far from tranquil as could be. He picked up his phone from the bedside table where it sat on top of yesterday's newspaper, next to the Glock G19 with its reassuring 15-round capacity. Except it could have been a 115-round capacity and he still wouldn't have felt reassured knowing who was on their way.

He watched the video again. Paused it again at the same point where the unidentified man came crashing through the front door of the house on Passover Lane, his face obscured by the young couple taking the selfie.

If he could only identify him, he might still have a chance.

He knew what went on in that house, knew who owned it too. Phil Kovitz. Big-time property developer with links to organized crime and a reputation for intimidation and bribery and crooked land deals.

The house was a honeytrap. Politicians and state legislators and aldermen, men good at opening doors and even better at opening their zipper, lured into compromising situations. He even knew the girl they used, the one who'd died. Kovitz's one-time mistress, Eleanor.

Normally that was all it took. The threat of the gutter press and jealous wives, of photographs and videos of a proud man caught with his pants around his ankles, sharing a mistress with a criminal like Florida Phil. It worked a damn sight better than weeks or months wasted around a negotiating table.

And this time there was an added bonus.

The unidentified man had gone too far. Eleanor had ended up dead. And in a very nasty way. Now that was a politician in your pocket for life. Men might risk the loss of their reputation and influence, maybe even their career, if pushed too hard. Few would risk spending the rest of their life behind bars.

That's what you call a valuable business asset.

So it was something to be protected at all costs. If the unknown man who'd killed Eleanor was unlucky enough to be caught by everyday police work, the asset was worthless. You can't pull many strings from a six-by-eight prison cell. The only thing that a man grown soft on the comforts that money brings is going to pull in prison is a train.

Hence the clearing of the decks. The elimination of anybody and everybody who might be able to identify Eleanor's killer. As well as anybody linked to them. He was okay with that. Sometimes things have to be done for the greater good. The trouble was, you could go on forever. Where did it stop?

And therein lay the crux of the matter. He'd expected it to stop before it got to him. His righteous indignation burned like a flare in the night sky. And his guts turned to ice-water.

With thoughts and emotions that raw running through his mind and hijacking his body, it was a miracle that he fell asleep. But he did. Even though he'd popped more pills than he could remember, determined to stay awake during the hours of darkness, grab a few hours' sleep during the middle of the day when he could.

But the body's a strange thing. It rarely does what you want it to. So his eyes were closed, his mouth open, snoring softly when the Topaz 28 Sportfish nudged the *Dead or Alive* as it drew alongside. Then Bormann proved the people who mocked him wrong, chewed his gum and laughed at the same time when he read the name of the boat. The sign painter could've saved himself more than half of the ink.

He was a large man, and heavy. The *Dead or Alive* dipped slightly when he stepped on board, more so when his compadre joined him.

In the master stateroom Lockhart stirred, some atavistic, subconscious survival instinct that still exists within us all despite the safety and comfort of our everyday lives responding instinctively to the subtle change, a movement that was out of rhythm with the waves.

Then he snapped wide awake.

He'd heard a sound that shouldn't be there. It was one he'd been expecting. Just not so soon. A careful footstep. A leather-soled careful footstep. Good for a city sidewalk or for kicking a man, the hard leather breaking delicate facial bones or rupturing internal organs. Not so good for creeping around the wooden deck of a boat in the middle of the night, surrounded by a silence so thick you could cut a piece of it with your knife to carry home with you.

Feeling stiff and unrested, he swung his feet off the bed, picked up the Glock from the table, its weight comforting in his hand. He wasn't going to sit and wait like some pitiful victim, hiding and hoping for the best until it was too late to do anything but die.

Outside, Bormann made an unexpected but welcome discovery. One that put a smile on his lips and a spiteful gleam in his eye. Because Bormann liked to hurt people when he got the opportunity. He picked it up, tested the point with his thumb. He couldn't have told you what it was called—a fishing gaff—but he could tell you what he was going to use it for.

It was a simple tool for a simple job, just a sharpened hook attached to a long wooden handle. Designed for hooking into fish to haul them from the water, swing them into the boat. And because fish are slippery slimy things that like to flap around a lot, the point was needle sharp. He swung it through the air, imagined the solid jerk as it bit into a man's arm or leg or even his neck.

Inside, Lockhart climbed the stairs from the master stateroom up to the salon. At the top he wiped his hands on his pants, switched to a double-handed grip on the Glock. Then crept stealthily towards the rear of the salon. The fighting chair was visible through the sliding glass doors. Beyond that lay the flat blackness of the night sea.

Then a sound from outside. He froze, head snapping to the left. Suddenly his resentment and anger flared again. He stared at the framed photograph on the wall, a copy of the one that seventy miles away Evan held up to the light in a bar in Key West, all but oblivious to what waited for him outside.

Was that what this was all about?

After all this time?

He couldn't drag his eyes away from the photograph even though it saddened him to look at it, the young man that he used to be, the heavy M60 machine gun balanced on his shoulder, a one-hundred-round bandolier wrapped around his hard body. He choked back a laugh at the Glock in his sweaty liver-spotted hands, imagined the weight of the M60 juddering in those same hands as he fired from the hip, cartridge links spewing into the air, the sound of five hundred rounds per minute moving through the chamber melding with the scream climbing from his throat. He saw himself, pivoting from the waist in a three-sixty-degree arc, spraying the walls of the salon and the ceiling and the flybridge above with a murderous rain of hot metal. Not stopping until the men who had dared come after him lay dead on the decks or blown away over the side, bodies shredded, their blood running between the deck boards and staining the sea. Didn't they know who he used to be?

Then his eyes shifted to the man in the photograph standing beside him. Hatred almost fifty years old stared back at him. Like a cold wind had sprung up sucking the warmth from his flesh, chilling his bones. Suddenly he felt like the old man he now was. Every damn day and minute of it. A pathetic figure, a man whose future was all behind him. And he felt afraid as he stared at the man he used to call a friend. The man who had sent the killers who waited for him somewhere outside.

Unlike Evan who didn't know and couldn't guess at what he held in his left hand, he knew exactly what it was. And he wondered if that was what waited for him, felt his scalp tighten as if a man had wound his fingers into his hair.

Looking for the last time at his erstwhile friend's arid features, he understood how a man's hatred can be nursed and kept alive, as fresh and vibrant as the day it was spawned, while the body that contains it withers and dies.

All you have to do is feed it.

He stood at the glass doors, listening, staring out at the Topaz 28 Sportfish tied up alongside. He cursed himself at having fallen asleep. If he'd stayed awake, he'd have heard it approach. He'd have had time to climb up into the flybridge or the tuna tower above it, shoot the bastards as they clambered awkwardly from one boat to the other. But he *had* fallen asleep. Now the roles were reversed. They were waiting for him. When he stepped outside there were likely two men and three directions he had to cover—port, starboard and immediately above.

He took hold of the handle. There was no way to slide it open without whoever was outside hearing, however well-oiled it might be. He stood, the Glock in one hand, the other on the door handle, listening hard. They weren't moving now, already in position. Waiting for him to make some pointless move against them. Like a cat waiting for a mouse to leave its hole, time on their side. No use trying to be cautious.

As he stood straining for any sound that might narrow the impossible odds, he heard something that at first made him think that he was indeed too old and it was high time he shuffled off this mortal coil.

He imagined that he heard music coming from outside.

Then when he realized that his mind wasn't in meltdown, that it was real, a spike of hope surged through him.

Only to die again just as quickly, replaced by a dread that was worse than before.

Because the music was too close. It was coming from the fighting chair. Played through a phone or some other portable device, placed there by the men who waited outside.

He knew the song. Could've quoted any statistics about it you cared to know. Sung the lyrics too if that's what you wanted.

Eleven minutes forty-one seconds long.

Released January 4, 1967.

Written by Jim Morrison, lead singer of The Doors.

The End.

And long before Francis Ford Coppola chose it for the soundtrack of the movie *Apocalypse Now*, the man who'd sent the killers after him had taken it for his own personal anthem.

It's surprising what a man with a sharp knife and a cruel streak can get done in eleven minutes and forty-one seconds.

He'd have laughed if his mouth wasn't full of dust. If it wasn't the final proof—as if he needed more—that he wouldn't live to see the sun rise. And that he'd pray for a merciful death long before that time came.

So fuck it all, I'll make you work for it.

He threw the door wide open, took two fast paces. Launched himself through the air. Up and over the padded bench between him and the fighting chair, aiming at the gap between them and the small protection that it afforded, diving headlong into the music and the wilderness of pain that awaited him.

From somewhere behind him and to his left a different sound, a whistling, the sound of something moving fast. The gaff cutting through the still night air in a murderous arc. Then an eruption of pain in his lower leg. The razor point digging into the meaty part of his calf, ripping through flesh and muscle and tendon as his momentum carried him onwards against Bormann's greater weight. A sudden jerk stopped him dead in mid-air. He hung suspended like a skydiver, arms extended in front of him, the Glock flying out of his hands. Then crashed to the deck, the searing white-hot pain of his ruined leg that colonized every cell of his being tearing a scream from his throat, melding with Morrison's crazy lyrics.

Then it was as if a man had thrown himself from the tuna tower, landed with his full weight on his back and shoulders. Mashing him into the wooden slats of the deck, pinned him squirming in the bottom of the boat like some record-breaking four-limbed wailing fish. The unforgiving deck came up hard and mercifully fast. Met his face with a bone-jarring impact, knocked the consciousness from him, music fading to black silence as Bormann twisted the gaff, hooked it deeper into his calf and dragged him along the deck.

'Shit.'

This from Bormann. He worked the gaff free, a look of disappointment on his face. The fun was over. For now. Until it was time to take the trophy. He stuck his large fingers in his large mouth, pulled out the gum he was chewing. He rolled it into a ball, stuck it on the bloodied point of the gaff.

'Don't want anybody to get hurt,' he told his partner. 'Not accidentally anyway. Now turn that shit off.'

44

If Evan thought he'd gotten bored sitting in a graveyard watching an empty house, Lydia Strange would have told him he didn't know his ass from a hole in the ground. Try sitting in your car watching people go in and out of the Jerusalem Tavern all night long. So she passed the time by nursing her hatred.

She didn't believe Guillory and her boyfriend the investigator.

How come her brother had left Guillory alive in the cabin and then gone off on an errand? One that had resulted in him getting killed. Had he forgotten to take any bullets along? Had to go back home for them? Silly me, I left them on the kitchen counter. They must think she was stupid. Which she wasn't at all. Just unbalanced.

So she'd followed Guillory, seen her go into the bar. Before long the fat detective turned up and stuck his fat head inside the door. But the conversation that followed when she came out and sat with him in his car didn't look to her like she was watching one police officer admit to another that she'd been in a house where a known pedophile had been viciously murdered. One that she'd previously assaulted.

Certainly not when they both got out and went into the bar together afterwards.

So. Two lies. If Guillory had been the only one she wanted she'd have waited and followed her home. Put a bullet in the base of her skull as she fumbled with her door key after all the booze she drank.

But she wasn't. She wanted Liverman, wanted him so bad her hatred was like a bitter taste on her tongue.

Thinking about Liverman made her think about her father. Good ol' Buck Strange. She could feel his hands on her now, the skin rough and calloused, the touch gentle. Her skin crawled. A shiver of revulsion that made her feel physically sick rippled across her skin, left it cold and clammy, as she thought about what he'd have done to her if Todd hadn't been there.

Todd was always there. Unlike their mother. She didn't remember very much about her. Just a child's intuition that she despised what she had brought into the world. Things were better when Aunt Daisy, her mother's sister, came to live with them. Daisy was a lot younger than their mother, prettier too with a better figure. Her mother said it hadn't had the life sucked out of it by two ungrateful children.

What she remembered most about her mother was that one day she just wasn't there anymore. They went down to breakfast and she was gone. Good ol' Buck said the whoring bitch had run off with another man. That's what they'd overheard him tell the police when they came to the house. It didn't stop them from dragging him shouting and cussing to the police station.

He hadn't come home that night while they beat him half-heartedly to see if he would crack. With just her and Todd and Aunt Daisy it had been one of the best nights of her young life.

Things changed after they released him. The sleeping arrangements mostly. Aunt Daisy wasn't sleeping in the spare room anymore. She'd been promoted to Good ol' Buck's bed.

From what Lydia could remember, the promotion came with a split lip and a black eye too. Daisy didn't seem to mind.

Except that one day she wasn't there anymore either. Only this time the police didn't come to the house. So maybe Good ol' Buck hadn't killed her too which is what Todd said had happened to their mother.

That left the three of them in the house. And she was the only girl. If Lydia had been paying more attention, she might have seen a pattern emerging. From her mother's age to the age of her younger sister Aunt Daisy and then on down . . .

She wouldn't ever forget the night she came within a hair's breadth of being promoted herself. Good ol' Buck had been a lot nicer to her after Daisy had left. She got as many fatherly hugs and chaste kisses on the top of her head as Todd got slaps and punches. And that was quite a few.

It was never any more than that. Despite what Todd said he was going to try to do to her one day. At the time she'd thought Todd was only saying it so that he could put his own hand down there to show her what he was talking about. In case she didn't understand.

She understood fast enough when it came to promotion night. She was still sharing her room with Todd at the time even though the spare was available. He said he was protecting her. She reckoned he just wanted to watch her undress even if she didn't have much to see.

Good ol' Buck got back later than usual from the bar. He'd taken to looking in on them before he turned in for the night. He always sat on the edge of her bed. Stroked her hair and kissed her on the forehead. She hated it, teeth gritted behind the strained smile. At least he kept his hands to himself.

Until promotion night.

Todd was in the bathroom when Good ol' Buck came into the room and sat on her bed. She'd smelled the beer and whisky on his breath all the way from downstairs, the cigarettes too. He smoothed her hair like he usually did. His hand was rough and calloused, the touch gentle.

Somehow, she knew it was going to be different tonight.

His hand moved down her cheek. Over her chin and onto her neck. She couldn't breathe, her limbs frozen. Eyes wide with terror. Then his hand was under her—

'Leave her alone.'

Todd standing in the doorway.

Good ol' Buck rising up without a word, his face twisted with fury. His arm uncoiling, backhanding Todd across the face. Snapping his head sideways into the door frame. Todd sagged, knees buckling.

Good ol' Buck was there to catch him. By the neck. He pinned him to the wall, fingers tightening around his throat. Lifting. Squeezing. A strangled wheezing coming from Todd's mouth, his face red and slick with sweat.

And Lydia unable to move, lying frozen in her bed.

Then a metallic click. Todd's hand came out of his pocket, the blade of his knife flashing in the light from the bedside lamp. Arm pumping. In and out, in and out. Burying the blade to the hilt in Good ol' Buck's belly and then his chest as his hands fell away from his son's neck. Over and over until he dropped to his knees, the shock and horror on his face the most beautiful sight she'd ever seen.

He fell onto his front like a wall collapsing, dust from the rug rising up into the air. Lydia was out of bed now, staring at the body twitching on the floor, mesmerized. When the blade slipped from Todd's fingers, she snatched it up. Dropped to her knees and sank the blade deep into her father's back, blood spurting, coating her face, her arms, as she thrust again and again.

Then into the kitchen after they dragged him down the

stairs. Undoing Good ol' Buck's zipper while Todd had his head in the closet looking for a saw. Kitchen knife in her hand, trying to decide where she'd stick it once she'd chopped it off. Then Todd's fingers around her wrist. Slapping her face with a force to match Good ol' Buck any day—

Raucous laughter brought her back to the present with a jolt. Her eyes snapped immediately to the bar across the street. A group of people had just come out. She scanned the faces flushed with good times and booze, didn't see Guillory among them. Then relaxed, her fingers caressing her cheek, the remembered slap like a fond memento to carry around with her.

And to bolster her resolve should it ever slip. Not that there was any danger of that. Because killing Liverman would be like killing Good ol' Buck all over again.

She got out her phone, called the number for Liverman that she'd memorized. She bit her tongue to stop herself from laughing at the childish charade she was about to play when it was answered.

Which it was immediately. Followed by silence apart from a man's breathing. She started with the first line that Todd had told her. Rolled her eyes as the man on the other end of the line gave the appropriate response. Then they ran through the rest of the stupid game together. She was surprised she didn't have to sing a song. The line went dead.

She kept the phone in her hand, waited for it to ring. Which it didn't immediately. That made faint alarm bells ring. Because Todd had told her that they always called back immediately. Except with all the trouble with Guillory and Garfield, it was understandable if they were more cautious than usual.

When it finally rang, it was Liverman's voice on the other end. She knew it instantly. Not just that it sounded to her like the sort of voice she'd expect to hear offering candy to a child from the back seat of a car, the unctuous tone masking the danger beneath. But because her brother had been a cautious man. He'd recorded all of his conversations with all of his clients. Even if it hadn't done him any good thanks to that bitch Guillory.

The amusement that she'd fought to control when she ran through the contact procedure was long gone, replaced by a cold loathing. If she closed her eyes, she'd see her father's face.

'Who is this?' Liverman said.

'Lydia Strange.'

The woman who is going to turn your head into a red mist.

'Ah. You're Todd's sister.'

'Yes.'

And your executioner.

'I'm very sorry for your loss.'

She thought then that if she hadn't already decided to kill him, the insincerity that coated his words as they oozed down the line would have clinched it.

'Thank you.'

'What can I do for you, Lydia? You don't mind if I call you Lydia?'

'Not at all.'

She tried to shut out the thoughts that crowded into her head at the sound of the solicitous voice, the same voice he used when he said *you don't mind if I put my hand there?* as he laid it on a trembling knee.

'Good. And please call me Joseph.'

Not Uncle Joseph? she wanted to scream, digging her fingernails into her own knee until they turned white.

'It's what I can do for you . . . Joseph.'

Her mouth twisted in disgust, wanting to spit. As if the name burned her tongue as she uttered it, couldn't get it out of her mouth fast enough.

There was a long pause then. Again, it was to be expected.

An unsolicited offer coming so soon after all the trouble was bound to arouse suspicion. She prayed that what she had to offer would be too much to resist, despite the increased risks. When it came, his reply was short and to the point.

'Go on.'

'I can deliver Guillory to you.'

There was a sharp intake of breath. As if the child he'd just touched had bitten his hand.

Again the pause.

'I don't want her *delivered*. I want the job your brother was paid to do finished. I assume that money came to you after his death.'

She was speechless for a long moment, couldn't believe the cheek of the man. Nor was he finished.

'His failure to complete the job has caused us a lot of unwanted and unnecessary'—he put a lot of emphasis on the word—'aggravation.'

She took a deep breath, let it out slowly. Put a lot of obsequious into her voice, despite the effort it took.

'I'm very sorry about that, Mr Liverman.'

'So I can rely on you to make good your brother's failure to deliver?'

'It's not as straightforward as that.'

There was a brief pause, did I hear that correctly? Then a great deal of indignant spluttering filled her ear, something about how dare you demand more money? She didn't care, wasn't even listening. Because Guillory had just come out of the bar looking very pleased with herself. If a little unsteady on her feet.

Hearing Liverman's complaints coming down the line, an uninterrupted stream of words, the indignation now infused with self-pitying whining, she was at the point of saying *fuck it* and forgetting about trying to be clever and killing two birds with one stone, just ending the call and going after Guillory in her vulnerable state. She could get to Liverman any time she liked. Her gun was in her bag on the passenger seat next to her. It would be satisfying to see Guillory's head explode as a high-velocity round from the Vanquish blew it apart, but could she really be bothered?

Just get the job done.

She cut the call.

Guillory had turned left, was walking away. The street was deserted. Why bother even following her home? Fifty yards ahead of Guillory she saw the darkened entrance to an alley. Shove her in, put a bullet in her head as she staggered drunkenly into the dumpsters and be on her way in under a minute.

She slipped out of the car. With her hand gripping her gun inside her bag, she crept silently after her, quickly closing the gap. Just not quickly enough. Another twenty yards and Guillory would be at the mouth of the alley. She broke into a run. Then her phone rang in her bag.

Liverman, calling her back.

She had to stop it ringing.

Because if Guillory heard it, she'd lose the advantage of surprise. The bitch might be worse for wear from the alcohol but she was a trained police officer after all. It would change the dynamics, shift the balance of power the wrong way. She dropped the gun, rooted in her bag for the phone. Snatched it up and declined the call.

When she looked up again Guillory was nowhere in sight. She froze. No way she could have made it to the end of the block. If she'd been following a man, she'd have said he'd ducked into the alley to relieve himself, had forgotten to go before he left the bar. Not a woman. Some women, maybe, but Guillory didn't look the sort.

She'd ducked into the alley for a different reason. That changed everything. She'd seen her. Or heard her running footsteps, heard the phone ring. Either way it was too risky now.

Right on cue the phone rang again. She answered it this time, head down, walking briskly back to her car. Waves of anger crackled down the line, the voice a petulant shout.

'Nobody hangs up on me!'

She pulled the phone away from her ear, stared at it. Was this guy serious? Then common sense kicked in. Swallow your pride and let him shout. It would be a very different sound coming from his mouth soon. She was at her car now. Glancing back the way she'd come there was no sign of Guillory.

'I'm sorry, Mr Liverman. Somebody came into the room. I had to cut the call immediately. They were still there when you called back. I've come outside to my car now.'

She started the car as she said it, but not because she needed to prove anything to him. In her rearview mirror she'd seen Guillory emerge from the alley. She wasn't hitching up her clothes as you would if you'd just had to make an emergency comfort stop. Nor was she turning left, the direction in which she'd been heading. She was standing still, arms held loosely at her side. Staring straight at Lydia's car. And despite the distance, Lydia felt the intensity of her stare in the rearview mirror. She put the shift into first, pulled slowly away, felt both relieved and stupid at how she'd almost let her impatience and anger get the better of her and spoil everything. When she looked again, Guillory was gone.

On the other end of the line Liverman had calmed down.

'You said things are not straightforward. Why is that?'

'Because Guillory was in Garfield's house before he was killed. She talked to him.'

The lack of reaction to what should have been an inflammatory remark only proved what she'd already figured out for herself. Liverman's own men had killed Garfield. To silence him. She needed to work on his fears that they'd been too late.

'She searched the house as well—'

'Okay, okay. No need to go on about it. Let me think.'

She smiled to herself, pictured the sweat running out of his greasy hair and down his face, the hands that she wanted to chop off for where he liked to put them flapping nervously, pulling at his collar.

'How much did he know about—'

'Will you shut up and let me think.'

She made *tsk, tsk* noises down the phone, thought about telling him not to talk to her like that. Maybe hang up again. Fun as it might have been, she resisted the temptation.

'Sorry.'

'How will you deliver her?' he said eventually.

Those were the words that came out of his mouth. What she heard was *how do you intend to kill me?* She composed herself, stripped all the excitement out of her voice.

'She lost an earring in the house. And I've got it.'

'How on earth—'

'It doesn't matter. I've got it and she wants it back. And she'll come alone.'

Then he said something that she wasn't expecting. Although she should have, because why wouldn't a man like him have a venal streak running through the middle of him, think everybody was the same?

'How much do you want for it?'

How do you explain to a man like him, a man who would sell a child to another monster like himself, that some things are not for sale? You don't even try.

'It's not for sale.'

The edge to her voice made him leave it there. Except he couldn't let it go completely.

'Why are you doing this if you're not interested in money?' A small titter of laughter, a strangely girlish sound, slipped out of his mouth. 'For your brother? Revenge?'

The mocking tone made the phone flex in her hand, made her teeth grind so hard she could barely speak.

'Yes. Revenge. For my brother.'

He heard the truth in her voice, regretted just a little that he'd mocked her. But not so much as to make him suspect that he was a large part of that revenge. Even so, he wasn't completely stupid.

'How do I know I can trust you?'

It was her turn to laugh then. And she did. And didn't care what he thought because there wasn't a thing he could do about it.

'You don't. You can walk away from it right now if you want. I won't contact you again. But maybe Garfield knew you'd send your thugs after him. Maybe he told Guillory what he knew to spite you from beyond the grave.'

She let her words sink in. Silence was her ally. Let his own mind do the persuading for her, the seeds of doubt she'd sowed taking root. Because it's human nature that the motivation to avoid something unpleasant is a lot stronger than the desire to achieve something positive. There are few words in the English language more powerful than a retrospective *if only*. Especially if you're sitting in a prison cell at the time in the secure wing to keep you safe from the general prison population of garden variety murderers and gangbangers.

It was a difficult line to walk, to get the balance of fear and encouragement just right. Because the last thing she wanted was for him to send his thugs to collect Guillory from her and not turn up himself. So she gave him a little encouragement, a reason to believe in her.

'I've got a condition.'

There was a sharp intake of breath from the other end of the line. The sort of sound that suggests a cautious man has just had his suspicions confirmed. Things are not so good as they seemed a moment ago. Which would make him all the more trusting when his suspicions were proved wrong.

'What condition?'

'I want to be there when you interrogate her.'

There was a short pause while he considered her request, made a quick assessment of how he could turn it to his own advantage.

'That shouldn't be a problem.'

'Good. Because I've got some questions of my own.'

He laughed at that, a sound that turned her stomach. It made her feel dirty, the feeling that they were in this together now. That it somehow made them the same.

'That won't be a problem either.'

'There's something else.'

Again the suspicious pause.

'I want us'—she felt physically sick to use the word—'to do it at the same location where you interrogated her the last time.'

That amused him too.

'What an excellent idea. That should make her more compliant even before we start on her. One last thing . . .'

She knew what was coming, had her answer ready.

'Will you be finishing the job?'

She had to wait for a moment to compose herself, glad in so many ways that the conversation was being conducted over the phone. He couldn't see the revulsion on her face as they'd talked. Nor could he see the smile on it now.

'Don't worry, I'll be finishing the job.'

45

EVAN WOKE EARLY THE NEXT MORNING EXHAUSTED AFTER A restless night of tossing and turning. The relentless chirping of the cicadas outside his open window had filled his subconscious mind with vivid and disturbing dreams. Running barefoot through the paddy fields and jungles of South East Asia, chased by a faceless man with teeth filed to points and something bloody clutched tightly in his bony left hand. A thing that shifted and changed each time he caught a glimpse of it. But in the end was always the same. Kate Guillory's sad face, streaked with blood, a gaping hole in her forehead.

He set off early and walked the length of Duval Street to clear his head, stopping only to grab some breakfast, withdraw a large sum of cash from the ATM and buy a pair of cheap binoculars and a clear plastic waterproof cell phone case.

Because you never know when you might be going into the water against your will. Ask George Winter.

Then he boarded the *Yankee Freedom III* at the ferry terminal in the Historic Seaport for the 8:00 a.m. departure to Fort Jefferson in the Dry Tortugas. He found a seat on the upper deck and settled in to enjoy the trip.

Except his mind wouldn't let him relax. Nor his churning gut, the vague feeling of dread that something that had started before he was born in a place he'd never been was waiting for him somewhere over the horizon. As soon as the boat had cleared the marina, he called Guillory. For something to fill his time as much as anything else, thinking it would be better than his own thoughts.

Shows how wrong you can be.

'Lydia Strange followed me when I left the Jerusalem last night,' she said.

He opened his mouth to ask her if she was sure, she'd had a number of beers after all, thought better of it. The fresh sea air was obviously good for the brain. And his wellbeing. He kept it simple.

'Really?'

'*No.* I wasn't imagining it. I'd only had a couple of beers anyway.'

'What happened?'

'She ran off again. She's up to something.'

Her words made him wish he hadn't made the call, had just stared at the endless blue of the ocean and let the wind blow his mind clear. Because he still hadn't told her about the Vanquish sniper's rifle that had been in his possession and was now in Lydia's. And she hadn't gone to the effort of snatching it out from under his nose in Crow's house for nothing.

He told her now.

A stunned silence came down the line in stark contrast to the noisy laughter and shouting of the kids surrounding him and leaning over the rails. He guessed she was re-living the meeting in the diner where there may well have been a high-powered rifle aimed at her head.

He wanted to tell her not to dwell on the past, concentrate on the future. He had the sense to leave that unsaid too. The sea air was sure working wonders today.

'Thanks for telling me,' she said eventually.

Quick translation: *why didn't you tell me earlier?*

'I didn't get the chance to tell you earlier.'

She let out a nervous stutter of a laugh.

'Good to know that your head might explode at any minute rather than just have it happen out of the blue, eh? That's the kind of heads-up to make your day.'

He didn't trust himself to speak. No answer would've worked, so he didn't try one. It wasn't a good note on which to end the call.

Immediately he called Crow to chew him out for sending him on what would probably turn out to be a wild goose chase while he should be at home doing what he could to put right the mess he'd caused.

Crow answered with his customary wariness at receiving a call on the telephone, a much over-rated piece of equipment in his opinion. He recovered when he heard Evan's voice.

'Hope you're enjoying yourself in the sun down there.'

With those few words he gave himself away.

If Evan had been a cynical man, he might have thought that Crow was talking just for the sake of it. To prevent Evan from taking him to task over all the things he hadn't told him. Things which he suspected Evan would have come up against in the course of his enquiries. Because Evan had never known Crow to make small talk in his life. So he'd let him believe it was working for a minute or two.

'Yep. On the ferry now. On my way to the Dry Tortugas National Park with the sun on my face and the sea breeze in my hair.'

'Ah, yes. Fort Jefferson. One of the largest brick fortifications in the Western Hemisphere. Bet you can't guess how many bricks it's made of.'

'A couple of thousand?'

'Stupid boy. Sixteen million.'

'Wow! You seem to know a lot of useless information.'

'Don't be impertinent.'

'I've got one for you. Why would a person file their teeth to points?'

The silence on the line was a lot more satisfying than the last one, the one with Guillory. Because, for once, it wasn't him who was the guilty party. It was a good feeling and he made the most of it.

'And don't give me any crap about ethnic groups and indigenous tribes in Africa and Asia doing it as an initiation ceremony during puberty to prove their manhood. I read all that stuff on the internet last night. What I'm interested in is why an American soldier, a man in a photograph standing next to Vaughan Lockhart, a photograph that you gave me and a man you described as *nobody important* would do it.'

This time the silence seemed to go on forever. For a moment he thought he might have gone too far, offended the old buzzard. Then a man sitting behind him tapped him on the shoulder.

'You're wasting your time, buddy, there's no signal.'

They were out of range of the cell phone towers on the mainland and he'd forgotten there aren't any in the Dry Tortugas.

Not only had he not gotten an answer from Crow, he was on his own.

Until he got to the Dry Tortugas, that is.

46

THE FERRY LOOPED AROUND TO THE NORTH OF THE DRY TORTUGAS and Howe Key, then dropped down and came into Fort Jefferson Boat Pier from the west. Bird Key Harbor was on the starboard side as it made its approach. So while everybody else's attention was on Fort Jefferson on the port side, Evan concentrated on scanning the harbor through his binoculars for a sighting of the *Dead or Alive*. There were only three boats in the harbor. A large, expensive-looking yacht was anchored off on its own. Then there was the most likely candidate, a sport fishing boat some distance away and a smaller boat close to that, partially obscured by it.

Trouble was, the wind was coming in from the north which meant the boats had swung around on their anchors and were facing the ferry. He couldn't see the name on the stern of the most likely candidate. He was no expert but from where he was three hundred yards away, it looked very similar to the boat he'd discovered George Winter drowned underneath.

It wasn't all bad. The wind direction worked in his favor too. Coming into Bird Key Harbor from the direction of Fort Jefferson he'd be approaching the *Dead or Alive's* bow. He figured if Lockhart was outside at all, he'd most likely be out on the stern deck, eating or fishing or just sitting there in the morning sun, trying to work the night's chill out of his body.

When the ferry docked, he waited until all of the other passengers had disembarked. Most of them made a beeline for Fort Jefferson itself, straight ahead. Looking back in the direction of Bird Key Harbor, he reckoned it was somewhere in the region of six to seven hundred yards to where the *Dead or Alive* was anchored.

All he needed now was a means of getting there.

And a weapon.

Because he had a bad feeling about the smallest boat.

Turning left as he disembarked, he wandered along the pier to where a number of National Parks Service boats and other smaller craft were moored. Beyond that was a section of beach reserved for dinghies. Pulled up onto the scrubby grass was a bright orange inflatable dinghy with an outboard motor as well as a couple of yellow kayaks. They hadn't paddled all the way from Key West, so he reckoned they must have come from the large yacht in the harbor. Jumping down onto the shore, he made his way towards them.

A couple of teenage kids, a boy and a girl, sat on the ground looking back out to sea. He hoped their parents, the owners of the yacht, were the sort who believed that children shouldn't have everything handed to them on a plate. That they should learn to appreciate the value of money and as a result didn't get an allowance that was bigger than what he made in a month.

He smiled to himself when he saw the looks on their faces. Their world had just ended. Here they were, sitting on a beach in the sun with the magnificent historic monument that was Fort Jefferson behind them and they looked like their dog had just died. They had no cell phone service. Hopefully the offer of some easy cash would ease their pain. Maybe they wouldn't even care if they lost one of the kayaks, a small gesture of defiance against heartless parents who would take them to a shithole where your phone doesn't work.

Five minutes later he'd secured himself the unlimited rental of one of the kayaks. The amount of cash that he'd handed over in exchange told him that these kids would do okay in life. Probably end up with a bigger yacht than daddy. There was only one proviso. The boy pointed in the direction that Evan was about to head off in.

'You see that yacht over there?'

Evan said he saw it.

'Don't get too close to it, okay. Not unless you want my father to radio for the coast guard to come and arrest you for piracy. Or shoot you with the rifle he keeps on board.'

Evan wasn't listening. He'd just seen something he was sure wasn't permitted in a National Park. Half-hidden under the other kayak was a speargun. It looked like there were some brightly-colored dead fish under there too. The boy saw him looking. A guilty grin crept over his face. Evan made a point of looking over to where the Park Rangers' boats were moored. Not very many dollars later the speargun was loaded and lying in the bottom of his kayak.

The boy gave him a push to get him underway and he started the long paddle towards the *Dead or Alive*. It had worked out better than he'd anticipated. This way he could approach silently. Even if Lockhart was vigilant and saw him coming, he'd be unlikely to make a run for it. Nobody he was hiding from would be coming after him in a bright yellow kayak.

As he got nearer, he saw that the smallest of the three boats was right alongside the sport fishing boat that he was now positive was the *Dead or Alive*. A surge of trepidation went through him as an overheard conversation came back to him—a charter boat skipper with a black eye complaining bitterly about two men forcibly commandeering his boat.

He picked up the speargun and laid it across his knees, then eased off paddling as he got closer, the kayak slipping slowly through the crystal-clear turquoise water. There was nobody in sight on either boat. He went past the *Dead or Alive's* anchor line and started down the side of it, coasting now, his left hand on the speargun across his knees. Then, with his right hand against the side of the boat, he pushed himself carefully to his feet, speargun held against the kayak to steady it.

With his arms stretched wide his head was facing downwards, the sun hot on the back of his neck. The fingers of his right hand closed around the wooden gunwale. He lifted his head.

Looked right into the barrel of a forty-five automatic.

Behind it two faces grinned at him.

'What took you so long, asshole?'

Hard-wired animal instinct kicked in, reflexes responding without conscious, time-wasting thought. He brought the speargun up fast towards the man with the gun. At the same time the other, bigger man stepped forward with a fishing gaff in his hand, knocking his smaller compadre out of the way.

Evan fired the speargun at the empty space where the smaller man had been a split second ago, already falling backwards as the kayak capsized. The larger man brought the gaff down in a murderous whistling arc towards the raised speargun.

The razor point snagged the barrel with a sharp jolt, the two men balanced on either end of their weapons. Evan wrenched the speargun hard towards him, pulled the man on the boat off balance, the lanyard on the gaff's handle looped securely around his wrist.

His back hit the water as his feet swept up through the air, slammed into the side of the boat. He powered them out like an Olympic swimmer pushing off after a flip turn, pulled the guy on the other end of the gaff in after him.

The guy landed on top of him, a tangle of thrashing arms and legs under the surface. Above them on the boat the guy with the forty-five stood at the gunwale, head moving side to side, peering at the inseparable jumble of limbs through the explosion of water, his gun arm trying to track Evan's body below his partner.

Evan dropped the speargun, threw his arms around the guy's body, clamped his hands on the ends of the gaff. Pulled it hard up under the guy's chin, across his throat, cutting off his air. With his own body completely submerged, he wrapped his legs around the man above him to stop him from kicking wildly, to pull him down like a 'gator drowning its prey.

In his panic the guy jerked his arm out, snapped the lanyard. Drove it back in again. Buried his elbow into Evan's gut. Evan jack-knifed, the air exploding out of his lungs. His hands came off both ends of the gaff, the pressure on the guy's throat gone.

Then Evan's breath sucked back in. He was still underwater. No air went in. A ton of salty seawater did. He kicked violently, head bursting into the sunlight in a spray of glittering water droplets, coughing and retching as the other guy twisted away from him back towards the boat.

The guy grabbed the gaff floating free on the surface, swung it and buried the tip deep into the gunwale, pulled himself up. His partner hauled him in. Then the two of them watched Evan as he flapped on the surface, spitting and retching, trying to control the involuntary spasms of his panicked lungs.

The one with the forty-five fired a shot into the water a foot to the side of his head.

'Get in, asshole.'

Evan didn't have a choice. In the perfectly clear water he'd be an easy target. In his sodden clothes and shoes, they'd shoot him in the back before he got ten strokes away. Wouldn't have to worry about blood on the pristine deck boards either. Save themselves a bitch of a job getting it out again.

He swam to the boat while the big guy worked at getting the point free from where it was stuck fast in the gunwale. Reaching up, he clamped his hand around the gunwale. He only had seconds to get in on his own. Once the big guy worked the gaff free, he'd be getting a helping hand—or hook. He felt the guy's eyes roving over his body. Where to sink the pointy tip of the gaff into first? The back of the shoulder? The upper arm? The forearm? So many fleshy places, so little time.

He hauled himself up, heard a sound that brought a smile to his face. A sharp snap.

'Fuck. Cheap piece of shit.'

The guy had broken the gaff in his hurry to get it free before Evan got on board.

Evan rolled himself into the boat, landed on the deck with a thump, a tangle of boneless limbs as the adrenalin rush subsided. He lay with his face pressed into the wooden slats for a moment, heart thumping against them, thankful that his blood wasn't running away between them. Not that the wood was clean or blood-free. Far from it. A pool of dried blood stained the slats just inches from his nose.

He pushed himself up, stared into the malevolent piggy eyes of the large guy, a face-off between two monsters from the deep dripping water onto the deck. He gave him a watery grin.

'No charge for the swimming lesson.'

The big guy's eyes bulged. He stepped forward but his partner put his arm out across his chest to stop him. Motioned to Evan with his gun.

'In the cabin.'

There was no sign of Lockhart inside. The two men had

been making themselves at home in his absence. There were two plates on the galley table. The pattern looked as if it had been licked off one of them, half-eaten pancakes and sausages on the other. They'd been pushed to the side in a messy pile, knives and forks heaped on top. Evan glanced at them, dismissed the idea immediately. What use would flatware be against a man with a gun? The big guy swept his arm across the table, sent the plates and everything on them clattering into the corner just in case.

But not before Evan saw that there had been another knife on the table, hidden by the plates. This one was long and thin, the blade curved. A filleting knife, used for gutting fish. From the blood that coated the blade, it was clear it had been used recently. Just not for gutting fish. And no sausage that Evan had ever eaten was full of fresh blood like that.

For reasons that he couldn't and didn't want to explain his mind was filled by the image of the man who had sent these killers. Not as he was now but as he had been almost fifty years ago when he posed for a photograph with something grisly in his left hand.

In that moment Evan understood what it was that the man held half-hidden from the scrutiny of the camera lens. He felt his gorge rise, a pricking at his scalp, and knew he didn't want to find Vaughan Lockhart.

47

THE GUY WITH THE FORTY-FIVE SET A NICE FRIENDLY TONE.

'Who the fuck are you?'

Evan told him who the fuck he was. If it was any of his business.

'Why are you looking for Lockhart? And who are you working for?'

Evan nodded towards the big guy.

'Bet you don't ask him two questions at once.'

If he thought the guy was going to react, attack him in the limited space of the salon, maybe create an opportunity, he was disappointed. The insult washed over him if he even understood.

'C'mon Hitch,' he said. 'What difference does it make anyway? Let's get this over with and get out of here. Someone might have heard that shot.'

Hitch hesitated for a moment, saw the sense in what his partner was saying.

'You get the gas can, I'll deal with this asshole.'

The big guy lumbered off, the whole boat rocking under his

heavy footsteps. Hitch motioned towards the stairs leading down to the master stateroom.

'Downstairs, seeing as you're so interested in Lockhart. He's waiting for you down there.'

Evan turned towards the steps behind him, saw bloodstains leading down the stairs, an image of the bloody filleting knife in his mind. He saw something else too. A loaded flare gun on the seat on the other side of the salon. With the mention of the gas can, it was easy to guess what they had in mind—another fatal fire, this time at sea.

Hitch saw him looking. He darted quickly across the floor, grabbed the flare gun.

'Uh-uh. Now get downstairs.'

The boat dipped slightly as, behind them, the big guy jumped down onto the stern deck like an excited kid. Hitch didn't pay it any attention. Which was a big mistake. As was his over-confidence, the confidence of a man with a forty-five automatic in one hand and a loaded flare gun in the other.

Evan hesitated at the top of the stairs, his hand on the bulkhead to steady himself. It didn't matter if they planned to douse the whole salon with gasoline and set it alight with the flare gun, or just the downstairs staterooms, concentrate the fire in those small rooms. Either way, if he went down the stairs he wasn't coming back up.

A grim smile flickered across his lips as he reflected that the man's cruelty would be his undoing. If he simply shot him in the back now and pushed him down the stairs, it would be all over. But where was the fun in that? He wanted to burn him alive.

That wasn't why he hesitated. Because he wasn't hesitating. He was waiting for something he knew would happen any second.

Hitch was impatient as well as over-confident. It's a bad combination. Even if you're the one with the pistol and the flare gun. So he made things easier for Evan. At the same time as his partner outside—who was a lot fitter and more athletic than his bulk and over-developed muscle would suggest—leapt up onto the gunwale, he raised his leg to give Evan a helping foot down the stairs.

Then the big guy did what Evan was waiting for.

He leapt from the gunwale onto the boat tied up alongside. He was a big man, weighed two hundred and thirty pounds. When his bulk suddenly came off the *Dead or Alive*, it dipped forwards and rocked to the port side. Evan tipped sideways. Not by much. But it was enough. Off-balance on one leg, Hitch didn't so much kick Evan's butt as topple forwards.

His foot went straight past Evan's thigh into empty air. Evan slapped his hand on the bulkhead to steady himself, grabbed Hitch's leg. Yanked it forwards. Hard. Threw himself backwards into him, arm pumping out like a piston as he pushed off the bulkhead. Drove the back of his head into Hitch's face, felt his nose flatten and crack with the impact.

Hitch's arms flew up and backwards like he'd been hit in the chest by a shotgun blast. He kept hold of the pistol in his right hand. The flare gun in his left sailed up and over his head, landed on the floor behind him. He crashed on top of it, pinned it to the floor between his shoulder blades. Then Evan landed on top of him like the roof just fell in, the back of his head smashing into Hitch's face.

With his arms splayed on the floor, Hitch curled his right arm and the gun in his hand in towards Evan's head. Evan threw his arm out. Clamped his fingers around Hitch's wrist, pushed back. Bigger and stronger than Hitch, he bent his arm open wide while Hitch punched at the side of his head with his left. Evan grabbed that one too, straightened his arm. With Evan on top, they lay on their backs on the floor looking like two men nailed to a cross together to save on nails.

Evan dipped his chin to his chest, drove his head backwards into Hitch's face, felt bone and cartilage give way. Over and over he powered his head backwards turning Hitch's face into a bloody pulp as the man struggled underneath him, a regular grunting in Evan's ear like a fat man fucking.

Then a loud bang. Just not loud enough. And not from the gun at the end of Hitch's outstretched arm.

The grunting had stopped, replaced by a high hysterical scream as the flare gun went off, an incandescent orange-white fire blazing up between Hitch's shoulders and around his neck and head like a halo straight from the burning pits of hell.

Flames licked at the back of Evan's head, singed his hair. He let go of Hitch's wrists, rolled off him and away. The flare was a magnesium inferno now, enveloping Hitch's whole head, filling the room with white smoke. Evan pushed himself to his knees, saw Hitch's gun on the floor. He snatched it up, was on his feet a second later, the gun pointed at Hitch's writhing body.

Hitch slapped uselessly at his head and face, did nothing more than set his sleeves on fire. Evan looked down on him and thought of all the people he'd never met—George Winter and a young couple taking a selfie video and Vaughan Lockhart—all of whom had died at the hands of this man and his partner. Who, by the sound of it, was at this very moment motoring away now that the tables had turned.

Amid the broken plates and scattered flatware on the floor he saw the filleting knife and the fresh blood on it. He thought again of Lockhart's dying moments and of the souvenir demanded by the man who had ordered his death. A man with teeth filed to points. A man who liked to wear a waistcoat made from small misshapen pieces of hide.

So he didn't just watch him writhe. Nor did he shoot him. Not for the satisfaction of it or to put him out of his misery. Instead, he took hold of his feet as the heels beat futilely against the floor and spun him around so that the fireball that used to be his head was facing toward the stairs. Then he ran him along the floor like a man pushing a heavy broom, leaned into the rigid legs, pushed him down the stairs, watched him bump down step by step.

He didn't feel an ounce of remorse.

Because Hitch had been a split second away from doing the same to him. And doing it deliberately. To add him to the list of those already dead. He had Hitch's own partner to thank for that reprieve, his heavy-footed enthusiasm to get the gasoline in order to burn him alive. So he didn't bother to even look for a fire extinguisher. What good would it have done anyway for a man whose flesh had melted from his face?

He stared down the stairs. The fire had already taken hold. Everything was made of wood, the stairs and doors and bunks and with the bedding to get things started. He couldn't see the bottom of the stairs, just the soles of Hitch's shoes poking out of the smoke climbing up towards him, the open stairwell the only way out for the developing inferno.

He turned away from the rush of heat and smoke, looked around for a lifesaver. Stupid. They wouldn't be kept inside. Then he saw something through the smoke that stopped him dead, something more imperative than the sliding glass doors and the fresh air and freedom beyond them.

A framed photograph on the wall. Identical to the one in his pocket. The one given to him by Crow that showed Lockhart, now dead downstairs, with another man whose teeth were filed to points. Just as he knew that Crow would never write the names of the people photographed on the back of the print for fear that it was an admission of weakness, a failure of his memory, a vanity even after all these years, he knew without knowing how that the photograph on the wall would give him the name he wanted.

He pulled it from the wall, smashed the glass against the corner of the galley table. Beads of sweat ran down his face as the heat from downstairs increased, the billowing smoke growing ever thicker and more noxious. He knew nothing about the layout of a boat like this—or any other for that matter—had no idea where the gas tanks were in relation to the blazing living quarters below.

Not far enough was as accurate as he needed to be.

He shook the broken glass from the frame, worked the photograph free. Eyes streaming from the stinging smoke while hot air burned his breathing passages, he darted through the sliding glass doors and out onto the stern deck. Then slammed them firmly shut. He turned the photograph over, felt a warm glow of satisfaction as he coughed and blinked away the tears. He'd been right. Scrawled on the back in ink that was almost fifty years old were two names. Lockhart, he knew. The other meant nothing to him. Beyond the fact that it had a spiritual ring to it, a fitting name for a man who chose to file his teeth to points.

He folded the photograph in half and then half again, squeezed it into the waterproof case with his phone. The kayak was long gone. He looked around, saw it heading as if driven by a homing instinct towards the expensive yacht. All hell would break loose when it bumped into the side.

Behind him the salon was now completely filled with black smoke, the orange flames climbing the stairs from below the only light. The glass doors would blow any second, a ball of fire exploding outwards. The deck wasn't the place to be when they did. There were no lifesavers in sight. Even with the adrenalin coursing through his veins, a seven-hundred-yard swim in clothes and shoes wasn't the best of ideas.

He ripped through the storage cabinets around the deck, throwing open doors and lifting lids, slamming them shut in frustration. No lifesavers. No surprise. He ran towards the gunwale. He'd take his chances in the water. Then a thought. The BCD he'd found before he discovered Winter dead. It might still be in the day head.

No time to worry that the day head was adjacent to the glass doors. He raced for it through the heat radiating off them, wrenched open the door, saw it under all of the rest of the diving gear. He pulled it out, pulled it on. Didn't bother clipping it on properly. Two fast paces and up onto the gunwale, legs tensing, momentum carrying him forwards and over the side.

No.

He was already falling. Arms windmilling. Trying to stop himself from toppling in. Clawing frantically at the BCD. Had to get the damn thing off. One arm out. Twisting in the air. His back hit the water with a massive slap, his weight taking him under despite the BCD. He popped to the surface. Wrenched his other arm out. Held the BCD above his head, kicking furiously. Then hurled it far out into the ocean.

Because when the glass doors exploded and rained down a shower of super-heated glass fragments on everything within a quarter mile, he wanted to be under the water, not suspended on the surface by the BCD.

Not waiting to see it land, he duck-dived under the surface, stroked strongly for the bottom. His feet were still in the air above the water when the doors blew, six feet under it when the shattered glass rained down on the surface then slowly sank, twisting and glinting, reflecting the sunlight, like a shoal of some strange new species of fish racing each other to the sea bed.

Thirty seconds later he broke water a few yards short of the glass-peppered BCD. He sucked the clean salty air deep into his lungs, floating on his back, spread-eagled under the hot sun until the weight of his sodden clothes threatened to sink him.

He twisted in the water and swam to the BCD, pulled it on and stuffed his shoes in the storage pockets.

Then, on his back again, he sculled himself back to shore. He looked like an upside-down turtle enjoying the sun on the bottom of its shell. It was more comfortable than trying to swim in the BCD. And he could watch the *Dead or Alive* as it burned, the National Parks Service boats tearing across the water to investigate. Seven hundred yards later with all official personnel in the vicinity fully occupied he clambered up the gently-sloping beach to the astonished stares of the two teenagers.

'You lost my kayak,' the boy complained.

Evan shook his head, couldn't help laughing.

'No. Last I saw of it, it was headed straight for your dad's yacht. He'd probably have the park rangers out looking for you now if they weren't so tied up.'

The boy looked across the water at the floating pyre that used to be the *Dead or Alive*. Evan was tempted to say, try to find a game that exciting to play on your precious phone, thought better of it. Instead, he shrugged off the BCD, dropped it on the ground next to the boy.

'Here, you can keep this as compensation.'

Then he made his way to Fort Jefferson where he fished the soggy, crumpled admission ticket that was included in the price of his ferry ticket out of his pocket. He ignored the look the attendant gave him as it was suspiciously and reluctantly accepted. On top of the fort's walls he found himself a nice warm spot in the sun. There, with his back to some of the sixteen million bricks, he waited patiently for the return ferry and his clothes to dry out.

Or at least he tried to. Because although he was good at a lot of things, patience was not one of them.

So he got out the waterproof case with his phone and the photograph he'd salvaged from the *Dead or Alive*.

He stared at it a long while. The object in the man's left hand didn't hold such a fascination for him now that he knew what it was. It was the man himself that he was interested in. Now that he knew the sort of man he was. He turned the photograph over to read the faded words again, hoping that maybe the smoke had gotten in his eyes when he'd glanced quickly at it on the boat. It hadn't. The names were the same—if the second one was a name at all.

Pentecost.

Just the one word. Not a full name like the name *Vaughan Lockhart* written alongside it.

What had happened between the two men who had posed together for a photograph with all the camaraderie of men whose friendship is forged in blood, that one of them should send two killers to murder the other on his boat? And after almost fifty years.

He closed his eyes, angled his face towards the sun to ward off the feelings of trepidation growing inside him. Elwood Crow had the answers. And he would be unable to stop himself from asking Crow about it. Then Crow would demand that he go after the man called Pentecost and his murderous gum-chewing lackey.

He almost laughed as the meaning of the name Pentecost came to him as a memory from long ago.

The day on which, according to Christian doctrine, the Holy Spirit descended on the apostles, manifesting itself as a strong wind and looking like tongues of fire. With the smoke from the *Dead or Alive* still visible in the distance and the image of Hitch's head engulfed in a ball of flame it was a little too reminiscent of the day he'd had so far.

But what put a chill in his bones that had nothing to do with the wet clothes drying on his skin was the knowledge that he wasn't done yet with the man who had filed his teeth to points. A man who cut a swathe through anybody who stood in his way with all the merciless efficiency and righteousness of an avenging angel.

An avenging angel who, as Crow would later tell him when pressed, had learned his trade in the jungles of South East Asia before Evan was born.

And something Evan could figure out on his own without help from Crow or anybody else, just his experience of the past days to guide him—an avenging angel with a loose end to tidy up.

48

Kate Guillory shifted down into second, put her foot to the floor. Evan's '69 Corvette Stingray surged as the big V8 engine responded instantly, catapulting her forwards to pass an ageing hippy in a vintage VW camper van. His pride pricked, the old fart stomped on the gas.

Normally it wouldn't have made a blind bit of difference as she blew him into the weeds. Except that's when her phone rang. She glanced at it on the passenger seat, concentration wavering momentarily, her foot inadvertently coming off the gas when she saw who was calling. A long blare on the horn from the camper van alongside snapped her eyes front. Straight into the strobe-like glare of an approaching eighteen-wheeler's lights.

On her right the old fart grinned, gave her the finger.

She jumped on the brakes. Wrenched the wheel to the right, cut back in behind him. The truck steamed past, the air pushed in front of it slamming into her like a horse kicked her in the chest, plucking at her hair and clothes.

She wouldn't be telling Evan about that one. He'd asked her to pick it up from the shop, not trash it. He'd been complaining that it wasn't running properly. The mechanic had said it was a problem with the gas pedal—it wasn't being pushed hard or often enough. He hadn't actually said that. But that's what she was going to tell him.

The phone was still ringing.

Great. With her hair still in her eyes from the truck's side draft and her heartbeat at one-twenty, she didn't need another reminder of her own mortality.

She leaned over and turned off the radio, abruptly silencing Whitesnake's *Here I Go Again* mid-chorus.

'Hello Lydia. Are you calling to give me Liverman's real name?'

A lot had happened since they'd last spoken. On that occasion—in the diner with Evan there too—Lydia said she needed time to think about it. Translation: time to figure out how to make it work for herself.

Guillory guessed she'd done that now. And seeing as since that meeting she'd learned that Lydia did indeed have a Vanquish sniper's rifle—courtesy of Evan himself—she approached the conversation with caution.

It wasn't just the gun. Lydia had followed her from the Jerusalem Tavern before changing her mind and running off. She'd seen her with Ryder. Would know she hadn't confessed her sins to him, her presence in the house where Garfield was murdered, as she'd told her she was going to do.

So Lydia would be as suspicious as she was.

The conversation would be an exercise in reading between the lines. If she'd asked him—and she never would—Evan would have said it was just two women having a conversation.

'No,' Lydia said. 'I've got something better.'

Better for whom?

'Really? What's that?'

'I can give you Liverman himself.'

It wasn't what she was expecting. Even so, it was easy enough to see through.

Or give me to Liverman.

It wasn't the time to ask difficult questions, questions that might make Lydia end the call. Like why did you follow me? And what made you back off?

Up ahead the VW camper van had gotten stuck behind a bus. The road ahead was clear. She shifted down again, blew past both of them. Gave the old fart his finger back. With the roar of the engine and the wind in her face she missed what Lydia said next, got her to repeat it.

'I've set up a meeting with him.'

'Who? Liverman?'

'Uh-huh.'

'What for?'

Lydia stifled a laugh, then continued, the amusement still in her voice.

'To discuss what to do about you.' She said it as if she was telling a friend how she'd just made an appointment for the pest control guys to come around, see what they could do about the ants in the kitchen. 'Someone gave him the impression I wanted to finish the job he paid my brother to do. I thought you might want to go in my place.'

Guillory listened to the oh-so-pleased-with-myself sound of her voice, her mind doing the translation, filtering out the facts. It was obvious that Lydia had told Liverman a similar story, had promised to deliver her to him. But why?

'Where will you be if I take your place.'

'Doesn't matter.'

It does if it's on a roof with the sniper's rifle, Guillory thought. Then she asked a question as if she was interested in taking things forward despite the lack of an answer.

'Where is the meeting?'

Lydia didn't bother to stifle the laugh that bubbled up from deep inside her.

'It's somewhere you've been before. Except you don't know where it is.'

A cold hand gripped Guillory's heart, her chest suddenly tight, as if she was back there already. The feel of a rough hood over her head, men's fists coming at her from all directions. And the smell. She couldn't ever get it out of her nose. Of dried blood and sweat and vomit. Her foot, her whole leg, was rigid now, locked on the gas pedal. Knuckles white on the wheel as the speed climbed, roadside trees a blur of green and brown. Grit and wind and water in her eyes, streaming back across her face. Drawing the air deep inside her body, cleansing her, if only for a minute before the wheel bucked in her hands, nearside wheels clipping the shoulder, a cloud of dust and debris billowing out behind the car.

On the other end of the line Lydia's sick, sing-song voice.

'I can tell you've guessed already.'

And Guillory wondered if that big eighteen-wheeler was coming at her now whether she'd pull in behind the camper van like before or just push her foot harder to the floor and put an end to it all.

'It's where they had you before.'

Then the moment passed. She eased off the gas, let out the first breath for five miles. Bit back the words on her lips—the place your brother picked me up from, to take me for a one-way trip out to the woods—said something less inflammatory instead.

'You're a sick bastard.'

Lydia giggled like a boy she had her eye on had just said how nice her hair looked.

'Not me. It was Liverman's idea.'

Guillory didn't believe a word of it, asked her the question she couldn't hold in any longer.

'Why would you do this?'

There was something different about the pause that followed. If one silence can be different to another. Guillory felt in her gut that Lydia wasn't about to come out with more of the same lies and half-truths. That instead she was making a decision about how much to say. How much of herself to reveal. In the words that she said next, Guillory would feel a bond of some sort develop between them.

Those are dangerous feelings.

'You know what Liverman is,' Lydia said. It was a statement, not a question.

'Of course I do.'

'Of course you do,' Lydia mimicked. 'You almost threw away your career because you attacked one of his kind. You've just jeopardized it again breaking into his house in the middle of the night. The night he was killed.' The mocking tone was gone now, replaced by a cold venom, a touch of hysteria behind it. 'And you ask me why I would hate a man like Liverman enough to want him dead? Or worse. Why should you be the only one?'

The flavor of Lydia's words—why wouldn't anybody hate a disgusting pervert of a pedophile?—was just a smoke screen. Something to hide behind as she worked her way towards her personal truth. So Guillory held her tongue, let her talk. She sure as hell wasn't expecting what she said next.

'Tell me about your father.'

An image instantly flashed across Guillory's mind. The closed door to her father's study, the door that was always open. Then it was gone, as fast as it came, left her asking the same question as she always did.

Had it been closed? Or had her mind closed it

retrospectively, a trick of the subconscious to protect her from the memories of what lay behind it?

She didn't share that with Lydia, kept it simple.

'No.'

The curtness of her reply, spat out like a bad taste, elicited a surprised giggle from Lydia. Like Guillory had made an inappropriate remark and Lydia had been unable to catch herself before it was out.

'Why not? Did he abuse you? Is that why you attacked Garfield?'

Guillory threw back her head, looked up at the sky. How far off-base can a person be? But the questions, asked as if they were the logical sequitur to not wanting to share your family history with a homicidal maniac who may well be planning to kill you, gave her an insight into Lydia's motivations.

'No. To all your questions. Why, did your father abuse you?'

She hadn't expected to hear a barely-controlled sob climb from Lydia's throat or to feel the phone shake in her hand as she launched into a vitriolic diatribe. But she didn't expect the response she did get, one which matched hers for close-mouthed brevity.

'No.'

She kept the surprised *oh!* to herself. Because Lydia hadn't finished.

'But he would have. If he'd gotten the chance.' The tone of her voice made it clear that there was a great deal of satisfaction, pleasure even, in preventing him from getting that chance. 'If my brother hadn't killed him first.'

Guillory couldn't deny it was the best reason—if the word *best* has any place in such circumstance—for Lydia to have turned out the way she had. Her brother too, starting his career of cold-blooded murder for hire with a very different killing. One with sufficient emotions—of fear and rage and disgust and relief—to more than compensate for all the perfunctory deaths that came after.

What it didn't do—and this was the important part—was explain why, if Lydia was on a personal crusade against the perverts and the abusers, she didn't simply kill Liverman without all the elaborate fuss of the meeting she had set up.

The answer was obvious. One that Guillory pushed from her mind because nothing could be gained by dwelling on it.

Lydia was after more than just Liverman.

The whole situation was unreal. It made her feel as if her head was on the block and the blade of the guillotine had failed to fall. And now she was in earnest conversation with the executioner, pointing at whatever obstruction had jammed the blade, a triumphant *there's the problem right there* on her lips.

'What's it going to be?' Lydia said. 'You want to do this or not?'

They both knew she didn't have a choice. If she wanted a chance at getting to Liverman, this was the only way to go. She'd been unable to find any trace of him on her own. The stupid, irrational act of breaking into Garfield's house had at least produced one positive outcome. She now understood how much her ordeal had affected her judgement. How much it had blinded her to the consequences of her actions, sent her spiraling down a bottomless self-destructive hole.

If you wanted the Lone Ranger, call Evan, not her.

A wave of relief washed through her, left her legs weak and her head light, the moment she made the decision. A huge weight had been lifted. Because however things played out, it had to be better than her life at the moment, watching her obsession eat away at everything good in it. She'd never have a moment's peace until she put Liverman behind her. Whether that happened as a result of his incarceration for the rest of his unnatural life, or as a result of a high-powered round blowing her head apart, it had to be better than this.

If Evan or Ryder had been there, Ryder's words would have been particularly apt.

It must be her self-destructive streak that attracts her to you. Like a moth to the flame. She gets it from her old man.

Because she knew that the self-destructive hole that she was spiraling down wasn't bottomless at all. Nor was the bottom very far away. And it had the taste of a gun barrel in her mouth.

Like father, like daughter.

She stomped her foot down, pedal to the metal. Kept it there as the car hurtled down the road, the feral grin on her lips at one with the throaty growl of the engine. And it matched Lydia's on the other end of the line in every way, but most of all in the way that it proclaimed that things were drawing to a close.

'I'm in.'

49

As was often the case, Evan reckoned he deserved a medal. This time it was for patience and self-control. The way things were going he was going to have to get himself down to the gym, build his chest up a bit, to fit them all on.

Because, despite his last conversation with Crow—the one where he'd asked him about the man with filed teeth—being abruptly terminated when he lost the cell phone signal, he'd sat on his hands the whole way back and not called him.

Some things needed to be discussed face to face. With the option of giving the old buzzard a clip around the back of the head, Guillory style, or maybe a poke in the eye, if he prevaricated. He flexed his fingers, warming them up, as he waited on Crow's doorstep.

And waited.

He was on the verge of giving the bell a third, much longer push when the door swung open.

'Sorry,' Crow said with a backwards and upwards flick of the head. 'I was busy upstairs.'

He was talking about his wife. She suffered from Alzheimer's

Disease and spent most of her life in bed. Evan knew this and it seemed plausible enough. Apart from the fact that he hadn't seen anyone coming down the stairs—because he couldn't see through doors—but he was sure he'd caught a glimpse of somebody disappearing up them as Crow opened the door. He didn't mention it. It was none of his business.

He was wrong about that.

Crow looked as penitent as any man who starts every day with the words *never explain, never apologize* on his lips can.

'I don't know at exactly what point our phone call was cut off,' Evan said once they'd gotten themselves settled into the back room, 'but I'd just asked you why a man would file his teeth to points.'

Crow went to speak. He looked a lot like his pet bird opening its beak and nothing coming out. Evan stopped him.

'Not just any man. An American soldier. A man in a photograph standing next to Vaughan Lockhart, a photograph that you gave me and a man you described as *nobody important.*'

Evan dug in his pocket. Crow watched in silence. Even the pet crow was quiet, wondering what Evan was about to produce, maybe hoping it was a worm. Rather than a can of them. Evan pulled out the original photograph that Crow had given him. It was crumpled and curled at the edges. He hadn't had the time or the inclination to put it in the waterproof case with his phone and the photograph from the boat before he made his hasty exit.

'Sorry. It got a bit wet.'

Crow took it from him, didn't say anything. As you wouldn't when you know a damn sight worse had happened than an old photograph getting ruined. He tried to smooth it flat nonetheless, gave up when he saw Evan's face.

Then Evan produced the photograph he'd taken from the boat. It was nice and flat, the waterproof case having done its job.

'So I got you another one.'

Crow took that one from him as well, turned it over when Evan told him to. His face remained as expressionless as if there'd been nothing written on the back.

'I assume Pentecost is the name of the man with Lockhart.'

Crow nodded, turned the photograph over again.

'First name? Last name?'

'Last. His first name is Avery. He never used it.'

'You want to tell me about him? And while you're at it, what the hell's going on here.'

Crow put the photograph on top of the other one on the side table, pushed himself wearily out of his chair. Evan reflected that much as he might have the old man on the back foot, Crow was still Crow after all. And Evan would wait for his answers until Crow was good and ready. But Crow didn't make his way towards the drinks cabinet to get them both a shot of the good stuff as Evan was expecting. Instead he began to pace the room. As if the story he was about to tell was not one to be told sitting down, where the demons he was about to describe could more easily get at you. As he moved away his pet bird launched itself into the air, settled on the seat Crow had just vacated. As a cat might, seeking out the residual warmth. Staring at it, Evan couldn't help but wonder which one of them he'd get more truth and sense out of.

'I don't know what's going on here,' Crow said.

Evan was out of his own chair in a flash, spooking the bird, sending it flapping away to the far side of the room.

'I wouldn't have sent you down to Florida if I did.'

Evan thought hard for a moment, decided to postpone the first poke in the eye for a little while longer. Crow caught sight of his expression, decided that a little bit of explanation wouldn't hurt.

'I know who Avery Pentecost is. Or was. I'll tell you about him in a minute. But I honestly don't know what's going on.'

Evan didn't miss the reference to the past tense—*was*. Did that mean that Pentecost was dead? If so, who was the old man with the filed teeth? One thing he did know—he wasn't going to find the answers until he'd brought Crow up to speed on everything that had happened in Florida.

So he took him through it from the beginning. Despite the time and trouble it had taken him to uncover, it was a very simple story. Not only that, it was as old as it was simple. The house on Passover Lane in Key West that was used as a honey trap and the woman who died in it at the hands of an important —and still unidentified—man with powerful friends. The inadvertent filming of that man's panicked escape from the house and the subsequent hunting down and killing of everybody whose lives had been touched by those events, however fleetingly or tangentially. Including Crow's friend George Winter.

'Hah!'

The sudden outburst from Crow stopped Evan mid-flow. He stared at Crow for a long moment. His expression suggested that he was unaware that he'd said anything remotely amusing. Crow smiled apologetically.

'Sorry. I couldn't help it.'

Evan couldn't move on until Crow had explained himself, told him to spit it out.

'It's ironic, that's all. The fact that the house is on Passover Lane. You do know what the Jewish feast of Passover is about?' He took Evan's silence as a denial, shook his head sadly. 'An avenging angel was sent to kill every firstborn Egyptian child in order to persuade the Pharaoh to release the Israelites from slavery. It's ironic that the house on Passover Lane gave rise to a similar bloodbath.'

Evan said that he could see the similarity, wondered not for the first time about the way Crow's mind worked. As far as he was concerned it was something much more down to earth, no help from avenging angels required.

'It's the same old, same old. Rich, powerful men protecting their own. Plus all the usual minor details. Some selective police blindness, that sort of thing.'

'Not your friend Cortez?'

Evan had been wondering when Crow would try to turn the story back on him, and then bring Guillory into it as well. If he thought it was going to deflect the attention away from himself, it wasn't going to work.

'No, not her. Anyway, I think this guy Pentecost is behind it all. He's the one orchestrating the clean-up. All I need to know now is who the hell he is.'

He gave a low sweep of his hand, over to you. Crow was shaking his head. Evan didn't know if it was meant to say I disagree or I'm not telling you. Either way, it was an unacceptable response. The time for pokes in the eye was on hand. Crow backed away, showed Evan his palms.

'They killed Lockhart as well?' he said.

Evan was tempted to ask him what he'd been doing for the past ten minutes while he was explaining. He'd just told him they'd killed everybody. The only thing he hadn't specifically mentioned was the glaringly obvious loose end—himself. They'd be getting to that soon.

'Yes, Lockhart too.'

Crow only shook his head more. He seemed tired and vaguely disgusted, something that sounded like *after all this time* muttered under his breath.

'What's after all this time?'

'That Pentecost would kill Lockhart.'

Evan took a deep breath, his chest swelling to make room for one more medal, one awarded for not throttling an old man, even under extreme provocation.

'How about you tell me what the hell you're talking about?'

'Good idea,' Crow said, sounding as if he'd been the one to suggest it. 'I thought you'd never ask.'

50

STRONG HANDS STREAKED WITH DIRT AND GRIME HAULED THE three grunts into the back of the slick by their pack straps. Behind them the rotor wash bent the elephant grass flat, blew the marker smoke every which way.

'Go! Go! Go!' the portside door gunner yelled.

'*No!*'

The urgent scream cut through the deafening roar as the big turbine geared up for lift-off.

'There's one more to come.'

The door gunner gawked at the man sprawled and panting at his feet like he'd just asked if there was time to stop for a quick picnic. Then he quickly scanned the area around the LZ for signs of a straggler making his desperate way towards the helicopter.

There was nobody in sight. Just the muzzle flashes of sniper fire from the banyan trees.

'So where the hell is he?' the door gunner yelled. 'Taking a fucking piss?'

Even above the sound of the engine and the rotor blades it

seemed that the silence that followed the question was the loudest sound of all. The door gunner stared at the three men struck mute, the adrenalin coursing through his veins lending a hysteria to his voice.

'Who is it, for Christ's sake?'

Lockhart, the man who screamed for them to wait, told him.

'Pentecost.'

The door gunner's face froze as if he'd been hit by a sniper's round. Then erupted in fury.

'*Jesus Christ!* I'm not getting my ass shot to hell for that crazy son of a bitch.'

Because he knew what had caused Pentecost to lag behind, what had stolen the words from his comrades' mouths.

Somebody suddenly yelled, his arm frantically pointing.

'*There!*'

Every head snapped around. Then a glancing shot hit the turbine cowling. That was it as far as the pilot was concerned. He wasn't giving the Vietcong snipers a second chance at a direct hit. The chopper started to rise.

All thoughts of the man still outside forgotten, the gunner opened up with his M60, sent a rain of fire into the trees, hot lead shredding leaves and trunks searching out the small, wiry men who hid behind them.

Next to him Lockhart was on his belly hanging halfway out the door. Legs held tightly by the other grunts, his arms hanging below the skids, waving frantically at Pentecost as he charged towards the LZ—as if he didn't know which way to run.

If anyone but the approaching man had seen his face as he risked his life for his friend they'd have seen the horror and anger collide in his eyes at the sight of what Pentecost clutched in his blood-stained hands. It sure as hell wasn't something he'd been issued with.

No. Not again.

Lockhart prayed for strength, not physical but the moral kind, to stop himself from shouting for them to haul him back in, leave the unhinged madman where he belonged. Except his humanity wouldn't let him leave any man behind, leave him to the mercy of the Vietcong at this very moment tearing through the grass, their machetes drawn.

It was a decision he would come to regret almost fifty years later.

'*Drop it!*'

Screaming into his face.

'Drop it, you sick bastard.'

Pentecost grinning all the more, eyes alight with something that no mere words could touch nor extinguish.

'They'll court martial you for Christ's sake.'

The grinning man didn't care. Or maybe it wasn't that at all. Perhaps he had some prescient vision in his deranged mind that in years to come men as culpable as himself, men guilty of far more heinous crimes, would quietly resign, the investigation into their atrocities discreetly buried.

Or maybe he just didn't give a damn.

The chopper continued to rise, the chance to save him disappearing by the second as the sniper fire kept coming. Appeals to his decency and threats of retribution had failed, so Lockhart tried a pragmatic tack.

'You can't hang on with one hand.'

And with those words the finger of blame pointed squarely at Lockhart for what came next.

On the ground Pentecost opened his mouth.

It wasn't to shout a last desperate plea as Lockhart's outstretched hands pulled further away. Or to cry out in shock and pain as a sniper's bullet caught him in the back.

Above him it was Lockhart who screamed.

'*No!*'

Then Pentecost stuffed his prize into his mouth, clamped his teeth tightly shut around it. Jumped like some giant flea, locked his blood-streaked fingers around Lockhart's left arm as the chopper rose and banked.

Lockhart stared in open-mouthed horror at the crazed face of the man clamped to his arm like a monstrous leech and felt his self-control stretch and then give way inside him.

He lashed out. A vicious open-handed slap across the mouth that grinned around its prize. Still the teeth kept their grip. So he grabbed the other end and pulled, his gorge rising, filling his throat with hot salty bile.

He'd be damned if he let go.

Pentecost swinging below him knew it too. And he would not forfeit his bounty. He let go of Lockhart's arm with his right hand. To punch him in the face? To pound the back of the hand tugging at his mouth? Who knows? It didn't matter.

Because in the split second that he hung suspended by one hand, his other poised to strike, a sniper's round hit the landing skid above his head then ricocheted harmlessly into the distance.

But the damage was done.

Both men flinched at the impact so close to their heads. Maybe if it had only been one of them, things would have been different. As it was, the combined force of their involuntary spasms jerked them apart. Left Pentecost hanging in mid-air. As if his rage and madness were sufficient to keep him aloft.

Then he dropped. Landed with a heavy splash in the paddy field below.

The last they saw of Avery Pentecost was as he loped unhurriedly into the trees like an animal that has returned to its natural habitat, the place where it can be what it truly is, do what it was brought into this world to do.

As they watched the excited Vietcong hard on his tail, one man voiced the thought running through all their heads.

'God help those VC.'

51

IN THE SILENCE THAT FOLLOWED CROW'S STORY EVAN WOULD HAVE sworn that he heard the sound of a helicopter retreating into the distance. It was only the beating of his heart, loud in his ears in the quiet of Crow's back room that was as nothing compared to the lull that had filled the slick almost fifty years before.

'Were you on that chopper?'

'I was the door gunner. I'd have gotten the hell out of there the minute I heard Pentecost's name.'

'Did you ever see him again?'

Despite what Crow had already spoken of, he hesitated. Looked off into the distance. Evan reckoned about nine thousand miles into the distance.

'No.'

'Tell the truth and shame the devil.'

Crow gave him a soft smile.

'I've never talked about any of this. Not to my wife'—he flicked his head up at the ceiling—'or to my son.'

Neither man realized it but what he'd just said would give an insight into what later happened to Evan. For the present, Evan wasn't going to let it go.

'Maybe they never asked.'

Crow nodded, that must be it.

'Seeing as you have asked, nobody actually ever *saw* him again. But men came back from patrol saying they thought they'd glimpsed, or felt like a sixth sense, somebody, something shadowing them. And they'd say they heard music. Always the same song. *The end* by The Doors. Sometimes they'd come across the body of Vietcong who'd been butchered. They looked like the animals had been tearing them apart.'

A shudder went through Evan, an image of a man with teeth filed to points filling his mind. At some point during Crow's story his pet bird had settled on his shoulder. Now, two pairs of black beady eyes peered at Evan. If he put his own eyes out of focus they appeared to move together, merge into one, the bird's beak seeming to come from the center of Crow's face. The effect was unsettling after a tale of a man gone back to nature and its atavistic ways.

'What happened to him?'

Crow shrugged, who knows?

'Rumors are what happened to him. Some people said he died over there.'

Evan knew him well enough to know that in Crow-speak what isn't said is often more important than what is.

'And what do the others say?'

Crow smiled as if he'd just been given the opportunity to deliver the punch line to a joke.

'That he didn't.'

'He came home?'

Again the shrug. It was one shrug too many for Evan, this pretence that Crow knew nothing about it, that he was as bewildered as the rest of them. Crow was good at a lot of things. Playing the part of a senile old fool wasn't one of them.

'Tell me what happened.'

'It's just rumors, remember.'

Those were the words that came out of his mouth. What Evan heard was *here follows some gold-plated truths*.

'People say he didn't come back, so much as he was brought back.'

Evan decided to mix a little naivety with a dollop of facetiousness, see what came out.

'To face charges for his crimes?'

Crow smiled indulgently. Silly boy.

'No. To take advantage of the skills he'd acquired in committing those crimes. You've heard of the Phoenix Program?'

His tone of voice implied that he expected a negative response. Evan didn't disappoint.

'It was a collaboration between the CIA, US special operations forces and military intelligence and the South Vietnamese, amongst others.'

Evan felt the first pangs of a faceless, nameless dread in his gut. It stemmed from his friendship with Crow. The knowledge that, stuffed full of information as he was, he rarely divulged any of it just for the sake of making conversation or filling the myriad holes in Evan's education. When Crow gave you a history lesson it was because it was pertinent to the present. The future, too, and your continued participation in it. So Evan's gut churned.

'The CIA described it as a set of programs that were used to attack and destroy the political infrastructure of the Vietcong,' Crow said, and laughed again, as he had about the irony of the house on Passover Lane. 'You don't need me to tell you what programs are.' He made air quotes with his fingers as he said the word. 'Most people who aren't having to explain their activities to a government committee would just come out and say torture and interrogation. Some assassination too, of course. The torture was particularly barbaric. Look it up on the internet if you feel like making yourself feel ill. Or maybe if you want to find out the sort of things the people you vote for will do in the name of democracy.'

Now Evan understood Crow's need to stand and pace while he talked. The vague sense of trepidation that had been growing inside him demanded movement. To be doing something, even if it was only pacing the floor like a man in a prison cell. He pushed himself to his feet, went to stand looking out of the window at Crow's back yard.

'That's all well documented,' Crow said.

Again, it was the unspoken words that mattered the most.

The things that are not well documented.

Then, as if to underline the veracity of what he was about to say next, Crow repeated his earlier caveat. That made Evan turn away from the window to look at him directly. Because Crow may as well have clapped his hands to get attention.

'This is all rumors, remember. But I've heard it said that some people thought the Phoenix Program was such a rip-roaring success in Vietnam, why not bring it, or something like it, home with us.'

'And that's what Pentecost was brought back for?'

Crow nodded slowly, mechanically. His mind was elsewhere, thousands of miles away in the jungles and paddy fields of South East Asia. From the hollow blackness in his eyes Evan knew that he was re-living atrocities seen or even participated in.

'Yes. To form and head-up a loose association of veterans with a diverse selection of skills.'

The word *skills* was a euphemism that might have been substituted directly for the phrase *set of programs* used to describe the capturing, torturing and killing of the Vietcong.

'And then to put those skills to work. When a job needed

doing that might not stand up to the scrutiny of the public at large.'

'With no accountability.'

Crow smiled at him. The boy was learning at last.

'You think that's what's going on here?' Evan said, telling himself that if Crow shrugged in response to this one, he'd poke him in both eyes at once.

'Don't you?'

'I don't know anything about it. Was Lockhart in this group?'

'There's not a published list of members.'

The rebuke was very different, the sharpness and force of it, to when Evan had asked if Pentecost had been brought back to face charges for his crimes. It made him feel as if he'd just asked Crow if he was a member himself. He turned quickly back to the window, stared out at the yard, for fear that Crow would see on his face the epiphany he'd just experienced.

It might have taken a while to get there, but once it was there, the thought wasn't going away. So Evan decided to ask him. Because he deserved to know. Crow had sent him on a seemingly simple errand to check on an old friend. And this is where it had led. That begged a question that he wasn't prepared to ask—did you know or suspect all this from the beginning? He asked the easier one instead.

'Are you a member of this group?'

He made the same promise to himself if Crow dared shrug.

'It's not a difficult question, Elwood.'

'I have known people who are.'

The words had a finality to them. Matter closed. And not just the question of whether Crow was or had been a member of the group of veteran assassins and practitioners of other black arts. It felt like the end of the whole affair. Crow had the answers he'd been after—his friend George Winter was dead and he knew who was responsible.

And that was it.

'Is that it?' Evan said.

'Is what what?'

'The end of the line. George is dead, no need to send a Christmas card this year. Pentecost did it. Move on.'

Crow studied him for a long while. Whereas it usually made Evan feel like a laboratory rat about to be dissected, it didn't do so today. He returned the stare in spades.

'What exactly are you proposing?' Crow said.

'You don't want to do anything about it?'

'Like what?'

Evan put his finger to his lips, pretended to give it some thought.

'Go after Pentecost.'

Crow nodded, sounds reasonable. Until you take the facts into consideration.

'To what end?' He held up a bony finger. 'And don't give me any claptrap about justice.'

'You don't care about your friend George?'

'I can't bring him back. And if I want to bang my head against a brick wall, I've got plenty of them right here.'

Evan considered doing it for him, see if he could knock any sense into him.

'They almost killed me.'

'Be happy they didn't.'

Evan had an answer for that. On balance, he'd rather have not had one and the situation not exist.

'Yet.'

'Ah. You think you're next.'

'I am the only one still alive who knows anything about it.'

'Nonsense. I know about it.'

'Yes, but they don't know about you.'

Crow nodded happily, always a silver lining.

'You're right.'

Again the conversation had the feeling of being at a natural end, all outstanding matters satisfactorily dealt with. Except Crow had some more advice for Evan, even if it wasn't worth the breath expended.

'You can't fight these people, Evan. They're everywhere. Cut off one limb and two more grow back in its place. Even if they haven't got official sanction, nothing will ever be done to them. You could spend your life gathering evidence of their activities—'

'Crimes.'

'Yes, crimes. Only to have it lost in the system. You saw how your friend Cortez's investigation was closed down before it even got started. You think that wouldn't happen again? Every step of the way. Until one day they decide, enough of this irritation and stomp on you like a giant cockroach. *Splat*. End of problem.'

It seemed to Evan that Crow was being deliberately obtuse.

'And if that foot is already raised to stomp me?'

'Hmm.'

Crow had the appearance of a man taking one last look at the crossword puzzle before throwing the newspaper away, the last clue unanswered. Evan wanted to point out that, unlike the crossword, there wouldn't be another one of him along tomorrow if he couldn't figure it out.

'What if I could make that go away?' Crow said.

Evan stared at him for a long time before answering.

'Would that be anything to do with talking to people you might have known in the organization in the past?'

Crow smiled, clever boy. He looked as if he was about to reach for his phone then and there.

'No,' Evan said.

'No, *what*?'

'No, it's not enough. They've killed five people—'

'They've killed a lot more than that.'

'—and tried to kill me. And if they can't be touched officially, that only leaves the unofficial option.'

'Let me ask you a question.'

Evan told him to ask away.

'Let's suppose that the man who killed the girl in the house was the President.'

He raised an eyebrow at Evan, got a *whatever* shrug back. Won't make any difference.

'Now assume Pentecost is the Director of the CIA.'

Again the eyebrow. This time the shrug was a little less *so what?*

'Would you still want to take up your personal crusade to bring them down? You. Evan Buckley, avenging angel extraordinaire. Fighting the good fight. Against all of that power and influence and money. I can hear the music playing now.' His voice took on the tone and fervor of a rousing call to action. 'Justice at all costs! Make the bastards pay!'

Evan fought hard to control the smile that threatened to break out and ruin his argument. Because it did sound ridiculous when put like that.

'You're saying that's what we're up against?'

Crow held up a hand, his head shaking fit to fall off.

'*You.* Not *us*. And even if it's not the President and the CIA, that doesn't mean it's nothing at all. They're still a lot bigger than you. Remember the last person who tried to win a fight like that?'

It was a dirty trick.

Because that person had been Evan's wife Sarah, incarcerated in a state asylum ostensibly for her own good after she lost her memory. In reality because she asked too many awkward questions, pushed the wrong people too hard.

Immediately Crow regretted saying it, saw the impact of his words on Evan's face. He moved on quickly, tried a different tack.

'What would it take to make you drop it? To make you swallow your pride. Because that's what it is at the end of the day—'

'And principles.'

'—swallow your *pride* and accept that there are some things you cannot change, some fights that you just can't win. And which aren't worth dying for in the trying.'

That was when Evan's phone rang, before he could think of an answer. At that point, there was no answer, however long he thought about it. What he didn't know was that he'd have one by the end of the call.

'That'll be Kate,' Crow said brightly.

If Evan had been listening to him, he'd have realized that the answer was right there in his words. But he wasn't. Because Crow was wrong. It wasn't Guillory.

It was Lydia.

52

'Do you believe in the saying, no pain, no gain?' Lydia said.

It wasn't an encouraging start. Nor did Evan feel that a quick *No* and then ending the call was appropriate. Because he wasn't as stupid as people thought he was, knew that what she was really asking was, are you prepared to suffer the pain for a gain that's not guaranteed?

'Depends on what the gain is,' Evan said.

Instead of answering, it seemed to him that she echoed Crow's question of a minute ago.

'What is it that you want?'

It struck him then how much things had changed. Not so long ago the answer would have been quick and unequivocal. To learn what had happened to his wife. Now that he had, something—or someone—else had taken its place.

To have Kate Guillory back as she was.

He didn't come out and say it. For one, she knew the answer before she asked the question. More importantly, if he'd opened his mouth and let his thoughts and feelings come pouring out, he'd most likely have given a fuller answer.

To have Kate Guillory back as she was before she was beaten and then taken out to the woods to be killed—by your brother.

That would have been counter-productive despite the small satisfaction it would have given him to say it. Because he knew in the secret oozings of his gut, that the crazy woman on the other end of the line had it in her power to give him what he wanted.

He also knew that she was equally capable of taking it all away in the time it took to gently squeeze the trigger of a Vanquish sniper's rifle.

Then the crazy woman proved him right, demonstrated that she knew exactly what he wanted.

'What is it that *she* wants?'

'Liverman.'

Spoken without a moment's hesitation.

'I can deliver him to you.'

'To me? Not her?'

'No.'

Sitting on its perch for once, Crow's pet bird chose that moment to caw loudly. It made Evan jump. Lydia too.

'What was that?' Then she answered her own question and he heard the smug satisfaction in her voice. 'You're at your friend's house. The old one who needs to get a better lock on his front door.'

There was no need to confirm it. All it did was remind him that she hadn't stolen the gun back for the fun of it.

'Why me?' he said again. 'Why not deliver him to her?'

Again she answered him with another question.

'Do you think she's learned her lesson? When she broke into the pedophile's house. Because if she has, she'll make it official. She'll bring her fat partner and all the rest of them into it. That's too good for Liverman. Because what have they got on him?

Nothing. A name she thinks she remembers while she had a hood over her head and men were beating the shit out of her. He'll walk away laughing.'

She was right.

He knew what effect that would have on her. He also knew what Lydia was going to say next. It made his mouth go dry, his stomach clench. Because it seemed all roads led in just one direction.

'But what if she hasn't learned her lesson? What if she does something else stupid? Something even more stupid? Like killing him. What then? A cop in prison has almost as hard a time as a pedophile. Would you want that for her? Would she want it for herself?'

She left the questions hanging in the void between them, let them do their work. He swallowed, his legs suddenly weak, dropped into the chair behind him. Across the room, Crow pointed at the drinks cabinet, a question on his face. Evan shook his head.

'I asked her about her father,' Lydia said.

Ordinarily the statement would have appeared to come from left field, a random comment thrown out. Just not today. Today its pertinence hit him like a slap around the face. Because it seemed that not only did all roads lead in one direction, he was the only one who didn't know where they ended up. Even if he had a nasty feeling about it.

'She wouldn't talk about him. Why do you think that is?'

He tried to block out her words and all the thoughts that they sent spinning through his mind. Seemed she wasn't happy leaving it there.

'You think he swallowed his gun? Maybe his little girl found him with his brains spattered all over the walls.'

The phone creaked in his hand. Suddenly he was aware of

Crow at his elbow, a glass of the good stuff held towards him. Maybe the old buzzard had better hearing than he let on. Or perhaps he simply watched the color drain from Evan's face as his whole body sagged into the chair. Evan took the glass gratefully, threw the contents down his throat. The fiery burn did nothing to stop the chill that climbed up inside him.

Still Lydia hadn't finished. Because she was enjoying herself.

'She lives alone, doesn't she? Maybe you'd be the one to find her.'

He wanted to end the call. Wanted to throw the phone against the wall. Stuff it down the pet bird's beak, anything to shut her up.

'You've made your point.'

'Good.'

He read a lot into that one word. Most of all, *don't question my decisions again*.

'What if I do what you want and meet with him. What then?'

'That's up to you. I'm just giving you a means of getting what you want. If you want it badly enough.'

There it was, the crux of the matter. If he believed that the only way for Guillory to move on was for Liverman to get what he deserved—either to spend his life in prison which was unlikely or to meet with an Old Testament type of justice which was what was being offered to him now—was he prepared to do it? And to live with another scar on his conscience.

Not forgetting that it was very likely that Lydia was setting them all up.

'What if I say no?'

'Then I offer it to her. And you risk living every day of your life wondering if today's the day you get a call or find her. Or maybe that won't ever happen. Maybe I'm being melodramatic and you just watch her go quietly insane as it eats her up. I reckon a gun in the mouth is better than that. Think about it.'

Except there wasn't anything to think about. Like Guillory before him he understood that whichever way it panned out, things were drawing to a close.

'I'm in.'

53

'THAT WAS HER, WAS IT?' CROW SAID AS EVAN SLIPPED THE TOXIC messenger that was his phone back into his pocket. 'The woman who took the gun.'

Evan held up his hand, pulled the phone out again, made a call.

'What do you want?' Ryder said by way of greeting.

'What did you mean when you said to me it must be her self-destructive streak that attracts her to me, she gets it from her old man?'

A heavy sigh came down the line.

'Jesus. I wish I'd never opened my mouth.'

That makes two of us, Evan thought.

'Did he kill himself?'

'You'll have to ask her.'

'Why?'

'Because it's not my place.'

'No. Why did he do it? You just as good as told me he did.'

There was a long pause as Ryder realized it was true. Even if it was only really the final confirmation. The seeds had been sown when he put the words *self-destructive* and *her old man* in the same sentence.

'He . . .'

Evan held his breath, the silence in the room absolute. Because Crow had heard Evan's questions. From where Evan sat, he looked as if he'd passed away silently while Evan wasn't looking, he was so still.

Ryder cleared his throat.

'He—'

Without warning Crow's pet bird let out a loud squawk, took to the air.

The moment was lost.

'No,' Ryder said. 'You'll have to ask her.'

There was no point pushing him. Evan swiped at the bird as it flew lazily past, missed it by a mile. It let out another harsh caw. He had no trouble interpreting—*gotta do better than that.*

'You're at that crazy old guy's place, are you?'

He wondered if that was how Guillory had described Crow when she'd mentioned him, decided he wouldn't say anything to Crow.

'Yeah.'

'Thought so.'

There was an awkward pause. The words that Ryder spoke next were as if he felt the need to give Evan something to make up for the refusal to discuss Guillory's past.

'Kate told you that we've got a lead on Garfield's murder?'

'Uh-huh.'

'So you don't have to worry either. I'm not going to lose any sleep over what you were doing in that house. You'll answer to a higher power than me for all of your crimes one of these days.'

The line went abruptly dead. As if he'd already said too much, didn't want to say more that he might regret. Evan didn't miss the word *either* and its implications, that he also knew Guillory had been in the house.

Although it was nothing compared to the sacrifice that Evan would shortly be faced with, Ryder had made his own personal offering, had sacrificed some part of his professional integrity.

After the call ended a thought struck Evan, one prompted by Ryder's reference to Crow. He looked over at the crazy old guy and immediately felt ashamed of what had just gone through his mind. Because it had occurred to him that it would be the easiest thing in the world for him to ask Crow to do some of the research that he was so good at, see what he could dig up about the death of a police officer called Guillory who had very probably taken his own life.

It made him feel dirty.

Grubbing around behind her back to see what he could find out instead of coming right out and asking her. He felt guilty too. Because he'd asked Ryder the questions in front of Crow. And Crow had witnessed Ryder's refusal to answer. He knew that the minute he was out the door, Crow would be digging away without having to be asked. He was tempted to tell him now that he didn't want to know what he discovered.

Nor did Crow say anything about it. Which only confirmed his suspicions. So they both acted like the call to Ryder hadn't occurred.

'That was the woman who took the gun, was it?' Crow said, referring back to the phone conversation they were allowed to discuss.

'Uh-huh.'

'What did she want?'

'To offer me a chance to get Liverman.'

'Get?'

Evan took a leaf out of Crow's book, shrugged, you work it out.

'You. Not Kate.'

Evan confirmed it. Him. Not Kate.

'Hmm. She's up to something. You think she's luring you there in order to kill you?'

He said it as if he'd just asked Evan if he thought it was going to rain. A sharp bark of nervous laughter exploded from Evan's mouth.

'Jesus, Elwood. Why not tell it how it is?'

That earned him a disapproving look that spoke volumes about what was wrong with the world today.

'It won't change anything if you pussyfoot around, refuse to call a spade a spade. Besides, maybe it's not you she's interested in. Perhaps she's using you to lure Kate there.'

'I'm bait, you mean.'

Crow shrugged, deal with it.

'What are you going to do?'

'I don't have a choice.'

Then he took him through Lydia's assessment of the situation and the irreparable harm—or worse—that might result for Guillory.

'You can't argue with that,' Crow said, which was as unhelpful as it was true.

It was then that Evan's long acquaintance with Crow paid dividends. If you accept that dividends in the wider sense are not always good things. Because it seemed to him that Crow looked very uncomfortable. If he'd been his namesake, the pet crow, he'd have been hopping along his perch, back and forth in his agitation. So Evan told him to do what he'd tell the pet crow to do if it had tried to swallow too fat a worm.

'Spit it out.'

'You remember that telephone number you gave me . . .'

Evan said that he did.

'I wasn't able to trace it . . .'

The penny dropped. As did, as far as Evan could see, even more shit onto his head.

'You called it? After giving me such a hard time. Accusing me of always jumping first, looking later.'

Crow stuck a bony finger down his collar, tugged at it.

'There was nothing else to do.'

'You could've tried doing that. Nothing.'

'That's rich, coming from you.'

This was a trick that Evan was familiar with. The guilty party attempting to shift the blame onto him. Guillory tried it all the time. With her, it invariably worked. Not with Crow. He held up a hand.

'This isn't about me.' Even as he said the words, he saw a gleam in Crow's eyes that said *oh yes it is.* He ignored it. 'What happened when you called?'

'I think there's some sort of coded exchange meant to take place. I failed it and they hung up.'

'So someone's on their guard.'

'Probably.'

'Likely to be suspicious if someone, let's call her Lydia, sets up a meeting.'

'Definitely.'

Evan blew out a great rush of air. He wiped the back of his hand across his forehead, flicked away imaginary sweat.

'Thank God you're going in my place.'

He didn't get the reaction he was expecting. Even though he was joking, he'd have expected to see at least a momentary look of horror on Crow's face before he caught on. Instead he got a look of serious consideration. As far as Crow was concerned the remark wasn't as stupid as it sounded. But what he said took the conversation in a different direction altogether. Or so it seemed to Evan.

'I asked you earlier what it would take to persuade you to drop the Pentecost matter.'

Evan nodded, yes, he remembered.

'It seemed to me that you were at a loss to know what to say.'

Evan said that was true as well.

'Are you any better placed to give me an answer after your telephone conversations?'

Evan didn't miss the reference to conversations, plural. Including the one with Ryder. Because he realized now what Crow was getting at. Crow answered for him before he had a chance to put it into words.

'What if I could guarantee that Pentecost will leave you alone for as long as you do the same. And'—he paused to make sure Evan was giving him his full attention—'arrange for Kate's problems to go away? Would that be enough to satisfy your pride and paranoia?'

Evan didn't even bother to say there was nothing paranoid about almost being burned alive on a boat, he was so taken aback by Crow's suggestion.

'You mean for Pentecost's organization to deal with Liverman?'

The shrug was back, why not?

'It's what they do, after all.'

Evan wondered if this was how it had happened with the house on Passover Lane. Two old friends having a discussion, maybe over a shot of the good stuff.

Got a bit of a problem in Passover Lane.

Really? Want us to sort it out for you?

If it's not too much trouble.

Not at all. Consider it done.

Then a raising of glasses, a celebratory *cheers*. And before you know it, five people are dead. That's what old friends are for.

Crow gave him time. Because he knew it was hard for the

boy. To be asked to decide whether the end justifies the means. And if so, to give the go-ahead. Easy once you've done it a few times. Not so easy the first time. So Crow made it easier for him.

'I can't guarantee anything, of course. You'll still have to go along with Lydia's plan, to meet with Liverman and his thugs. And risk the possibility of Lydia herself on a rooftop with the gun she stole, waiting for you.'

It struck Evan then that pride is indeed a strange beast. Because when Crow had told him to swallow his pride and not pursue Pentecost, pride was a bad thing. Now it was pride again that had prevented him from immediately taking Crow up on his offer. Clicking his fingers as it were, *deal with it,* from the comfort of an easy chair. But once an element of uncertainty and personal risk were introduced, that same pride demanded his participation.

Crow hadn't finished either.

'There's a price to pay, as well.'

'That's not a problem,' Evan said, disappointment that Crow should think the monetary cost of what he was suggesting would sway him lending a sharper edge to his voice. He still had a substantial sum stashed away, a generous bonus paid to him on the successful outcome of a recent case. The one where he'd first come across Crow, in fact. Crow was well aware of it, too.

Crow held up a finger. It wasn't his middle finger in a response to Evan's tone. Nor was it his index finger, raised to interrupt him, give him further information before he made his decision.

Except it was exactly that. Evan just didn't know it yet. Because Crow was holding up the little finger of his left hand.

'Upstairs, first door on the left,' Evan said. 'Be quick.'

The look on Crow's face made the smile on Evan's lips at his joke slip away almost before it appeared. It wasn't the time for levity. There was none of the usual *stupid boy* accusations either.

That's when the realization took hold. Crow never did anything for no reason. Crow gave a small nod when he saw the change in Evan's eyes. And if his demonstration wasn't sufficient, he made it clearer.

'They don't want your money. They've got more than they know what to do with already.'

Still the finger was held aloft. As if Crow was waiting for Evan to put it into words before he dropped his hand. It came out as a squeak when he tried.

'They want your finger?'

'Only the tip.'

There was no hint of humor in Crow's voice despite the words. Evan didn't feel like laughing either. He swallowed as if his fingertip had already been cut off, fed to him.

'Why?'

'Because they can. Because they provide a service that nobody else does. Call it a demonstration of how committed their clients are.'

The tip of Evan's finger seemed to grow cold as Crow spoke to match the chill in his gut. Without thinking, he wrapped the fingers of his right hand around it. In his mind he saw his left hand on a wooden chopping block, fingers splayed wide, a meat cleaver held high. He was aware that Crow had said something else, something he'd missed. What he hadn't missed was the change in Crow's voice as he said it, his voice very different to when he was talking of clients and commitment as if it were a corporate business deal of some kind.

'What was that?'

Crow's face said he wasn't happy repeating himself. His tone of voice reinforced the point.

'I said because Pentecost has a cruel streak running through him a mile wide.'

Although he'd never seen him apart from in an old

photograph, the name brought an image of a mouth filled with teeth filed to points. Then a sudden feeling of nausea at the thought that maybe the razor-sharp meat cleaver he'd imagined a moment ago was just wishful thinking.

'He doesn't . . .'

Crow shook his head slowly, a *don't be silly* half-smile on his lips. Like a dentist who's just deliberately filled the syringe with water and not novocaine telling you that it's not going to hurt.

'Of course he doesn't bite it off. I don't know where you get such stupid ideas from.'

Evan bit back the protest on his lips. It wasn't worth the breath.

'Good to know.'

Crow studied him now, well aware of what he'd set in motion. Except for Evan it wasn't just a simple question of whether he would pay the price of the tip of his finger to get Guillory her life back.

'What would I tell Kate? I caught it in the blender?'

'I'm sure you'll think of something.'

Evan didn't miss the fact that Crow was already talking as if he'd agreed to go ahead. There was no *if* about it. Again he had the mental image of his hand on a wooden chopping block. Except this time the scarred wood was stained red. He saw himself looking down at it in horror and disbelief in the instant before the pain kicked in. As if it were somebody else's hand, somebody else's fingertip separated by a half inch of empty space from the rest of the finger.

He felt like pinching himself. The situation was unreal. He'd had his share of injuries over the years, inflicted on him as he equally inflicted them on others. In the heat of the moment, the midst of a fight, the adrenalin flowing. But to sit in a comfortable chair in a pleasant living room with the sun slanting through the windows and decide whether to sacrifice the tip of his finger as if they were discussing chopping a dead branch off a tree in the yard.

Suddenly a thought went through his mind. As if his subconscious was desperately scraping the barrel for any other explanation. There was only one that came to mind. And the more he looked at Crow's wrinkly old face staring back at him, the more likely it seemed. Crow was playing with him. A test to see how far he would go, what he would agree to, however outrageous and unreasonable. Would he agree to physical pain and mutilation to go with the scars on his conscience?

'You're not just making this up?'

Crow didn't answer, let the silence speak for him, his lips a tight line, eyes unblinking. The hope that had burned briefly inside Evan flickered and went out.

'Didn't think so.'

It had been a last-ditch attempt by his subconscious to put off the inevitable. Now he accepted it. He couldn't have told you how it made him feel. The chill of his fear battling it out with the warmth that was spreading through his veins as he saw Guillory's pain taken away as cleanly as the tip of his finger.

Sacrifice.

An act of slaughtering an animal or person or surrendering a possession as an offering to a deity.

Crow had been right to assume that the decision was already made. It was all business now.

'Before or after.'

'After. Sometimes a long time after.'

'So you never know when they're coming.'

Crow gave a gentle shrug, I don't make the rules.

'I told you. He's a cruel man.'

'What if you die first?'

'They wipe out your whole family.'

Evan was out of the chair before the word *family* had left

Crow's mouth. Then he saw the faint smile on the dry old lips. He dropped back into his seat, his own mouth turned down.

'I thought this wasn't a laughing matter.'

'You're right, it's not. Sorry, I shouldn't have said that. All debts are considered paid should you die before they call you.'

Evan wished there was a way you could frame words and hang them on your wall. Because something as rare as an apology from Crow was worth displaying, showing off to visitors. Then Crow ruined it all.

'So at least there's an upside if Lydia is waiting on a rooftop with her Vanquish preparing to shoot everybody who turns up for your meeting.'

Before Evan could repeat that it wasn't a laughing matter there was a sharp bang on the ceiling from upstairs. He looked up, in his mind the memory of the person he thought he'd caught sight of disappearing up the stairs when Crow opened the door to him.

Crow didn't look up. Which said everything. So neither of them mentioned it, didn't bother to suggest that maybe Crow's wife had fallen out of bed. It was his house after all. He could have as many visitors as he liked.

But he was up to something.

There was something else. Crow was staring at him more intensely than he usually did which was bad enough. The chill in his gut seemed to grow colder. There was more to come. Crow had saved the worst to last.

'What?'

Crow shook his head slowly.

'It doesn't matter.'

Any other day Evan would have grabbed him by the throat and shaken him. Not today. Because somehow, he knew what Crow had decided not to ask. The unvoiced question sucked all the anger and frustration that he might have felt towards Crow out of him, left him feeling hollow. In a way it was worse than if Crow had said he'd made a mistake when he said fingertip, he'd meant right arm.

'I don't know,' he said.

Crow heard the truth in those few words. He understood the raw and tangled emotions that lay behind them and acknowledged the unfairness of the unasked question.

'Fair enough.'

Because without knowing how, Evan had known that Crow wanted to ask him whether he'd have agreed to the loss of a fingertip to get his wife Sarah back. He didn't want to think about it now. What purpose would it have served? He got up to go.

'I'll let you know as soon as Lydia gets in contact again.'

He said it in the full knowledge that Crow had not listed all of the potential dangers he might face. That a fingertip was not all that was at stake. That by meeting with Lydia in Guillory's place he might well be making a sacrifice of himself. Because who could say whether Pentecost and his men when given his location by Crow might not decide to kill two birds with one stone, wrap up for good all the loose ends connected to Passover Lane and forego their fee of a severed fingertip.

What he could never have known was that the man tasked with the assignment after Crow made his call had a very personal reason to hate him, to exercise his discretion and expand the brief he'd been given to include Evan himself.

54

KATE GUILLORY FELT LIKE SHE WAS SIX YEARS OLD.

That was how old she'd been the last time she'd been told to wait in the car. This time it had been Ryder doing the telling, not her father, and she was parked a couple of blocks away from the derelict warehouse where she was supposed to meet Liverman. The backs of her legs weren't stinging either.

'You're too emotionally involved,' he'd said.

It made sense. She could accept it. So long as she ignored the fact that what he was really saying was *you can't be trusted*. That, and the words muttered under his breath as he left her in the car to join the rest of the team taking up their positions.

Not after what happened at Garfield's house.

Patricia Malloy, the female officer who had taken her place was a good likeness, except—and she better see a good deal of head nodding coming from Buckley's direction—her eyes were like dark pissholes in the snow compared to the denim blue of Guillory's own eyes. She was carrying a few pounds of extra weight around the middle too. And it wasn't just the Kevlar vest.

Despite the irregular circumstances giving rise to the

operation, everybody was upbeat about it. If everything went to plan, the two thugs who butchered Garfield would be dead or in custody by the end of the day. If they survived the takedown, one or both of them was bound to turn, to deliver Liverman himself to them. If they were lucky, they'd also find evidence at the scene of the gang's aberrant activities. And if Guillory could find comfort or relief in any of that, so much the better.

So she was feeling like a very relaxed six year old sitting in the car.

And that wasn't right.

Because every night she relived the horrors of her ordeal. Found herself sitting bolt upright in her bed in the small hours of the morning. Covers thrown from the bed, her skin cold to the touch and slick with sweat, a nameless anxiety gnawing at her stomach, making her heart race in her chest. Studying the aerial photographs of the location at the briefing she'd been aware of sly glances in her direction, knew her face betrayed her as she saw herself tied to a chair in one of the old buildings. Now here she was, a couple of blocks from the scene. On a street she last drove down in the back of a van with a hood over her head. Facing the imminent arrival of Liverman and the men who'd beaten her senseless come to finish the job. She'd have expected it to have worked her gut into a twisted knot, left her chest tight and breathless.

It hadn't.

Which meant one of two things.

She was over it.

Ha!

The sudden bark of laughter that burst from her mouth would've had Ryder congratulating himself for making a good call when he confined her to the car.

Or they were in the wrong location.

Because she'd have felt something. Hooded and semi-conscious as she was when she was delivered to the men who'd interrogated her, she'd still have felt something approaching this place. Sounds or smells that her mind hadn't acknowledged on a conscious level but had stored deep in its bowels would respond now with a pricking at the back of her neck or an irrational fear that she couldn't shake.

There was none of that.

Then the radio crackled into life.

White Toyota Corolla approaching.

She smiled to herself and it wasn't one that Evan would have wanted turned on him. Lydia was making her play. Because in her mind she was immediately back standing outside the Jerusalem Tavern staring at a car that had been following her. A white Toyota Corolla. Even though there are hundreds of thousands, maybe millions of them in the country, she knew it was the same one. Then, it had been driven by Lydia Strange. Now, who knows? It didn't matter. It was just a distraction, a decoy.

Right on cue, her phone rang. She didn't even bother to look at the display.

'Where to now?' she said.

On the other end of the line Lydia laughed.

'You didn't think I was just going to tell you, did you? So that you could invite the fat detective and all the others along, spoil the fun.'

'Where to?'

Lydia tut-tutted down the phone.

'Just listen. Liverman is going to be here soon. Your boyfriend Evan is already here.'

Guillory swallowed her surprise at the mention of Evan's name. On the other end of the line, Lydia's voice had slowed.

Like she was concentrating on doing something while she talked. Her words confirmed it.

'The crosshairs of my sight are on the bridge of his nose right ... about ... now.'

A feeling was growing rapidly inside Guillory that they'd all underestimated Lydia Strange. Not just her murderous abilities but the depth of her hatred and obsession too. Something bad was coming, something that had been festering inside her for a long time. She tried to keep her voice flat, kept it short, which helped.

'Where?'

'Stop saying that! Things have changed. Two people are going to die today.' Her voice was empty. There was no pity, no shame, no guilt, no regret. There wasn't even anger. Just a blankness that was worse than any fury Guillory had ever seen or felt. 'Liverman is one of them. I'll be doing the world a favor getting rid of that sick fuck. You decide who the other one is.'

Maybe it was because she was tired or perhaps it was the emotional rollercoaster that had been her life since she couldn't remember when, but she wasn't thinking. She opened her mouth and the knee-jerk response popped out.

'You're insane. I'm not going to ...'

She felt Lydia's self-satisfied smirk coming down the line as the words died in her mouth, imagined her face with its look of physical and mental undernourishment coming alive with the mischief she'd set in motion. Something gave in her belly at the realization and she felt an ache in her bladder. Then Lydia's mocking voice.

'Figured it out?'

'Of course I've figured it out, you fucking lunatic. If I don't turn up, that only leaves Evan.'

She got out of the car, stalked around to the driver's side.

Dragged a hand over her face then rested her elbows on the roof, stared at her distorted reflection in the paintwork. For once the outside was a good indicator of what was going on inside. What dirty tricks had Lydia used on Evan, what impossible situation had she put him in? She guessed it was the same as the one she was in.

He thought he was saving her.

She raised her fist to slam it into the car roof, held it there, knuckles white, arm vibrating so hard the whole car shook. But she wouldn't give Lydia the satisfaction of hearing her frustration and anger.

It was all for nothing anyway. Because Lydia was wrong. Her brother's death had nothing to do with her or with Evan. She just wanted to lash out. Somebody was going to pay and she didn't much care who it was, looking to fill the blackness of her bleak, empty eyes with the reflected pain of another.

'This won't make it right, you know,' Guillory said, her voice little more than a whisper, imbued with the weary acceptance that her own words wouldn't change a thing. 'It won't put an end to whatever happens when you close your eyes at night.'

That got a sharp bark of laughter that suggested Lydia had left her meds behind a long time ago. It didn't mean she couldn't put her finger right on the spot.

'Hey! Get your own head straight before you start trying to fuck with mine.'

Once the finger was there, it seemed Lydia had a talent for sniffing out pain, poking and probing, seeing if she couldn't open up some old wounds that might not be as healed up as people tried to pretend.

'You want to tell me about your father yet?'

The image of the door to her father's study was instantly back in her mind. Except it was different this time. As it sometimes was when she was down. It was still closed. But now it was opening. She didn't want it to open. Not now. Not with everything else that was going on. Not ever.

She screwed her eyes shut, the vision exiled back to where it came from, the stain of its recalling papered over with the urgency and horror of the confrontation that lay ahead.

'Sure. He was the best, most decent man I ever knew. Anything else?'

Lydia hadn't expected an answer, had just wanted to make her point. Her voice was filled with scorn when she replied.

'Yeah, right. Just don't go lecturing me on what happens when you close your eyes at night. So. What's it going to be?'

'Where do I go?'

'*Aw*. How sweet. Take me! Except I might be the unstable lying bitch you think I am. What did you call me? A fucking lunatic? Yeah, well, maybe I'll kill everybody in sight just for the fun of it. Don't bring your fat partner or any of the others. There's somebody watching to make sure. I know you don't believe there was ever anybody with a sniper's rifle aimed at your head last time we met. Maybe there wasn't. Maybe you don't believe me now. Doesn't matter, it'll be your boyfriend's head you're risking if you want to take a chance. It's funny, he's the one I got the gun from. What's that phrase?'

Guillory couldn't stop herself from glancing up at the rooftops and darkened windows all around, choked back the urge to scream down the phone at her.

Poetic justice, you stupid bitch.

She had no idea what half-assed notion had made Evan take the rifle from Lydia's mad dog of a brother. But he'd be the one paying the price for his stupidity. Fate catching up with him at long last. Because if the correlation between cause and effect was always so clear cut, he'd have been in the ground a long time ago.

Now it was in her power to send fate on its way once more with her foot up its ass.

'Just give me the address.'

Lydia snickered, nice try.

'Uh-uh. Start driving. I'll direct you. And don't bother calling him. If he touches his phone you might as well turn around, save yourself a wasted journey. Unless you've got a bucket and a mop in the trunk.'

55

Evan got halfway out of his car, stood with one foot on the ground, one foot still in the car. He looked around at the derelict factory buildings surrounding him on three sides and felt his heart and his spirits fall. The place was soulless and depressing as hell, a reminder of the passing nature of all things. Not just our own flesh and blood but also the things we build. Things that once were new and exciting are soon old and forgotten.

People might say that in the face of all that transience, the only thing that endures is love. Looking at the desolation and decay around him and with the prospect of meeting a deviant like Liverman looming over him like a black cloud, Evan would've ventured that evil is hanging on in there too.

He looked around at the broken windows and busted-in doors, some of the buildings with their roofs sagging under the weight of so many years of neglect, and wondered which one of the squalid rooms Guillory had been taken to and tied to a chair to have the will to live systematically beaten out of her. They couldn't have chosen a more fitting place.

It should have brought him some comfort that being here

himself meant that she didn't have to return to this place. The place where her life was put on hold by a deviant and his sadistic thugs and a mad dog who traded people's lives for cash.

The comfort was notable by its absence of course, a nagging dread eager to take its place. Because, like her, he'd been around the block a time or two, knew that things were never as simple as they seemed. They sure as hell weren't simple today, caught between the mad dog's unbalanced sister and the goodwill of a man with teeth filed to points.

He quickly scanned the rooftops of the nearest buildings, didn't see the prone outline of a body nor the flash of sun on a sniper's scope. As if he needed reminding of the inadequacy of the simple three-point plan he'd put together in the fifteen minutes' Lydia had given him to get there.

Act like bait.

Stay alive.

And if the cavalry doesn't arrive, shoot anything that moves.

The sound of an approaching car jerked him from his thoughts. More than a hundred thousand dollars' worth of Range Rover SUV was negotiating its way across the cracked and pitted asphalt. It looped around then stopped thirty yards away, his own car shielding him from it. The front doors opened as one. Two large men stepped halfway out, as if mirroring his own stance. He was face to face with the men who'd ripped open Garfield's throat and beaten Guillory. Back again, hoping to finish the job.

That thought put a grim smile of satisfaction on his lips. It faded just as quickly as in the back of the SUV he made out the shapeless form of a whale of a man, the evil of his presence seeming to flow from the shiny ostentatious vehicle like a toxic cloud seeking out new flesh to touch and sully.

Liverman.

A personification of all their hatreds and fears, an abstraction made all too real.

Kate Guillory's nemesis.

Then one of the men ducked his head back inside the car, relayed the news of Evan's presence and Guillory's absence to the monster in the back. Seconds later his head was back out again, staring malevolently at Evan across the weeds and discarded trash.

'Where's Guillory?'

Evan hoped for the sake of the human race at large that he hadn't needed to consult with his master to come up with an opening like that.

'In that building over there.'

He nodded at the shell of a building behind them. Their heads whipped around as if they expected to see her standing there with a shotgun in her hands. By the time they'd turned back his gun was in his hand. Trouble was, so were theirs.

It was a Mexican standoff of sorts, if two against one counts.

This would be as good a time as any for Pentecost's man to make his presence felt, Evan thought to himself.

Ask and you shall receive.

Without warning two gunshots rang out. So fast as to be almost one continuous sound, the sharp crack of their reports bouncing off the buildings surrounding them, racing each other into the distance. Both driver and passenger standing at the front of the SUV jerked violently as if a truck had rear-ended their car. Pools of bright red blossomed on their chests, rapidly staining the white of their shirts with arterial blood. The shooter, whether Lydia Strange or Pentecost's man, had opted for the safe shot. Both men hung suspended for a split second, mouths open in surprise or pain, then crumpled to the ground. Four hundred and fifty pounds of arrogant bodyguard-cum-interrogator rendered instantly useless by two quick squeezes of an index finger.

Good riddance. And a good start to a day of bloodletting.

Evan had ducked instinctively at the sound of the shots. Now he stood back up, looked behind him to where the shots had come from. He thought he saw the quick flash of sunlight on glass, couldn't be sure. One thing was crystal clear. If the shooter had wanted him dead, he'd be slumped over the car now, a ragged hole punched in his back or the top of his head blown away. Did that make it Pentecost's man? Or was Lydia simply clearing the minor pieces off the board, making room for the main players?

Because he knew now that it had never been her intention for it to be only Liverman and himself, knew that Guillory's arrival was imminent.

He had to get to Liverman before she arrived. Because he didn't want to think what she would do, face to face with him, here in this godless place. And if he had to haul him from the car for whoever was on the roof to do what they had set out to do, so be it.

He came around from behind the car door, ran towards Liverman's car. Halfway there, in the middle of the open ground between the two cars, a small explosion of concrete kicked up a yard from his left foot, a split second ahead of the whipcrack from above and behind him. He froze. Recognized the shot for what it was. Then a voice riding on the back of the echoes as they bounced from building to building. A voice he knew.

'Don't move.'

A barked instruction, sharp as the shot that preceded it.

Lydia Strange. Not Pentecost's man.

He ignored it. Took another step towards Liverman's car. Then a second warning shot, the round ricocheting off the ground no more than six inches from his foot, splinters of concrete and grit peppering his leg and shoe.

The instruction behind it a scream this time with a hysterical intensity that only a fool would ignore.

'*I said don't move!*'

He didn't move. He was out of time anyway.

Kate Guillory's car came bucking and bouncing across the rutted ground in a cloud of dust, nose-dived to a stop beside his car. She was out of it before it stopped rocking on its suspension, staring at him standing exposed in the open ground. She took in the two men slumped dead across the SUV, her head snapping instantly to the rooftops. Back and forth from one building to the next.

'It's Lydia,' he called.

She gave him a look. Who else would it be? Then she trotted across to join him. Neither of them asked the other what they were doing there. What would've been the point? They were where they were, a maniac with a sniper's rifle on the rooftops above them. Deal with it.

Nor did he say anything about a man that Pentecost might have sent. He might need that breath another day.

'Waiting for me?' she said. 'I put on some lipstick for you.'

In those few words and the hint of a smile that went with them he knew that this would end today, one way or the other. Because the old Kate Guillory was back standing beside him. Whether she hung around for more than the next five minutes was anybody's guess.

And Lydia's call.

He indicated the pockmarks in the ground.

'She asked me to wait here.'

Guillory nodded. She knew why.

She wants us all together.

'Nice way of asking. Where is she?'

He pointed to the rooftop behind them.

'The shots came from over there.'

She followed his finger briefly then turned her attention to the SUV. The mass of flesh that was Liverman was visible behind the driver's seat, a faint misting to the glass as the heat and sweat poured from his skin.

'Cover the passenger side. I'll get him out.'

Without a glance at the rooftop she marched around to the rear driver's side door. In her purposeful stride he saw some hidden intent at work. Just as he knew something that she didn't —the potential and now unlikely intervention by Pentecost's man—she knew something she wasn't sharing with him. Because it seemed to him as if her movements were a direct challenge to the woman on the roof.

He guessed that she had arrived at an understanding with herself, her personal Armageddon. If she couldn't be who she was before, she wouldn't be anybody at all. Just a memory in the minds of the people who'd loved her before the sick deviant cowering in the SUV had stripped her life away, left only the bare bones of the person she used to be.

He forced his teeth to unclench, his breathing to resume. Moved his finger outside the trigger guard for fear that in the rage that colonized his body like a cancer he would inadvertently squeeze the trigger. Because he didn't want to squeeze that trigger. Not unless the barrel of the gun was already firmly between Liverman's teeth, the sound of his pleading filling his ears.

He took up his position by the rear passenger door. On the other side Guillory pulled at the door handle like she wanted to rip it off. It was locked. She could easily have reached in through the open driver's door and released it. But where's the fun in that? She reversed the gun in her hand, smashed the window with the butt. Small cubes of glass showered Liverman's lap, forced a strangled squeak from between the too-full lips. If he hadn't been the size he was, she'd have dragged him bodily through the jagged hole.

She wrenched the door open. Then stopped abruptly.

Watching her face over the wide expanse of the SUV's shiny roof Evan saw something pass behind her eyes. Something that lives inside all of us, and not so deep as you might think, a reminder of a time when we were little better than the wild animals we hunted. It made him very glad he wasn't Joseph Liverman. Or whatever his real name might have been. Because soon the only name he'd go by would be *dead meat*. And it wouldn't be any kind of meat that even the hungriest maggot or a half-starved rabid dog would foul its mouth with.

He watched her as she went to the back of the car, raised the tailgate. He knew when she'd seen what she was after by the smile that crept over her painted lips. If you could call a sour twist of the mouth like that a smile.

Liverman wasn't going anywhere. So he joined her at the back of the car. Together they stared into the interior.

He saw a rough sackcloth hood.

She saw an old friend.

He saw dried blood and vomit.

God only knows what she saw—and he wasn't telling.

She picked it up. Held it almost reverently. As if it were a priceless religious relic. In a way it was, or at least it had a sacred quality to it.

It was her salvation.

They exchanged a look as she held it tightly in her hand. So many things passed between them in that look, but one thought more than any other.

This is what has stood between us.

In a perfect world he'd have been able to bite back the inappropriate comment that surged up from inside him. In the real world even armor-plated teeth wired tightly shut couldn't have kept it in.

'Not sure the color suits you.'

There wasn't a second's hesitation before her reply was out. Not even the fastest flicker of surprise in her denim-blue eyes, as full of light now as he'd ever seen them. Just a look that said she'd have been disappointed at anything less.

'Not any more, it doesn't.'

They both knew who the color would suit.

He took the hood from her. It felt as if she offered it to him. Together they went around to Liverman's door. He leaned into the car and pulled the hood down over Liverman's head, shutting off the incoherent stream of pitiful sub-human sounds as efficiently as a falcon's hood stills a restless bird. Then together, her with a strength spawned somewhere deep inside her, one that harnessed all the pain and fear and anger that she'd carried with her ever since the filthy hood had been over her own head, they hauled Liverman's three hundred pounds out of the SUV as if it were nothing, no more than a person-shaped bag of foul hot air.

She forced his arm up behind his back, jammed his body against the side of the car to stop him from sliding bonelessly to the ground, held him there. For a moment he didn't see Kate Guillory beside him, saw instead something out of a medieval history book, an executioner displaying the condemned man for the pleasure of the jeering crowd.

He thought she might taunt Liverman, maybe slap or punch his head, the blows sudden and unexpected, make him suffer like she had in some small way. It was an unworthy thought, one that made him feel dirty. He knew her better than that.

Besides, it was beyond that.

It was the moment of truth.

They all knew it. In the past minutes he'd forgotten all about

Lydia on the roof behind them, watching as the scene played out for her amusement. He guessed Guillory had too.

Now, with Liverman out of the car, the three of them stood facing the rooftops with the sun behind them, their shadows stretching away ahead of them like their hopes and fears for the future. Waiting in the sudden stillness like gladiators before the emperor. Sweating from exertion or fear, hearts racing, minds filled with so many different thoughts, none of them good.

Liverman praying to any god who would listen that he hadn't pushed Guillory to a place where she no longer cared about anything beyond her rightful revenge.

Evan wondering where the hell Pentecost's man had gotten to and how his whole life might now be forfeit and not just the tip of his little finger.

And Guillory, standing proud, chest and chin thrust forward. Challenging the maniac Lydia Strange to put up or shut up, make good on her threats. Take two of us, let the other walk away.

Then in the distance the sound of police sirens. Because Guillory had called in her location as she bounced across the rutted ground to the confrontation that now engulfed them.

For a brief moment Evan thought that they might stay as they were, frozen, waiting, until the police arrived. That Lydia might shuffle backwards on her belly and make her escape.

Guillory had other ideas.

Because today it had to end. One way or the other.

She looked at him, a question on her face. He nodded, happy to be asked. Even if he knew it wouldn't have made a blind bit of difference whatever he did.

Then, like a snooty waiter in some fancy restaurant, she took hold of the top of the hood over Liverman's head, pulled it off with a flourish. As if she were lifting a silver cover to reveal the chef's culinary creation below.

Except there was no mouth-watering delicacy. Just Liverman's sweat and tear-streaked face, a line of drool making its way down his chin like a demented slug or snail had slithered from his slack mouth and was making its slimy bid for freedom.

The birds had grown suddenly quiet. The stillness of the afternoon had a strange breathless, watchful quality, as if the natural world itself awaited the inevitable outcome of the events now unfolding.

As Guillory swept the hood through the still air with a final flourish reminiscent of a matador's cape, a single gunshot shattered the silence.

Kate Guillory's head exploded.

That's how it looked to Evan as the round blew Liverman's head apart. Gore spotted his own face but nothing like it did hers on the far side of Liverman. Blood and gray brain matter and glistening white bone and lank greasy hair spattered her face and hair and clothes, coating her with what remained of the monster who had haunted her dreams and tormented her in her waking hours.

Except unlike Garfield's bile and vomit that she'd scrubbed from her skin with a manic, almost hysterical intensity, she'd have worn the gore that now dripped from her face like a badge of honor, paraded through the streets with it drying on her face in the warm sun.

Evan knew as surely as she did herself that Liverman's blood and gore had done more than cleanse her of the horrors of her ordeal. With the raising of the hood she had allowed it to wash away some part of her humanity.

As had he for being a willing party to it.

One more small sacrifice paid by each of them, a step taken into another place where justice and vengeance are without distinction.

It seemed to him that she stood now waiting for a greater

price for that crime to be demanded, for payment to be swiftly made. He turned away from her defiant pose to face it with her, looked to the rooftop. Saw the sun reflect on the glass of a sniper's scope.

It wasn't aimed at Guillory.

And his heart swelled inside his chest to see that it was pointing directly at him.

56

ON THE ROOFTOP LYDIA STRANGE'S EYES WERE FIXED AND unwavering. But it wasn't Evan's chest or head that her gaze was focussed on. It was the blue sky and the wispy clouds above that her sightless eyes stared at.

She lay on her back, her throat cut from ear to ear. A quick, silent death at the hands of the man who had taken her place with the stock of the Vanquish sniper's rifle now tucked snugly into his shoulder, his eye at the scope as pitiless as the sun. He'd crept up on her as the echoes of her first two shots reverberated around the disused buildings, her concentration on the scene below total. Then, after she fired her second warning shot into the ground at Evan's feet and screamed at him to stay where he was, he made his move.

Hand clamped over her mouth as he dropped with his knee onto her back. Head pulled sharply up, the razor edge of his knife slicing more sharply still through cartilage and muscle, through veins large and small and the carotid artery. Holding her tightly as her small body twitched and convulsed, her life's blood draining through a convenient hole in the roof, dripping into the empty building below. Quick, maybe painless. Another of the damaged ones sent on her way to find an easier path in the next world.

As the echoes of his first shot—the one that reduced Liverman's head to a red mist—subsided, he resumed chewing his gum, wiped the sweat from his bald head overheating in the sun. The job as described was complete.

But people are only human. Even men who think nothing of cold-bloodedly slitting a young woman's throat as part of the assignment they've been tasked with have their own hopes and fears, insecurities too—even if that might come as a surprise to the person having their throat cut.

So Pentecost's man moved the crosshairs of his scope. If he was going to do this, he'd have to be quick. The sirens were louder now, closer. Except he didn't pan to the right, to the woman standing defiantly, her whole body seeming to scream for his attention.

Me too!

No, he panned left. Towards where Evan Buckley stood staring directly at him. The crosshairs came to rest on the spot between his eyes. Just above the bridge of his nose. There was confusion and doubt in those eyes. The man on the roof understood why. Because the young woman had screamed at him before she died. Buckley had no reason to suspect that she was not still behind the gun.

He stopped chewing once more. Controlled his breathing. His finger tightened on the trigger.

The shit would hit the fan like never before if he made the shot.

But would it make life any better? Take him back to how things were in a half-remembered time that in his heart he knew had never existed?

The sirens were very loud now. He blocked them out. Concentrated.

And because a man who can take another's life without a twinge of sadness or remorse can himself still feel unwanted and unloved, he'd imagined this moment many times. It always ended the same way. With Buckley's head exploding in an eruption of blood and gore as Liverman's had a moment ago. Except in his dreams he didn't have to deal with the fallout.

With his father's rage.

Because Caleb Crow's father was still a force to be reckoned with. Despite his age and the jovial Uncle Elwood front he chose to present to the world. Caleb would bear the brunt of his anger if he pulled the trigger now, killed the man that his father treated like more of a son than he ever had his own flesh and blood.

From his vantage point he saw the approaching police vehicles in the distance. He didn't have long.

His finger tightened on the trigger.

A hair's breadth from the point of firing.

Then Buckley moved.

Except he didn't dive to the ground or for the cover of the vehicle, turning in the air and sending a rain of bullets blindly his way like some movie hero. Instead he stepped sideways to stand in front of the woman, an attempt to shield her.

The woman wasn't having any of it.

She was fast. In the blink of an eye it was her standing in front of Buckley.

Stupid bitch.

Didn't she have eyes in her head? Had she not stood side by side with him many times, seen that he was a good half head taller than her? A half head that he could easily blow apart with just another thousandth of an inch tightening of his finger.

Except it wouldn't have mattered, not if she'd been eight feet tall and four feet wide or if her head had barely come above his belt. It didn't matter that it was a stupid, pointless gesture that could have gotten them both killed and saved him the price of a bullet into the bargain.

None of it mattered.

Because she'd made her point.

They both had.

Caleb could no more have pulled the trigger in the face of what was playing out below him, such raw, unashamed emotion and selflessness, than he could have put out his own eyes with his knife.

Now Buckley was pushing at her, using his weight to shove her to the ground out of harm's way while she squirmed and slapped at him.

If Caleb's throat hadn't been so damn thick, the lump so fucking huge, he'd have laughed at their ungainly struggle to protect each other.

He shimmied backwards and made his escape as the police and emergency vehicles poured into the scene, their flashing lights like a ritual celebration of death and disaster. And because he was a confident and professional man despite the moment of madness that had almost overwhelmed him, his movements were careful and unhurried as he made his way along the escape route that he'd identified earlier. He even had time to remove the gum from his mouth and wrap it carefully in the silver foil from whence it came, then put the little warm bundle in his pocket.

Because his father hated gum with a passion and anyone who chewed it, and heaven help a hapless fool who might stick it to the underside of a table or chair.

57

'WHAT IS *WRONG* WITH YOUR FINGER?' GUILLORY SAID, MAKING NO attempt to hide the irritation and frustration in her voice. She swiped at his hand, missed by a mile. 'Apart from the fact that it spends too much time up your ass. You haven't left it alone since we got here.'

Evan was in the middle of telling Crow how, when Ryder and the rest of the police had turned up, he was forced to sit on the writhing jumble of limbs that was Guillory and himself in an attempt to control them. In the ensuing maelstrom he'd ended up with Evan's elbow in his eye—deliberately Ryder later said—and in turn had bruised Guillory's left breast with a wild swing of his own arm. A minor scuffle had then broken out over who would rub it better.

But Crow was more interested in what Guillory had just said, a mischievous gleam in his eye.

'You want me to take a look at it for you, Evan?'

Evan responded with a tight *no, thank you*.

'Maybe it needs amputation.'

Guillory had something else to say too.

'Big baby. Want mommy to kiss it better?'

Better be quick about it, Evan thought to himself and let go of his finger. He sent an arid smile towards both of them. But mainly at Crow. Because Crow had taken him aside when they arrived and said that there was one minor detail that he'd omitted to mention. Evan was free to discuss his pact with the devil with as many people as he saw fit—but if he chose to do so, the price would be very different. And Crow could not in all conscience recommend that Evan try his luck getting by with only one thumb. The proviso covered talking to Guillory herself. At first, he'd thought that Crow was having a joke at his expense. His expression had convinced him otherwise, a look on his face that suggested he'd be more likely to laugh at an old blind man falling down a flight of stairs. So he let Crow have his fun and left Guillory in her state of ignorance.

That ignorance explained her and her colleagues' bafflement at what had occurred on the rooftop. Who exactly had killed Liverman and his two thugs? And who had cut Lydia Strange's throat?

'We haven't found any evidence of who else was on that roof,' she told them.

Scandalous, the state of modern-day policing Crow had said. More resources should be made available.

It's a tough one Evan had admitted. He was sure they'd get a break sometime soon.

She stared at them sitting in front of her like a pair of naughty schoolboys with their hands in their laps. Even if she didn't know exactly what was passing between the two men, she wasn't stupid. They were up to something, had some guilty secret that she was not privy to.

One thing she did know—she'd have more chance of getting an answer out of Crow's pet bird that was now sitting on Evan's shoulder looking into his ear.

'Can I ask you something, Elwood?'

'Of course, my dear.'

Evan cringed, just about stopped himself from pulling his head down between his shoulders. It took a braver man than him to use that word.

'At what age do grown men stop acting like little boys?'

If she was expecting a shy, penitent smile or a guilty shrug she was disappointed.

'At a hundred and ten. Why?'

'Only a year to go,' Evan chipped in.

The conversation deteriorated from there until it was time to go. Standing at the front door, Evan had the impression of somebody watching him from the darkness at the top of the stairs, light from an upstairs window reflecting dully on a man's bald head.

A memory scratched at the back of his mind wanting to be let in. Pushing Guillory down to the ground as he stared at the rooftops. The flash of sunlight on something round and shiny and smooth.

Guillory got tired of waiting, grabbed his collar to tow him out of the house.

'When do I get to meet Caleb?' he said to Crow.

The question threw Crow for a moment.

'I'm sure you've already met him. Both of you.'

Evan shook his head. So did Guillory.

'Definitely not.'

Now it was Crow shaking his head, in confusion more than denial.

'How strange. Only the other day he said what a nice couple you and Kate make.'

Time to go, Evan thought, writing the remark off as just another of Crow's attempts at matchmaking.

If only he knew.

Then again, maybe he did. Because the carrying case he'd

glimpsed in the corner before Crow moved deliberately to block his view looked very familiar. It would have answered all of Guillory's questions too.

Then he heard music playing softly from upstairs, a song he recognized and which didn't surprise him—*The End* by The Doors. He knew then that he'd never hear it again without the image of a mouth with teeth filed to points filling his mind.

He caught Crow staring at him. It made him shiver. Behind Crow he saw something that he'd never noticed before. A heavy black overcoat hanging on a hook. It looked as if his pet bird had been sitting on his shoulder when he last wore it, a large dollop of birdshit dried on the shoulder. He glanced down at the threadbare cardigan sweater that Crow always wore, wondered if he wore it when he left the house. Or if he had something similar, but warmer.

Because a crazy thought had hijacked his mind that he couldn't shift. He'd never seen Pentecost in the flesh. All he had was a mental image as the security guard Rodriguez described him. The back of a car can be dark, the gaps and teeth in an old man's mouth hard to make out if you've stared at the glare off the water for too long. Who knows what you might think you've seen if you're already feeling flustered and under pressure after two rude and aggressive men quiz you?

'*Evan!* What is wrong with you? If it's not your finger, it's your head you've got up your ass.'

Guillory's shout from halfway down the path made everybody laugh.

The moment passed, the stupid, irrational thought gone from Evan's mind.

For now.

BOOKS BY JAMES HARPER

The Evan Buckley Thrillers

BAD TO THE BONES

When Evan Buckley's latest client ends up swinging on a rope, he's ready to call it a day. But he's an awkward cuss with a soft spot for a sad story and he takes on one last job—a child and husband who disappeared ten years ago. It's a long-dead investigation that everybody wants to stay that way, but he vows to uncover the truth—and in the process, kick into touch the demons who come to torment him every night.

KENTUCKY VICE

Maverick private investigator Evan Buckley is no stranger to self-induced mayhem—but even he's mystified by the jam college buddy Jesse Springer has got himself into. When Jesse shows up with a wad of explicit photographs that arrived in the mail, Evan finds himself caught up in the most bizarre case of blackmail he's ever encountered—Jesse swears blind he can't remember a thing about it.

SINS OF THE FATHER

Fifty years ago, Frank Hanna made a mistake. He's never forgiven himself. Nor has anybody else for that matter. Now the time has come to atone for his sins, and he hires maverick PI Evan Buckley to peel back fifty years of lies and deceit to uncover the tragic story hidden underneath. Trouble is, not everybody likes a happy ending and some very nasty people are out to make sure he doesn't succeed.

NO REST FOR THE WICKED

When an armed gang on the run from a botched robbery that left a man dead invade an exclusive luxury hotel buried in the mountains of upstate New York, maverick P.I. Evan Buckley has got his work cut out. He just won a trip for two and was hoping for a well-earned rest. But when the gang takes Evan's partner Gina hostage along with the other guests and their spirited seven-year-old daughter, he can forget any kind of rest.

RESURRECTION BLUES

After Levi Stone shows private-eye Evan Buckley a picture of his wife Lauren in the arms of another man, Evan quickly finds himself caught up in Lauren's shadowy past. The things he unearths force Levi to face the bitter truth—that he never knew his wife at all—or any of the dark secrets that surround her mother's death and the disappearance of her father, and soon Evan's caught in the middle of a lethal vendetta.

HUNTING DIXIE

Haunted by the unsolved disappearance of his wife Sarah, PI Evan Buckley loses himself in other people's problems. But when Sarah's scheming and treacherous friend Carly shows up promising new information, the past and present collide violently for Evan. He knows he can't trust her, but he hasn't got a choice when she confesses what she's done, leaving Sarah prey to a vicious gang with Old Testament ideas about crime and punishment.

THE ROAD TO DELIVERANCE

Evan Buckley's wife Sarah went to work one day and didn't come home. He's been looking for her ever since. As he digs deeper into the unsolved death of a man killed by the side of the road, the last known person to see Sarah alive, he's forced to re-trace the footsteps of her torturous journey, unearthing a dark secret from her past that drove her desperate attempts to make amends for the guilt she can never leave behind.

SACRIFICE

When PI Evan Buckley's mentor asks him to check up on an old friend, neither of them are prepared for the litany of death and destruction that he unearths down in the Florida Keys. Meanwhile Kate Guillory battles with her own demons in her search for salvation and sanity. As their paths converge, each of them must make an impossible choice that stretches conscience and tests courage, and in the end demands sacrifice—what would you give to get what you want?

ROUGH JUSTICE

After a woman last seen alive twenty years ago turns up dead, PI Evan Buckley heads off to a small town on the Maine coast where he unearths a series of brutal unsolved murders. The more he digs, lifting the lid on old grievances and buried injustices that have festered for half a lifetime, the more the evidence points to a far worse crime, leaving him facing an impossible dilemma – disclose the terrible secrets he's uncovered or assume the role of hanging judge and dispense a rough justice of his own.

TOUCHING DARKNESS

When PI Evan Buckley stops for a young girl huddled at the side of the road on a deserted stretch of highway, it's clear she's running away from someone or something—however vehemently she denies it. At times angry and hostile, at others scared and vulnerable, he's almost relieved when she runs out on him in the middle of the night. Except he has a nasty premonition that he hasn't heard the last of her. Nor does it take long before he's proved horribly right, the consequences dire for himself and Detective Kate Guillory.

A LONG TIME COMING

Five years ago, PI Evan Buckley's wife Sarah committed suicide in a mental asylum. Or so they told him. Now there's a different woman in her grave and he's got a stolen psychiatric report in his hand and a tormented scream running through his head. Someone is lying to him. With his own sanity at stake, he joins forces with a disgraced ex-CIA agent on a journey to confront the past that leads him to the jungles of Central America and the aftermath of a forgotten war, where memories are long and grievances still raw.

LEGACY OF LIES

Twenty years ago, Detective Kate Guillory's father committed suicide. Nobody has ever told her why. Now a man is stalking her. When PI Evan Buckley takes on the case, his search takes him to the coal mining mountains of West Virginia and the hostile aftermath of a malignant cult abandoned decades earlier. As he digs deeper into the unsolved crimes committed there and discovers the stalker's bitter grudge against Kate, one thing becomes horrifyingly clear – what started back then isn't over yet.

When Jessica Henderson falls to her death from the window of her fifteenth-floor apartment, the police are quick to write it off as an open and shut case of suicide. The room was locked from the inside, after all. But Jessica's sister doesn't buy it and hires Evan Buckley to investigate. The deeper Evan digs, the more he discovers the dead girl had fallen in more ways than one.

A ROCK AND A HARD PLACE

Private-eye Evan Buckley's not used to getting something for nothing. So when an unexpected windfall lands in his lap, he's intrigued. Not least because he can't think what he's done to deserve it. Written off by the police as one more sad example of mindless street crime, Evan feels honor-bound to investigate, driven by his need to give satisfaction to a murdered woman he never knew.

Join my mailing list at www.jamesharperbooks.com and get your FREE copies of Fallen Angel and A Rock And A Hard Place.

BAD CALL – A PSYCHOLOGICAL THRILLER

Ralph Da Silva has screwed up. Big time. He's had four Tequilas too many for lunch and now he thinks he might have killed somebody—somebody important. Somebody with a lot of very unpleasant friends. The question is—can he get himself out of the country before they strap him to a chair and get the electrodes out. One thing is certain—he can't afford to make another bad call.

To Rills Smills, without whom none of this would have been possible.

Printed in Poland
by Amazon Fulfillment
Poland Sp. z o.o., Wrocław

79791340R00231